Shadow

A Reiko Watanabe/Inspector Aizawa Thriller

by

Matthew Legare

Copyright

Mailing List

Join my mailing list! You'll receive updates, deals, and the free prequel novella, *Conspiracy in Tokyo*! Just visit www.matthewlegare.com to sign up.

Thanks!

Author's Note

In addition to using the Western calendar, the Japanese also divide their history among eras named after the reigning emperors. For example, modern Japanese history is comprised of the Meiji Era (1868 – 1912), the Taisho Era (1912 – 1926), the Showa Era (1926 – 1989), and the Heisei Era (1989 – 2019), and the Reiwa Era (2019 – present). The events of this novel take place in 1931 or Showa 6. Additionally, there are references to the Tokugawa Era, which covered the years of 1603 – 1868 when the Tokugawa Shogunate ruled Japan through a military dictatorship, reducing the emperors to mere figureheads.

Many Japanese terms that have not entered the English lexicon have been italicized, followed by a brief translation. Those words that have gained familiarity in the West (e.g. geisha, yakuza, shogun) are not italicized.

There are also common suffixes used throughout the novel such as *san* (formal for both males and females) *chan* (informal for females) and *kun* (informal for males).

In Japan, surnames come before given names (e.g. Watanabe Reiko), but in order to make the story more palatable to Western readers, characters' given names will come before their family names (e.g. Reiko Watanabe).

Acknowledgments

The seeds of this novel were planted long ago and I am grateful to all those who have supported and guided me while it grew. Jay, for his years of mentorship, Caroline T. Johnson for her fantastic cover design, my family and friends for their encouragement, my Japanese friends who helped with cultural nuances and translations, and to my beta readers, especially my other half, Jenny, who read the novel many times over and always offered better and better feedback.

December 1931

Sixth Year of the Showa Era

CHAPTER ONE

Reiko Watanabe quickened her pace through the crowded streets of Tokyo, praying that she wasn't too late. The assassination was imminent but one phone call to the Police would stop this madness. She cursed the kimono that wrapped her legs like rope, forcing her to take small, plodding steps. Crossing the street, her *geta* clogs crunched over a thin carpet of snow, slowing her down even further. But there, at the end of the block, was the telephone booth. Nothing could stop her now.

However, the lingering stares from passersby slowed her pace. Did they suspect something or were they just gawking? The sight of a geisha running in full dress must have been an odd sight, even in Asakusa, the neighborhood of *ero guro nansensu* – erotic grotesque nonsense.

A kimono-clad sumo wrestler waddled past like a moving mountain. Tattooed hoodlums stood guard outside gambling dens, the lairs of the yakuza. A pair of unshaven men in tattered coats traipsed by, the unfortunate victims of this terrible depression that had swallowed Japan's economy.

A group of ragged-looking children huddled around a cart grilling *yakitori* chicken skewers, savoring the sweet smell. Rickshaws carried passengers through the streets, sharing the road with an occasional honking automobile. On the corner, a Buddhist minstrel, masked by a straw basket, played a morose tune with his flute. Across the street, a band wearing samurai costumes performed jazz music.

Nothing unusual for Asakusa, but every eye seemed to follow Reiko as she approached the telephone booth. In their stares, she felt the watchful eye of her lover, Masaru Ryusaki. Entering the telephone booth provided a temporary refuge, allowing Reiko to examine the reflection in the glass. Her *shimada* wig was still in place, but a face full of white paint couldn't hide cheeks turned pink by the cold. Hardly a dignified look for a geisha.

With trembling hands, Reiko pulled out a five-sen coin, enough to make any local call in Tokyo. She was about to slide the coin in, but a loud knock on the glass startled her. A man in a dark brown tunic and peaked service cap stood outside the telephone booth. The uniform of the Imperial Army. No, it couldn't be Lieutenant Nakajima. Not here.

Too frightened to look the soldier in the face, Reiko glanced at his shoulder insignia and noticed they were solid red with only one yellow star each. She expelled a relieved sigh. The soldier was a *nito-hei* – a simple private – and not the officer she dreaded.

"My humblest apologies," the soldier said, clicking his heels. "But I am shipping out to Manchuria soon! Please allow me the honor of your company!"

Although he stood at full attention, the red in his face told her that this soldier had been drinking, probably more than ever before in his young life. No wonder he had the impudence to actually flirt with a geisha. More and more units were being sent to Manchuria to settle that *incident* in northeastern China. Reiko pitied anyone going to that subzero hell, but seeing the soldier's brown uniform filled her with venom.

"Try the brothels in Yoshiwara," she said. "You can't afford me."

The soldier gave a hurt look and an apologetic bow before stumbling away. Reiko sighed in relief and reminded herself that there was no reason Lieutenant Nakajima would be in Asakusa. Not now at least. That bastard Nakajima. All of this was his fault. Like some evil spirit, he had turned Masaru Ryusaki from her pampering lover into a madman who plotted the assassination of politicians. Her thoughts drifted to Masaru, who had no idea his geisha mistress was about to betray him. Reiko Watanabe never considered herself to be an especially moral person, but even she couldn't turn a blind eye to murder.

Only one police officer could be trusted with this information. After all, Masaru claimed to have many sympathizers inside the Tokyo Metropolitan Police Department but only one sworn enemy. Countless curses against an "Inspector Aizawa" had etched the name into her mind. Reiko picked up the receiver and dropped the five-sen coin into the slot.

"*Moshi moshi*," a woman's chipper voice answered.

"Yes, operator? Connect me to the Metropolitan Police Headquarters. Inspector Aizawa's office."

"Hold, please."

The line went quiet and Reiko gripped the telephone cord.

Moments later, a man's sharp voice came through.

"Inspector Aizawa speaking."

"There's going to be an assassination," she said, lowering her already husky voice.

There was a brief pause. "Who is going to be killed?"

"Baron Fumio Onishi…there's an emergency session of the Imperial Diet today. He'll be shot as soon as he exits the House of Peers."

"Who's going to shoot him?"

"A man. He's short with a mustache like Charlie Chaplin."

"What's his name?"

Reiko searched her mind but couldn't remember. Masaru Ryusaki had several followers who believed in his brand of right-wing patriotism. Hours before, she had served the tea as Masaru ordered the assassination of Baron Onishi for his many crimes – corruption, weakness, and greed. The little mustached man barely spoke, but his eyes blazed with such murderous delight that it sent a shiver down her spine.

Soon after, Reiko excused herself to fetch some alcohol, saying they'd need something to celebrate Onishi's death with. Instead, she rushed to the nearest telephone booth where she now found herself betraying the man she loved.

"I don't know his name," she finally said.

"Is anyone else involved?"

Above all, that was something the Police could never discover. Masaru Ryusaki was not just her lover but also the only source of income she had. If he were arrested, then she wouldn't last very long in this depression. But once this insane assassination plot failed, she could persuade him to give up on politics and return to their normal lives...or so she hoped.

"Hello? Are you there?"

Instead of answering, Reiko hung up the receiver. Exiting the telephone booth, she sucked in the cold air. Its bite helped steady her as she rejoined the stream of humanity through Asakusa's streets.

She expected a sense of shame, but her betrayal left only a detached, numb feeling. Masaru was expecting her, but he would have to wait a little longer. A nearby Shinto shrine had a hypnotic draw and beckoned her closer. Passing underneath the *torii* gate, she entered the realm of gods and spirits.

After washing her hands at the purification fountain, Reiko approached the worship hall and tossed a few coins into the offering box. The shrine was crowded today, filled with people praying for help. What were they asking for? Probably employment, judging from the wrinkled kimonos and patched coats they wore. It seemed that the gods had abandoned Japan in the past two years, leaving behind economic misery and political turmoil.

Absent or not, a heavy rope with bells hanging from the shrine served as a direct connection to the Shinto pantheons. Reiko shook it and felt certain that she had captured their attention. It was up to the gods to help Aizawa now.

CHAPTER TWO

Inspector Kenji Aizawa stared out the car window, examining the Imperial Diet Building in the distance. Like something out of the ancient past, the sprawling structure's two pillared wings were thronged by reporters. Holding them at bay were squads of *junsas*, the rank and file of the Tokyo Metropolitan Police Department.

Sergeant Toru Murayama parked the vehicle. "Think we're too late, Inspector?"

"Nobody has radioed anything in yet," Aizawa said. "But we'd better hurry."

A rush of cold air bit into Aizawa's face as he stepped from the automobile. His shoes crunched against the snowy courtyard and he sank into his overcoat. December in Tokyo was usually mild but winter had come early this year along with a fresh dusting of snow the night before. Sergeant Murayama lumbered alongside him, exhaling puffs of frosted breath, like a sumo wrestler in a dark blue uniform.

They approached the Diet with rapid steps, taking in the building's enormity. Reporters mostly clustered around the sides where both houses of the legislature were meeting. Located on the left wing, the House of Representatives was comprised of party politicians elected by the masses. Representing the aristocracy, the House of Peers was situated in the Diet's right wing. That was where Baron Onishi would step straight into the path of an assassin's bullet.

Although that woman sounded desperate enough, Aizawa wondered if her call was just an elaborate scheme to make a fool out of him. Japan had a long history of political assassinations, but given the enemies he'd made in the past few months, Aizawa felt safer keeping it to himself and Sergeant Murayama for now. Many policemen allowed personal emotions to cloud their duty, but Murayama was uncomplicated. No politics, just strict obedience to the chain of command.

As they neared the throng outside the House of Peers, several regulars from the big newspapers – the *Asahi*, *Nichi Nichi*, and *Yomiuri Shimbun* – were there. A few reporters had set up a radio transmitter under a banner labeled JOAK. If the Japanese Broadcasting Corporation had sent men to get a live feed, the Diet probably wasn't passing a budget bill.

"What's going on?" Aizawa asked a nearby reporter.

"Wakatsuki just resigned," the reporter said, keeping his attention focused on the building. "The Diet is adjourned for the rest of the year, but they're holding an emergency session right now. But it's doubtful the Emperor will appoint a new prime minister today."

So that was it. Prime ministers had short careers these days and Reijiro Wakatsuki was no exception. There were more politicians ready to take his place, all hoping to be more effective than their forgettable predecessors.

Aizawa thanked the reporter and surveyed the crowd for short men with Charlie Chaplin mustaches. Damn that woman. Couldn't she spare more details? Still, a wall of grim-faced *junsas* in their dark uniforms, gleaming short swords, and peaked caps was enough to intimidate most citizens. Perhaps this would-be assassin had already been scared off.

Aizawa made his way through the crowd and up the steps while Murayama followed close behind. A senior *junsa* stood at the center of the wall of policemen. As they approached, he stepped forward and saluted.

"Inspector Aizawa," the *junsa* said. "What brings you here?"

"Special investigation," he said, shutting down further inquiry. It would have been easier to order the *junsas* to scour the area for men with toothbrush mustaches, but he dismissed the thought. Better to let Sergeant Murayama sift through the crowd while he grabbed the Baron and escaped out the back. Cowardly? Yes, but also the safest course. At least until he knew for certain that this mysterious informant wasn't some rival officer's wife.

Aizawa leaned close to Sergeant Murayama. "I'll get the Baron and exit through the back. Keep an eye out for our man."

"It won't be easy in this crowd," Murayama said. "I could use some help."

Aizawa shook his head. "Just keep watch out here. Remember, short, Charlie Chaplin mustache."

Sergeant Murayama scratched his own thick mustache and started back down the stairs before disappearing into the throng.

Aizawa turned his attention to the Diet's entrance. The doors were now wide open. A stream of distinguished-looking men in frock coats and three-piece suits began to exit. They walked past the mob of reporters, held at bay by the wall of *junsas*. He glanced at his watch. 5:05. Any minute now, the Baron would exit with this flood of Dietmen.

Aizawa braced himself, half-expecting bullets to cut through the crowd.

CHAPTER THREE

Aizawa recognized only a few notable politicians. There was the illustrious Prince Fumimaro Konoe, who wore a toothbrush mustache but was far too tall to be the man in question. Iesato Tokugawa also stood out with his paunchy gut. How strange that this doughy man was not only the House of Peers' president, but also the patriarch of the Tokugawa Clan, the same family who had ruled Japan through their military dictators, the shoguns, for some two hundred years.

After a few more nondescript politicians filtered out, a man in a black frock coat and top hat emerged from the Diet Building. Tall and statuesque, Baron Fumio Onishi leaned on a cane and surveyed the crowd like it was his personal fiefdom. His chiseled face, highlighted by silver hair and matching mustache, was the Japanese aristocracy personified.

How fitting, since according to the newspapers, Onishi was descended from over thirty generations of *daimyo* lords. His own father had played a leading role in the Meiji Restoration, toppling the Tokugawa Shogunate and returning full power to the Emperor. Aizawa suppressed an urge to kowtow then and there.

Instead, he darted up the steps and bowed deeply before the Baron. Straightening up, Aizawa presented his *meishi*, his formal business card.

"Inspector Kenji Aizawa," Baron Onishi read aloud in a dry voice, before tucking the *meishi* into his coat pocket. "And what may I do for you, Inspector?"

"Baron, forgive me for being so direct, but your life is in danger."

The Baron raised a silver eyebrow. "Is that so?"

"I received a call a few minutes ago—"

"From who?"

"I'm not sure, but she warned me that someone intends to shoot you outside the Diet."

Baron Onishi's face remained placid. "I see. Today is the eleventh, correct?" he asked, rubbing his chin.

"Yes…but I don't see how—"

"That makes three this month…"

"Three, Baron?"

"Death threats. I've received about fifty since September."

"Did you report them?"

"I considered it, but there are so many nationalists in the Police these days," Onishi said.

The Baron did have a point, but such flippancy toward a police inspector took him aback.

"Baron, perhaps I'm not being clear. I'm here to offer my protection."

The Baron scoffed. "After my speech about the Manchurian Incident, I'm surprised you're not here to arrest me."

Aizawa remembered the flurry of editorials denouncing Baron Onishi's "unpatriotic criticism" of the invasion of Manchuria. After all – the newspapers argued – Chinese soldiers had attacked a Japanese-owned railway without provocation and threatened to kick Japan out of the region entirely. The Japanese Empire would collapse without the endless amount of raw materials from Manchuria. Faced with such a grave choice, the most elite unit of the Imperial Army – the vaunted Kwantung Army – took action and invaded while politicians bickered like children.

"Perhaps this is no idle threat, Baron. I suggest we take cautionary measures."

"I shall do no such thing." Baron Onishi gestured to the chattering mass at the bottom of the steps. "Those reporters down there will want to know what I have to say about the day's events. Japan is seeking a new prime minister, or perhaps you've been too busy chasing pickpockets to notice?"

Maybe the coming assassination wasn't political at all. The thought of someone shooting this arrogant bastard on account of his personality made sense. The forces of *giri* and *ninjo*, duty and emotion, tugged at Aizawa. If this pompous fool didn't care for his own safety, then you shouldn't either, *ninjo* argued. But emotion shouldn't cloud the mind of a police officer, *giri* countered. As always, *giri* won, even though its resolve was waning.

"I understand your obligations, Baron," Aizawa said. "But I feel it best to go back inside and—"

Baron Onishi drew in his breath just loud enough to make an irritated hiss. "Japan should see its political leaders standing without fear, not cowering behind bodyguards. I hope you understand, Inspector."

With that, the Baron strode down the steps and the wall of *junsas* parted for him. Feeling like a whipped dog, Aizawa followed. At the foot of the stairs, Baron Onishi's appearance electrified the sea of reporters, setting off a series of flashing camera bulbs. Shielding his eyes, Aizawa glimpsed the Baron striking a refined pose, like a *kabuki* actor about to deliver his finest performance.

Aizawa reviewed the crowd for anything suspicious, before considering that this assassin might be one of the *junsas*. A frightening thought, but like the Baron said, there were so many nationalists in the Metropolitan Police Department these days. He squeezed through the line of policemen and glanced back and forth, looking for short men with Charlie Chaplin mustaches. Nothing.

Aizawa shook his head. It was a police officer's job to be suspicious, but the past few months seemed to have made him paranoid beyond his thirty years. Japan had changed too, from a nation of mostly law-abiding people into a land of fear, assassination, and plots.

"Baron Onishi," a reporter near the front called out. "Have you heard anything from the Emperor's advisers?"

The Baron maintained his poise and answered, "No, but should His Majesty ask me to form a government, I will accept with great fortitude."

"Baron, if you become prime minister, will you pull out of Manchuria?"

"I will present our case to the League of Nations," Onishi replied.

"What will your economic policy be?" another reporter asked.

"There are no easy solutions regarding the depression. We cannot rely on international trade anymore, especially with the United States. Their so-called Smoot-Hawley Tariff has crippled our economy."

A universal revulsion swept through the crowd. Because of America's foolish protectionism, ships full of Japanese exports were anchored in Tokyo Bay, causing thousands of layoffs. As Baron Onishi continued to answer questions, off to the side, the JOAK booth burst to life with commentary.

"Special bulletin! Special bulletin! This is the Japanese Broadcasting Corporation with important news regarding the nation! Prime Minister Wakatsuki resigned earlier today after one of his ministers, Kenzo Adachi, refused to attend cabinet meetings with him. Rumors abound that the next prime minister will be either Baron Onishi or Tsuyoshi Inukai, the president of the Seiyukai Party. Stay tuned as Japan's future will be decided in the coming days."

Aizawa surveyed the crowd again. Toward the back of the throng, a diminutive figure wearing a brown coat and flat cap cut across the courtyard and approached with rapid steps.

Aizawa pushed and elbowed his way through the reporters, who were too fixated on Onishi to protest. He soon emerged from the back of the crowd and could see the oncoming man more clearly. His face was grim and determined, his eyes were focused on Baron Onishi, and underneath a slender nose, was the mustache.

CHAPTER FOUR

The man kept coming, now only a few meters away. Aizawa reached for his Colt 1911 automatic pistol, secure in its shoulder holster. It was a good weapon, sturdy and reliable, but rarely used. Being a police officer in Japan was seldom dangerous, thanks to an inculcated respect for hierarchy. Shame was the foundation which Japan was built upon, and that – not his gun – was Aizawa's usual weapon.

Perhaps a show of authority was all he needed. Aizawa marched forward to intercept the man.

"Police! Stop right there!"

Aizawa grabbed the little man's shoulder as he bolted past. Out of nowhere, a fist connected hard with Aizawa's face and drove him down into the snowy ground. Dazed and numb from the cold, he released a deep groan. Pushing himself up, he looked around for his attacker. The little bastard had turned around and was heading toward the crowd again.

Aizawa again reached for his pistol, but hesitated. There was no way he could get a clear shot now, unless he wanted to read "Insane Police Inspector Guns Down Reporters" in tomorrow's newspapers. Aizawa hopped to his feet and a sudden energy launched him forward.

He grabbed the man's collar and heaved him back. Losing his balance, the little man gripped Aizawa's coat, pulling them both down. Slamming against the snow-covered ground, Aizawa gasped for breath and looked up. Somehow, the man had already righted himself and with one sharp thrust, slammed a foot against Aizawa's cheek.

Aizawa's face throbbed with pain. How did that little bastard get up so quickly? The man brought his foot up again, his mustache twitching in preparation for the final blow.

Instinct took control as Aizawa hooked his legs in a sweeping motion, sending his attacker crashing to the ground. Fueled by adrenaline, Aizawa lunged atop the man and drove a firm punch across his face. A burst of blood spewed out of the little bastard's mouth, staining the snow red. Gathering the rest of his strength, Aizawa landed another punch and the little man crumpled onto the snowy ground. Noticing the commotion, a few reporters broke away from Baron Onishi and encircled them.

"Inspector, who is that man?"

"Was he trying to harm Baron Onishi?"

"Or former Prime Minister Wakatsuki?"

Aizawa paid no attention as he handcuffed the man. Sergeant Murayama and two *junsas* pushed their way through the throng and helped Aizawa to his feet.

"Are you all right, Inspector?" he asked. A nod was all Aizawa could give as he gasped for breath. Murayama hoisted the little man to his feet and examined his face. "Little too thin to be a Charlie Chaplin mustache."

Taking deep gulps of air, Aizawa fumbled through the man's clothing. Tucked into his waistband was the gun. Aizawa pulled it out and noticed it was a Nambu automatic, standard issue for the Imperial Army.

"Inspector, is that an Army pistol?" a reporter called out.

"Do you think the Imperial Army is involved in some way?" another followed.

The thought of military involvement knotted Aizawa's gut. He tucked the Nambu into his coat before anyone could take a photograph. Guiding the prisoner into Murayama's arms, he said, "Take him back to Headquarters, Sergeant. I'll clean up here."

Murayama and the *junsas* snapped salutes before dragging the little man through the courtyard, trailed by a group of noisy reporters. Aizawa turned back and shoved his way through the gauntlet. One reporter blocked his path and asked, "Inspector, the *Asahi Shimbun* has a duty to its readers. Who was that man?"

Aizawa couldn't resist. "Don't you recognize Charlie Chaplin?" He pushed the *Asahi* man aside and continued on. Several *junsas* led Baron Onishi back into the Diet, while the rest of the squad restrained the press from following. Aizawa ascended the stairs after them. Behind him, the reporters shouted questions that soon lost any individuality and melted into a singular, droning noise.

*****

Reiko clutched the bottle of chilled Kirin beer, stinging her fingers with cold. Ignoring the pain, she continued to rehearse a placating story in her mind. With all the parties being thrown for soldiers going to Manchuria, many stores had simply run out of alcohol. A believable excuse for being gone so long.

As she hurried through the streets of Asakusa, a man and woman strolled by like a pair of haunting memories. Extravagantly dressed – even for Asakusa – they were the epitome of the *mobo* and *moga*, the modern boy and modern girl. These were the flappers of Japan who wore skirts, smoked cigarettes, and indulged in everything modern, from jazz to premarital sex. The *mobo* in his double-breasted gray coat and fedora, and the *moga* in her fur-trimmed black dress and cloche hat could have been her and Masaru only months earlier. Reiko stared down at her black kimono, dotted with a pink cherry blossom design, and neatly tied *obi* belt.

An icy breeze cut through her, as if punishment for her treachery. Mistresses didn't betray the men they loved. Those who did were poison women, the femme fatales of Japanese lore. Another gust of wind blew life into the Rising Sun flag mounted outside of Masaru's *machiya*, a humble, two-story dwelling. Reiko sighed as she approached. Most buildings in Tokyo were either *machiya* townhouses or *nagaya* row houses. After two thousand years of natural disasters, the Japanese still built homes out of paper and wood.

Only eight years ago, Tokyo was utterly destroyed by the worst earthquake in its history, followed by a firestorm that turned what remained of the city into a burning hell. Recently, the newspapers detailed how the Manchurian city of Chinchow was bombed from the air and shelled with artillery. Reiko shuddered to think what would happen to these wooden buildings under the same bombardment. Assassinations might give way to civil war and turn Tokyo into a charred wasteland again.

But there was no time to think about that now. With a deep breath, she shed Reiko Watanabe and donned the persona of the dutiful geisha, Harutora. *Spring Tiger* was a fine name during the cherry blossom season, but it seemed out of place during these months of ice and snow.

She slid the *machiya*'s door open and stepped inside the small *genkan* vestibule. After taking off her snow-crusted *geta* clogs, Reiko entered the main room, hoping the gods were still with her.

CHAPTER FIVE

"Welcome back, Harutora," Masaru Ryusaki said as Reiko slid the door shut behind her.

Across the room, Masaru knelt with a sheathed *katana* sword at his side. The rest of him was less menacing. A dark blue kimono and gray *hakama* pants hung from his long, wiry frame and a thin nose held up horn-rimmed glasses. A clean shave and hair parted to the side gave him a fresh-faced, bookish appearance. When they'd first met back in March, Masaru had been the very image of a *mobo* playboy; educated, worldly, and modern. Although only thirty years old, he now looked like a samurai from the Tokugawa Era.

Reiko set the beer bottle down and bowed. "Forgive my latenesss, Masaru."

Drawing herself up, she feigned a detached calmness, even though his sparsely furnished *machiya* had begun to resemble a prison. A typewriter was nestled on a low-lying table where Masaru propagated his ideas. Up above, a mounted 'god shelf' – where the Shinto deities were enshrined – watched over them both in a never-ending, all-seeing gaze.

She averted her eyes to the charcoal heater where they warmed themselves during this cold winter. A phonograph lay off to the side where only months before, they'd listened to jazz records together while dancing the fox-trot. Next to that was a tabletop Sharp radio from which the melancholy tune of "Sake, Tears or Sighs?" seeped out.

"I thought you didn't listen to jazz anymore, Masaru," Reiko said, making her way over to the heater.

"I'm waiting on confirmation," Masaru said.

"On whether or not Chaplin-san——"

"His name is Makoto Kuroki and he will soon be honored as one of our greatest patriots!"

"Ah yes. After he shoots Baron what's-his-name, right?"

"Baron Onishi." Masaru rubbed his chin. "It should have happened by now."

Reiko laughed, warming her hands by the heater. "Hopefully he didn't stop by a bar on his way to the Diet."

"Kuroki-san isn't a drunk."

"Speaking of alcohol, most of the stores were cleaned out! Too many parties for boys going to Manchuria, I suppose." Reiko shuffled back over to the bottle. "But I did manage to find something," she said, presenting the beer to him. "It's Kirin. Your favorite."

Masaru took the bottle with a triumphant smile. "Tonight, we will toast the death of Baron Onishi!"

She knelt beside him and frowned. "Does it have to come to this?"

Masaru nodded. "The government has been corrupted and weakened by big business and democracy. Baron Onishi only cares for the rich. If he becomes prime minister, the poor will starve, millions more will lose their jobs, and Japan will be at the mercy of the League of Nations. That old fool will pull out of Manchuria and disgrace our soldiers. He doesn't realize that Japan must fight more wars to survive…"

"Against who?"

"China…Russia…America…the whole world if necessary! Soon, we will have a leader who understands that."

Reiko swallowed hard. "What happens after the Baron is…shot?"

Masaru's smile broadened. "With Onishi dead, His Majesty will have no choice but to offer Tsuyoshi Inukai and his Seiyukai Party the government."

Reiko gave a dry laugh. "I didn't know you were still a Seiyukai member!"

"Minsei, Seiyukai. There's no difference between them."

"Same shit, different smell?"

Masaru's handsome face shone with approval. "However, once Inukai becomes prime minister, he will appoint General Yori Sakamoto as the army minister. By the end of the week, General Sakamoto will declare martial law, abolish the Diet, and become the new shogun!"

"A return to the Tokugawa Era?" Reiko asked.

Masaru nodded. "Japan needs a strong leader who will rule on behalf of the Emperor, take control of the economy, and stand up to the League of Nations. The Kusanagi Society will be in charge of inciting a riot that will justify martial law. Then, the New Japan will begin!"

Mention of Masaru's patriotic group prickled Reiko's skin. Small in numbers but bursting with limitless patriotism, the Kusanagi Society recruited downtrodden young men who blamed politicians, foreigners, and big business for everything wrong with the nation. She hated attending those gatherings with Masaru, singing patriotic songs and pouring drinks for men like Makoto Kuroki who constantly questioned when the government would be overthrown.

Reiko hid her concern and asked, "What will your position be in the New Japan?"

Masaru lifted his head high. "I'll serve as General Sakamoto's senior adviser. He'll need my guidance in building a pure and just society."

The position sounded more like the shadow shoguns of the Tokugawa Era, government ministers and lords who ruled behind paper screens. Reiko asked, "Is Inukai-san aware of your plans?"

Masaru scoffed. "I would never trust a politician. But Inukai will become aware of them when our new shogun tears down the Diet Building and puts something more fitting in its place. Perhaps a landfill?"

"As long as you don't touch Asakusa, I'll be happy."

"You'll still have your tea houses and cinemas. But in five years, you won't even recognize Japan." Masaru released a satisfied sigh. "I have Lieutenant Nakajima to thank for this great victory. Without him, this would never have happened." He set the bottle of beer down. "Let's have a drink. To Hajime Nakajima!"

Reiko almost blanched but maintained a mask of composure. "I'd rather not. I don't think the Lieutenant would return the toast."

"He's an Army man. They don't appreciate women."

"Like you?" Reiko leaned closer.

Masaru swallowed and ignored the question. "Thankfully, Nakajima-san steered me back to the path of purity and patriotism."

Curses rang out in Reiko's mind. That devil soldier had ruined everything. It was Nakajima who encouraged, begged, and subtly shamed Masaru into concocting this insane assassination plot. If he hadn't appeared, then she'd still be in her world of movie theaters in Asakusa and afternoon shopping in Ginza.

"Still, I feel uncomfortable around him. Like he thinks I'm stealing you away from him and—"

The forlorn dirge of "Sake, Tears or Sighs?" cut off and was replaced by the crisp voice of a radio announcer.

"Special bulletin! Special bulletin! We interrupt this program to bring you breaking news from outside the Diet Building."

Masaru leaped to his feet and leaned closer to the radio. Reiko clutched her kimono tighter.

"During a press conference given by Baron Fumio Onishi, a violent scuffle broke out in the Imperial Diet's courtyard between an unidentified man and Police Inspector Kenji Aizawa."

Anger flickered behind Masaru's glasses.

"Details are unclear but the man was taken into custody. Baron Onishi was safely escorted back into the Imperial Diet. Police have not released any further information."

Masaru clicked radio knob off. Blood drained from his face, leaving him pale and trembling. Did he suspect anything? She searched his numb expression for any sense of betrayal but there was no emotion. Suddenly, it ignited in rage.

"Aizawa! Him again? Damn him, damn him, damn him!" He grabbed the Kirin beer and hurled it to the floor, shattering the bottle into pieces. "Why must he hound me when my only crime is patriotism?"

Reiko kept quiet but gave a sympathetic nod.

"No, he won't win this time," Masaru said, grabbing the *katana* tightly in his hand. "Aizawa will soon learn that his loyalty to those villains in the Diet will cost him dearly! The gods punish the unrighteous!"

The sword rattled louder in Masaru's grip and Reiko feared what was coming. Smashing bottles was bad enough, but he might go lopping off a few heads with that thing.

"Masaru, please control yourself!"

Masaru's fury melted away as he set the sword down.

"You're right. I must be calm. Then I can think...and plan."

He dropped to his knees. An innocent vulnerability shone behind his glasses, the kind she hadn't seen in months.

"Masaru, please, it's over. Forget about Nakajima...forget about the Baron...forget about all of them..."

"Harutora...Reiko...sing me a song."

"How about 'Cherry Blossoms, Cherry Blossoms'?"

He closed his eyes. "Jazz."

Now it made sense. He didn't want the geisha Harutora; he wanted the *moga*, Reiko Watanabe. Her suspicions were correct. Underneath that samurai shell, there was still a *mobo* inside Masaru Ryusaki. Perhaps with a little jazz, she could bring him out and put an end to this madness.

She sang the opening bars of "The Japanese Sandman" from memory. Masaru quivered and nestled his head on her lap. Fitting, since it had been the song playing when they first met, so many months ago. Before that bastard Nakajima ruined everything.

She stopped and said, "I've always loved the lyrics to that song."

Masaru kept his eyes closed. "They're just nonsense."

Reiko sighed. "Those are the best kind."

CHAPTER SIX

Pacing back and forth, Second Lieutenant Hajime Nakajima's footsteps echoed throughout the empty halls of the Imperial Diet Building. According to the wall clock hanging above a nearby conference room, it had been over ten minutes since the Diet session ended. Baron Onishi must be dead by now!

Lieutenant Nakajima smiled and gripped the heavy saber at his side. He'd use it soon enough during the revolution that would save Japan from the claws of evil. But for now, he continued to pace and wait for the conference room to open.

Some of the most powerful men in the government were behind those doors; chief among them was Nakajima's superior officer, the Vice-Army Minister, General Yori Sakamoto. The General was scheduled to be in meetings all day with these lesser creatures, scheming politicians from the Seiyukai Party and its president, Tsuyoshi Inukai.

Disbelief swept over Lieutenant Nakajima as he once again realized his proximity to these men. This lowly son of rice farmers stood in the halls of the Imperial Diet, nerve center of the Japanese Empire.

Not that it would be around for much longer. Soon, his *sensei*, his teacher, Masaru Ryusaki and the Kusanagi Society would dynamite buildings and cause riots throughout Tokyo, spreading panic and chaos. Nakajima would play an important role too, storming the Diet with a platoon of soldiers and declaring martial law. A new era would dawn when General Sakamoto was declared shogun and began cleansing Japan of impurities.

Lieutenant Nakajima imagined scores of unpatriotic Dietmen standing before a firing squad, including Tsuyoshi Inukai, discarded like a useless puppet. Then, with his mission in the home islands accomplished, Nakajima could transfer to Manchuria and die a beautiful death for the Emperor, like a cherry blossom fluttering to the ground on the last day of spring. Only then would this lowly son of rice farmers attain godhood.

Suddenly, a parade of dark uniforms turned the corner and forced Nakajima off to the side. Police officers clustered around a tall, stern-faced man and escorted him down the hall. A glimpse of a silver mustache was enough to identify Baron Fumio Onishi.

Kuroki had failed! Perhaps there was still time to draw his saber and strike the villain down—but he dismissed the idea. Ryusaki-sensei would have another plan. He always did.

Another man in a black suit, fedora, and overcoat trailed behind the squad of policemen. Lieutenant Nakajima studied his squared face with thick eyebrows that highlighted a pair of dark, focused eyes. Even thicker sideburns lined his face while a bright red mark spotted his cheek. His mouth was turned downward, out of which hung a lit cigarette.

It had to be Inspector Aizawa...the man Ryusaki-sensei hated with such fury. With their backs turned to him, there were so many opportunities to strike them both down, but again, Nakajima suppressed the urge. Time was needed to correct today's failure.

After Aizawa and the other police officers disappeared around a corner, Lieutenant Nakajima turned back toward the conference room, its doors now wide open. Amid pleasant chatter, Tsuyoshi Inukai and General Sakamoto exited first, followed by a pair of grinning Seiyukai Party bureaucrats. Inukai was dressed in an elegant dark suit that clashed with his white hair and goatee; his wrinkled, sunken face with taut skin resembled a mummy with fur. But this frail little man was president of the conservative Seiyukai, the second largest political party in Japan.

Towering over him was General Sakamoto, whose own finely trimmed gray goatee surrounded a confident smile. His dark brown uniform was identical to Lieutenant Nakajima's, although Sakamoto's was ornamented with several awards. Service medals from the Russo-Japanese War, a campaign badge for the Siberian Expedition, and the most prestigious, the Order of the Golden Kite dangling at his throat, were like Shinto charms in this den of devils.

A well-built man in a three-piece suit with neatly combed gray hair and a strong jaw exited last. The glittering Rolex around his wrist was more than enough evidence that the man belonged to the *zaibatsu*, Japan's capitalist cliques.

The man's loathsome face was constantly in the newspapers these days; Isamu Takano, the banker. Though less insufferable than the liberal Minsei Party, the conservative Seiyukai was known for its connections to the *zaibatsu*.

Contempt swept over Lieutenant Nakajima. To strut around with a Rolex while unemployment numbers soared higher every day was almost unforgivable. Heartbreaking letters from his mother flashed in his mind, all detailing how his childhood village and many others like it were ravaged by famine. But nobody in the capital seemed to care much about poor rice farmers. His thoughts drifted back home, back to the northeastern Tohoku region. He was a boy again, watching an entire summer's rice harvest packed up and shipped south to Tokyo. After the rice his sister, Chitose Nakajima, went too.

Loud chattering returned Nakajima to the present and he snapped to attention. General Sakamoto acknowledged him with a nod but Takano and the politicians walked past without even a glance.

"Farewell, General," Inukai said. "I'll be in touch."

"I'm sure you will, Inukai-san," General Sakamoto said with a gracious smile.

After exchanging bows, the Seiyukai politicians and Takano walked down the hallway. Only after they were out of earshot did Sakamoto speak.

"Anything to report, Lieutenant?"

Nakajima's jaw tightened. "Kuroki has failed, sir."

Sakamoto's smile vanished. "No, your *sensei* has failed, Lieutenant."

Shame wrapped around Nakajima's throat but he managed to choke out, "General Zakamoto...I..." before trailing off.

Damn it all. Even in Tokyo, at the side of one of the most powerful men in the Imperial Army, he still felt like a callow rice farmer. He never learned how to completely control his Tohoku accent, turning 's's' into 'z's'. But there was no time for self-pity. Not while Japan slid toward the abyss of corruption and decadence.

"I apologize, General..."

General Sakamoto's smile returned, more subdued but still confident. "Lieutenant, when you finally see combat, you'll realize that there is no shame in withdrawing from the battlefield when the enemy is too strong. It only means you must alter your strategy. Tell Ryusaki-san I wish to meet with him. Tonight."

Lieutenant Nakajima bit his lip and nodded. Ah, how kind the gods were to let him serve under men like this.

"But first," Sakamoto added. "We must attend to His Excellency, Baron Onishi."

CHAPTER SEVEN

At Baron Onishi's request, they retreated to his personal office. Aizawa posted two *junsas* to stand guard outside before ordering the rest of the squad to disperse the crowds around the Diet and search the perimeter, just in case there were any other assassins out today.

The office was furnished with a portrait of the Emperor hanging above a polished desk, decorated with a candlestick telephone, files, and an ashtray. Aizawa stubbed out his smoke but still needed another to settle his nerves. He pulled out a green-and-yellow pack of Golden Bat cigarettes, humbly offering one to the Baron first.

"No thank you, Inspector. I do not smoke Japanese cigarettes." Onishi reached into his coat and presented a pack of Pall Malls to sample. "Shameful as it is, I must admit that American tobacco is superior to ours."

A valid point. Golden Bats left a bitter aftertaste and were rumored to be cut with tobacco dust. Still, they remained the most popular brand in Japan, if only because of their low price. The lure of foreign tobacco proved too great and Aizawa accepted the pack of Pall Malls. Lighting up further dulled the remaining pain from his cheek. He couldn't fault the Baron for his taste.

"What you did out there," Onishi said, turning his head, "was very brave."

"I was merely doing my duty," Aizawa said.

Despite his top hat and Pall Malls, the Baron was still Japanese and had to sympathize with that. Aizawa took a drag on his Pall Mall and handed the pack over.

"Keep it," Onishi insisted. Aizawa slid the cigarettes into his coat pocket, unable to tell if the Baron was being generous or thought the pack was now contaminated.

*****

Lieutenant Nakajima walked down the deserted halls of the Diet, keeping an eye out for Baron Onishi. Where had that wrinkled villain slithered off to? He couldn't let the Baron leave until General Sakamoto spoke to him first. Time was not on their side. Any minute now, Onishi could be offered the government, and all of their carefully laid plans would be ruined.

He turned a corner and almost collided with a police officer.

"My apologies, sir."

Nakajima nodded and said, "Pardon me, but was that Baron Onishi you escorted in here?"

"Yes, sir."

"My superior, General Sakamoto, wishes to have a word with the Baron."

Although there were traces of hesitation on the policeman's face, the mention of General Sakamoto had its intended impact.

"Follow me, Lieutenant," he said, as they started down the hall.

*****

Aizawa smoked in silence for several minutes before the office door opened. A *junsa* presented himself with a salute.

"Sir, the area has been secured," he announced

Aizawa said, "Good work. Baron, would you please accompany me back to Headquarters and give a statement?"

Before Onishi could answer, the *junsa* added, "Also, there is an Army officer who wishes to speak with the Baron."

Aizawa nodded but kept his hand near his pistol, just in case. Stubbing out his cigarette, Aizawa followed the *junsa* and Onishi into the hallway. A young officer approached them. Cloaked in a dark brown uniform and with an emotionless mask for a face, he looked like a toy soldier come to life. Yellow aiguillettes looped around his right shoulder marked him as a staff officer attached to the Army Ministry. Without acknowledging Aizawa's presence, he strode up to Onishi and bowed.

"Lieutenant Nakajima, Your Excellency," he said.

The Baron returned the bow.

"Excellency, my superior, Vice-Army Minister Zakamoto, requests an audience with you."

The Lieutenant's accent was folksy and rural, probably from the Tohoku region, famous for its endless rice farms. These days, the Army and Navy were filled with young men eager to escape the grinding poverty and famine of the northeast.

Other than that, the Lieutenant was practically a photographic print of the officers he'd served under while in the Army, during the ill-fated Siberian Expedition to crush the Bolshevik Revolution some ten years ago. Cold and aloof, officers were like a species above their men. Even now, Aizawa fought a reflex to stand at attention.

"Very well, Lieutenant," Baron Onishi said before turning to Aizawa. "I shall visit your Headquarters and give my statement afterward, Inspector."

"Perhaps I should accompany you, Baron."

Onishi waved his hand. "That won't be necessary. I know General Sakamoto personally." He turned to the Army officer. "Please lead the way."

Lieutenant Nakajima spun around on his heel and led the Baron down the hall, his heavy saber clanking against his left boot. Police officers weren't used to being snubbed, but in the pyramid of Japanese society, the Military and aristocrats were both a tier higher, making the slight more acceptable. Aizawa leaned over to the two *junsas*.

"Follow him and be on your guard. As soon as he's done, escort him back to my office. Even if I'm not there, send him to *my* office. Understood?" The *junsas* saluted and trotted off after the Baron. If Onishi had business to attend to, then so did he.

Aizawa headed back toward the Baron's office, called Police Headquarters, and asked for Murayama.

"Sergeant Murayama here."

"Is Chaplin-san awake yet?"

"Not yet. You really nailed him. The *junsas* are calling you KO Kenji."

"Please tell me there's more," Aizawa said.

"His name is Makoto Kuroki and he already has a record with us. A month ago, he stole a bag of rice and spent a week in jail. When he got out, Kuroki pickpocketed some salaryman on the subway. The salaryman trailed him to a brothel in Yoshiwara and called the Police. But listen to this. Kuroki apologized and explained that since he was laid off from his job at the cannery, he couldn't afford to see his favorite whore any longer. The salaryman was so sympathetic to Kuroki's situation that he dropped the charges."

"What was the name of the brothel he was arrested at?" Aizawa asked.

"The Water Temple," Murayama said before adding, "A yakuza joint. Owned by the Okamura Gang to be specific."

Aizawa tensed at the name and remembered raiding their gambling den a year ago. He was sure that the Okamura Gang hadn't forgotten either. Was the underworld also involved with this assassination? Regardless, he needed to get over there fast.

"Good work, Sergeant. I'll pay a little visit to the Water Temple. In the meantime—"

"I'll begin questioning our guest," Murayama said with a soft chuckle. The Sergeant's interrogation methods always left Aizawa with a bad taste, but a spasm of pain in his cheek discouraged any pity this time.

Aizawa hung up and reviewed the facts. Makoto Kuroki, unemployed and destitute, had robbed a man and spent the money on prostitutes instead of food. Such a man might not want a last meal, but chances were he'd want a last lay.

CHAPTER EIGHT

Aizawa looked out the taxicab window as the Diet Building shrank behind him. Traveling northward, they were soon out of the government district of Nagatacho with its modern cement buildings and bending around the elaborate moat that ringed the Imperial Palace. A leftover from the Tokugawa Shogunate, the structure radiated such heavenly authority that Aizawa turned his unworthy gaze eastward to the steel-and-brick towers of Marunouchi.

Aside from the Diet, few places were more despised these days than Tokyo's financial district. Newspaper editorials ranted against the greedy men who schemed and swindled while common people lost more and more each day. For the past year, the Metropolitan Police had been bombarded with letters demanding the arrest of Japan's real criminals – the *zaibatsu* capitalists.

Continuing northward, the taxicab drove through his home neighborhood, the working class Ueno district, and passed by the largest park in Tokyo. Although it was shrouded in darkness, Ueno Park filled Aizawa with childhood memories: playing baseball with friends, viewing the cherry blossoms with his parents, and taking his little sister to the zoo.

He sighed. Tokyo was a city of duality, made up of Marunouchis and Ueno Parks, the old and the new, the living and the dead. He'd seen the city die before, during the Great Kanto Earthquake, only to be resurrected like some vengeful spirit. Whatever Tokyo was now, Kenji Aizawa's duty was to maintain law and order in it.

Several minutes later, the taxicab ground to a halt. Outside, the walled district of Yoshiwara stood like a relic lost in time. Created some three centuries ago in the Tokugawa Era, it had withstood revolutions and disease but had nearly succumbed to the Great Earthquake. Somehow Yoshiwara had survived, although it now looked mortally wounded. Gone was the splendor of old Japan with its poetry-emblazoned gate and garishly dressed courtesans. Now, Yoshiwara had devolved into just another vice district, like an old whore whose syphilis had finally caught up with her.

The driver turned around and said, "Sorry sir, but this is as far as I can go. That'll be one yen, please."

"Stay here. I won't be long," Aizawa said, handing a one-yen coin over.

The driver gave a sly smile. "Take as long as you want in there, I don't judge. Besides, it's not as if I have anywhere to be."

Every business had taken a hit apparently, even the one-yen taxis that drove anywhere in Tokyo for a single yen per trip. It looked as if the water trade – as the Japanese so delicately called prostitution – was no exception. Only a small trickle of men in overcoats and winter kimonos filtered through the main gate like factory workers beginning their shifts.

Aizawa hopped out of the car and joined their ranks. Brothels lined the streets of Yoshiwara like noodle stands. Before the depression, he'd been a frequent customer. But only duty brought him here these days.

Aizawa walked down the main street of Naka-no-cho until he reached the Water Temple. It was a simple, two-story wooden structure with *noren* curtains that proclaimed its name at the entrance. Pleasant and inviting, but also owned by the Okamura Gang. He needed to make sure his toys were ready before he went in to play. He felt for his Colt automatic, snug in its shoulder holster. Aizawa took a deep breath and entered.

*****

The silence was suffocating. Reiko searched for an excuse to leave the *machiya*, but her mind went blank. Masaru would suspect something…or did he already? No, judging by that empty stare on his face, she was the last thing on his mind. He hadn't said a single word since she'd finished her song. Not even a 'thank you' after she cleaned up all that broken glass.

Walking over to the radio, she turned it on, filling the room with a tune that was jazzier than "Sake, Tears or Sighs?"

"What's the name of this?" Masaru wondered aloud.

"'Minnie the Moocher'*,*" Reiko answered. Not the best song to lift someone's spirits, but that's what geisha were for. "Masaru," she cooed, kneeling next to him, "it's over now."

He glared back from behind his glasses.

"You don't understand. I can't ignore my duty to the Emperor and my ancestors."

That reminded Reiko of her own duty as a geisha; to lift Masaru out of the swamp of self-pity. That meant more jazz. She hummed the melody to "Minnie the Moocher" and ad-libbed her own scat. Masaru sat grim-faced but at least she was having a good time.

"Ryusaki-zensei?" a folksy voice called from outside.

Hajime Nakajima. What did that country monkey want?

"Turn that off," Masaru said, pointing at the radio. Reiko leaped up and turned the knob, then resumed her post. "Come in, Nakajima-san."

The sliding door whooshed open and Lieutenant Hajime Nakajima stepped inside. Fresh snow clung to his black boots and khaki cape, draped over his frame. With one swift motion, he parted the cape, revealing the rest of his dark brown uniform. Red collar patches, red and gold shoulder insignia, yellow aiguillettes, and a brass star centered in the crimson band on his peaked service cap looked like drops of blood and piss in a sea of shit.

Despite his clothes, Lieutenant Nakajima looked dashing with a strong jaw, soft cheeks, and warm brown eyes underneath his cap's black leather visor. He cast a glare toward Reiko, like a man discovering a thief in his home. Turning his attention toward Masaru, Nakajima gave a deep bow, like a samurai appearing before his *daimyo* lord.

"*Zensei*, I have urgent news."

"I know that Kuroki has failed," Masaru said. "I'll find another man to kill Baron Onishi…"

"Yes, but General Zakamoto wishes to speak to you."

Masaru's eyes widened. "What?"

"He's here in Asakusa…at the Dragonfly Tea House."

Panic struck Masaru's face. "Is he calling the plan off?"

Nakajima shook his head. "The General regards this as merely a setback."

Masaru sighed and smiled. "Come Harutora. Let's show General Sakamoto a good night."

Nakajima's face distorted with irritation. "*Zensei*, should we really bring…her?"

The Lieutenant no longer looked like a samurai. More like a dog begging for scraps. Reiko stood and bowed. "Yes, perhaps I should be turning in for the night." Her brain was already overloaded with intrigue.

Masaru shot her a paralyzing look and turned back to Nakajima. "You don't expect us to pour our own drinks, do you?"

*****

"For the last time Inspector, we don't keep records of our customers," the woman said from behind her desk. Wearing an elegant kimono and heavy wrinkles down her cheeks, she possessed the look of a former prostitute turned brothel mistress. And one didn't rise from the depths of Yoshiwara without learning to keep your mouth shut. "If you're not planning on becoming one, I suggest you leave."

From behind her little wooden desk, the brothel mistress guarded the entrance to the main entryway, closed off behind a *shoji* screen door. If this were any other brothel, a flash of his *meishi* card would be sufficient, but it was always better to tread carefully with the yakuza, especially the Okamura Gang. Still, something was off. Yakuza thrived in the illegal shadows of society; protection rackets, organizing construction workers, and above all, gambling. But prostitution was legal so long as it was licensed. No matter. Right now, he needed to focus on more important matters.

"I'm only interested in one of your customers. Makoto Kuroki. Little man. Charlie Chaplin mustache. He was in here a month ago with some stolen money. Sound familiar?"

The woman shifted her eyes down but said nothing.

"I…I can't say anything," she said, squirming in her seat.

"Not if you want to keep your tongue!" a voice shot out from behind them. Aizawa drew himself up as the *shoji* door slid open. A man stepped out, clutching a *wakizashi* short sword. His young face was partially obscured by a flat cap but it didn't shadow the glow of alcohol in his cheeks. His stocky body was draped in a light gray kimono and black *hakama* pants, so loose-fitting that a horned *oni* demon tattoo was visible on his chest, cushioned by bright, swollen skin.

"Who are you?"

"He's with the Metropolitan Police," the mistress said, standing to attention.

"Police?" he sneered, lowering his sword slightly. "What do you want? Our license is up to date…"

"I'm just asking a few questions."

"We don't have good memories here," the man said, sake clinging to his breath.

Aizawa searched this yakuza for any signs of an impending attack. The status of being a police officer was usually enough of a shield, but alcohol mixed with youthful arrogance could make an explosive cocktail. He decided on a compliment to diffuse the tension.

"New tattoo?"

The yakuza smiled and opened his kimono further, showing it off. It was a red-faced *oni* demon, snarling and swinging an enormous club. The red ink glistened in the pale electric light. "Like it? It's my first. Just got it a few days ago. The demon symbolizes strength. It's also my nickname." He chuckled. "That's why I'm on security duty here."

Aizawa forced a smile. Any yakuza who chose that as his first tattoo had something to prove. But so far, the *wakizashi* hung harmlessly at his side, easing Aizawa's fears.

"Demon-san, I tried to tell Inspector Aizawa that we don't keep records," the mistress said.

"Aizawa?" Demon snapped, bringing the *wakizashi* up close. "The same Inspector Aizawa who raided that gambling den last year?"

Aizawa tensed. That raid not only earned him an accommodation, but also the undying hatred of the Okamura Gang. Members of the yakuza rarely attacked police officers, but the intense hatred in this hoodlum's bleary eyes was cause for concern.

Aizawa reached for his gun but like a rushing tsunami, Demon slammed him up against the wall. Air rushed out of Aizawa's lungs. The yakuza hadn't lied about his strength. Grasping Demon's wrists, it took everything Aizawa could muster to keep the *wakizashi* from plunging into his throat.

"Our gang was almost ruined because of that raid. What's worse, you made us all lose face," Demon hissed, as the sword shook in his hand. "You owe us, Inspector. Now pay up!"

CHAPTER NINE

A fiery pain ripped through Aizawa's muscles as he struggled to keep the sword at bay. He scanned the room, searching for help. The brothel mistress backed up into the corner, wide-eyed with mute horror. No customers came in or out, although it was doubtful whether Demon would stop even in front of witnesses.

"I think I'll bring your head to Boss Okamura," Demon said with breath like poison gas. "We'll crack it open in front of the whole gang like a watermelon. Then, I'll get a new tattoo to celebrate. Maybe a severed head?"

Aizawa's gaze shifted to the snarling tattoo on the yakuza's chest, set against raw, pink skin. He could still attack Demon's one weak spot. Summoning the last of his strength, Aizawa pushed Demon back as far as he could with one hand and used the other to dig his nails into the inflamed flesh.

Demon threw back his head and spat out an agonized scream, letting the *wakizashi* drop slightly. Aizawa threw a heavy right cross and sent the hoodlum stumbling across the foyer and up against the other wall. Within seconds, Demon collected himself and stood, grasping the *wakizashi* for a renewed attack. Catching his breath, Aizawa plunged his hand into his coat and drew the Colt automatic. Demon froze and tossed the sword to the ground.

"You win, Inspector," he sighed, extending his hands out to be cuffed.

Nothing would please Aizawa more than to have Sergeant Murayama give this hoodlum the works, but members of Tokyo's crime families couldn't be treated like normal criminals. The Metropolitan Police and the yakuza maintained a delicate balance that was rarely upset. Aizawa didn't need any more trouble at Headquarters.

Instead, he strode over to Demon and gave him another firm punch right on his bloody tattoo. The yakuza collapsed onto the floor, clutching his chest and gasping.

"Let's try this again. Makoto Kuroki. Short man. Charlie Chaplin mustache. When did you last see him?"

"Last night. He was one of Yuki's regulars," Demon said with a wheeze and twisted his head toward the brothel mistress. "Bring that little fool out."

The woman nodded and disappeared behind the *shoji* door. Demon struggled to pick himself up but Aizawa forced him back to the floor with another kick to his tattoo. The yakuza's face contorted in pain but he kept quiet. The brothel mistress returned with a plump-faced young girl, no older than fourteen, wearing a green kimono and an empty expression.

"Yuki," Demon wheezed. "Answer the Inspector's questions."

The girl nodded.

"Yuki-san, do you remember Makoto Kuroki being here last night?" Aizawa asked.

"Yes. Kuroki-zan was one of my regulars."

There was no mistaking Yuki's distinct dialect from the Tohoku region. She couldn't be the same woman who had called him. Instead, her accent summoned images of that Army officer from earlier, Lieutenant Nakajima. Tohoku boys typically joined the Army and Navy, while Tohoku girls did their tour of duty in the brothels of Tokyo and Osaka.

"Yuki-san, are your parents rice farmers?"

She nodded.

Everything aligned with clarity. Licensed prostitution wasn't the yakuza's preferred business, but gambling and money-lending were. The girl's parents had probably fallen into debt with the Okamura Gang and had sold her off to save the farm for another season. In return, Demon and his bosses made a profit from each lay Yuki gave from now on. During famines, only the locusts ate well.

"What did Kuroki-san say last night?" Aizawa asked.

"That he wouldn't be coming back. He wouldn't tell me why. It was heartbreaking."

"Heartbreaking? Did you love him?"

"No," Yuki said. "He was a good customer. Until he lost his job."

"Did he love you?"

"Maybe. He has no friends or family." Yuki sighed. "Such a pitiful man."

"He does have *one* friend," Demon gasped. "He was here last night…even paid for Kuroki's lay."

"Who?"

Demon shook his head. "Didn't give his name."

"Describe him."

"Tall and thin. Wore a nice suit and horn-rimmed glasses," Demon said.

The description sounded hauntingly familiar. "Tell me more," Aizawa said.

"He only paid for Kuroki-san's round. Instead of treating himself, he kept going on and on about some patriotic society he led."

An ominous chill swept over Aizawa. "A patriotic society? What was its name?"

"I can't remember…there are hundreds these days. The Dark Ocean Society, the National Foundation Society, the Black Dragon Society…"

Aizawa lifted his foot over Demon's tattoo. "Think harder."

The yakuza's eyes widened. "Something to do with a sword…that's right. It's from that story where the sun goddess gave her grandson the invincible grass-cutting sword from heaven…the Kusanagi!"

Aizawa's foot hit the ground with a hollow thud. The Kusanagi Society. That meant Masaru Ryusaki. It had to be him. All the details fit. He should have known that bloodthirsty samurai would be involved somehow.

"Tell me exactly what he said or I'll peel that tattoo off your chest."

Demon nodded. "He tried to recruit me. Lots of yakuza have ties to patriotic societies. Some genuinely love Japan while others just use it as a way to make a few extra yen. I don't care about politics, but I humored this fool as he went on."

"Did he mention anything about Baron Onishi?" Aizawa asked, raising his foot again.

"No, he didn't," Demon said, his face tightening with fear. "Just that the Kusanagi Society needed patriotic men in the coming days. Typical right-wing bluster. Once Kuroki finished I asked them both to leave. That's all I know, I swear!"

Some yakuza he turned out to be. Still, Aizawa felt some gratitude toward this sniveling creature for unmasking his old enemy. He turned to the women. While the brothel mistress shook in fear, Yuki stood there like a department store mannequin. The kid had already braced herself for years of service in Yoshiwara and the cruelest part of all was that it was entirely legal. Such an unjust system gave rise to men like Masaru Ryusaki and his Kusanagi Society, willing to kill whoever they wanted in the name of reform.

Aizawa bowed and began walking toward the exit, but paused in front of Demon. "If you hear anything about the Kusanagi Society or Masaru Ryusaki...come directly to me."

Demon nodded and whimpered in agreement. Aizawa marched out of the Water Temple and slammed the sliding door behind him. The thought of Ryusaki controlling Kuroki, along with other puppet assassins, filled him with anger and dread. Masaru Ryusaki's involvement meant that a dark plot was wrapping itself around Tokyo like some giant octopus.

A light snow fell and dusted Yoshiwara with a dreamlike atmosphere. Aizawa lit a Pall Mall and soaked in the warmth from the lighter. Winter was the best time for plots.

CHAPTER TEN

Back at the Metropolitan Police Headquarters, Aizawa took the elevator to the second floor. A century ago, it could have been the shogun's torture chamber but it now served as the 'interrogation and processing level.' A *junsa* escorted a middle-aged woman with puffy eyes and tear-stained cheeks past him. No doubt she was one of the many housewives caught thieving everything from rice to *koi* fish out of ponds, just so the family could have something to eat. Aizawa shook his head and hoped the courts would show leniency. At least her type confessed easily. For the holdouts, there were other methods.

Officially, torture had been banned some fifty years ago, during the Meiji Era. But behind closed doors, police officers had perfected the art of slapping, beating, and brutalizing without leaving marks that would show up in court and complicate matters.

Entering the interrogation room, Aizawa reminded himself that duty to the Emperor wasn't always pleasant. He gave the room a once-over. On the wall, a portrait of the Emperor cast a paternal, yet judgmental gaze onto his subjects. After all, His Majesty was not just a mere monarch, but also the Son of Heaven and direct descendant of the sun goddess Amaterasu. Simply seeing the Emperor's disapproving face was enough to break some suspects. But not Makoto Kuroki.

Sergeant Murayama stood naked to the waist, bathed in sweat and clutching a bamboo sword. Swollen and battered, Kuroki sat handcuffed, beaming a triumphant smile.

"Sorry, Inspector. He still hasn't talked," Murayama said, buttoning his tunic back up. "This little worm has armor for skin."

Kuroki gasped out a laugh. "Patriotism has given me the strength of a hundred men! I am harder than any bamboo you can beat me with."

Aizawa sighed. This was going to be difficult.

"I'm impressed, Kuroki-san," Aizawa said. "Yuki-san would be too if she could see you now."

Kuroki's smile dropped and his mustache twitched. If brutality didn't work, perhaps shame would.

"She's heartbroken that you've been arrested," Aizawa said, taking a seat across from him.

Kuroki's eyes dropped.

"You were her best customer. What will she do for money? Don't you care about her?"

"I did…but…" Kuroki lifted his head with a newfound confidence. "My mission was more important than any woman."

"Your mission? You mean assassinating Baron Onishi?"

"I wasn't going to assassinate anyone."

Aizawa sighed again. This was going to be *very* difficult.

"You weren't? Don't tell me you were carrying that Nambu around for protection. Besides, it's illegal for a private citizen to own a firearm."

"The pistol was my brother's," Kuroki said.

"An Army officer?"

Kuroki bit his lip and nodded. "A lieutenant in the Imperial Guard."

Aizawa gave an impressed nod. The Imperial Guard? Obviously, not all Kuroki men were short.

"He shot himself last year to protest that treasonous London Naval Treaty," Kuroki continued.

"Is that so?" Murayama snorted. "An Army man concerned about the Navy! That's a first!"

"That evil treaty limits our battleships three to one against Britain and America," Kuroki said. "My brother knew the politicians would try to poison the Army with some shameful treaty next." Kuroki's eyes began to water. "I tried to follow him into the Army, but," he paused, mustache twitching and fists tightening, "I couldn't pass the height requirement." A heavy sigh followed. "I tried and tried but was always rejected. Instead, I planned to follow his example."

"By committing suicide?"

Kuroki nodded. "Yes, in front of that treacherous bastard, Baron Onishi. Do you remember the speech when he called the Imperial Army 'bandits in uniform stealing Manchuria like thieves in the night'? How shameful! Tomorrow morning, while fat *zaibatsu* capitalists and politicians drink their morning tea, they would read about how Baron Onishi's fancy clothes were splattered with the blood and brains of a true patriot."

Aizawa laughed. "Are these really your words? Or were they given to you by your *sensei*…Masaru Ryusaki?"

Kuroki's eyes widened.

"Oh yes, I got that information from the Water Temple too. You realize that Japan is one national family, right? What would the Emperor think if he knew about your plans to assassinate one of our political leaders?"

Kuroki's entire frame began to tremble. "I told you…I was going to shoot myself!"

Aizawa waved his hand. "A convenient story if you got caught…I'm sure Ryusaki will find another unemployed patriot to correct your failure…"

Kuroki sprang out of his chair and lunged across the table like a mortar. They tumbled over, Kuroki's small hands locking around Aizawa's throat like a vice. How could this little bastard be so strong? A fighting spirit must have blazed inside Kuroki's tiny frame like an inferno.

The attack didn't last long. Like a mother tiger protecting her cub, Murayama intervened and pulled Kuroki off, then hammered a thunderous punch into his gut. After a pathetic groan, Kuroki sank to his hands and knees, cursing between wheezes and gasps.

The Sergeant helped Aizawa to his feet and gestured to the bamboo sword again. "Want me to give him another round?"

A tempting offer, but Kuroki wasn't the type to break from a beating or forced shame. Besides, time was not on his side. He needed to know what Ryusaki was plotting soon. Two options remained. One, bring out tortures usually reserved for Communists; bamboo slivers under the fingernails and lit matches held underneath genitals. Or two, throw him in an unheated cell in the dead of winter to have him 'chilled.' Neither was appealing, but the first seemed especially dishonorable.

"Sergeant," Aizawa said, turning toward the door. "Chill him."

"Inspector," Kuroki wheezed. Aizawa turned back and met the cold pair of eyes drilling into him. "Patriotism has hardened my spirit. Do your worst."

Aizawa turned to Murayama. "You heard him, Sergeant. Do your duty."

Closing the door behind him, Aizawa sighed. Needing a smoke, he fished out a Pall Mall and remembered Onishi. The Baron must have arrived by now. He cursed his forgetfulness and started toward the elevator, away from the agonized howls that echoed throughout the hall.

CHAPTER ELEVEN

The elevator doors opened on the third floor, Headquarters for the First Investigative Section. Detailed with solving the major crimes of Tokyo, Aizawa and his peers had their hands full since the depression began.

Earlier in the year, an unemployed man beheaded his landlord with a samurai sword after he was evicted. Labor unions caused unrest so often that the Police doubled as strikebreakers. Every other week, gamblers who couldn't pay back their debts to the yakuza were fished out of the Sumida River. Even the most heinous of all Japanese crimes, arson, was on the rise. It was all too easy to ignite one of Tokyo's many wooden buildings, usually to collect insurance money, but sometimes as a megalomaniacal suicide.

Aizawa reached his office and dismissed the *junsa* standing guard. He entered and found Baron Onishi sitting stone-faced across from his desk, littered with papers, files, and a bloated ashtray. It was small and cramped, but all his. The Baron probably disapproved of such messiness, despite his placid expression. Aizawa felt the need to explain how a private office was a rare prize, one he was awarded after his former partner made superintendent, but settled for a deep bow instead.

"Welcome Baron," he said, sitting behind his desk. Onishi simply nodded as his eyes scanned the tiny office. "I apologize about the mess. May I offer you anything? Tea or one of your cigarettes?"

"No thank you."

So much for humor. Besides, Baron Onishi looked far more interested in a framed newspaper article on the wall, with the headline "Inspectors Shimura and Aizawa Raid Yakuza Gambling Den!"

"Your partner?" Baron Onishi asked, returning his full attention to Aizawa.

"My superior now. That case earned him a promotion."

"Shouldn't we meet with him?"

Aizawa coughed. "We will, but may I please ask you a few questions first?"

Baron Onishi nodded.

"Are you familiar with Masaru Ryusaki or the Kusanagi Society?"

"I've never heard of either," Onishi replied with an irritated look. "Are they related to the man from earlier?"

"His name is Makoto Kuroki, a member of the Kusanagi Society."

Aizawa reached into his desk drawer and removed a slim book. He hadn't looked at it in months but kept it around for just such an occasion. Its cover burst with such radiant color that it almost hurt his eyes; a *katana* sword surrounded by bright pink cherry blossoms. An image straight out of a samurai fairy tale. He handed it to the Baron, who studied it like vermin under a microscope.

"*The New Japan*," Baron Onishi read aloud. "By Masaru Ryusaki."

Aizawa nodded. "He leads the small but dangerous Kusanagi Society. That's who wants you dead, Baron."

Onishi sighed. "Another right-wing group? They're growing like weeds."

"Thank the depression. Every unemployed hothead is starting his own patriotic society." Aizawa lit a Pall Mall. "This group takes its name from the Kusanagi, the invincible grass-cutting sword forged by the gods."

"Such childish fantasies," the Baron scoffed.

"But men like Ryusaki know how much people love those stories. He founded the group earlier this year with the purpose of overthrowing the government."

"I take it this man is incarcerated now?"

"No, he's not." Aizawa swallowed hard and took another drag. "I need to tell you some things, Baron. But I also need your guarantee that they will not leave my office."

Onishi set the book on the desk and nodded his agreement.

"Back in March, there were rumors about a plot hatched by Ryusaki and other nationalists. I infiltrated the Kusanagi Society and learned how it was planning to stage riots in front of the Diet. Dynamite would be planted around the building and throughout Tokyo. This, in turn, would allow the Army to declare martial law and install a general as the new shogun."

Aizawa bit his lip, trying not to let his rage show. Only six years ago Japan had finally given voting rights to all men, not just the wealthy like Masaru Ryusaki. For centuries, men like him ruled Japan while commoners toiled away in silence. And now this madman wanted to abolish what little democracy there was?

"So, the Imperial Army was involved?" Baron Onishi asked, bringing Aizawa out of his thoughts.

"Ryusaki bragged about how there was a junior officer in the Army Ministry who acted as a liaison to some of the top brass. Once news of his capture reached their intended shogun, he panicked and backed out. The entire scheme then collapsed."

"I have never even heard any of this."

"It was kept out of the newspapers," Aizawa said and took a drag on his cigarette. "By him." He pointed to Shimura's picture on the wall.

"A fellow conspirator?"

"I'm not sure, but definitely a sympathizer. He's changed. I'm not sure why, but he ordered Ryusaki's release because 'his motives were sincere.'"

"I take it you don't share his views."

Aizawa took another puff before stubbing the Pall Mall out. "Crime is crime, regardless of how sincere the intentions might be. I have a duty to the Emperor to uphold the law. Everything else is secondary."

"What happened to Ryusaki?"

"I lost track of him. Moved out of his old place and went underground. Baron, with your help, I can finally locate Ryusaki and bring him to justice. But you must appeal to my superior for protection."

Confusion showed on Baron Onishi's face. "I must beg for protection from a man who favors assassins and fanatics?"

It did sound insane when said aloud. Still, at least he'd had the foresight to send the Baron to his office, rather than directly to Superintendent Shimura. Here they could rehearse in privacy.

"Baron, I must obey my superior, regardless of how I personally feel. Being a Dietman, surely you can understand. Isn't public service a constant war between duty and emotion?"

The Baron gave an understanding nod. All Onishi needed was an extra push to become a willing ally in the coming war.

"Baron, Kuroki might not confess anytime soon. As of right now, he's insisting he only wanted to kill himself as a protest."

"How selfless of him."

"Men like him are worse than crooks. They're idealists, and that means they don't break easily. While we're waiting for a confession, Ryusaki will send a second, third, and fourth assassin."

"What do you suggest?"

"Nationalist or not, Superintendent Shimura is still a police officer. If you tell him about the death threats you've received and request protection, then he'll be obligated to keep the case open and I can continue the investigation."

"And what about this mysterious informant of yours?"

"I think it's best if we keep that between us."

Onishi sat in dignified silence. Proud men might not fear death, but they could hold grudges.

"Inspector, I do not fear these...*soshi*," the Baron said, practically spitting the last word out like phlegm. Once a title applied to strong warriors with pure spirits, it had long been synonymous with political gangsters like Ryusaki. "But I understand your obligations and I will not interfere with your duty."

Aizawa smiled. Now, he had to convince Shimura.

CHAPTER TWELVE

Followed by Baron Onishi, Aizawa entered Superintendent Shimura's office and presented his superior with a deep bow. In his dark uniform and flashy epaulettes, Joji Shimura cut an impressive figure, amplified by a pair of intense eyes guarded by round spectacles. His long face hadn't aged much since his promotion to superintendent last year, but streaks of gray through his hair showcased the stress from his new position. There were no chairs in the office since Shimura always fortified himself behind a massive oak desk and below a portrait of the Emperor. Nevertheless, the Superintendent rose and greeted them with a bow.

"May I introduce the honorable Baron Onishi," Aizawa said at attention. "Baron, Superintendent Shimura."

"It is an honor," Shimura said with a smile.

No words from Onishi, only a stiff bow. Aizawa glanced around the office, letting his mind run. What did the Baron think of the file cabinets labeled "Subversive Persons & Dangerous Thinkers"?

"You have something to report, Inspector?" Shimura said, still smiling.

"Yes sir, there was an incident outside the Imperial Diet earlier. A young nationalist, Makoto Kuroki, was attempting to assassinate the Baron."

"I'm pleased you finally informed me," Shimura said as his smile began to fade.

"My humblest apologies, sir. I was busy conducting Kuroki's interrogation."

"Has he confessed?" Shimura asked.

"No, sir...he insists he was going to commit suicide as a form of protest."

"Ah, I see."

"The Baron saw the entire incident," Aizawa said.

"Yes," Onishi said, clearing his throat. "The Inspector and this young man engaged in an altercation in the courtyard."

"Did Kuroki-san shoot at you?"

"No," Onishi conceded. "But I agree with the Inspector's conclusions."

"And Inspector, did you see him draw his pistol?"

"No, sir."

"Then there is very little evidence that he was planning to harm anyone."

A lingering soreness on Aizawa's cheek argued otherwise. "He did assault a police officer."

"Yes, and he will be prosecuted for that. But both illegal possession of a firearm and assault are a far cry from assassination."

"That being said, I have received several death threats recently," Onishi interjected.

Shimura's eyes widened behind his glasses. "I'm shocked to hear this, Baron. Why didn't you hand them over to us?"

Probably because you'd frame them on your wall. An unfortunate truth, but aloud Aizawa said, "Kuroki will confess eventually, sir. However, in light of these threats, perhaps granting the Baron protection would be best."

Onishi gave a firm nod. "I find this agreeable, given the current political climate."

An insincere smile molded onto Shimura's face. "Of course, Baron," he said, reaching for his phone.

"Thank you, Superintendent," Onishi said. "But I'd like the Inspector to personally take charge of my security."

Shame and humiliation flickered on Shimura's face. "If you insist, Baron."

"I do," Onishi replied. Although his face was dry, Aizawa could see pools of joy in the Baron's eyes. A lifetime in politics must have sharpened one's tongue.

"I'll have one of the *junsas* from earlier escort you home and stand guard tonight, Baron," Aizawa offered. Onishi gave a satisfied nod.

"If you would excuse us, Baron," Shimura said. "I need to speak to the Inspector privately."

"Very well. I'll wait for you outside, Inspector."

After a series of bows, Onishi turned and walked out. Once alone, Shimura dropped his artificial smile.

"Why did you wait until now to report this to me?"

"I apologize sir...my duty was elsewhere."

Shimura sank into his chair. "Inspector, housewives are poisoning landlords because they can't pay rent, children are dropping out of school to become pickpockets, and fathers are pimping out daughters for extra yen. But you're concerned with a madman intent on shooting himself."

"And the Baron."

"Why do you think so?"

"Political assassination has a long history in Japan. Prime Minister Hamaguchi was shot last year and Prime Minister Hara was killed ten years ago, both by right-wing nationalists. Baron Onishi admitted he's received many death threats."

"Were any from Kuroki?"

"I don't know."

"And why were you at the Diet today?"

Yes, why was he there? Instinct warned against revealing his anonymous informant, just in case Shimura maintained ties with Ryusaki.

"No special reason, sir," Aizawa said. "I heard about Prime Minister Wakatsuki's resignation and felt there might be unrest."

A pair of narrowed eyes conveyed Shimura's doubts.

"I expect a confession out of Kuroki soon," the Superintendent said. "Dismissed."

Aizawa bowed and slunk out of the office, closing the door behind him with a heavy sigh. He couldn't dismiss a murky premonition that this was his last case. A word from Superintendent Shimura that he harbored "dangerous thoughts" would be enough to demote him back to *junsa*. If he was lucky.

Aizawa turned and walked back to his office where Baron Onishi waited outside the door with a uniformed escort.

"You're to guard Baron Onishi around the clock," Aizawa said. "He is never to leave your sight. You'll be relieved tomorrow afternoon."

The *junsa* snapped a salute. At least Onishi would have some protection. Aizawa considered but dismissed the idea that this policeman was a secret member of the Kusanagi Society. Although there were sympathizers – like Shimura – most of his fellow officers placed duty above politics. Besides, today had left Aizawa so fatigued that he was in no state to guard anyone himself.

Still, he needed to find Masaru Ryusaki fast. Tomorrow, Aizawa would follow up on any leads concerning his old enemy's whereabouts. That is, unless Kuroki confessed first.

"Inspector, I forgot to tell you," Onishi said. "I agreed to attend a meeting in Marunouchi tomorrow afternoon. It should take about an hour."

"With who, Baron?"

Onishi frowned at such an intrusive question but answered anyway. "Prominent men in politics, military, and finance. Tsuyoshi Inukai, General Sakamoto, and Isamu Takano, who's a major donor to the Seiyukai."

Aizawa rubbed his chin, picturing the three-headed beast. Being so close to such powerful men might be useful in the investigation.

"I will personally take over your protection tomorrow afternoon, Baron," Aizawa said.

"Excellent. We will meet you here at four o'clock then," Onishi said. "Until then, I'll retire to my estate and wait for His Majesty's summons."

After exchanging bows, the Baron walked toward the elevator with the *junsa* trailing close behind.

CHAPTER THIRTEEN

Reiko hadn't set foot inside the Dragonfly Tea House in years but found it more or less the same; a simple one-room tea house illuminated by several paper lanterns. But once the sliding doors were shut, it seemed as if Masaru, Lieutenant Nakajima, and she were miles away from Asakusa and in someone's private, picturesque world.

Inside the main room, a wall scroll of Mount Fuji hung ornately. Below it sat a general, kneeling in front of a low-lying table like a monk in meditation. Reiko now understood why she'd been dragged along. Not only to pour drinks but to compete with General Sakamoto's uniform. It was a matter of prestige. How many medals was a geisha equivalent to?

"General Sakamoto," Lieutenant Nakajima said with a bow and clutching a bottle of sake. "May I present the honorable Masaru Ryusaki, *zensei* of the Kusanagi Society."

Masaru gave a deep bow, the lowest Reiko had ever seen. Not expecting an introduction, she bowed too.

General Sakamoto stood and returned the greeting, though at a higher level.

"I am honored to see you again, General. My apologies for making you wait, but there seems to be a shortage of alcohol in Asakusa," Masaru said as Nakajima placed the sake bottle and four cups on the table. Sakamoto smiled and nodded. Late or not, after Kuroki's failure it would have been unthinkable for Masaru to show up empty-handed. With the introductions concluded, they knelt around the table, forcing Reiko off to the side. Still, Sakamoto's eyes gravitated toward her.

"And she is?"

Masaru beamed. "This is Harutora, the finest geisha in Tokyo."

Reiko gave a deep bow, touching her forehead against the *tatami* mat. "Pleased to meet you, honorable General."

"How charming," Sakamoto said. "I adore geisha but the Lieutenant thinks they're a distraction."

Nakajima said nothing.

"Femininity is lost on some men," Reiko said. "Like coins to a cat."

Sakamoto chuckled. Masaru smiled and gave a quick nod to continue.

"Masaru has told me much about you," Reiko said.

"Oh?" Sakamoto's thick eyebrows rose. "Such as?"

"Your honorable service to the Emperor," Reiko said. "And how you're the only hope for Japan."

The General rubbed his chin. "He exaggerates."

"I disagree." She gestured to his glittering medals with her paper fan. "Such a colorful uniform is the cloak of a true hero, one who does not frighten easily."

Sakamoto gave a hearty smile. It was almost too easy. Inflating a man's ego was the geisha's primary duty. Everything else was a distant second.

"Let's have a toast," Reiko said, filling up the cups. She handed one to each man. Masaru poured her a shot and she lifted her glass. "To our great General Sakamoto! Kanpai!"

"Kanpai!" Lieutenant Nakajima and Masaru chorused and downed their cups. General Sakamoto leaned closer to Reiko.

"I've heard geisha take secrets to the grave. Is that true, Harutora-san?"

"Of course, honorable General."

"I'll share a secret with you if you promise not to tell."

Reiko tittered and pressed the fan against her mouth.

"Last year, I bought this tea house," General Sakamoto announced, gesturing around the room.

Reiko removed the fan from her lips and said, "Oh? You must have all sorts of geisha who entertain you here."

Sakamoto shook his head. "Unfortunately not. My men and I," he glanced at Nakajima, "meet here to discuss our plans in secret, away from prying eyes. But junior officers don't appreciate geisha these days. They feel they're creatures of decadence and luxury."

"That's our best trait. Besides, what do junior officers know about geisha? Only colonels and higher can afford us."

Sakamoto gave a pleased smile and said, "You're quite the talker, Harutora-san."

"A woman's tongue is her sword, General. And one that never rusts," Reiko said, matching the General's smile.

That earned a bout of laughter from Sakamoto. Masaru nodded in approval while Nakajima remained stone-faced.

"I haven't had the company of a geisha since before the depression," General Sakamoto continued. "They're like a painting come to life."

"Harutora's dance is like a work of art," Masaru said.

"Is that so?" Sakamoto remarked.

"Oh, but there's no music," Reiko said. "It would be like swimming without water!"

Masaru glared a warning and Reiko realized she had little choice. After a quick bow, she said, "Please enjoy the Dance of Spring."

She rose to her feet and snapped open her paper fan, decorated with fluttering pink cherry blossoms. She twisted it around to reveal a tiger stalking through the mist. A gift to reflect her geisha name: Harutora, *Spring Tiger*.

It had been years since she'd done the Dance of Spring, a movement written to celebrate the cherry blossom festival. Normally, the twanging melody of a *shamisen* provided her rhythm, but the motions were still ingrained in her muscles from endless hours of training.

Reiko held the fan high, representing the radiant sun melting the harsh winter snow. She snapped it shut and slowly opened it, inch by inch, just as the cherry blossoms bloomed in the spring sunlight. Pressing the open fan to her chest, she paused in intricate poses to illustrate the beauty of the season, so many months away. Finally, she lowered the fan to the floor as the cherry blossoms broke free of their trees and fluttered to the ground in a dignified death.

General Sakamoto stared with admiration, as if he were studying a new exhibit at a museum. Masaru looked on with beaming pride but Lieutenant Nakajima shot her a contemptuous glare so cold it prickled her skin.

The dance concluded, Reiko bowed and knelt again. The General and Masaru glowed with approval. For most men, geisha were as potent as alcohol or opium, lulling them into the most susceptible stupor. She figured that only now could Masaru discuss his failure without shame choking him.

"Another toast," Masaru said, holding out his cup.

Reiko took the hint. She grabbed the bottle and poured a shot for Masaru and the General.

"To the Emperor!" Masaru toasted.

"The Emperor!" Sakamoto repeated before they downed their shots.

Masaru exhaled and added, "And to the New Japan! Inspector Aizawa only postponed our inevitable victory!"

"Is this the police officer who arrested you in March?" Sakamoto asked.

Masaru grimaced. "The same." His long fingers wrapped around his *katana* handle. "He's nothing more than a watchdog for the Diet and the *zaibatsu*."

· "But he poses a great risk to our plan. What if he breaks your assassin?" Sakamoto asked, scratching his goatee.

"Kuroki-san won't confess. I chose him for his loyalty and strength," Masaru insisted.

"How did you come across this man?" General Sakamoto asked.

"It was a month ago, after I reactivated the Kusanagi Society. I was selling my book on the street when he approached me. He'd been laid off and rejected for Army service, his lifelong dream."

"Is that so?" Sakamoto said, rubbing his chin.

"Kuroki-san didn't meet the Army's physical requirements. I took pity on his situation and gave him the book for free. General, I've never seen such patriotism inside a man! Although unfit for military service, I drafted him into the Kusanagi Society. He passed out pamphlets and helped sell my book on the streets of Tokyo."

"He seems very devoted."

Masaru nodded. "When you ordered Baron Onishi's assassination, I knew he was the perfect man to carry it out."

"Yet, he failed…"

Masaru swallowed and made no reply.

"What's worse, this Inspector Aizawa might connect the two of you," the General said, wedging a Golden Bat between his lips. On instinct, Reiko leaned over and lit the cigarette with a match. After all, a dutiful geisha was always there to serve men.

Masaru adjusted his glasses. "General, let me deal with Aizawa before he gets too close."

General Sakamoto shook his head. "Far too risky to kill a police inspector. Besides, he will be dealt with after we take power."

Masaru gave a twisted smile.

"But that doesn't solve our problem," Sakamoto continued. "Baron Onishi will be on his guard now. And should he become prime minister, all hope is lost."

Masaru rubbed the back of his head, showing his humiliation.

"Yes, of course, General. Forgive me for my earlier impudence. I'll find another patriot to strike the Baron down."

Sakamoto took a long drag on his cigarette before saying, "That won't be necessary."

"*Zensei*," Nakajima broke in. "I will kill Baron Onishi!"

CHAPTER FOURTEEN

Nakajima's announcement silenced the room for several moments until the General finally spoke.

"Before we left the Diet," Sakamoto said in between drags of his cigarette, "I arranged a meeting with Baron Onishi."

Masaru nodded along, dumbfounded.

"The meeting will take place around 1700 hours tomorrow. Lieutenant Nakajima will be positioned in a window across from the Marunouchi Building, armed with a rifle. From there, he will have a clear shot when Onishi enters the west entrance."

Words finally escaped Masaru's mouth. "But…how do you know he will go in there?"

"Because it is the entrance closest to the Takano Bank office."

Disgust tightened Masaru's face. "Isamu Takano?"

General Sakamoto held up a stifling hand. "Tsuyoshi Inukai of the Seiyukai Party will be there too. Believe me, I do not wish to associate with these scheming foxes, but I will for the sake of the plan."

"General, perhaps killing Baron Onishi is unimportant," Masaru said.

Through the wisps of cigarette smoke, Sakamoto raised an eyebrow.

"Even if he becomes prime minister, my Kusanagi Society can still cause an incident that will justify martial law and make you shogun. Then we can dispose of the Baron at our leisure," Masaru said, punctuating his face-saving plan with a tap on his *katana*.

Sakamoto shook his head. "Impossible. Our numbers are too small."

"But if you would allow me to hold rallies out in the open instead of selling my book in the back alleys of Tokyo I could—"

"Enough!" Sakamoto roared, slapping his hand on the mat. "Baron Onishi must die before he becomes prime minister!"

"Yes, of course, General," Masaru said with a supplicating bow. "But what if Lieutenant Nakajima is…captured?"

General Sakamoto took a final drag and stubbed out his Golden Bat. "*If* that happens, the Metropolitan Police have no jurisdiction over Army officers. He'll be turned over to the *Kempeitai*, the Military Police—"

"And the *Kempeitai* is controlled by the Army," Masaru continued, nodding his understanding.

"Regardless of what happens afterward, the Lieutenant has requested to be transferred to Manchuria," Sakamoto said, slapping Nakajima on the back. "He'll make a fine platoon commander."

A smirk cracked Lieutenant Nakajima's glassy face. "It is my sacred duty to die for the Emperor, but I wish to fight for him first."

Masaru clapped his hands and turned to Reiko. "Another toast!"

Of course, a toast for Japan's future shogun. Aizawa would probably be interested in this turn of events, but hadn't she done enough already? Forcing a smile, Reiko poured three shots. Masaru was beaming, but there was concern behind his glasses. Perhaps at losing his most die-hard follower to Manchuria? Or was it from losing face in front of the General? Probably both.

General Sakamoto looked at ease, a man accustomed to strategies and tactics going his way. As always, Lieutenant Nakajima was handsome, icy, and mechanical; like a ceremonial gun ready to be fired. And how did she look? Hopefully, the white face paint hid her worry.

"To the New Japan!" Masaru raised his glass. "Banzai!"

*****

It was almost midnight when Aizawa arrived back in Ueno after completing his paperwork. The neighborhood was a far cry from the pleasure palaces of Yoshiwara or the government efficiency of Nagatacho. But here was where he'd grown up and chosen to remain. In better times, the neighborhood was home to working-class families; men who labored in factories and women who sewed in textile mills. Now they worked at whatever they could.

But despite the hardship, a woman stood by a small box labeled "Relief for the Tohoku Famine." That poor girl Yuki flashed in his mind. Several passersby stopped and gave whatever they could. Even in this misery, Tokyoites could still be generous.

Aizawa dug deep into his pockets and tossed in a few coins. He turned the corner and entered his compact *nagaya* with an exhausted sigh. After changing into a kimono, Aizawa sat near his charcoal heater to warm up. He'd pawned whatever knickknacks he could part with, leaving a hollow, cave-like lounge.

Only a low-lying table, an electric lamp, and a small family altar remained. Inside was a small statue of the Buddha, serene and merciful. He cast a gaze downward onto a framed photograph of his parents, his little sister Tokiko, and himself out for a stroll in Ueno Park. Although faded and wrinkled, it remained the only picture of the Aizawa family that had survived the Great Earthquake.

Shame prodded him to light incense and pray for the souls for his family and all those who were lost on that warm September day. After finishing the ritual, Aizawa opened his copy of *The New Japan*, taken from the office. He scanned through it, searching for any clues to Ryusaki's present whereabouts.

The first half was a self-aggrandizing biography: a descendant of twenty generations of samurai, Masaru

Ryusaki had spent his early youth intoxicated by decadent American culture and became a *mobo*, a modern boy.

He'd even studied in San Francisco, drinking beer in speakeasies and writing essays about how Japan should adopt American-style democracy. But according to the book, his views changed when he returned to Tokyo in 1923, one week after the Great Earthquake. Upon seeing the smoldering ash that had been the Imperial capital, Masaru Ryusaki realized his sins and sobbed for hours.

He was reborn as a stalwart patriot. When his parents died, Ryusaki was left with a small fortune and decided to go into politics. Joining the conservative Seiyukai Party, he was elected to the Diet in 1928. The book was littered with passages exposing the corruption he'd seen in the government, and Ryusaki even boasted about showing up to a session in full samurai armor, clutching his family sword as a subtle threat to his political rivals.

It didn't work. Ryusaki lost his seat in the 1930 election and shortly afterward, he'd written this drivel. The second half of the book was a political rant disguised as a manifesto. Unpatriotic politicians should be assassinated. Extravagant fortunes should be seized and redistributed to the poor. The book explained how the Meiji Restoration of 1868 – which toppled the Tokugawa Shogunate and restored the Emperor to power – had allowed a clique of greedy and corrupt men to dominate politics. A modern-day Showa Restoration – named after the current Emperor's reign – would abolish the corrupt and weak civilian government and install a new type of shogun to rule on behalf of His Majesty.

Most disturbing was Ryusaki's insistence on war. Japan, he argued, had to fight China for control of Manchuria, the Soviet Union for Siberia, France for Indochina, Britain for Singapore, and America for the entire Pacific Ocean.

Each passage reminded Aizawa of the plot that had crawled out of Ryusaki's mind months before. He snapped the book shut and tossed it onto the table. If Aizawa had to gamble, after Onishi's assassination, Ryusaki would use his spy in the Army Ministry to declare martial law and install a new shogun just like what he'd attempted in March. As the old saying went, "Fall down seven times, stand up eight." But Aizawa was just as determined. If this was going to be his last case, it would also be Ryusaki's last plot.

CHAPTER FIFTEEN

Reiko opened her mouth with an enormous yawn and looked around. Sunlight trickled into Masaru's *machiya*, and onto Masaru himself, who lay beside her. Although she didn't remember much from last night, the meeting with General Sakamoto remained clear. But everything after that – the drinking games, songs, and stumbling through Asakusa with Masaru for late-night sex – was hazy.

She rose, stirring Masaru awake. After grabbing a nearby mirror, she stared at what looked like a geisha melting in the morning sun. Streams of white greasepaint had peeled off, and her *shimada* wig was about to wobble loose.

"What time is it?" Masaru groaned.

"Early," Reiko said, setting the mirror aside. Even though this was Masaru's place, her morning routine always included a little music. She shuffled over to the Sharp radio and clicked it on. "My Blue Heaven" poured out and filled the entire *machiya* like opium smoke.

As Reiko hummed along, Masaru rose and joined her beside the radio. They stared at each other in silence, letting the melody speak for them. As if entranced, Masaru slid his arm around Reiko's waist and took her arm. How many times had they danced to this tune over the past few months? He guided her for a few fox-trot steps until her legs strained against the kimono. Letting out a panicked cry, Reiko tumbled backward and hit the ground with a thump.

Masaru sank to his knees and steadied her upright. "Are you hurt?"

"Just embarrassed." She laughed. "One day, I'll figure out how to fox-trot in a kimono."

Masaru smiled and helped her up. "I'm sorry. I don't know what came over me."

"Don't apologize," she said. "I wish you did that more often."

Masaru's smile vanished and he turned the radio off. "I'll need an alibi tonight," he said. "When the assassination occurs."

Reiko gave a bitter sigh. "Why don't you ask one of your followers to entertain you?"

"Don't be like that. The Police won't question the sincerity of a woman."

Did that apply to poison women as well? It didn't matter. Jazz had briefly resurrected the old Masaru. Perhaps a more potent injection would bring the *mobo* back to life.

"All right then," Reiko said. "Meet me at Harlem."

Masaru curled his upper lip. "Why there?"

"Don't play coy. It's where we met."

He sighed. "Fine. I'll meet you there at around four o'clock."

A smile enveloped her face. Although the situation looked bleak, an evening at Harlem was her best chance to snap Masaru permanently back to sanity. "Now, if you'll excuse me," Reiko said, "I need to go change into something I can fox-trot in."

*****

Aizawa checked his watch and cursed. It was ten past four already, and he dreaded keeping Baron Onishi waiting. Frustrated, he quickened his pace back to Metropolitan Police Headquarters. Although he'd spent the entire morning and afternoon searching all over Tokyo, he had nothing to show for it. Every old lead and contact proved useless in his search to find Masaru Ryusaki's new residence. The Ryusaki family estate in the Roppongi neighborhood had remained derelict since March. He was most likely slumming in the eastern part of the city, but there were hundreds of holes that spider could crawl into.

Aizawa reviewed the timeline again in his mind. A year ago, Ryusaki published his book. In January, he founded the Kusanagi Society, which began collecting members and high explosives. In March, Aizawa infiltrated the group and personally arrested its *sensei*. But after his release, Ryusaki had vanished like a bad dream.

Metropolitan Police Headquarters came into view along with a sleek Roll-Royce Phantom parked outside the steps. They must have seen him approaching because the *junsa* hopped out of the back seat and held the door open for Onishi. The Baron exited and fixed Aizawa with a disapproving stare.

"Forgive me, Baron," Aizawa said after bowing. "I've had a busy day."

"So, you've found this *soshi* who wants to assassinate me?"

"No…not yet."

"I see. And what about the other *soshi*? Has he confessed?"

"No…not yet." Aizawa turned to the *junsa*. "You're dismissed. Good work. Go home and get some sleep."

The *junsa* saluted, gave a respectful bow to Baron Onishi, and marched off.

"He never left my side once, except when I had to relieve myself," the Baron said.

Aizawa didn't know whether or not that was a compliment but allowed himself a proud smile as he followed Onishi into the Rolls-Royce.

*****

Lieutenant Nakajima steadied the shaking Arisaka rifle in his hands. Was he nervous or just cold from the crisp air seeping in through the open window? Whatever it was, he couldn't let it affect him. His destiny was approaching fast. Baron Onishi would soon appear on the street below, directly in his crosshairs.

After kicking the regular staff out, by orders of General Sakamoto, he'd spent the afternoon converting the Army recruiting office into a makeshift sniper nest. Even though he hadn't fired a gun since his graduation from the Imperial Army Academy, such details didn't matter. Soon, all of the corrupt villains in Tokyo would fear for their lives.

In his mind, Nakajima reread a letter he'd received from his mother, little over a month ago. In agonizing detail, she had told him about the hunger pains, the grinding poverty, and their rice farm ravaged by famine. Most likely, she conceded, the whole Nakajima family – his mother, his father, and his older brother – would all starve to death by spring. Unfortunately, they'd already sold their only daughter, Chitose, to the brothels years ago. That well had gone dry long ago.

But once General Sakamoto became the new shogun, he'd seize extravagant fortunes from men like Baron Onishi and redistribute them to the poor. If only his family knew that help would soon arrive. Ah, he couldn't wait to fire a bullet straight into the heart of evil, saving not only his family but the entire nation.

From the open fifth-story window, Nakajima surveyed the bustling Marunouchi district for what must have been the twentieth time. It was toward the end of the work day and dozens of salarymen, stock traders, and finance drones crisscrossed each other, exiting the enormous eight-story Marunouchi Building, the Maru-Biru, directly across the street. Inside, men in three-piece suits decided the fate of millions through schemes and intrigue.

Below, Marunouchi was a sea of American cars. Model A Fords, Plymouth Chryslers, and Buick Coupes flowed by like the Sumida River. Added to their ranks was a flashy Rolls-Royce that slid to a halt in front of the Maru-Biru. The chauffeur hopped out and opened the passenger door. Baron Onishi emerged, donned his top hat, and headed toward the Maru-Biru's entrance. Every god in the Shinto pantheon screamed to open fire.

Nakajima angled for a clear shot, but pulsating adrenaline distorted his aim. The crosshairs finally aligned with Baron Onishi's gray face but before he could pull the trigger, a tramcar surged by, obscuring his view. When it passed, Onishi was already entering the Maru-Biru, followed by a man in a black overcoat and fedora.

Inspector Aizawa.

Lieutenant Nakajima slid the crosshairs over the Inspector's head and for a brief moment, considered pulling the trigger. No, such a fate befitted scheming villains like Baron Onishi, not honorable men carrying out their duty. The Inspector would have to be dealt with some other way.

But for now, he'd wait. The Baron would have to exit sometime.

CHAPTER SIXTEEN

Reiko gripped the receiver as a low voice answered.

"Metropolitan Police Station."

"Yes, is Inspector Aizawa there?"

"No, may I take a message?"

Reiko hung the receiver up and heaved a deep sigh. She'd called three times today but Aizawa was nowhere near his office. Looking up, she stared at the worried reflection in the telephone booth glass. She still wore eye shadow, mascara, and lipstick, but white greasepaint no longer hid her face.

Instead of a *shimada* wig, her hair was a chic bob topped with a blue cloche hat. In place of her kimono, she wore a dark blue pea coat, pleated wool skirt, and held a beaded handbag. A pair of brown leather gloves and matching heels completed her transformation from geisha to *moga*, a modern girl.

Reiko stepped out of the telephone booth where a cold breeze met her. Rubbing her gloved hands together, she tried to soak up the last remaining rays of sunlight. Soon, electric lights would bathe Ginza in a neon glow. The fancy foreign restaurants, department stores, boutiques, and nightclubs held a charm second only to Asakusa. Not only was Ginza the most modern part of Tokyo, rivaling Times Square, Piccadilly Circus, and the Bund, it was also where she and Masaru had met back in March. She'd always be thankful for that.

Unfortunately, there weren't many people taking in Ginza's beauty. While a steady stream of automobiles and rickshaws passed through the street, most pedestrians looked like the wealthiest Tokyoites. As they tossed their cigarette butts onto the pavement, a few ragged-looking men in worn-out coats scooped them up, thirsty for tobacco.

Looking up, Reiko saw Masaru walking toward her. He had undergone a similar transformation himself. Instead of a kimono, a blue suit and overcoat framed his slender body. A matching fedora topped his head, partly concealing his dour face.

Reiko couldn't suppress a smile at the sight. Masaru had returned to his roots as a *mobo*, a modern boy. Appropriate, since they were headed to Tokyo's best jazz club, Harlem, where nice *mobos* took their *mogas*.

"Harutora," he said, looking her over.

"It's Reiko now."

"Yes...Reiko. You look stunning."

She smiled. "You look handsome yourself. Like a Japanese Harold Lloyd."

He scanned his outfit with less enthusiasm.

"I'm sorry for being late. I needed to change into clothes that wouldn't draw attention here."

"Don't apologize. You look good in a Western suit," she said, taking his arm.

They walked across the street and into an alley. Harlem was made to look like an American speakeasy, unmarked and exclusive. After knocking, the door opened and they entered a secluded world of jazz. Trumpets squealed, saxophones blared, and the air was hazy from cigarette smoke, just as she remembered it. Most comforting of all were the portraits of the living gods of jazz, still hanging in the lobby. Duke Ellington, King Oliver, and Cab Calloway smiled back like old friends.

A smiling waitress, clad in kimono and white apron, led them to a table across from the small dance floor and even smaller band, clad in black suits and blackface. Smallest of all was the clientele, made up of what looked like homesick foreign diplomats, businessmen and their mistresses, and a paltry showing of *mogas* and *mobos*.

"Anything to drink?" the waitress asked.

"A gimlet for her and I'll have a Kirin beer," Masaru said.

The waitress bowed and soon returned with their drinks. The blackface band struck up "Alligator Hop." Reiko sipped her gimlet and tapped a foot to the beat. Masaru took a swig of his beer before slamming it down.

"Masaru, you can stop pretending that you hate jazz. Nakajima isn't here."

Masaru said nothing and took another gulp.

"Does this place remind you of San Francisco?"

Masaru stared at the blackface band and empty dance floor before responding. "Not really. The government had outlawed alcohol, so we had to drink in secret."

"In speakeasies, right?"

He nodded. "The first time I went to one, there was a raid. I begged a policeman on my hands and knees to let me go, telling him what shame an arrest would cause my family."

She leaned in. "What happened?"

Masaru gave a bright smile. "The officer lifted me up and said, 'Son, I'm just looking for a bribe.'"

Reiko giggled and said, "Go on..."

"Another time, King Oliver himself asked me onstage and requested I sing 'Royal Garden Blues' in Japanese. I don't think I'd ever been happier."

So, the *mobo* was trying to escape that samurai armor. When the band commenced with "The Charleston," she saw an opportunity to help bring him out even further.

"There's plenty of space on the floor," she said, sipping her gimlet. "I wish some dashing *mobo* would ask me to dance."

Masaru looked hesitant, but when Reiko pouted her lips and gave a wistful stare, he stood and stretched out his hand. She took it and together they strolled out to the dance floor with "The Charleston" in full swing. Masaru led, animated by the music.

They kicked their legs, stepped the steps, and waved their arms. They flowed with the song, like a ship adrift during a storm. "The Charleston" was confidence, passion, and freedom put into tempo. She resisted the urge to kick off her heels to gain extra mobility and dutifully spun when Masaru twirled her.

The music stopped, followed by sparse applause, allowing her to catch her breath. Masaru mopped sweat from his brow and smiled brightly. She couldn't contain a sigh. He looked so handsome when he smiled like that. What would Lieutenant Nakajima think if he could see them now? She tensed at the thought of that devil soldier shooting at Baron Onishi from an open window, like some sort of American gangster.

Of course! Aizawa must be with Onishi at the Marunouchi Building! She glanced at her watch. Half past four. There might still be time left if she hurried.

"Would you excuse me, Masaru? It's so hot in here. The cold air might do me some good."

Masaru nodded her dismissal. She eased out of the main hall, threw on her pea coat, and fled out the front door. Sprinting, she crossed the street and entered the phone booth. After depositing five sen, she called the main office of Takano Bank.

"Takano Bank," a voice answered.

"Is Inspector Aizawa there?" she cried out, her voice ricocheting off the glass.

"Hold please."

As moments passed in silence, Reiko gripped the receiver tighter and prayed she wasn't too late.

CHAPTER SEVENTEEN

Isamu Takano's office was larger than Aizawa thought possible in the overcrowded beehive of Tokyo. Carpeted floor, a large oak table, stock ticker, and a beige globe perched atop a mahogany desk looked like something out of Wall Street. Only a framed portrait of the Emperor in ceremonial uniform rooted the office in Japan.

Three men were gathered around the table. Takano was easiest to identify by his three-piece suit and flashy Rolex, but also because his chiseled, distinguished face made regular appearances in the press.

According to the newspapers, Takano Bank had risen to prominence at the turn of the century, even loaning the government money during the Russo-Japanese War. However, two years before the stock market crash on Wall Street, Japan suffered its own financial panic that almost ruined Takano along with countless other bankers.

But strangely enough, Takano was one of the few *zaibatsu* who had somehow survived the 1927 crisis and the depression so far. His ability to weather economic storms led to the joke that Isamu Takano didn't pray to Daikoku – the god of wealth – but employed him as a bank teller.

Tsuyoshi Inukai's beard and diminutive figure identified him, but Aizawa had never seen the third man, a tall Army officer. The man's mask-like face was decorated with hooded eyes and a gray goatee, and his dark brown uniform was encrusted with glittering medals. Most impressive were the gold-colored shoulder tabs with three stars, proclaiming his rank of *taisho*, a full general.

Bows were exchanged, differing according to prestige and stature, with Aizawa always lowering himself the deepest. Not that it bothered him. Outsiders rarely saw the machinery of government stripped bare, and here he was with a front-row seat.

"Baron Onishi, thank you for joining us," Takano said after bowing. "Allow me to introduce Inukai-san. And you are already acquainted with Vice-Minister of the Army, General Yori Sakamoto."

"And this is Inspector Aizawa of the Metropolitan Police," the Baron said flatly.

The three men traded concerned looks with each other.

"While I have the utmost respect for the Police," General Sakamoto began, "I would prefer to conduct this meeting in private. Even Army Minister Minami doesn't know I'm here."

"Such intrigue," Takano said with a laugh, offering the Baron a seat. The others sat back down, leaving Aizawa to stand near the belching stock ticker.

Onishi said, "I understand your concern, General, but the Inspector is not investigating anyone here. He's concerned only for my safety."

"Yes, I heard about the incident outside of the Diet. I'm glad you're safe," Inukai said, then shook his head. "No one is more hated than Dietmen these days."

"Bankers are a close second," Takano said, chuckling. "The nationalist press claims we all must have Chinese ancestry to be so money-hungry."

"If the Baron feels unsafe here, perhaps we could relocate the meeting somewhere else," Sakamoto said.

Baron Onishi forced a smile and looked over at Aizawa who understood he was being dismissed. His glimpse behind the paper screen had been fleeting. It was, after all, taboo to see *kabuki* actors without their makeup. He gave a departing bow and walked out of the office. Aizawa closed the heavy wooden door behind him but made sure to leave a slight crack open. If he had learned one thing from Superintendent Shimura, it was that there was nothing dishonorable with a policeman eavesdropping.

After predictable small talk, Takano steered the conversation to the business at hand.

"Gentlemen, the Imperial advisers are meeting with His Majesty to decide who to appoint prime minister. Whoever it is, he will have a difficult time governing. Baron Onishi, you may have the support of aristocrats in the House of Peers, but the political parties in the House of Representatives will block whatever policy you enact. Inukai-san, remember that the Minsei Party is still the majority bloc in the Diet and will not yield ground to your Seiyukai.

"I suggest a coalition government. Onishi-san becomes prime minister, Inukai-san becomes finance minister, and General Sakamoto becomes the army minister, thus creating a united front against the Minsei Party."

"And what about the Imperial Army?" Baron Onishi asked. "We must rein in its wanton behavior."

"As army minister, my first order will be to purge these hotheaded extremists from active duty," General Sakamoto cut in.

"Up until last month, weren't you one of those hotheads, General?"

"Times change, Baron. Certain incidents…tempered me."

"Regardless, General Sakamoto is willing to serve in either of your governments," Takano said diplomatically.

"However," Inukai cut in, "leaving Manchuria is out of the question. Regardless of the insubordinate way it began, our forces will soon occupy the entire region."

"I agree, Inukai-san," Baron Onishi said. "Withdrawing now will cause a tremendous loss of face. But we cannot have further military action without approval from the civilian government. The League of Nations frowns upon flagrant militarism. It reminds them of the German Kaiser during the World War. Many in the West already see our empire as the Yellow Peril. We will gain a reputation as some sort of South American nation if we do not re-establish discipline."

"The Army will obey whatever orders I issue," General Sakamoto said. "Currently, that boy warlord, Chang Hsüeh-liang, has garrisoned the bulk of his troops in the southern city of Chinchow. Enemy forces also control Harbin in the north. These two strongholds are all that remain of the opposition in Manchuria."

"What about Chiang Kai-shek?" Baron Onishi asked.

"The Generalissimo is too busy fighting the Communists in China's southern provinces to assist his allies up north. He's no threat to us," Sakamoto said. "As Takano-san mentioned, the Chinese are a greedy race of merchants and mercenaries. Their soldiers fight for loot, not China."

"And the Soviet Union?"

General Sakamoto laughed. "Another fake warrior playing with his toy sword."

High-heeled footsteps approached, prompting Aizawa to look up.

Takano's secretary gave a polite bow and said, "Inspector, there's a call for you."

Aizawa nodded and followed her out of the hallway and into the main lobby, where a phone receiver waited on her desk.

"Inspector Aizawa," he answered.

"If Onishi isn't dead yet," a husky female voice said, "then don't let him leave through the west exit. There's an assassin in the building across from the Maru-Biru."

"Who is this?"

The line went dead and the woman faded back into anonymity. An operator came through with a perky, "*Moshi moshi?*"

Aizawa slammed the receiver down, startling the secretary. He gave an apologetic bow before walking toward the window and stared out at the nondescript office building across the street. Dusk was setting in and it was almost impossible to examine any silhouettes in the windows, all tightly shuttered – except one on the fifth floor. An open window on a cold day was unusual, but given his mysterious informant's call, it now looked downright sinister.

Calling for reinforcements was unlikely since he'd have to obtain approval from Superintendent Shimura. All he could do was get the Baron to safety, and that meant sneaking him out the back door. After all, the voice had said nothing about other assassins lurking about. Then he would be free to confront this shadowy enemy face-to-face.

CHAPTER EIGHTEEN

Aizawa marched back to the heavy oak doors, where the discussion had shifted from Manchuria to the depression.

"Baron, trade with America is the lifeblood of our economy," Takano's irritated voice seeped through the crack between the doors.

"My position is firm on both issues, Takano-san," Onishi said. "Relying on trade with America has nearly ruined us. It was their Smoot-Hawley Tariff that exported the depression to our shores. And as for devaluing the yen, gold is the only stable commodity in an unstable market."

With the grace of an alley cat, Aizawa slid into the room and shut the door behind him. The four men looked up, but only General Sakamoto showed visible annoyance.

"I sincerely apologize," Aizawa said after bowing. "But I must speak to the Baron."

Onishi stood up. "Pardon me, gentlemen." He spun around and met Aizawa outside of the office.

"I'm sorry to interrupt, Baron," Aizawa said, lowering his voice.

Onishi held up a hand. "Not at all. I should thank you for ending my pain."

The meeting must have been truly terrible for the Baron to accept such loss of face.

"You need to leave now. But not the same way we entered. I'll have your chauffeur bring the car around to the east exit," Aizawa said. "I'll come to your place immediately after."

Baron Onishi nodded. There was no need to go into detail. Not now, at least. Onishi dug into his pocket, retrieved his own *meishi* card, scribbled something on the back, and handed it to Aizawa.

"Here's my address and telephone number. I'll await your arrival at my estate. Please excuse me while I say goodbye to these…gentlemen," the Baron said before returning to Takano's office.

Aizawa made a brisk walk to the exit. He hated leaving the Baron unguarded, but if things went well, he'd arrest Ryusaki's assassin and put an end to this madness for good. Of course, he'd have to handle the coming moments with skill in order to avoid a bullet in his brain.

*****

Cramped in his sniper's nest, Lieutenant Nakajima gripped the Arisaka rifle like a statue. Staring out its scope with an unblinking eye, he surveyed the area outside of the Maru-Biru. The only movement came from Onishi's chauffeur, smoking a cigarette near the gleaming Rolls-Royce.

There. That's where he would kill him. Soon that polished Rolls-Royce would be soaked in Baron Onishi's poisonous blood and become his hearse. With that enemy vanquished, Nakajima would quickly dispose of the Arisaka and report back to General Sakamoto before transferring to the Manchurian front. His only wish was to arrive before the fighting was over.

Suddenly, the Maru-Biru's main entrance opened. The chauffeur flicked his cigarette away and stood at attention. Nakajima curled his finger around the rifle's trigger and waited for the Baron's distinctive top hat and silver mustache to appear.

But only Inspector Aizawa emerged and walked over to the chauffeur. After a brief conversation, the chauffeur entered the Rolls-Royce and sped away. No! His mission couldn't end in such inglorious failure! Had the Inspector spotted him in the sniper's nest?

Frantically, Nakajima scanned the area in hopes of spotting Baron Onishi sneaking away, but there was no sign of him. He moved his rifle scope across to the Maru-Biru's third floor, where the offices of Takano Bank were. Maybe he could still get a shot. He could barely make out General Sakamoto in his brown uniform and glinting medals, along with Takano and Inukai in their three-piece suits, but the Baron was nowhere to be found.

Even more troubling, Aizawa advanced across the street. He zigzagged, making it impossible to draw a bead on him. In mere minutes, the Inspector would be here to arrest him. Such failure demanded suicide. If only he'd shot Onishi when he had the chance. If only…but it was too late for self-pity.

Lieutenant Nakajima fought a nausea rising in his stomach and set the rifle down. With a trembling hand, he drew his saber. While it wouldn't have the dignity that ritual suicide did, self-impalement was still an honorable death. He closed his eyes and took a deep breath.

"Hajime," a voice from the darkness called out.

Startled, Nakajima opened his eyes. He looked around but nobody was there. Suddenly, a small figure of light in a white kimono floated from out of the corner and approached him. It flickered in and out like a dimming light bulb, but its features grew more defined as it approached. Through the translucent skin, he recognized the eyes and soft cheeks of his older sister, his *oneesan*, Chitose.

"You cannot die yet Hajime-kun," she whispered. "Continue your mission."

Her image faded as quickly as it had appeared. Nakajima sank to his knees, trying to make sense of what happened. Suddenly, the world snapped into focus. The gods must have sent Chitose-oneesan to stop him. They still had use for this lowly rice farmer. The same corruption and evil that had killed his sister were now poisoning the entire nation. Only men like him could save Japan. His duty to the nation was more important than his own pitiful life. Death could wait. He sheathed the saber and vowed that he would not fail again. But first, he had to deal with Inspector Aizawa.

CHAPTER NINETEEN

Aizawa entered the office building's lobby and scanned a nearby directory. Most were ordinary businesses: insurance companies and accounting firms. However, the Army Recruitment Station-Marunouchi District in Suite 505 stood out. Aizawa took the stairs, adrenaline propelling him forward. Reaching the fifth floor, he caught his breath and made his way down the hall. Many offices were empty, more casualties of the depression, but 505 still looked occupied.

Aizawa stopped in front of the Army Recruiting Station, drew his Colt automatic, and knocked. No answer. A small sign on the door listed 0700 to 1700 as operational hours. Perhaps they had gone home? He slowly opened the door and scanned the darkened room. Lights from across the street cast gloomy, elongated shadows on recruiting posters of gallant-looking soldiers in steel helmets.

He took a few cautious steps in, allowing his eyes to adjust to the darkness. The door slammed shut behind him. Aizawa swept his pistol around, but before he could get a bead, a rifle butt came into view and slammed into his stomach, deflating him like a popped balloon. The pistol tumbled out of his hand and bounced on the floor. Air shot out of Aizawa's lungs as he collapsed to his knees.

Steadying himself on his hands, Aizawa looked up and saw the outline of an Army uniform in the last bit of light from outside: peaked service cap, brown tunic, and white gloves. The man's face was obscured not only by shadow and darkness but also by the rifle held in firing position. Aizawa's breaths grew tighter, knowing each one could be his last.

"Lie down," the Army officer said in a low and obviously disguised voice that couldn't hide traces of a Tohoku accent.

Aizawa was in no position to argue and flattened himself on the floor. The officer walked backward out of the office, slamming the door shut behind him. Aizawa leaped to his feet, retrieved the Colt, and ran after his attacker. After only a few steps, a sharp pain throbbed in his gut, almost doubling him over. Aizawa leaned against the wall and steadied himself. The hallway was deserted, but heavy footsteps going down the stairwell were still audible.

Aizawa took several deep breaths until the pain subsided. He was in no shape to pursue any further. Instead, he reviewed the man's accent and remembered that Army officer from yesterday – Lieutenant Nakajima, General Sakamoto's adjutant. Although he'd caught his breath, Aizawa felt a tightness renew in his chest.

General Yori Sakamoto was the shadowy wire-puller behind Masaru Ryusaki. But that presented a whole new problem. How could a callow police inspector arrest a general who was on his way to becoming the next army minister?

The answer was that he couldn't. Not only was Sakamoto too high up, he was also an Army man, which meant the Metropolitan Police had little authority over him. Aizawa would have to enlist the help of the *Kempeitai*, whose loyalty would probably lie with the General rather than the law. If he went to the press, the Police would force any newspaper that published the story to quickly retract it. The only hope was to keep Baron Onishi alive long enough so that if he did become prime minister, he could have General Sakamoto transferred far away or forcibly retired.

He needed to get to Onishi's estate before Nakajima got there first.

*****

Nakajima slammed the taxicab door shut and snapped, "The Army Ministry. As fast as you can!"

"Y-yes sir," the driver said, putting the cab into gear. Within moments they sped off. Nakajima watched the Marunouchi Building shrink in the rear window and expelled a relieved sigh.

"Shipping out to Manchuria?"

Nakajima was taken aback. How did this cabbie know his orders?

"What are you talking about?"

"Your rifle…I just assumed…"

Nakajima looked down at the Arisaka, practically glued into his hands. Thankfully, a soldier carrying a rifle wasn't too out of the ordinary.

"Keep driving," he snapped. The cabbie nodded and went quiet.

Nakajima leaned his head back and gathered his thoughts. Somehow, Aizawa had seen him in that sniper's nest. How could he be so careless? A vocal, ruthless part of him wished he'd opened fire while Aizawa was lying on the ground. However, such an execution was unworthy of an honorable man simply obeying his duty. But if Aizawa interfered again, Nakajima might not have the luxury of being so merciful.

Ryusaki-sensei would know what to do next, as always. Now, he just needed to reach him. Earlier in the morning, Ryusaki-sensei had confided that he would be at that den of decadence, Harlem. Taking advantage of his need for an alibi, Reiko Watanabe had suggested it. The thought of that corrupt woman sucking money out of Ryusaki-sensei like some bloated tick made him shudder. Masaru Ryusaki was a great man, but he had weaknesses. It was times like this that Nakajima was thankful for never giving in to cravings for flesh, satiating himself through prayer and patriotism.

When they were well out of Marunouchi, he said, "Pull over at the next phone booth. I need to make a call."

CHAPTER TWENTY

Reiko watched Masaru tap his foot to "Sing Me a Song of Araby" with unrepressed glee. She smiled as the jazz cleansed him of evil spirits. A few more songs and he'd be back to his old self. Polishing off the last of her gimlet, she savored the sweet taste and her victory over Lieutenant Nakajima. She'd tear Masaru away from his grip, saving Japan and herself in the process. That country monkey would be transferred to the barren wilderness of Manchuria, leaving her and Masaru to spend the rest of the days at Harlem just like they were always meant to.

"Excuse me," the waitress interrupted, "but are you Ryusaki-san?"

Masaru stopped tapping his foot and nodded.

"There is a telephone call for you," she said. Masaru stood and followed her to the side where he took the receiver. She couldn't hear any of the conversation over the music, but a dark cloud swept over his handsome face, leaving him agitated and sullen. No, not yet. Not when she was so close to finally having the happy life she'd been denied for so long. She cursed the gods for being so cruel.

Masaru hung up and stalked back to the table. "We have to leave," he snapped.

Reiko forced a smile. "One more dance? I'll ask them to play 'The Japanese Sandman.'"

He shook his head. Any traces of the *mobo* were fading fast.

She gripped his hand. "Masaru, please..."

"Get your things or I'm leaving without you." He shook her hand away and slammed a few yen on the table. Reiko followed him as they donned their coats and hats, silently saying farewell to her old friends. Hopefully, she'd see them again one day.

They exited out into the alley and made their way to the main street. Ginza was now bathed in neon lights advertising Lion Dental Cream, Meiji Milk Chocolate, Yamasa Soy Sauce, and Ramune Soda. Banners proclaiming a sale hung from the same multi-storied Matsuya Department Store where Masaru had bought her countless outfits before. They'd walked happily down this street many times before, but now it seemed like a funeral procession.

"Masaru, what's wrong? Who was that?"

He said nothing until they stopped in front of the telephone booth where she'd called Inspector Aizawa.

"That was Nakajima-san...Baron Onishi has escaped again."

Perhaps the gods hadn't abandoned her.

"This is a sign," Reiko said. "Forget about the Baron and Nakajima. Forget about everyone except us."

After a moment of heavy silence, Masaru said, "I can't ignore my duty."

An intoxicating anger pulsed through Reiko. It burned in her belly and leaped from her mouth. "Your duty? What about your duty to me? What happens if you're thrown in prison...or killed? I'll be out on the street or in a brothel with a broken heart!"

Crying wasn't easy for her, but Reiko dug deep. She remembered every cut and blister she got while sewing in that textile mill her parents called their home, when the Great Earthquake turned Tokyo into ash, and when she saw Louise Brooks in *Diary of a Lost Girl* for the first time. Most importantly, she pictured the bleak future unfolding before her. Tears soon moistened her cheeks.

"Reiko," Masaru said with softening eyes.

"I'm worried about you," she said, sinking to knees, "and for us."

Even with stockings on, the cold pavement stung her legs. But Masaru soon knelt down and placed a hand on her wet cheek, warming her a little.

"Reiko...I had no idea you were so concerned."

"Please, Masaru, don't leave me. I just want our old life back."

"I won't ever leave you, Reiko…" The *mobo* shone briefly behind those round glasses. "But I must save Japan…"

"Masaru, you're not like them. You're not a murderer. Turn your back on Nakajima, Sakamoto, and their plots. We'll hide in our own little world where nobody can find us."

His gaze darted between her and the telephone booth, like a child torn between two parents. She sympathized. In Japan, there were few things more shameful than selfish individualism. As the old saying went, "The nail that sticks up should be hammered back down." Soon, Masaru's eyes were also bleary and his face contorted in turmoil. Two Masaru Ryusakis inhabited her lover and she was witnessing one of them die. Wiping his eyes, he took his hand away and stood up.

"I'm sorry Reiko…but I cannot turn back now."

He stepped past her and into the telephone booth.

"Hello, Metropolitan Police Department?" she heard him say. "Get me Superintendent Shimura."

Reiko couldn't hold back another flood of tears that turned Ginza's neon lights into a shimmering blur.

*****

Lieutenant Nakajima marched through the halls of the Army Ministry with heavy footsteps, passing by an open conference room. Staff officers in dark brown uniforms crowded around an enormous map of Manchuria that detailed the latest enemy troop movements. Only a few took notice of the Arisaka rifle in his hands but none protested.

He halted outside of General Sakamoto's office and announced, "Lieutenant Nakajima entering!"

"Get in here now," the General's voice boomed from behind the door.

Nakajima entered, set the rifle aside, and snapped to attention. As with most top brass, Sakamoto's office was Spartan and dull, with a pair of crisscrossed Rising Sun flags the only island of color in a gray lake. The General stood behind his desk, arms crossed and brow furrowed.

"What the hell happened back there?" Sakamoto demanded. "All of a sudden, Baron Onishi left the meeting, saying he had 'urgent business' to attend to!"

"Sir, Inspector Aizawa sabotaged our plans!"

Sakamoto's eyes widened. "What?"

"He nearly caught me at the Recruiting Office, but I escaped."

"Did you kill him?"

"No, sir…"

"Did he see your face?"

"I…I don't think so…it was dark…"

General Sakamoto slammed his fist down. "You fool! He must have spotted you in the window!"

Shame forced Nakajima to droop his head. "I'm sorry sir…but I called Ryusaki-zensei. He is arranging for Aizawa's superior, Superintendent Shimura, to take him off the case."

Sakamoto gave a skeptical look. "A police officer?"

Nakajima nodded. "He aided our cause back in March. In exchange for his help now, Ryusaki-zensei promised to appoint him superintendent-general of the entire Metropolitan Police after the Showa Restoration."

A renewed glee softened Sakamoto's face. "Excellent! That will leave Baron Onishi unguarded! I'll secure a staff car for tonight. You'll drive out to Baron Onishi's estate in the Azabu Ward and deal with him once and for all." He rummaged through a desk drawer and withdrew a Nambu automatic pistol. "Take this for tonight. It's less cumbersome than a rifle."

Sakamoto handed the Nambu over and Nakajima accepted with both hands.

"Th-thank you, sir…"

The General laid a paternal hand on Nakajima's shoulder. "If only I had your youth again, Lieutenant."

Nakajima felt the formalities of rank bend slightly enough to ask a personal question.

"Sir…I must ready myself…for tonight and for service in Manchuria…what is it like to take a life?"

"First kills are like first lays," the General said. "The more you think about it the worse it will be."

That didn't help. But Sakamoto must have seen confusion manifest in Nakajima's face and elaborated.

"I was around your age when I killed my first man, a Russian officer during the Battle of Mukden. It felt…mechanical and detached. I pried a Nagant revolver from his hand as a trophy and…I wanted to hate him, but couldn't." General Sakamoto clapped his hand on Nakajima's shoulder. "Do not hate your enemy. Hate the evil he represents. Baron Onishi is unimportant. What he represents, this corrupt political system, must die…tonight."

Nakajima tucked the Nambu into his belt and snapped to attention.

"General, I swear that either Baron Onishi dies tonight or I will!"

CHAPTER TWENTY-ONE

Following the address on the *meishi* card, Aizawa took a taxicab over to Onishi's estate and found the Baron in the middle of dinner. A gracious host, Onishi invited him to join. Not since before the depression had Aizawa eaten so much sashimi, grilled squid, eel, and rice. Did the Baron dine like this every night or was he just trying to impress this simple police inspector? Not that he needed to. His *yashiki*, the spacious manor inherited from his *daimyo* ancestors, was enough. Added to that was his wife, the Baroness Sachiko Onishi, who, despite her gray hair, retained a regal beauty in an elegant purple kimono. The Baron had also changed into an evening kimono and *hakama* pants, looking more like a *daimyo* lord than a British gentleman.

The meal concluded, Aizawa bowed his thanks as a horde of servants cleared the table and served tea.

"How do you like it, Inspector?" the Baroness asked.

Aizawa nodded. "It's very good."

Baron Onishi smiled. "It's jade dew. The leaves are grown in the shade to accentuate the taste."

Even the tea here was aristocratic. Or perhaps the Baron was fishing for compliments from his commoner guest. Many Tokyoites never entered the southwestern part of the city, let alone the affluent Azabu Ward. Even the Metropolitan Police rarely made visits here since the rich had a way of policing themselves.

"Your family *yashiki* is most impressive, Baron."

"Thank you," Onishi said, sipping his tea.

"It's from the Tokugawa Era," the Baroness elaborated. "The Shogunate ordered all the *daimyo* to construct homes in the city as a way of submission. The Onishi family is originally from out west, near Shimonoseki."

"Despite this, our family's true allegiance was always to the Imperial throne," the Baron said, in case Aizawa had any doubts.

"Of course. Do you have any children, Baron?"

Onishi nodded. "A son, currently serving in the diplomatic corps. He's at our embassy in Washington. Do you, Inspector?"

"I'm not married yet."

"Siblings?"

"I had a younger sister."

An awkward silence stifled the conversation, hinting that they should retreat back to the solid footing of guard and guarded.

"How was your meeting today?" the Baroness asked.

"A waste of time," Baron Onishi scoffed. "It was mercifully cut short by Aizawa-san. What was that all about, Inspector?"

Aizawa set his teacup aside. "I received another call…" He decided to leave out the chase with the shadowy Army officer. "I believe General Sakamoto is behind the plot to assassinate you, Baron."

Onishi's glacial face began to melt with concern, perhaps from realizing that he had more enemies than previously thought.

"The Army Ministry is a hive of intrigue," the Baron said. "Sakamoto is an ambitious man who clearly wants to become prime minister himself one day."

"He wouldn't be the first general to scheme his way into office," the Baroness said. "And they claim Dietmen are intriguers. Hypocrites!"

Baron Onishi laughed. "Unfortunately, our history is written by intrigue. Now I see what all that nonsense was about going off the gold standard."

"Gold standard?" Aizawa asked.

"Takano brought it up today. His bank has been engaged in currency speculation, purchasing millions from American banks. They stand to make a fortune if we leave gold and convert their dollars back into yen."

"And the bankers wonder why they're hated," the Baroness sneered.

"General Sakamoto is no better," Baron Onishi continued. "Last week, he came to my office in the Diet, asking what my economic policy would be."

"Last week?" Aizawa asked.

Onishi nodded. "Sakamoto claimed to have secret knowledge about Prime Minister Wakastuki's impending resignation. It's well-known that I'm being considered as his successor, so Sakamoto must have wanted to ingratiate himself into my cabinet as army minister. The General said that going off the gold standard would allow for a larger military budget. Fools! Don't they remember the inflation that occurred in Germany?"

The Baroness laughed. "Imagine, financial advice from a military man! It's like discussing religion with a stray dog!"

"Indeed. Which is why I flatly refused. Takano also suggested some ridiculous plan of reviving the economy through increased trade with America." Onishi shook his head. "Don't these fools understand that the United States is our greatest enemy?"

America again? Most Japanese seemed to have dual feelings toward the United States. Love for baseball, Hollywood, and jazz; resentment toward immigration laws, unequal treaties, and that dishonorable Smoot-Hawley Tariff. But for the Baron, America evoked only an icy contempt.

"Baron, if you become prime minister, what will your policy be toward America?" Aizawa asked, hoping the bait was good.

The Baroness laughed. "Oh, I should leave. I never like to be around my husband when his former mistress is discussed." She rose and bowed her way out of the room, leaving Aizawa to wonder what scab he'd picked open.

Baron Onishi finished his tea before responding. "Come with me, Inspector."

Aizawa followed the Baron down the hall and into a large room, furnished with leather chairs and a suit of red samurai armor mounted in the corner. Beside it was the *daisho*, the ceremonial swords of the Onishi Clan. The long *katana* and the short *wakizashi* looked so serene sheathed, but Aizawa wondered how many heads they'd lopped off and stomachs they'd opened over the centuries.

But what dominated the room was an enormous bookcase, crammed full of texts, mostly in Japanese, though on one shelf the books had exotic, foreign words on their spines. The Baron pulled one out and handed it to Aizawa.

The book was in English, and as Aizawa flipped through the pages, only a few words appeared familiar: *Japan*, *America*, and *war*.

"*The Rising Tide of Color* by Lothrop Stoddard. In it, the author argues that Japan will lead the peoples of Asia to war against the United States." Onishi pointed to another book. "*The Passing of the Great Race* warns that if America allows too many Japanese immigrants, it will be poisoned from within. Foolish, but American lawmakers apparently read it because they restricted all Japanese immigration, similar to the shameful way they barred Chinese entrance into their country."

The Baron gestured to another book. "This is my personal favorite. *The Great Pacific War* by Hector Bywater. Fiction, but many American military men wish it were fact. It details how a treacherous Japan destroys the Panama Canal and provokes America into a long naval war. They win, of course."

Aizawa closed Stoddard's book and handed it back. "I'm sure there are Japanese novels where we win."

Baron Onishi filed the book away and said, "The point is that they want war with us, Inspector. During our war with Russia, I served at the Japanese embassy in Washington. After Admiral Togo's great victory at Tsushima, a group of American Navy officers extended their congratulations to us. However, they warned us that their fleet was far stronger than the Russians, and could blockade Japan so quickly that our empire would capitulate in a month."

"I heard Americans were tactless," Aizawa said.

"And gluttonous! They devoured California from Mexico, Hawaii from its natives, and the Philippines from Spain. If they can expand their territory, why can't Japan? Although I opposed the Army's invasion of Manchuria, I'm more appalled with the insubordination it showed toward the civilian government." The Baron shook his head, looking like a disappointed father.

"Japan is now an international pariah," Onishi began again. "And America will take advantage of our weakness. In 1923, they pressured the British to end their alliance with us. Now, our economy has been wrecked by their tariff. But when Manchuria is occupied, Japan can use the resources of that vast land and become completely self-sufficient, free of American imports."

"Don't we need American imports, though?"

Baron Onishi's face darkened. "We must show the Americans that our people can withstand any hardship. My first act as prime minister would be to reduce trade between America and Japan to a trickle."

A tightness wrapped around Aizawa's throat. "That might lead to war, Baron."

"We are already at war, Inspector. But in this conflict, the weapons are tariffs and stocks."

Suddenly, Aizawa felt like a firefighter working from inside a burning building.

"Inspector." He heard the Baroness's voice and turned around. "You have a call."

Aizawa excused himself and followed the Baroness to a candlestick telephone around the hall.

"Aizawa here."

"Inspector," Superintendent Shimura's sharp voice said. "I'm releasing Kuroki-san."

"What! Why?"

"Return to Headquarters and I'll explain. There is no further need to guard Baron Onishi."

"But, sir, I must disagree—"

"Return to Headquarters, Inspector. That's an order."

After a harsh click, the line went dead. Aizawa hung up the receiver and considered what to do next. He couldn't leave Onishi unguarded, even for a few hours. Any backup would have to be approved by Shimura, unless he called in a favor. He picked up the telephone and called Police Headquarters, then asked for Sergeant Murayama.

"Murayama here."

"Aizawa here."

"What can I help you with, Inspector? I'm almost off duty."

"I need you to spend a few hours at Baron Onishi's *yashiki*. At least until I can convince Superintendent Shimura to change his mind."

"Doing what?"

"Walking around the premises and eating his food. There's plenty here. I'm sure he wouldn't mind. Grilled squid and eel."

A few moments of silence went by. "You owe me for this, Inspector."

Aizawa smiled and gave him the Baron's address. He hung up and glanced at his watch. Almost nine o'clock. He returned to Onishi's study and bowed his apologies.

"Unfortunately, Baron, my superior has called me back to Headquarters. However, my replacement, Sergeant Murayama, will be here soon."

Baron Onishi nodded and continued browsing his bookshelf. "How will you get back?"

Aizawa hadn't thought about that. The least Shimura could have done was send a staff car. And he didn't want to spend any more of his money on one-yen taxicabs.

"Inspector, can you operate a motor vehicle?"

"Yes, I drove supply trucks in Siberia."

"Why don't you drive my Rolls-Royce back?" Onishi asked, turning toward him.

Aizawa examined the Baron's face for any expression of reluctance but couldn't find a trace. Imagine driving up to Police Headquarters in that. Even officers on the take would sneer. But it was either that, take a taxi, or walk.

"Are you sure, Baron?"

Onishi nodded. "Until this whole incident is over, it's yours."

First the Pall Malls, now this. "Thank you, Baron," Aizawa said, bowing. "I'll return it as soon as this case is closed."

Baron Onishi gave a solemn nod. "I'm sure you will."

CHAPTER TWENTY-TWO

The cold night air drilled into Lieutenant Nakajima's face like needles as he crouched in the brush, surveying Onishi's *yashiki* estate with binoculars. The homes in Azabu were spread out enough that each neighbor was at least a five-minute walk. Both he and the staff car that General Sakamoto loaned him were now thoroughly camouflaged.

Scanning the *yashiki* courtyard, Nakajima saw a taxicab pull up. A large uniformed police officer jumped out and met Inspector Aizawa in the courtyard, momentarily illuminated by several paper lanterns. Damn it all. Ryusaki-sensei had said there would be no bodyguards tonight! It was too late now. He'd have to fight his way in, guard or no guard.

After exchanging salutes, the burly policeman disappeared into the *yashiki* while Aizawa hopped into a Rolls-Royce, parked next to a Mercedes Benz. Such ostentatious luxury! Meanwhile, his comrades faced Chinese bullets in Manchuria and his family slowly starved.

The Rolls-Royce roared to life and drove off into the night. Nakajima stood and fastened the chinstrap on his service cap. Although he'd already prayed before he followed General Sakamoto's directions here, Lieutenant Nakajima closed his eyes and asked the gods for their guidance.

"Hajime-kun…"

He opened his eyes and twisted his head around.

"Kill him, Hajime-kun," Chitose-oneesan said, the wind carrying her voice across time and worlds. "Kill the Baron."

Nakajima nodded and turned back to the *yashiki*. Ah, how kind the gods were to reunite them before battle. He reviewed the field one last time and settled in on a chauffeur tending to that sleek Mercedes Benz. He set the binoculars aside and drew the Nambu pistol, entrusted to him by General Sakamoto.

Sprinting out from the brush, he crossed the driveway, coming up behind the Mercedes. Undetected by the chauffeur, who busied himself underneath the car's hood, Nakajima pressed the pistol against the nape of the man's neck. The chauffeur shivered, rattling the Nambu slightly.

"Be quiet," he said. "Take me to the Baron or I shoot."

Trembling, the chauffeur backed out from under the hood and nodded. Contempt swept over Nakajima. Servants should always die for their masters, even if they were villains. Still, it was unwise to shoot his best chance of finding Onishi.

They traipsed through the snowy courtyard and into the *yashiki*. Neither removed their boots, tracking watery footprints on the floor. The hallways were dark and empty, amplifying their footsteps. Nakajima divided his time looking backward and forward, seeing mostly darkness, and on occasion, Chitose-oneesan, staring at him with glassy eyes.

"Identify yourself!" a gruff voice cut through the darkness. Dim lighting revealed an enormous policeman striding toward him, reaching for his sidearm.

Nakajima slid the pistol from the chauffeur's neck and answered. One shot in the gut slammed the policeman onto the floor, and another to the head ended his misery. His first kill. Just a man doing his duty. A wave of nausea welled within him until he felt a soothing hand press on his shoulder. Chitose-oneesan stood beside him, easing his sickness. What was it that Sakamoto had said? *'Do not hate your enemy. Hate the evil he represents.'* And now, his enemy's blood oozed down the *shoji* sliding door he'd been protecting. The chauffeur fainted and joined the police officer on the floor. No matter. Chitose removed her hand from his shoulder and pointed the way.

Nakajima tore open the doors and surveyed the room. It was obviously a study, evidenced by the enormous bookcase and leather chairs. Onishi stood beside a magnificent *daisho* and a suit of armor with such stoic poise, they may as well have been one. Lieutenant Nakajima eyed the Baron with a steely gaze. They had fought this battle before, at different times and in different forms.

Purity versus corruption.

Patriotism versus treason.

Good versus evil.

*****

Baron Onishi looked him up and down, allowing only a sneer. Nakajima drew himself up for the words he'd prepared. After all, the Baron should know why he was going to die.

"Baron Onishi! In the name of the Emperor and the Japanese people, you are to receive *tenchu*, divine punishment!"

"So…Sakamoto sent his adjutant," Onishi hissed.

"Do you know why you must die?" Lieutenant Nakajima held his head high. "Because—"

"I don't care what foolish reason you have," Onishi snapped. "Just shoot and hurry back to Sakamoto."

Damn him. Nothing could shame this pompous aristocrat. Not the noble actions of the Army in Manchuria, or the masses of unemployed, or the Tohoku famine. A bullet was too easy. Nakajima holstered the Nambu pistol and drew his saber.

With a guttural shout, he rushed toward Onishi. A hideous crunch filled the study as the sword plunged straight into the Baron's midsection, cutting through muscles and organs. The charge slammed them both against the suit of armor, toppling it over with a loud clang. Onishi glared back with cold contempt, before looking down at the blade that now pierced his gut. Nakajima gave a sharp twist, contorting the Baron's face with pain.

Hysterical shrieking diverted Nakajima's attention to the entrance. A silver-haired woman rushed toward them, her face panicked and enraged. Nakajima slid the saber out from the Baron, dropping him to his knees. Blood washed over the pieces of armor, now strewn across the floor.

"Get away from him!" the woman cried, putting herself in between the Baron and himself. "If you're going to kill my husband, then kill me first!"

Nakajima scoffed. Kill a woman? Ridiculous!

"Stop hiding behind your wife, Onishi-zan," Nakajima said.

Disgust appeared on Baroness Onishi's face alongside rage and panic.

"You impudent peasant," she sneered.

There was no time for this. Sheathing the sword, he pulled out the Nambu and aimed it straight at her face.

"Move. Now."

"What kind of man are you? Pointing a gun at a woman?" she said, swatting the Nambu away. On the floor, Baron Onishi hacked and wheezed. "I spit on your ancestors, your family, and you!"

A chorus of gasps erupted from behind. Nakajima turned and found three servants gathered by the doorway, their faces disfigured in horror. He spun the pistol around and ordered them out. But despite their transparent fear, they remained still.

"Get out," the Baroness commanded. "Call the Police."

The servants nodded and obeyed, retreating from the room. Ah, such loyalty was admirable, even if it was to the corrupt Onishi family. He turned back to face the dying Baron.

"Leave me," Onishi said to his wife. "Please."

"Never," she said, kneeling beside him. Her tears fell to the floor, mixing with his blood. "My life ends with yours."

Perhaps these well-fed aristocrats did have a sense of honor. Nakajima lowered the pistol. Baron Onishi's face rapidly drained of color, but maintained a grim resolution. Clutching him in her arms, the Baroness was soon awash in his blood.

"Get me…get me," Baron Onishi strained through gasps, "our family sword."

The Baroness nodded and started for the *wakizashi* short sword, still perched on the *daisho*. Ah, the Baron was going to commit *seppuku*. An honorable death, but resentment welled deep inside Nakajima. Baron Onishi's death was to be assassination, not ritual suicide. He looked up and saw Chitose-oneesan in the corner, staring at him with wide, burning eyes.

"Kill them, Hajime," she said. "Kill them both."

As the Baroness shuffled back to her husband, clutching the *wakizashi*, Nakajima took aim and fired. A massive hole exploded out of the Baroness' temple, spraying the bookshelf with gore. Her dainty body collapsed onto the floor like a marionette with its strings cut. Baron Onishi's composure finally cracked and he vomited an agonized scream. Now he held her and stroked what was left of her gray hair. His pained face looked ready to shatter into a thousand pieces.

"Now you know loss, Baron," Lieutenant Nakajima said, the Nambu hanging by his side. "Now you are the hungry farmers, the unemployed, the girls sold like cattle. The New Japan begins with your death." He took aim once again. "*Tenchu!*"

He saw Chitose-oneesan smile and opened fire.

CHAPTER TWENTY-THREE

Standing at full attention before Superintendent Shimura's desk, Aizawa tried not to let his anger show.

"Sir, please reconsider," he said.

"Kuroki-san is not a threat to anyone. When I released him, he personally apologized to me for the trouble he caused."

"Sir, Kuroki was close to confessing. We just needed to chill him a little longer."

"Enough!" the Superintendent said, bolting from his chair. "We have real crimes to contend with, Inspector. Why should the Metropolitan Police concern itself with some brainless patriot who only wants to kill himself?"

Aizawa clenched his jaw and tightened his fists. "Sir…I beg you to reconsider. Baron Onishi's life is in danger. This might seal his fate."

Shimura sank back into his chair. "Our duty is to maintain law and order, not follow aristocrats around like servants. Besides, rich men can afford bodyguards."

Aizawa maintained an erect poise, despite the anger and frustration pulsating through his body.

"As you wish, sir. Then the case is closed?"

Shimura narrowed his eyes. "I didn't say that. If you think Onishi's life is in danger, then convince me in a report. I want a sound theory with a motive, not just conjecture."

"Yes, Superintendent," Aizawa said, forcing the words out.

"You're dismissed, Inspector."

*****

Back in his office, Aizawa reviewed his notes and scribbled out a summary of the plot's details so far. At the center of it all was General Yori Sakamoto, future shogun and wirepuller of Masaru Ryusaki, who in turn had puppeteered Makoto Kuroki. But why would Sakamoto want Baron Onishi dead? He thought back to what the Baron had said over tea.

Last week, General Sakamoto met with the Baron and demanded the government go off the gold standard in order to increase the military budget. Onishi refused. Frustrated, the General must have decided to simply overthrow the government rather than take power through legitimate means. As shogun, Sakamoto could increase the military budget tenfold.

What was he planning? A new war most likely. But with who? There were so many potential enemies. The Chinese were almost finished in Manchuria, but the Kwantung Army could still press southward onto Peiping, Tientsin, and Nanking. Soviet Russia was another possible enemy that many in the Army leadership wanted to fight. A *"fake warrior playing with his toy sword,"* as Sakamoto had called it. However, according to the Navy brass, Japan's greatest enemy was the United States. With an increased military budget, a decisive battle at sea would turn the Pacific Ocean into a Japanese lake.

Aizawa lit a Pall Mall and pictured how the coup would unfold. Shortly after Baron Onishi's death, Ryusaki's *soshi* would dynamite the Imperial Diet and other government buildings, causing riots and mayhem. General Sakamoto would call in troops and declare martial law, installing himself as shogun. It was so simple, and yet it all hinged on Baron Onishi's assassination. If he became prime minister, he'd have the power and influence to transfer Sakamoto far away from Tokyo and order the entire Metropolitan Police to hunt Masaru Ryusaki into the bowels of the city.

Aizawa took a deep drag on the Pall Mall and considered his options. He couldn't mention Ryusaki until he had definite proof. Superintendent Shimura might tell him that he was a suspect, possibly compromising his mysterious informant. He could tail Makoto Kuroki, though he doubted that would turn up much. Is that all that Superintendent Shimura wanted to tell him? The entire exchange could have been handled over the telephone. So why wasn't it?

Unless…it was to draw him away from the Baron. His chest tightened as he reached for the phone.

"Hello, operator? The Onishi estate in Azabu, please."

Aizawa took enormous drags in between rings and waited. Suddenly, a panicked voice picked up.

"Hello?"

"This is Inspector Aizawa. Is everything—"

The voice cut him off with a sob.

"Inspector, something terrible has happened…" Another choked gasp. "The Onishis…the Onishis have been murdered!"

The words slapped Aizawa hard. "Who did it?"

"I don't know who…he put a gun to my neck while I was working on the Baron's Mercedes. The other servants saw that he wore an Army uniform. After he…after he… murdered the Baron and Baroness…they say he fled into the woods and disappeared."

Lieutenant Nakajima. It had to be him.

"Let me speak to Sergeant Murayama."

Another sob. "He's also dead…"

Aizawa steadied himself. There would be a time to mourn, but not now.

"When did this happen?"

"About twenty minutes ago. I fainted during it…I'm…I'm so ashamed…"

"Have you called the Police?"

"Y-yes…they're on their way…"

Aizawa slammed the receiver down and took a final drag on his Pall Mall. He had to concentrate and not let his mind wander. He'd need to focus on the coming battle ahead. But haunting, mocking images passed by, distracting him; Sergeant Murayama's wife and three children without a man to provide for them, the slaughtered remains of the Onishis, and Masaru Ryusaki laughing in his face.

CHAPTER TWENTY-FOUR

Inside her apartment, Reiko's eyes darted between wall posters of Louise Brooks in *Diary of a Lost Girl* and Anna May Wong in *Piccadilly*. If anyone could understand her predicament, it was these ladies. What hell they had endured for men. She sat on her Western-style bed while Masaru stared out the window in tense silence, arms folded behind his back. A good mistress would offer words of encouragement, but his earlier behavior in Ginza had left her bitter. Now, all she wanted was a smoke.

"Where are your cigarettes?"

Masaru kept his back turned and said, "In my coat pocket."

Reiko hopped off her bed and walked across the cold wooden floor to the coat rack. Digging through Masaru's long blue overcoat, she pulled out his Golden Bats along with a folded pamphlet. She opened it up and stared at a strange illustration; a giant samurai in full armor about to bring an enormous sword down on the Imperial Diet Building.

"What's this?"

Masaru turned around and smiled. "Ah yes, I wanted to show you that. Tomorrow, my followers will pass those pamphlets out all over Tokyo. The Kusanagi Society will have to increase its ranks to cause the incident that will bring General Sakamoto to power." He glowed with triumph. "Now, after months of persecution, our hour or triumph is at hand!"

Reiko nodded and stuffed the pamphlet back into the coat pocket. Lighting a cigarette, she took a deep puff and turned up the electric heater next to the bed. Even with the heater at full power, it remained freezing inside the cramped apartment.

She retreated back to the bed. Masaru drew away from the window and sat beside her.

"Reiko…I'm sorry."

She took a deep drag. "For being such a coldhearted man?"

His long fingers twirled her bobbed hair.

"A patriot must love his nation above everything…but don't ever think that you're not important to me," he whispered into her ear.

She held the cigarette between her fingers and faced him. "How important?"

He smiled. "You're my morning sun…my cherry blossom in full bloom."

Trite words, but what else could she expect from a writer? Still, it lowered her defenses and soothed her bitterness. Reiko took another drag and studied his features. Although he could be cruel at times, at least Masaru was handsome…in an overeducated, rich-boy way. Not every mistress could say that.

"Masaru…what will happen to us…in the New Japan?"

He reached over and took the cigarette from her. "A man needs the support of a woman, in mind and body."

"So you'll keep me around as your mistress?"

He took a drag and eyed her. "Reiko…our nation is in peril. Every citizen will have to sacrifice in the coming months. There will be no room for selfishness in the New Japan."

Words that proclaimed the coming of a new era. Like a tsunami, if you stood tall against it, you'd be swept away. The only hope was to seek higher ground and hope it passed you by. Her eyes darted between the Louise Brooks and Anna May Wong posters, then to her *shimada* wig perched next to the open closet full of drop-waist dresses, pea coats, and her black kimono. The whole room seemed to swirl around in a typhoon of banality.

The shrill ring of the nightstand telephone ripped her out of self-pity. She grabbed the receiver and snapped, "What?"

"Put Ryusaki-zensei on the phone," Lieutenant Nakajima said, his buzzing accent digging into her ear.

"Is that Nakajima-san?" Masaru asked, the smoldering cigarette hanging from his lips.

Her heart sank as she handed over the receiver.

"Lieutenant? Yes! Excellent work," Masaru said, punctuating every statement with a sharp nod. "A great victory over evil! Yes, I will see you tomorrow. For the New Japan! Banzai!"

Beaming, Masaru hopped off the bed, hung up the receiver, and stubbed out the Golden Bat in a nearby ashtray.

"Baron Onishi is dead!"

The words made the apartment feel even colder. Still, better to remain on Masaru's good side.

"Justice has prevailed. We can thank the gods for this great victory," she said, hoping the words didn't sound too mechanical or forced. "What will happen now?"

"Tonight, we celebrate! And tomorrow, we will throw Nakajima-san a party for his departure to Manchuria." He took in a deep breath. "He told me he's going to pray at the Yasukuni Shrine, like a true soldier."

At least that miserable country monkey would finally be out of her life. She'd silently toast that his death in Manchuria would be painful and ignominious. Reiko cursed that bastard Nakajima for what he'd turned Masaru into. Now she was the mistress to a murderer. There was no going back. At least she'd tried to stop it all.

"Unfortunately, he had to kill a police officer," Masaru said, donning his fedora.

"A police officer?" she spat out.

"Some sergeant. It's regrettable to kill a man who was only doing his duty, but this is war." He balled his fist. "If only it had been Aizawa...but I had Superintendent Shimura call him back to Police Headquarters. No matter. He'll be disposed of soon enough."

Sympathy washed over her: for the Baron, for that police officer, and for the fate that awaited poor Inspector Aizawa.

But her pity was soon drowned out by a swelling hatred for that devil soldier who had spoiled her happy life.

"I'll return shortly," Masaru announced, buttoning up his overcoat. "With a bottle of Kirin beer to celebrate."

He slipped on his shoes and practically leaped out the door, leaving Reiko alone with her anger. If the gods wouldn't punish that country monkey, she would.

She grabbed the receiver and said, "Connect me to Metropolitan Police Headquarters please."

One short ring later, there was an answer.

"Metropolitan Police," a curt voice said.

"Yes, please put me through to Inspector Aizawa."

"Hold please."

Moments of silence passed.

"Inspector Aizawa here." He sounded listless and numb.

"Your assassin is heading to the Yasukuni Shrine," she said and slammed the receiver down. Her burning hatred began to cool. The shame of an arrest would permanently stain Nakajima's honor, but with luck, Inspector Aizawa would gun that bamboo sword down before he could even reach Manchuria. Reiko collapsed onto the bed with a deep sigh. Moments later, the door swung open with a loud creak. She poked her head up and found Masaru standing in the doorway empty-handed.

"Are the stores closed?" she asked.

He shook his head. "I was thinking…we should join Nakajima-san in prayer at Yasukuni. Both of us have shameful pasts. We've been selfish, decadent, and acted like foreigners. Going forward, we must behave like true patriots."

"But Masaru, it's so cold outside…"

"Cold? While we lounge next to an electric heater, our brave soldiers face the cruel Manchurian winter!"

Trying not to let her panic show, Reiko cursed how easily the Japanese were governed by shame.

"Alright, Masaru…I'll get dressed."

CHAPTER TWENTY-FIVE

Aizawa hung up the receiver and puffed away on his Pall Mall. The past few minutes had turned into a nightmare before becoming a bizarre fantasy. That disembodied, husky voice had come to his aid again, even if it was too late for the Baron.

He reviewed the facts. Onishi's assassin wore an Imperial Army uniform. According to the mysterious informant, he was heading toward Yasukuni, where all of Japan's war dead lay enshrined. All the pieces fit and pointed the way to a final showdown with Lieutenant Nakajima.

Aizawa stubbed out his cigarette, then grabbed his overcoat and fedora. He felt for his Colt pistol, snug in its chest holster. He'd need it soon enough. The *junsas* could clean up at the Onishi estate.

*****

Snow crunched under Lieutenant Nakajima's boots as he approached the enormous *torii* gate of the Yasukuni Shrine. During the day, the sides were lined with booths of shrine maidens selling trinkets and charms to soldiers departing for Manchuria, all guaranteed to make them invincible in battle. But the shrine was deserted after dark, except for the thousands of souls that dwelled here. He couldn't face the gods with unclean hands, still stained with the Baron's foul blood. He washed them in the nearby purification fountain and then headed past the main *torii*, into the very soul of the Japanese Empire.

The main worship hall came into view with its white banner and chrysanthemum crests: white for the color of death and chrysanthemum insignia representing the Imperial throne. After depositing a few coins as an offering, Nakajima shook the bell and clapped his hands. He bowed his head in prayer as the gods surrounded him. Once men, they had been exploded, stabbed, and shot into godhood, and now saturated this lowly rice farmer with their divine presence. He would soon join their ranks, but for now, he continued in silent prayer; for his dead sister, for the Emperor, for the New Japan, and that his death in Manchuria would be utterly glorious.

Several minutes of silence passed until the sound of crackling snow interrupted him. Nakajima turned and found two figures rapidly approaching. Ryusaki-sensei wore a long blue overcoat and fedora, looking more like a salaryman than the leader of the Kusanagi Society. Reiko Watanabe lurked behind him, like a snake slithering quickly to keep up. Instead of her geisha rags, she also wore Western clothes: a fancy pea coat, cloche hat, and high heels, as if flaunting her decadence.

"Ryusaki-zensei...I'm honored by your presence."

"Your patriotic actions were so moving that I decided to join you in prayer, Lieutenant," Ryusaki-sensei said with frosted breath. "On behalf of our nation, I thank you."

Nakajima suppressed an inner glee and remained stoic. "I only did my duty, *zensei*."

Ryusaki-sensei beamed. "We must thank the gods for this great victory."

Such a triumph over evil would rank among the greatest victories of Japanese history right alongside the Battles of Tsushima and Mukden. But somehow, Reiko Watanabe's presence sullied the moment, like a stinking odor.

"What is she doing here?"

Ryusaki-sensei gave Reiko a once over. "She's my alibi for tonight." He turned back to Nakajima. "But she's come to pray as well."

"Is that so?"

Reiko gave a firm nod and bowed. "I have come to give thanks to the gods...and to you, Lieutenant."

The statement sounded hollow and forced, but Nakajima savored every syllable. In time, her words would become genuine. When the New Japan came, Reiko Watanabe would be purged of her selfish individualism forever. Ah, if this creature of decadence could be turned into a true patriot and an honorable woman, then there truly was hope for the rest of the nation.

*****

Aizawa ground the Rolls-Royce to a halt at the bottom of Kudan Hill, gateway to the Yasukuni Shrine. A black sedan sat parked in front of the steps that led to the main entrance. Aizawa hopped out and drew his pistol, then inspected the other automobile. It was empty but there was a metal five-pointed star on the car's grill, the symbol of the Imperial Army. Nakajima was still here.

Aizawa swept his gaze to and fro as he passed underneath the main *torii* gate and into the shrine grounds. Nobody in sight, but a fresh track of footprints leading from the courtyard to the main shrine was cause for concern.

Stone lanterns along the sides lit the way, stretching out his shadow across a thin carpet of snow. In the near distance stood the statue of Masujiro Omura, father of the Imperial Army, who seemed to stare at him with hostile accusation. How could he have forgotten? Passing underneath that *torii* gate had transported him into the Shinto pantheons. And here he was, brandishing a gun like some sort of bandit.

It had been months since he'd visited any shrine, let alone Japan's most sacred. But even he could feel the touch of the countless souls that rested here, all pointing the way out. Whatever crime had been committed, it didn't give him the right to desecrate their resting place with an arrest.

Aizawa retreated back through the courtyard and under the *torii*, returning to the land of mortals. He'd spring the trap here. Crouching behind the Army staff car, he peered out into the darkness, lighted only by the moon and two enormous stone lanterns that marked the entrance. He kept his pistol trained and waited. Frosted breath poured from his nostrils as he struggled to keep himself steady in the chilly night air. But a flood of images shook him: Sergeant Murayama dead, the Onishis dead, and General Sakamoto as the new shogun.

The snow crunched as three figures came into view. Two massive stone lanterns at the entrance illuminated them enough to distinguish key features. Though he was dressed in a long blue overcoat and fedora, Masaru Ryusaki's horn-rimmed glasses were an easy giveaway. But he couldn't identify an extravagantly dressed woman on Ryusaki's left. Attired in a dark brown uniform, peaked cap, and cape was Lieutenant Nakajima, walking alongside his *sensei* on the right as if he were departing for the Manchurian front.

"Police!" Aizawa shouted, standing up.

The three of them stood paralyzed with confused faces. Keeping the Colt automatic trained on them, Aizawa inched away from the staff car.

"You're all under arrest. Surrender and—"

A flash of fire erupted and struck the car window beside him. With his pistol drawn, Lieutenant Nakajima took refuge behind one of the stone lanterns, while Ryusaki and the woman dashed off into the darkness.

Aizawa ducked back behind the staff car's hood and returned fire. Nakajima shot again, shattering what was left of the car's passenger window. Aizawa took aim at his attacker and fired, only to miss and send a bullet whizzing into the snow.

Another bout of gunfire erupted, tearing more holes into the staff car. This needed to end soon before a bullet found its way into the gas tank. But that stone lantern provided the Lieutenant with an excellent defense and one that wouldn't explode any time soon.

Suddenly, the shooting stopped and Nakajima shouted, "Don't shoot! I'm coming out!"

A strange turnabout, considering the Lieutenant had the advantage. Regardless, Nakajima soon stepped out from behind the stone lantern with his arms raised and the pistol holstered. The heavy saber jangled at his side.

Aizawa gestured for the Lieutenant to put his hands on the bullet-riddled staff car. Nakajima nodded and obeyed. Aizawa shoved the Colt against the Lieutenant's neck and disarmed him of his Nambu pistol and saber. After handcuffing Nakajima, Aizawa looked around for any trace of Ryusaki, but the coward and his little whore had melted away into the night.

A good police officer always tempered his emotions, but rage seized Aizawa. He spun Nakajima around and slammed him up against the car. "By sunrise, I'm going to make you wish you had turned that gun on yourself." In the moonlight, the red and yellow rank insignia gleamed on the Lieutenant's shoulders. Nakajima gave no response except for a glassy-eyed stare, like a shark in an aquarium.

CHAPTER TWENTY-SIX

Aizawa kept a tight grip on Lieutenant Nakajima's handcuffs as the elevator door opened, depositing them onto the second floor of Police Headquarters. Screams and shouts echoed throughout the halls, giving this murderer a sample of what awaited him. Aizawa shoved the Lieutenant into an empty interrogation room and released his grip. Losing his balance, Nakajima fell to his knees and struggled to upright himself.

"Don't bother," Aizawa said with a right cross. Nakajima tumbled backward into a corner, wincing in pain. "That was for what you did back in Marunouchi. Now, here's what's going to happen. You're going to tell me where Masaru Ryusaki has been living these past few months. If not, I'm going to beat your face into a bloody smear."

Nakajima looked up and gave a cold glare. Aizawa slammed a foot into his gut. The Lieutenant released a rush of air, but quickly recomposed himself.

"I know that you were Ryusaki's spy in the Army Ministry during the March Incident. I know General Sakamoto is behind this new plot to become shogun. And I know you killed Baron Onishi. As they say in baseball, three strikes and you're out."

Nakajima lost no composure. "If you say so, Aizawa-zan."

Aizawa grabbed Nakajima's collar and hoisted him up.

"You're from Tohoku, right?"

The Lieutenant nodded.

"What will happen to the Nakajima family when they read that their beloved son is on trial for assassinating a statesman?"

Nakajima lifted his head. "When they realize it was Baron Onishi, the whole village will give my family a banzai cheer!"

"And what about the families of those you murdered? Sergeant Murayama had a wife and children."

For a moment, the Lieutenant's eyes softened with regret before hardening to stone. "Unfortunate casualties. Sometimes our airplanes bomb civilians in Manchuria."

Shame wasn't working, so Aizawa landed another right cross and Nakajima collapsed on the floor. Aizawa followed up with more kicks to his gut and back, before grinding his heel against Nakajima's cheek. Aside from stifled gasps, there was no sign of fatigue. The Lieutenant was like a samurai encased in invisible armor.

A bright glare blinded Aizawa, but he felt his fists connect again and again with Nakajima. Across his cheeks, in his gut, and on his chin. Not just the Lieutenant, but his blows reached out and landed on General Sakamoto, on Superintendent Shimura, and on Masaru Ryusaki.

A droning noise brought him back to the interrogation room and turned into the sound of deep breathing. Aizawa loosened his tie and sank to his knees in exhaustion. Anger was getting him nowhere. He needed to calm down before proceeding any further. Nakajima righted himself up and leaned against the wall. Blood trickled from his mouth and stained his uniform like crimson tears.

"You can beat me all you like…but I will never betray my *zensei*."

Aizawa said nothing and took large gulps of air. With every breath, his temper began to cool.

"Ah, the gods are kind," Nakajima said, almost laughing. "They have given me the strength to defeat you."

"What are you talking about?" Aizawa snapped.

"They aid those who are purehearted."

"You're pure?"

Nakajima gave a sharp nod.

"You're a murderer," Aizawa said.

"And what are you?" Nakajima asked, seemingly staring straight through Aizawa and at the Emperor's portrait, hanging across the room.

"A man whose duty it is to catch murderers."

"No, you're a mercenary for a corrupt government."

"And you're not? I was in the Army too. A good soldier obeys orders no matter what."

"Only if the orders are pure. Ryusaki-zensei taught me that loyal insubordination is sometimes the only pure path to take. I was once like you, Inspector, a slave to the evil men who run the government," Nakajima said, his eyes wide and inflamed. "But Ryusaki-zensei broke my chains. Only then could I see her…"

"Who?"

"My sister…Chitose Nakajima. Ah, I can see her ghost, standing in this very room. She tells me how pleased the gods are!"

Aizawa believed in ghosts as much as anyone else, but something told him that Lieutenant Nakajima might spend the rest of his life in an insane asylum rather than prison.

"Don't you understand, Inspector? You're a soldier too, carrying out your duty. But the gods do not want us to be enemies…let me show you the path toward purity and patriotism!"

Aizawa grunted. "Well, I hope you'll pray for me then."

A loud knock reverberated throughout the room.

"Come in," Aizawa said.

A *junsa* entered and snapped to attention. "Inspector Aizawa, Superintendent Shimura wants to see you right away."

Aizawa stood and walked toward the door. "Watch him."

The *junsa* nodded.

"Inspector," Nakajima called out. "I will pray for you. A true patriot is trapped inside you. Let him out."

Aizawa sighed. At least someone was praying for him.

*****

Aizawa entered Superintendent Shimura's office and stared straight into Masaru Ryusaki's serpentine face. It had been the first time he'd seen him up close in months. Decked out in a fancy blue suit and red silk tie, he hadn't changed since March. The bastard still radiated such arrogance it was almost toxic. But here he was, inside Metropolitan Police Headquarters. Had he actually turned himself in? Ryusaki stood in front of the Superintendent's desk, holding his fedora with a taunting smirk. Aizawa fought an urge to pummel him then and there.

Instead, he straightened up and said, "Masaru Ryusaki, you're under arrest!"

Ryusaki laughed and cocked his head. "On what charge?"

"Murder. Conspiracy. Treason. I'm sure there are others that I missed," Aizawa said, grabbing Ryusaki's lapels.

"Unhand him, Inspector," Shimura said from behind his desk.

"But, sir—"

"That's an order."

Aizawa released his grip but fixed Ryusaki with a penetrating stare.

"Ryusaki-san isn't under arrest. In fact, he is here to lodge a complaint."

For a moment, Aizawa lost his voice. "A complaint?"

Shimura nodded. "He claims that you attacked his friend…a soldier."

Aizawa balled his hands into fists. "Lieutenant Nakajima assassinated Baron Onishi. He also killed the Baron's wife and Sergeant Murayama."

"Yes, I heard about that," Shimura said. "I didn't order Murayama to guard Baron Onishi. Why was he there?"

Aizawa swallowed hard. "On my orders. I didn't want to leave the Baron alone."

Superintendent Shimura's eyes narrowed behind his thick glasses. "We will discuss that later. But for now, you are to explain your actions outside of the Yasukuni Shrine."

"My actions?"

Ryusaki cut in with a sharp laugh. "Don't you remember how you attacked us, Inspector?"

"That's a lie," Aizawa said, slamming a fist on Shimura's desk.

"It's the truth," a low, female voice interrupted.

For the first time, Aizawa noticed that woman from Yasukuni, standing off to the corner. He'd been so fixated on that crafty spider Masaru Ryusaki, he hadn't even noticed his little whore. She was pretty and with bobbed hair, eye shadow, and lipstick, the woman looked like a *moga*, a modern girl. Before the depression, *mogas* were a common fantasy. But nowadays they looked more like spoiled children playing dress-up and cheap Japanese imitations of the American flappers.

"This is Reiko Watanabe...Ryusaki-san's...associate. Watanabe-san," Shimura said, beckoning her over. "Please tell us what happened."

The *moga* stepped forward but kept her eyes lowered. "Lieutenant Nakajima is about to ship out to Manchuria...so we decided to pray for him at the Yasukuni Shrine. As we were leaving, Inspector Aizawa confronted us ..." Watanabe trailed off with a pitiful sob. Then, she lifted her head and stared back at him with bleary eyes. "Nakajima-san only drew his weapon after...after Inspector Aizawa began shooting at us!"

Aizawa stood in silence for several moments, letting each word sink in. He disregarded what Watanabe had actually said and scrutinized that husky voice of hers.

He'd found his mysterious informant at last.

CHAPTER TWENTY-SEVEN

Suddenly, Aizawa felt like a soldier marching across a minefield. One misstep would explode in his face. If he confronted Watanabe about the anonymous phone calls, she'd deny everything. Even worse, Ryusaki would realize her betrayal and see to it that she wouldn't survive the night. But he couldn't let her lies go unchallenged.

"Those are Ryusaki's words," he growled. "Not yours."

Watanabe stepped back and gave an offended look. "You shoot at us…try and frame Masaru for murder…and now you accuse *me* of lying?"

"What do you mean, Watanabe-san?" Shimura asked.

"Just what I said, Superintendent. Inspector Aizawa has been harassing Masaru for months even though he's no longer active in politics." Reiko Watanabe's face burned with the passion of an animal defending its home. "Superintendent Shimura, you said a politician was just assassinated. The Inspector must be trying to frame Masaru out of spite!"

Aizawa couldn't help but be impressed. If he didn't recognize her voice, the theatrics might have fooled him. However, Superintendent Shimura nodded along as if hypnotized.

"Watanabe-san, can you testify to the whereabouts of Ryusaki-san and Lieutenant Nakajima?" Shimura asked.

She nodded with enthusiasm. "Yes! I've been with them both for the past day. They were nowhere near this Baron Onishi."

"Watanabe-san speaks with the sincerity that only a woman can," Ryusaki cut in from behind her. "I suspect that Inspector Aizawa is unable to solve this case, so he chose to frame me for the Baron's assassination. There are many patriotic societies in Tokyo that could have killed him for his slanderous remarks against the Imperial Army."

"Do you have any idea who?" Shimura asked.

"No," Ryusaki said. "But I will gladly keep you informed if I hear anything."

"Thank you, Ryusaki-san. I'm sure Inspector Aizawa will appreciate your assistance."

Aizawa blinked in numb silence. He knew that Shimura sympathized with the Kusanagi Society, but it seemed impossible that he would actually ignore his duty as a police officer after everything that had happened. Masaru Ryusaki would escape again…only this time, he'd leave a trail of blood behind him. It became harder to breathe, as if the office had filled with toxic fumes, and Aizawa was the only one without a gas mask.

A loud knock on the door rang out.

"Enter," Shimura said.

Three more figures crammed themselves into the tightening office. They were all soldiers, uniformed in the same shade of dark brown as Lieutenant Nakajima, but with black collar patches instead of red. Two imposing sergeants wore white armbands with red kanji characters that read "Law Soldier." The officer leading them had no armband, but his suspicious eyes behind oval-shaped glasses were ominous enough. They were from the *Kempeitai*, the Military Police.

"Superintendent Shimura?" the officer asked.

Shimura stood and snapped a salute. The officer clicked his heels.

"Major Takumi Hatsu, *Kempeitai*. We've been informed that you're holding an Army officer prisoner. Second Lieutenant Hajime Nakajima. Please release him into our custody."

"How did you—" Aizawa began, but Shimura cut him off.

"When Ryusaki-san told me about what happened at Yasukuni, I contacted the *Kempeitai*. You should know that military personnel are outside of our jurisdiction."

Aizawa bit his lip. No wonder Nakajima had surrendered so quickly. He must have received assurances from Ryusaki and Sakamoto that even if he were arrested, he'd be a free man by morning. Like a fool, Aizawa had played right into their hands.

No, these *kempei* wouldn't win without a fight. Too much had happened for him to submit quietly. A fire rose in Aizawa's stomach and leaped out of his throat.

"Superintendent, if we turn Lieutenant Nakajima over to them, he'll never face justice!"

Major Hatsu's eyes widened behind his glasses. "How dare you? The Metropolitan Police has no authority over an Imperial soldier!"

"And the *Kempeitai* has no jurisdiction over the Metropolitan Police!" Aizawa bypassed Hatsu and leaned over Shimura's desk. "Superintendent, are we unable to stop a murderer because he wears the Army uniform? The pride of the Metropolitan Police is on the line!"

Superintendent Shimura said nothing, keeping his gaze low and defeated.

"You challenge the authority of the Imperial Army?" Major Hatsu demanded.

Aizawa straightened back up and glared at the three *kempei*. "If you try and take Nakajima, then I'll throw you in jail with him."

A heavy silence smothered the room. Ryusaki and Watanabe backed away in stunned silence. The three *kempei* didn't speak, but behind his glasses, Major Hatsu's eyes boiled with fury.

"Enough!" Superintendent Shimura roared, standing up. "Inspector Aizawa, I order you to cooperate with Major Hatsu. The Army and Metropolitan Police are brothers, serving the same father, our Imperial Majesty."

"Thank you, Superintendent," Major Hatsu said as the anger drained from his face. "I will give you the full report after we interrogate Lieutenant Nakajima." He saluted and marched out, followed by the two sergeants, each one pausing to shoot Aizawa a hateful glare before leaving.

"Thank you, Superintendent," Ryusaki said. "And I promise to help Inspector Aizawa in any way that I can."

"Thank you, Ryusaki-san," Shimura said. "You can go now."

After quick bows, Ryusaki and Watanabe exited the room. Shimura sank back to his desk like a popped balloon. Was this even the man who had inspired him to become a detective? No, this was the shadow of a once honorable police officer.

"Inspector…"

"Three people are dead."

"Inspector…"

Rage swept aside protocol. He pounded his fists against Shimura's desk. "Does that mean nothing to you?"

The Superintendent lifted his gaze to meet Aizawa's. "Inspector…"

"Murayama was one of us. How could you let his murderer go?"

"I didn't order Sergeant Murayama to guard Baron Onishi. That was your doing."

The shame of his failure hurt far worse than any physical pain he'd endured in the past few days. Like a bullet lodged deep in his gut, it burrowed deeper and deeper.

"Regardless," Superintendent Shimura began again. "That *moga* just provided Masaru Ryusaki with a firm alibi."

"Sir, we can still bring him to justice. If only…"

"If only what, Inspector?" Shimura asked with narrowing eyes.

"If only you would help me, like when we raided that yakuza gambling den last year…and countless times before."

"Why should I help you now, Inspector?"

Aizawa steadied himself and said, "Because you were the man who taught me to take pride in the Metropolitan Police. Before we became partners, being a police officer was simply my job. You transformed it into my duty."

"I never wanted these," Shimura said, gesturing to his rank epaulettes. "But after that raid, the Superintendent-General promoted me. It turns out that my predecessor had been forced to resign amidst rumors of corruption.

"That was not the worst of it," Shimura continued. "After my promotion, Dietmen sent me presents and then asked me to send detectives to trail their opponents. I had to look the other way when some politician was mixed up in a criminal investigation. I never imagined that so much corruption festered within our government. So when you arrested Ryusaki back in March, I was touched by his sincere patriotism despite his breaking the law."

Giri and *ninjo*, duty and emotion, the common curse among the Japanese. Aizawa almost sympathized but the parade of bloody ghosts haunted his mind.

Superintendent Shimura sighed. "But when Baron Onishi made that contemptible speech denouncing the Imperial Army's actions in Manchuria, calling them 'bandits in uniforms'…I couldn't forgive that insult. His words dishonored my comrades who died during the war against Russia and the men fighting for our country as we speak! The Baron represented everything wrong with the government…which is why he needed to be punished."

Aizawa felt his throat tighten.

"But all of that is inconsequential. The morning sun will soon bring the dawn of the New Japan. Tell me Inspector, will you be a part of it?"

Aizawa swallowed and gave the offer consideration. If General Sakamoto and Ryusaki became the leaders of a new government, wouldn't his policeman's duty oblige him to follow their orders? He shuddered at the thought.

"I don't think Ryusaki would want me in the 'New Japan,' sir."

Shimura stood and placed a hand on Aizawa's shoulder. For the first time in months, the Superintendent resembled his old partner.

"*I* want you there, Inspector…at my side like in the old days. We'll be working together again, fighting for justice…"

That probably meant locking up anyone who disagreed with Ryusaki. Aizawa searched for an escape. Reporting Shimura's actions to the Superintendent-General was unlikely, since disregarding the chain of command was almost unthinkable in the Metropolitan Police. Besides, Aizawa wasn't sure if the top brass also sympathized with the Kusanagi Society.

"Perhaps if I…visited a shrine and prayed on it," was all he could say.

Superintendent Shimura gave a warm smile and clapped Aizawa's shoulder. "I'm sure you'll come to the right conclusion. Dismissed."

After a bow, Aizawa marched out the door, down the hall, and into the sanctuary of his office. With a deep sigh, he looked over at the framed newspaper: "Inspectors Shimura and Aizawa Raid Yakuza Gambling Den!" He wanted to laugh but needed a smoke more. Aizawa fished the pack of Pall Malls out of his pocket and plucked the last one out. It was back to Golden Bats after this, but for now, he could enjoy this little luxury. He held the cigarette up before lighting it.

"For you, Baron."

CHAPTER TWENTY-EIGHT

Lieutenant Nakajima's and Major Hatsu's footsteps echoed throughout the virtually empty Army Ministry. The pain from Aizawa's punches still lingered on Nakajima's sore face, but it began to dull. The two *kempei* sergeants had uncuffed him immediately after they left Police Headquarters, but Hatsu never broke his watchful stare on him, always keeping a hand near his saber. They halted in front of General Sakamoto's office and Hatsu banged on the door.

"Major Hatsu and Lieutenant Nakajima!"

The words echoed through the halls like a reveille.

"Come in," Sakamoto ordered.

They entered and greeted the General with salutes. Major Hatsu approached Sakamoto's desk and presented him with the Nambu pistol that Inspector Aizawa had confiscated earlier. General Sakamoto laid the weapon on his desk before dismissing Major Hatsu with a curt nod. Once alone, he examined Nakajima's raw, pulpy face like a father whose son had been bullied.

"You look like you need a cigarette," Sakamoto said.

"No thank you, sir."

"That's right, you don't smoke. What's the reason again?"

"Purity. My body must be clean if I am to be a polished sword for the Emperor."

General Sakamoto chuckled and returned to his desk. "Did you tell them anything?"

"Aizawa already knew about the plot."

"No matter. It's too late. Baron Onishi is dead and Japan is forever in your debt."

"Thank you, General," Nakajima said with a bow. "I was only the human bullet that struck the Baron down. You and Ryusaki-zensei were the men who pulled the trigger."

General Sakamoto smiled. "Yes, we owe a great deal to Ryusaki-san. If he hadn't enlisted Superintendent Shimura's help, you'd still be rotting in that dungeon." He opened a drawer and removed a slip of paper. "And I wouldn't be able to give you this."

Nakajima took the paper and scanned the details.

Second Lieutenant Hajime Nakajima was to report to Tokyo Station at noon on December 14th, Showa 6, for immediate departure to the Manchurian front. He was hereby reassigned to the Kwantung Army's Tenth Infantry Division as a platoon commander.

Ah, the ticket to godhood was now in his hands.

"Without any more weak-kneed politicians interfering, the Kwantung Army will be free to march on Chinchow and finish off that stinking wanton youth, Marshal Chang Hsüeh-liang," Sakamoto said. "And you'll make there just in time to join them."

"General…" Tears ran down Nakajima's swollen cheeks. "I am honored."

"You'll need this," General Sakamoto said, extending the Nambu automatic.

Lieutenant Nakajima tucked the pistol into his belt and dried his tears. In all probability, he'd be dead by this time next year, and if not, he'd make sure to lead his platoon on a suicide mission. Hajime Nakajima would only be able to see the birth of the New Japan through the spirit world, enshrined forever at Yasukuni.

"General, when will it begin?"

Sakamoto appeared confused. "What?"

"The coup that will bring you to power."

"Ah yes," the General said. "Soon. Very soon. But you mustn't concern yourself with that. Your duty in Tokyo is over, Lieutenant." He smiled again. "Ryusaki-san is organizing a grand *sokokai* for you, the soldier who saved Japan from the poisonous reign of Baron Onishi."

Ah, a *sokokai*…the celebratory send-off for all military men when they first enlisted or went off to battle. He remembered the one his family had thrown him before he departed for the Imperial Army Academy in Tokyo. The entire village turned out, partly to wish him well and partly because there was free food. Most villagers never left the Tohoku region, forever shackled to their rice paddies. At least the Nakajima family had another son. They could afford to lose one. Just like their daughter. No, he couldn't think about that now. He'd have an eternity for that later.

Nakajima clicked his heels, snapped a salute, and said, "General, we will meet again. At Yasukuni."

General Sakamoto returned the salute but said nothing.

*****

During the taxicab ride back to Asakusa, Reiko sat in silence, nodding and smiling while Masaru crowed in victory.

"Did you see the look on Aizawa's face? Ah, I'll savor that for the rest of my life," he said with a laugh. "The humiliation must have been shattering. I hope he doesn't kill himself before," he cast a conspiratorial glance toward the driver, "the New Japan dawns. A more fitting punishment would be to throw him inside Sugamo Prison for the rest of his life, like an insect in a jar." He lapsed into fits of malicious laughter.

"Yes," was all she could say as she studied him. Cruelty and hatred distorted his handsome face into an ugly mask. She prayed it wasn't permanent.

The taxicab halted as a procession of men paraded past. Made up of factory workers and university students, they carried red flags and banners that read "Down with the Minsei and Seiyukai! The Social People's Party is the Future!" Like children picked last for a baseball game, the social democrats were now demanding their turn.

Shouting "Banzai to the Proletariat," the Social People's Party marched by, raising their fists into the air.

"There's quite a lot of them," Reiko said.

"The depression has given the social-democrats new life." Masaru balled a fist. "We must act before they do. The other patriotic groups are divided and disorganized. I must recruit more men into the Kusanagi Society for the approaching…incident."

"Maybe you could use them. It sounds like you both hate capitalism and want justice for the poor."

Masaru scoffed. "I would, except they've been infiltrated by Communists who want to remove our sacred Emperor from the throne! His divine rule is what sets us above the rest of the world. Their loyalties are with Russia, not Japan."

Reiko gave a dumb nod and kept quiet. The last of the procession finally passed, allowing the taxicab to speed off.

"When my group is a respectable size, the others will follow my lead," Masaru continued, slamming his fist into his palm. "Imagine it, Reiko. All the patriotic societies of Tokyo will be combined into one army under my command!"

She didn't want to imagine it but nodded anyway. Was this to be her life in the New Japan? A nodding doll? Repulsed, she turned away and stared outside as the taxicab sped through Tokyo. Tofu vendors, magazine kiosks, and noodle shops flew by. A stream of salarymen headed home after a long day at the office, passing a group of scruffy, forlorn men who leaned against a wall.

For better or for worse, this was her home. What would it look like under Shogun Sakamoto's rule? She doubted a return to the Tokugawa Era, but she'd seen footage of rallies and parades in Moscow and Rome. Most likely it would look like that.

But Reiko Watanabe wouldn't march. Maybe it was best to skip town. Shanghai was a good choice, with its Japanese community and nightclubs. Then again, the newspapers were full of stories of anti-Japan boycotts there, along with reports of Chinese mobs attacking anyone who even looked Japanese. After Manchuria was finished, another *incident* might erupt there.

So Shanghai was out. What about San Francisco? No, the United States had banned all immigration from Asia. Maybe she should just stay in Japan. After all, she'd heard nice things about Osaka. But what would she do for work? How many rich Osakans needed a mistress in their lives?

However, the thought of leaving Tokyo filled her with a sadness that stretched out into infinity. But if she remained, Reiko Watanabe would be the mistress of one of the most powerful men in the Japanese Empire. Besides, how many other men would marry a woman like her? She was almost twenty-five, practically an old maid. Her virginity was long gone, auctioned off during her geisha training. Worse still, her family name was lower than dirt. Masaru Ryusaki was far better than she, or most women, could ever hope for.

What would his position be in the New Japan? Oh yes, General's Sakamoto's senior adviser. He could also double as the minister of executions with that sword of his.

Suddenly, the taxicab halted. They were back in Asakusa, right outside of her four-story Western-style apartment building. Relief bathed her. She needed to be alone with her thoughts.

"Reiko," Masaru said. She turned to face him. "I must request your presence tomorrow night…at seven o'clock. We're throwing a *sokokai* for Lieutenant Nakajima."

A bitter laugh escaped her lips. "I'm sure he'd prefer I not be there."

Masaru held up a stifling hand. "Nakajima-san is…unfamiliar with women. Do not take it personally. But it is your duty as a geisha to entertain my men."

She clutched her skirt, realizing that there was little choice in the matter. "Fine."

"Good. Oh, and Reiko…" Masaru's stern demeanor evaporated, replaced by a face of sweet sincerity. "Thank you. Without your help, Aizawa might have won."

She had betrayed both men now. With agonizing difficulty, she forced another smile.

CHAPTER TWENTY-NINE

Aizawa awoke to the sound of knocking. He lifted his stiff neck from the desk and wondered how long he'd been asleep. A glance at his wristwatch said it was almost ten o'clock. Nobody could fault him for falling asleep at the office, not after the night he'd had. After a loud yawn, he lit up a Golden Bat to wake himself up. Despite being advertised as "Sweet & Mild," the bitter tobacco stung his mouth, recently spoiled by Pall Malls. Still, there was something therapeutic about the Golden Bats, as if he could taste Japan with every puff. He felt like a tourist returning home at last.

The knocking began again, prompting Aizawa to open the door. A *junsa* stood at attention, clutching a manila folder.

"Sir, here is the Onishi report and photographs."

Aizawa accepted the folder, dreading what grotesque images lurked within.

"You also have a visitor, sir."

"A visitor?"

He half-expected Reiko Watanabe to drop by with another clue. Instead, the yakuza from the other night, Demon, appeared behind the *junsa* and gave a supplicating bow.

"That will be all. Thank you," Aizawa said.

The *junsa* saluted and walked off. Aizawa beckoned Demon into his office and tossed the manila folder on his desk. The hoodlum had sobered up and calmed down since they last met, entering with timid steps. Once inside, Aizawa examined him for a few moments, enjoying a few more drags on his Golden Bat before speaking. Several rolled up prints were underneath Demon's arm, and although he had changed into a nicer kimono and *hakama* pants for the visit, he still clutched that threadbare flat cap in his left hand. Looking closer, Aizawa noticed that Demon's hand was bandaged, partly concealing a missing pinky finger.

Cutting off one's own finger was the sincerest of all yakuza apologies. Aizawa wondered what angered Demon's boss more; trying to kill a police officer or not succeeding?

"I see you lost your pinky," Aizawa said in between puffs.

Demon gave a smile of transparent insincerity. "Yes, as penance for my behavior the other night. Boss Okamura was very upset."

"I'm sure he was," Aizawa said, stubbing the Golden Bat out in the ashtray. "Tell him better luck next time."

"Regardless, he wants no further trouble with you and has ordered me to cooperate fully." Demon gave a deep, apologetic bow and unrolled the prints from under his arm. Laying them out on the desk revealed three pornographic woodblock prints. Painted in the old *ukiyo-e* style*,* the prints showed *daimyo* lords in bed with courtesans, Japanese soldiers screwing Red Cross nurses, and an octopus molesting a helpless damsel with slimy tentacles. Cheap thrills for those who couldn't afford a real woman.

"A gesture of goodwill, Inspector. Straight from the Water Temple."

Aizawa wanted to throw the prints back in Demon's face, but he had enough enemies at the moment. Instead, he nodded his gratitude.

"Is that all?"

Demon maintained his fake smile as he presented a pamphlet from inside his flat cap. It showed an image of an armored samurai, taller than Mount Fuji, and ready to obliterate a pint-sized Diet with his enormous *katana* sword. The other side was filled with columns of Japanese characters.

"Purity and Patriotism are the foundation of the Kusanagi Society! Join our ranks to save Japan from corruption and evil. The esteemed patriot, Masaru Ryusaki, will speak today at 1:00 underneath the statue of Saigo in Ueno Park."

"This morning, one of Ryusaki's men visited the Water Temple and gave me that," Demon said. "Apparently, they thought I might be interested in politics. I'm honoring our agreement to keep you informed, Inspector."

Aizawa set the pamphlet on his desk, next to the pornographic prints. "Thank you, Demon-san. That will be all."

Demon smiled and gave another placating bow. He scurried out the door, like a roach retreating to a crevice. Aizawa glanced at the pamphlet and let his mind wander. Even back in March, the Kusanagi Society never numbered more than a few members. Ryusaki had planned on the support of the many other patriotic societies in Tokyo to aid his plot. But now, here he was holding an open recruiting rally. It made sense. Ryusaki would need plenty of foot soldiers to overthrow the government.

He returned to the manila folder. An innocuous label read: "Photographic Evidence-Onishi Estate." Aizawa braced himself and opened the folder. Three ghosts stared out from black and white photos. Sergeant Toru Murayama was sprawled out on the floor and clutched his stomach. A gaping hole split his forehead open. The Onishis held each other in a gory embrace. The Baron stared back at the camera, despite bullet wounds taking a good chunk of his face away.

Disgusted, Aizawa closed the folder. Dark thoughts clouded his mind. Sergeant Murayama's widow and children without a provider. Baron Onishi's unsuspecting son receiving a late-night telegram. General Sakamoto convening a special session of the Diet to announce martial law. Where would Kenji Aizawa be in the New Japan? Probably on his knees and with his neck stretched out, waiting for Ryusaki's blade to fall.

No, there was still time left. Even if he couldn't arrest Ryusaki, he'd drop by Ueno Park to see who turned out to listen to him rant. Such harassment might even cause him to lose face in front of his followers, sabotaging his plot before it even started. If he was really lucky, he might even shame Ryusaki into confessing. But some leverage was needed. He opened the folder back up. The photographs would do nicely.

CHAPTER THIRTY

Despite the sunny day, Ueno Park was cold and ugly. Although beautiful in springtime with forests of cherry blossoms, its trees were now gnarled by a glaze of ice and snow. But the park still had its visitors. Many were homeless who used the public benches and steps as makeshift beds. However, Sunday was the one day of the week most Japanese had off and Ueno Park was filled with children, families, and couples out for a stroll.

Aizawa walked south and passed a diamond field where two teams of teenagers played baseball. He fought off an urge to watch and kept moving. Baseball was so ingrained in the national psyche that it seemed almost unpatriotic not to like this foreign sport. Babe Ruth, Lou Gehrig, and Lefty O'Doul were held in as much esteem as the generals who commanded the Kwantung Army in Manchuria. If there ever was a war with America, hopefully it would be settled on the baseball field.

After passing Kiyomizu Temple on his right, the unmistakable, pudgy figure of the great samurai, Takamori Saigo came into view. This simple statue of Saigo walking his dog had become inseparable from Ueno Park and a beloved icon of Tokyoites. Aizawa remembered how after the Great Earthquake, people plastered the statue with missing persons notices, desperately trying to locate their loved ones. Today, however, a sizeable crowd had clustered around it, but there was no sign of Ryusaki. He checked his watch: 12:58.

A few minutes later, cheers and "banzais" erupted through the crowd as Masaru Ryusaki made his way to the statue. He had changed out of his fancy Western suit and into a dark blue kimono with gray *hakama* pants, held up by his slender, spidery frame. Dark eyes surveyed the crowd behind oval glasses and his spindly fingers clutched a full-sized *katana*, sheathed at his side. Rather than the *sensei* of a patriotic society, he looked more like a university student on his way to a samurai costume party. How old was he again? That's right, they were the same age, thirty. What different paths they'd taken.

Aizawa was soon swallowed up by the throng's somber ranks. Here were the unfortunate orphans of layoffs and factory closings. Here were the Emperor's forgotten children who had fallen through the cracks and into the Kusanagi Society. How many were there? Ninety? A hundred? A few of them looked familiar.

A wall of seven men formed in front of Ryusaki. Underneath their flat caps and fedoras, Aizawa recognized their unshaven, grim faces. They were the same seven men who, months earlier, had helped Ryusaki found the Kusanagi Society. Now they looked like dutiful soldiers, conscripted again into another war.

Ryusaki held up his sheathed *katana* and the crowd hushed.

"Men of Yamato," he began, using the archaic name for Japan, "why are you here today? You are here because greedy men oversold stocks in Marunouchi and on Wall Street. You're here because pretty ladies in New York, London, and Paris aren't buying silk stockings grown by our farmers and made in our textile mills. You're here because our leaders abandoned us."

Although Ryusaki looked like an adolescent playing dress up, there was an intensity to his voice matched only by politicians, Shinto priests, and yakuza bosses.

"We cannot look to the Imperial Diet for support. I served in the House of Representatives and know that the system is a farce. The Minsei Party and Seiyukai are both owned by the *zaibatsu*, despite the sham elections they hold. The government has become so plagued with these termites, that it should be the duty of every patriot to tear it down and rebuild it from scratch."

Throughout the crowd, many men nodded in agreement.

"That's what the great samurai, Takamori Saigo, attempted." Ryusaki held his sheathed blade up, pointing its handle toward the statue. "He realized that although the Meiji Restoration had toppled the shogun, it had brought shadowy cliques of corrupt villains to power. In 1877, he led a civil war to purify the government...but was unsuccessful. Although he met defeat, our nation now honors him with a statue like the patriot he was."

Ryusaki brought the blade down, resting it by his side.

"A true patriot acts on behalf of Japan and the Emperor. Corruption must be cleansed from our national body...with blood if necessary. Perhaps you heard that Baron Onishi met his end last night? Another sign from the gods."

Soft murmurs and grunts of approval echoed throughout the men.

"Our empire is at a crossroads. Either build a New Japan founded on justice and patriotism...or else. We already received a warning of what our fate will be...in the form of the Great Kanto Earthquake."

That moistened several eyes. Everyone in Tokyo lost someone on that day. Aizawa couldn't suppress his own memories of that sunny September morning from flooding back. Of the watermelon he and his little sister ate before he donned his white summer uniform. Of his parents who wished him well before he set off for the Police station. Of the thunderous roar that shook the entire Kanto region, especially Tokyo. Of the collapsed houses with pulverized bodies underneath. Of the flames that consumed the debris, turning the Imperial capital to ash. Of the mobs that murdered Korean immigrants and Communists, who they claimed were poisoning wells. Of seeing his own house, smashed, burned, and ground into dust. And how he couldn't stop any of it.

"The Great Kanto Earthquake was punishment from the gods for allowing Japan to fall so deeply into decadence. Should we allow our nation to continue down this corrupt path, an even greater punishment awaits us."

What could be worse than the Great Earthquake? Japan sinking into the sea? Still, the crowd nodded its understanding. If the claim was sincere enough, the Japanese would believe anything, especially the preposterous.

"Fellow patriots, I need your help. This sword," Ryusaki said, holding the *katana* high, "was forged by my ancestors during the era of civil wars. Now it symbolizes the Kusanagi, the invincible grass-cutting sword. As *sensei* of the Kusanagi Society, it is my sacred duty to carry out what Takamori Saigo began and save the nation from the evil men who rule it from the shadows. The New Japan will be born in one explosive act of patriotism! But I need your help. Will you come to Japan and the Emperor's aid when they most need you?"

The seven founding members threw up their arms and roared, "Masaru Ryusaki, banzai!"

The crowd echoed back a triple banzai cheer. Ryusaki bowed to the sound of vociferous applause and descended into the welcoming arms of the throng. Making his way through the crowd, Aizawa made his presence known with a grin and a slight bow. Behind his glasses, Ryusaki's eyes widened with surprise then narrowed with hate. Sensing an intruder, the crowd zeroed in on Aizawa and buzzed like hornets defending their queen.

Swallowing hard, Ryusaki said, "A moment, please." The crowd bowed their respects, releasing him from their protection. Aizawa and Ryusaki walked away from the crowd and over to a nearby bench, occupied by a sleeping man with tattered clothes. After a gentle nudge, Ryusaki slid a few sen coins into the half-awake man's pockets in exchange for the bench. The man bowed his gratitude and staggered away.

"You're generous, Ryusaki-san," Aizawa said, taking a seat next to him.

"Poverty is an evil I'm fighting against. Corrupt men with authority is another."

"Speaking of which," Aizawa said, gesturing to the *katana*. "It's in my authority to point out that it's been illegal for civilians to carry swords in public ever since the Meiji Era."

"I have a permit," Ryusaki said, staring straight ahead at the crowd, still gathered near Saigo's statue.

"I see…"

Ryusaki cracked an arrogant smile. "Let's drop the act. Can't you see that I've won, Inspector?"

"Judging from your speech, it sounds as if you haven't won just yet. Riots that justify martial law require lots of manpower. How many of those men over there do you think will join the Kusanagi Society? If the economy improves, they'll go back to work and forget all about the New Japan."

"Are you here to arrest me or not?" Ryusaki snapped.

"Actually, I thought you'd like to see your work up close."

Ryusaki grimaced as Aizawa pulled the photographs from his coat. He accepted the grisly pictures and examined them with a vapid expression. Aizawa could only hope that somewhere inside Ryusaki's soul, there was still a spot susceptible to shame. But his heart sank when Ryusaki's cold gaze turned into a triumphant smile.

"The gods are kind. Japan is free from another corrupt, self-serving politician."

"And what about Sergeant Murayama? He had a wife and children," Aizawa said, snatching the photographs back.

"Acceptable casualties in pursuit of a just cause. Tell me Inspector, do you know how many innocents died during the Meiji Restoration?"

So much for shame. He should have known someone as vainglorious as Masaru Ryusaki had long since moved past it.

Ryusaki stood up and began to walk away. Aizawa tucked the photographs back into his coat, then sprang to his feet and followed.

"Not so fast," he said, grabbing Ryusaki's shoulder and spinning him around. "I'm taking you back for questioning…at my home. Shimura can't help you there."

Behind his horn-rimmed glasses, Ryusaki's eyes widened in a combination of rage and fear.

"Unhand me," he said, slapping Aizawa away. He looked back at the throng, huddled around Saigo's statue. "Patriots of the Kusanagi Society…this man here is the personification of the corruption rotting our nation! He is Inspector Aizawa, the careerist watchdog for big business and politicians like Baron Onishi! Police officers like him keep the wealthy in power and the downtrodden in the gutter!"

The crowd edged closer and soon formed a pincer movement around Aizawa, encircling him. He scolded himself for acting so rashly since, after all, he was deep in enemy territory. Saved by his loyal hornets, Ryusaki smiled and disappeared into their midst. Aizawa tried to force his way after him, but a fist slammed against his face. Stinging with pain, he fell to his knees and looked up. The crowd began shouting and cursing at him, the symbol of this corrupt system that had left them bitter, humiliated, and angry. Drawing closer and closer, they soon blocked out the afternoon sun entirely.

CHAPTER THIRTY-ONE

A sharp kick dug into Aizawa's back, forcing him back onto the ground. Through a steady buzz of insults, he could make out a few distinct jeers.

"*Zaibatsu* mercenary!"

"A tin sword for politicians!"

"Enemy of patriotism!"

Sporadic blows slammed against his ribs and into his back. Aizawa groaned in pain and fought to stand. It was unthinkable for most Japanese to kill a police officer, but these men looked angry enough to try. Like sharks in a feeding frenzy, the crowd grew wilder. As he scrambled to his feet, Aizawa ripped the Colt automatic out of the holster and held it high above his head.

The faces in the crowd contorted in fear like devils struck with a Shinto charm. A moment later they scattered in all directions, most running down the staircase of the south entrance. No matter. In the distance, he could still make out Masaru Ryusaki, running deeper into the park due north.

Holstering his pistol, Aizawa gave chase on foot. He soon passed the Kiyomizu Temple and the baseball field. But there was no sign of Ryusaki. Doubling back, he sprinted across the path, passing a *koban*, a police box, on his left. He wanted to enlist a *junsa's* help in searching the park but knew it was hopeless. There were just too many places to vanish in this damn park.

Aizawa slowed to a walk and caught his breath. A nearby bench shimmered like an oasis. Off to its side, a large group of children had gathered near a *kamishibai* storyteller and his paper theater. He plopped down on the bench, but the children paid him no attention, enthralled by the smiling old storyteller.

"Who wants to hear the story of Peach Boy Taro?" he asked.

A moan rang out from the children.

"That's an old one," a little boy whined.

"Ah, but this is a new version," the storyteller said. "Have you heard about when Taro went to Manchuria?"

No, the children hadn't heard that story and begged for him to go on. The storyteller slid in the first paper frame. Taro was still born from a peach, but instead of sailing to an island to fight *oni* devils, he enlists in the Imperial Army and goes to the Manchurian front. A new slide showed Taro in uniform and snapping a salute. In the next frame, he was joined, not by his usual friends – a dog, a monkey, and a pheasant – but rather a tank, an airplane, and a machine gun. In the final frame, Taro and his friends stormed the enemy stronghold, filled with *oni* wearing Chinese uniforms.

"Banzai! Banzai! Banzai!" the children cheered, throwing their arms up. Aizawa wondered what other stories would become militarized next. He pictured future generations learning fairy tales about Masaru Ryusaki and his band of patriotic assassins outwitting corrupt villains in the Metropolitan Police.

Aizawa concentrated on where that crafty spider Ryusaki could have crawled off to. He had many sympathizers throughout Tokyo, but men sometimes preferred a woman's company in times of crisis. He could only pray that Reiko Watanabe would help him one more time.

*****

Lying back on her Western-style bed, Reiko stared blankly at the latest issue of *Kinema Junpo*. The articles and photographs of movie stars usually captured her attention, but it was impossible to concentrate today. With the Baron dead, the new prime minister would be announced any time now. Tsuyoshi Inukai would appoint General Sakamoto as army minister and, unknowingly, the future shogun of the

Japanese Empire. She kept an ear to the Sharp radio near her bed for a special bulletin in between the marathon of jazz melodies.

Reiko returned to the issue of *Kinema Junpo* and tried to focus. Several articles highlighted the major motion pictures of 1931, including *The Public Enemy*, which starred that flame-haired tough guy, James Cagney, as the gangster scourge of America. Her other redheaded idol, Clara Bow, was in two films this past year, both forgettable except for her performances. Charlie Chaplin was back in the comic-love story *City Lights*, which hadn't been released in Japan yet. Neither had the monster movie *Frankenstein*, but *Dracula* had been playing since October. Japan had also contributed to the world of cinema with its first sound picture, *The Neighbor's Wife and Mine,* a light-hearted comedy about a playwright dealing with a noisy jazz band next door. Masaru had taken her to see it at least a dozen times over the summer, along with the social satire *Tokyo Chorus* and *Sword of Justice*, a period picture about a samurai rescuing his *daimyo* lord's kidnapped daughter from bandits.

A loud knock banged at her door. The landlady perhaps? No, Masaru had already paid her rent this month. Reiko sprang out of bed and stole a glance in the mirror. She looked presentable enough in her dark blue sweater with white stripes and matching black fluted skirt, an outfit she'd copied from Anna May Wong in *Piccadilly*. It used to drive Masaru wild, but now she wondered if she'd spend the rest of her life in a kimono.

The knocking began again.

"I'm coming," she groaned before opening the door.

Inspector Kenji Aizawa blocked the doorway, framed by a long black overcoat. He removed his black fedora, revealing a close-cropped head of dark hair that accentuated a pair of thick sideburns and eyebrows that hung over a stern, unblinking gaze. His squared jaw completed the look of a man on his way to audition for a gangster picture.

Panic erupted inside her. The Inspector didn't seem like a man who would beat a woman for information, but everyone had their breaking point. And a tenseness on his face suggested that Aizawa had almost reached his.

Without a bow, the Inspector forced his way inside and shut the door. Like a wild animal, he stalked around the room, looking under her bed and inside the closet. After an irritated grunt, he returned his attention to her and snapped, "Where is he? Where is Masaru Ryusaki?"

"I don't know, Inspector, but I suggest you leave before I call Superintendent Shimura and—"

"I'm going to get right to the point, Watanabe-san," he said, waving a hand. "I know the alibi you gave last night was a lie and that you're the one who's been informing me about Ryusaki's plans."

Such straightforwardness for a Japanese man! She didn't know whether to be offended or relieved to be spared idiotic small talk. Still, better to just deny everything and ask him to leave.

"I honestly don't…wait, how did you find my apartment?"

The Inspector gave a confident smile. "Easily. You had an altercation with your landlady back in March. She said you hadn't paid the rent and the Police were called in. I simply consulted the report."

She sighed, recalling the incident. It was right before she'd met Masaru, who then began paying her rent, saving her from eviction.

"That may be, Inspector, but—"

The jazz music on the radio cut out and gave way to a crisp announcer.

"Special bulletin! Special bulletin! Important news regarding the nation! His Imperial Majesty has now offered the government to Tsuyoshi Inukai, president of the Seiyukai Party. Inukai-san has now become the twenty-ninth prime minister of Japan. Further details about his cabinet have not been released, but it is suspected that Korekiyo Takahashi will serve as finance minister. In accordance with this, Prime Minister Inukai has issued a statement that has effectively ended gold exports. Citizens are to be advised of a sudden inflation of prices as high as forty percent. Please stay tuned for more details."

The announcer faded out, replaced by the jazzy melody of "My Blue Heaven."

"That broadcast means a coup d'état," Aizawa said, staring at the radio. "Unless you tell me where Ryusaki is."

"Inspector...I..."

He snapped his neck around and snarled, "Stop lying! I recognize your voice. You're the woman who called me. Why do you deny it?"

Yes, why was she still lying? He could see right through her, so what was the point? Maybe there was a little loyalty left in her. Still, the game was over. Time to forfeit.

"It's over, Inspector. We lost."

The muscles in Aizawa's taut, squared face looked ready to snap like ropes. "No, we haven't. Tell me where he is or I'll—"

"Or you'll what, Inspector?"

Reiko clenched her fists and braced herself. But the Inspector backed off and began pacing back and forth between the posters of Louise Brooks and Anna May Wong.

"You don't realize what's at stake..." he muttered. "You don't understand what he's capable of."

Reiko let out a bitter laugh. "No one understands Masaru Ryusaki better than me."

The Inspector stopped in his tracks. "Then why won't you help me now?"

"Even if you arrested him, he has enough friends to make sure he'd be out by morning. Just like last time."

Shame flashed across the Inspector's face, forcing him to look away. Instead, he focused his attention toward the open closet, stuffed with pea coats, drop-waist dresses, cloche hats, skirts, a black kimono, and her *shimada* wig.

"You're a geisha?" he asked.

"Yes."

"And a *moga*?"

"Yes."

He turned back to her. Shame and anger had left his face, replaced by an eerie confusion. "Who are you, Watanabe-san?"

Reiko let the question settle in her mind. She'd been meaning to ask herself that for years and always put it off, probably because she wouldn't like the answer.

"Whatever I need to be," was the best she could offer.

"I'll tell you what you are. You're a woman accustomed to being spoiled and pampered. Does Masaru Ryusaki spend all of the money he gets from General Sakamoto," he gestured to the open closet as if it were a sewer, "on that?"

Reiko could tell where this was going. "Yes, yes. I know there's a depression, and I'm some selfish little *moga* with ritzy clothes and gaudy jewelry. I should be ashamed, but I'm not."

The Inspector clutched his fedora so tight it looked ready to rip apart. "Tonight while you sleep in your warm apartment, think of the men forced to live on benches in Ueno Park and our soldiers in Manchuria."

"Don't try this with me, Inspector, because I gave up on shame long ago. You think the depression has hurt working men? My heart goes out to them, but do you shed tears for the unemployed secretaries and salesgirls? All of whom were laid off because businesses figured they couldn't afford to employ women any longer?"

Inspector Aizawa said nothing but continued with an accusatory stare.

"And when the working women of Japan were fired, what did their bosses tell them? 'Get married! Your husband will take care of you!' Never mind the fact that no man wants to settle down and start a family in these troubled times! So I had to make a choice, Inspector. You see, shame only works for those who have pride to lose."

The Inspector broke his stare and pulled a packet out of his coat. He removed two glossy photographs and tossed them on the bed, like a gambler playing his last hand. A few quick glances told her all she needed to know. She'd seen bodies like that before; her parents after their little house of wood and paper collapsed and turned them into butchered meat. Well played, Inspector.

"You may not have pride, but you must have some honor left," he said. "That policeman was Sergeant Toru Murayama. He leaves behind a widow and three children. The Baron and Baroness Onishi died in each other's arms. According to the official report, it took three *junsas* to pry Onishi's grip off his wife."

Reiko turned, straining to keep the tears at bay. How pathetic. Shame had worked after all. After a moment, she composed herself and faced the Inspector.

"Watanabe-san, Japan is faced with two futures. Either we are a nation of laws," he pointed to the photographs, "or that."

Reiko sighed and rubbed her temple. She must have looked like she needed a smoke because the Inspector offered her a lit Golden Bat. After a few drags, she sat back on the bed.

"At least give me time to think it over. I'll telephone you later."

"No, my line might be bugged," the Inspector said, donning his fedora. He gathered up the photographs and crammed them inside his coat. "Meet me in a public place."

Reiko glanced over at the issue of *Kinema Junpo*. "What about the cinema?" She handed the magazine over. Aizawa thumbed through it with a tepid expression.

"One that's not crowded," he said. "What about *The Neighbor's Wife and Mine?*"

"The talkie? It sells out every show."

Aizawa flipped through a few more pages. "How about *Sword of Justice?*"

She'd seen the film back in October, with Masaru, and remembered grabbing his hand during the thrilling sword fights. "That's fine. It's playing at the Denkikan Theater."

"How long will you take?" the Inspector asked, tossing the magazine aside.

"As long as I need," she said. "And by the way, Inspector I know how to lose a tail. So please don't get any ideas about following me back to his house."

The Inspector said nothing as he walked out, leaving Reiko alone with her thoughts and the fading strains of "My Blue Heaven."

CHAPTER THIRTY-TWO

Aizawa stepped out of the apartment building and back into Asakusa's stream of people. If Azabu was the city's most refined area, then Asakusa was its evil twin. The further east you went in Tokyo, the deeper you sank.

Completely destroyed during the Great Earthquake, Asakusa had rebuilt itself as the capital of *ero guro nansensu*, erotic grotesque nonsense. Whenever a store was robbed or a mistress murdered, the suspect was likely hiding out here. A ferocious chill blew off the Sumida River, only a few blocks away, prompting him to walk faster. Rubbing his hands for warmth, Aizawa regretted leaving Baron Onishi's Rolls-Royce back at Metropolitan Police Headquarters. However, one look at some of the riff-raff clustered in Asakusa's narrow alleyways told him that such an alluring target wouldn't last long in this part of town.

Aizawa soon passed by the Kaminari Gate, which led to the oldest Buddhist temple in Tokyo, the Senso-ji. Throngs of people passed under it, while groups of rickshaw men called out for business. An appealing thought, but Asakusa's streets were so crammed full of life that it was quicker to be carried by their current. Aizawa turned and found himself on a street packed with souvenir shops, selling everything from toy soldiers and model battleships, to parasols and masks of *oni* devils.

Aizawa turned again and was on a less crowded street, packed with food carts and stalls. Men and women slurped bowls of noodles near a ramen cart, merchants hawked sweet chestnuts, while scruffy children lined up at a stall selling Glico caramel candy. As Aizawa passed, they eyed him like pickpockets sizing up a mark. He made another detour and strolled past the gambling halls. Each entrance was guarded by narrow-eyed men with tattoos creeping up their necks and down their arms, the uniform of the yakuza gangs. Aizawa kept his head low and kept walking.

Up ahead was a street band wearing samurai costumes, led by a smiling woman in light green kimono and twirling a trumpet like a baton. They struck up a number of songs, "Tokyo Bushi," "Dinah," "Bye Bye Blackbird," and even a jazzy version of the national anthem, "Kimigayo." It was astounding that such frivolity still existed in Japan. Asakusa was like a hospital patient who hadn't been told its condition was fatal.

Aizawa turned the corner again, leading him into the Rokku, the theater district. Rows of neon marquees advertised Bela Lugosi in *Dracula*, Tokihiko Okada in *The Lady and the Beard*, and Kinuyo Tanaka in *The Neighbor's Wife and Mine,* which had a line out the door.

The Denkikan Theater was less busy. Posters for *Sword of Justice* hung outside, showing a dashing samurai, wearing a top-knot and brandishing a drawn *katana*, facing down an army of grubby-looking bandits. A beautiful woman in an elegant kimono cowered beside him, obviously the love interest.

Still standing since the turn of the century, the Denkikan had somehow withstood the Great Earthquake, as if protected by the gods of cinema. How many of those old films had disappeared on that sunny September day? Entire worlds had been lost forever, burnt along with Tokyo's past.

Aizawa bought a ticket and entered a deserted lobby, decorated with placards that promised talkies by early next year. He walked past an unmanned usher stand and into the theater. The flickering projector light illuminated a sparse crowd. Some moviegoers were transfixed while others – with unshaven faces and threadbare clothes – snored away. Movie theaters always offered a temporary refuge for the homeless, especially in winter.

Next to the screen stood a *benshi* narrator who provided live dialogue and commentary for silent pictures. He had already begun his act and was halfway through a grainy news film. No matter, since once admission was paid you could watch the show as many times as you wanted. However, most people left when the *benshi* did, since bombastic narration of these silent pictures had given them voices long before the talkies premiered.

The screen panned over a column of marching soldiers in heavy coats and steel helmets. An intertitle declared, "The Kwantung Army advances in Manchuria!"

"March on brave soldiers!" the *benshi* cried. "Ah, our soldiers are human bullets for the Emperor!"

A military march rang out from an upstairs piano while onscreen, armored cars and tanks rumbled across the snowy plains. Another intertitle exclaimed, "Triumph at Tsitsihar!" A wide shot showed soldiers waving Rising Sun flags from rooftops and raising their arms in a banzai cheer.

"After a fierce battle, the Kwantung Army expelled the enemy forces from the city of Tsitsihar. The Chinese bandit defenders have fled across the Soviet border in disarray. Now, only Chinchow and Harbin remain in enemy hands. Soon, Japanese and Chinese will work together like brothers to keep Manchuria cleansed of banditry and warlords forever! Banzai to the Kwantung Army!"

"Banzais" erupted from the audience, even from those who looked asleep. The march died out, replaced by a morose tune. Onscreen, a line of soldiers carried white boxes with bowed, sullen heads. "Funeral service for fallen comrades," read the intertitle. The *benshi* said nothing, but the film had its desired effect. No matter how bad things got in Tokyo, the soldiers had it worse. You couldn't escape shame, even at the cinema.

CHAPTER THIRTY-THREE

Rubbing her gloved hands together, Reiko cursed Masaru with frosted breath. Why did he make her come out here in the cold, just to entertain that rice farmer? If he expected her to dress like a geisha, then he was in for a disappointment. Hajime Nakajima wasn't worth applying elaborate makeup and asking her neighbor to tie her *obi* belt. On an icy night like this, she couldn't imagine wearing anything but her blue pea coat, matching cloche hat, brown leather gloves, and most of all, stockings.

Asakusa was its usual lively self, and the streets were clogged with its spawn. Reiko imagined Inspector Aizawa wading through the crowds like a turtle in a sea of sharks. His words and those horrific photographs haunted her mind as she considered her options. She could lead Inspector Aizawa directly to Masaru, but with powerful allies like Superintendent Shimura and General Sakamoto, another arrest would be futile. They'd ensure Masaru's release again and where would that leave her? Probably without a head.

However, if she kept her mouth shut, she'd be the mistress to one of the most powerful men in Japan. But what about those who might die in the approaching coup? Maybe she could convince Inspector Aizawa to leave town since he'd probably be standing before a firing squad by the end of the year.

Both were bad options, but which was worse? She'd have to decide later since Masaru's *machiya* was already in view, alive with lights and song. Reiko entered the *genkan* vestibule and found a row of shoes next to a pair of black boots. She removed her heels and tore off her cloche hat before walking into the main room of the *machiya*.

Seven men, wearing kimonos or rumpled Western suits, knelt alongside Hajime Nakajima, who had unbuttoned the collar on his uniform. Empty beer bottles lay scattered on the floor and not a single man looked sober, not even the Lieutenant. They gathered around a crackling phonograph that blared "If Ten Thousand Enemies Should Come," that horrible song the Army played over the radio before announcing the capture of some insignificant Manchurian town. Bawling the lyrics, they almost slumped over before the song was even finished. Only Lieutenant Nakajima maintained perfect poise, despite a red glow in his soft cheeks.

From the side, Masaru approached and embraced her.

"Masaru!" she squealed, squirming away. His face was also a deep crimson, explaining his lapse in modesty. Men were always so quick to forget their inhibitions after a few toasts. "You've been drinking too much!"

"Yes, and I want you to join me," he said, handing her a bottle of Kirin beer. Suddenly, his bleary eyes narrowed, and he leaned in closer. "Why aren't you dressed as a geisha?" he whispered.

Reiko had been so focused on the weather that she didn't consider how the rest of the Kusanagi Society might react to a decadent *moga* instead of the elegant geisha they were used to. She tried to think of some placating excuse when one of the patriots called out, "Ryusaki-sensei, who's the *moga*?"

"What? Don't you recognize me?" Reiko turned and struck her most refined pose.

The Kusanagi Society stared with slackened jaws before showering her with smiles.

"That's Harutora-san?"

"What a looker!"

"A great patriot like Ryusaki-sensei deserves such a beautiful woman!"

Reiko looked back at Masaru with a bright smile. The Kusanagi Society was too drunk to care whether she was a geisha or a *moga*...except for Lieutenant Nakajima, who sat fuming in silence beside the phonograph.

Reiko raised the beer bottle and said, "A toast! To Second Lieutenant Hajime Nakajima and our great victory! Kanpai!"

"Kanpai!" the men toasted.

Masaru raised his bottle. "Another toast! It was you seven patriots who helped me found the Kusanagi Society earlier this year. As our ranks continue to grow, I will never forget the faith you placed in me."

The men gave a loud cheer. Masaru leaned over to Reiko and said, "Ask the Lieutenant what he wants. This is his *sokokai* after all."

The final indignity. Time to play the dutiful geisha again. She took a swig of her beer and knelt beside him.

"Nakajima-zzzzzan," she hissed, hoping her contempt would show. "What do you want to do? We could play games…do they play games up north? Rice picking, perhaps? Or I could sing one of your little military songs…"

"I want to know why you're not wearing your geisha costume," he snapped.

Reiko forced a smile and gripped her skirt. "Now now, Nakajima-san…I know the Army hasn't taught you much about women, but geisha don't always wear face paint or kimonos."

The patriots chuckled drunkenly and Nakajima's face reddened further.

"I can't decide whether you're worse as a geisha or as a…*moga*," Nakajima said, practically vomiting the last word.

"That's enough, Nakajima-san!" Masaru said. "Show Reiko proper respect. Without her, you might still be Aizawa's prisoner."

Nakajima lowered his head. "Forgive me *zensei*. I don't drink very often."

Reiko released the grip on her skirt and stood. She wasn't going to let him get away with weeks of snide comments and turning Masaru into this assassination-plotting madman. If this was to be the last time they saw each other, she had a few things to say.

"Attention everyone! In honor of Nakajima-san's departure, I would like to perform a one-act play titled *Lieutenant Nakajima's Manchurian Adventure*!"

Masaru and his patriots – except for Nakajima – applauded. Reiko sprang up and darted back to the *genkan* vestibule. In a gray and brown pile of flat hats and fedoras, the bright red band and brass star on Nakajima's peaked service cap seemed to burst out with color. She plopped it on her head and tugged on the black boots. Marching out, she snapped a salute and clicked her heels.

"Lieutenant Nakajima, reporting for duty!" she said. A few patriots chuckled while Nakajima stared with wide, hateful eyes. She bent over and started the phonograph again. The scratchy trumpets blared and "If Ten Thousand Enemies Should Come" served as background music for her finest performance.

"Come on men, follow me!" Reiko kept her salute as she paraded around the *machiya*, stomping her boots. "Ah, wait, is the enemy this way or that way? Damn it all…Manchuria is so vast! I think I'm lost…I haven't been many places outside of my rice farm in Tohoku! Brrrr…and it's so much colder here!"

She chattered out a rattle of machine gun fire. Drunken laughter filled the room.

"I've been shot! The gods are so unfair! I didn't even get to kill a single enemy soldier! And even worse," she sank to her knees, clutching her gut, "I still don't know what it's like to be with a woman!"

Now even Masaru laughed. Time to close the curtain.

"Banzzzai to th-the…accckkk…" she coughed, gurgled, and keeled over dead, tongue out for good measure. Applause followed laughter. Reiko bolted upright and bowed. She spun around and saluted Lieutenant Nakajima, who looked like a grenade ready to explode.

"Disgraceful!" he screamed, leaping to his feet. "*Zensei*, she insults the honor of the entire Army!"

Masaru gave a dismissive laugh. "An Imperial soldier shouldn't give the words of a woman much weight, Nakajima-san. I'm sure that she was only teasing."

Reiko showed her glee with a triumphant, taunting smile. "Of course! It's all in good fun, Lieutenant." She tore off the service cap and slapped it onto Nakajima's head. "You'll probably need that."

Lieutenant Nakajima shook with impotent fury as his explosion of anger fizzled out like a bottle of Ramune Soda. She already pitied the poor Chinese soldier who would face him when it bubbled back up. She slipped off the boots and returned to the *genkan*.

A little man in a brown overcoat and flat cap stood there, removing his snow-crusted shoes. His face was swollen with bruises but that Charlie Chaplin mustache was all she needed to recognize Makoto Kuroki. Without a word, he walked past her and into the main room. Reiko tossed the boots aside and followed him.

"Kuroki-san," Masaru said. "I'm glad I persuaded Superintendent Shimura to release you!" The patriots chuckled. "Now you can drink to our great victory and enjoy Lieutenant Nakajima's *sokokai*!" Masaru extended a bottle of Kirin beer with a grin.

For several moments, Kuroki stared blank-faced at his *sensei* until, with one fluid motion, he reached into his coat and pulled out a revolver. Without a word, he pressed it under his chin and curled a finger around the trigger.

CHAPTER THIRTY-FOUR

A silent, thick tension swept over the *machiya*. Reiko clamped a hand over her mouth, stifling a scream. Nakajima edged closer to Masaru while the other patriots sat wide-eyed, staring at their *sensei* for guidance.

"Kuroki-san," Masaru said, still holding the beer bottle. "What are you doing? Put that gun down!"

"I'm sorry *sensei*…but I must kill myself…it's the only way to regain my honor."

"What are you talking about?"

"Ryusaki-sensei…we have been betrayed!"

Reiko's heart skipped a beat, but she kept herself steady.

Like a striking viper, Nakajima lashed out and knocked the revolver out of Kuroki's hand. The little man vomited a pained cry and fell to his knees. Reaching into his coat, Kuroki presented a red pamphlet with yellow characters. A hammer and sickle emblem was stamped at the bottom.

Lieutenant Nakajima traipsed across the *machiya* and inspected the revolver. "This is a Russian gun," he said, holding it up. "A Nagant. Kuroki-zan, where did you get this from?"

Kuroki bit his lip as the tears flowed. "From General Sakamoto. Last night…after Superintendent Shimura released me, there were three soldiers waiting. They drove me to the Army Ministry to meet with General Sakamoto personally. I was so honored…I thought he was going to congratulate me—" he gave a pitiful sob "—but instead he offered me a deal. He guaranteed me entrance into the Army and service in Manchuria…if I…if I assassinated you, *sensei*!"

Masaru's face drained of color. "Assassinate me? Why?"

"I don't know…but he gave me that gun and this pamphlet so we could blame it on the Communists. Forgive me *sensei*…it's my dream to follow my brother into the

Imperial Army…I shamefully accepted the offer…I was going to assassinate you tomorrow after Lieutenant Nakajima departs for Manchuria…"

No one spoke, but Reiko could almost hear the curses echoing in Masaru's mind.

"But I couldn't deprive Japan of you, *sensei*…that's why I wanted to kill myself in front of you…to show you how truly repentant I am!" Kuroki's words devolved into soft, pitiful sobs.

Masaru leaned over and said, "Your actions speak louder than words, Kuroki-san. I forgive your moment of weakness. The Kusanagi Society still needs the service of such a sincere patriot…but you must tell me what Sakamoto is planning."

At once, Kuroki looked like a man reborn. Wiping his tears, he said, "General Sakamoto said that if I didn't assassinate you, he'd have the *Kempeitai* arrest you and then…and then torture you into confessing that you're secretly a Red!"

With a ferocious growl, Masaru hurled the beer bottle across the room. It shattered near the phonograph like an artillery shell.

"That traitor! General Sakamoto must be working for the Seiyukai! He used us to get rid of Baron Onishi!"

The patriots of the Kusanagi Society hissed like snakes ready to bite.

"We cannot rely on a new shogun to carry out reform…we must do it ourselves," Masaru said, pacing back and forth.

"How *sensei*?" Kuroki asked.

Masaru gave a dark look. "The body of Japan has become infested with parasites," he began. "The treacherous advisers who surround the Emperor. Communist traitors and greedy capitalists. And above all, every politician in the Diet. We'll have to kill these vermin one by one. Within a week, ten evil men will die. Then, twenty more. By the end of the year, every villain in Tokyo will fear for his life!"

The Kusanagi Society roared a triple banzai cheer, amplified by bloodlust.

"But first...General Sakamoto must pay for his treachery," Masaru said.

Lieutenant Nakajima stood at attention. "*Zensei*, I volunteer!"

Masaru gave a solemn nod before turning to Reiko. "Leave us. This is no place for a woman. I'll call for you later."

She couldn't agree more. After a deep bow, Reiko grabbed her cloche hat, put on her shoes, and slid open the front door without looking back. Asakusa was still busy and bursting with life, oblivious to the plots and intrigue being hatched right behind her. Although her legs trembled slightly, she walked away from the *machiya* with quickening steps.

*****

"Surrender now, or I shall punish you with my sword of justice!" the *benshi* declared as the samurai hero confronted a horde of bandits at their camp onscreen.

"Ha ha, arrogance will be your downfall samurai," the *benshi* gave voice to the bandit chief. "It's fifty to one!"

"I am never outnumbered," the *benshi* said in his most heroic voice, "as long as the gods of justice are on my side!"

Things didn't look good for the samurai, but since the movie wasn't even half over, it was doubtful he'd die just yet. A slender silhouette crept across the screen, just as the samurai drew his sword and rushed toward the enemy.

"Would the young lady please take a seat?" the *benshi* asked politely, but with enough hiss to let his annoyance show.

Reiko Watanabe ducked in and out of rows, peering and prying in the darkness. After a sheepish scan of the aisles, she zeroed in on Aizawa and took a seat next to him.

"General Sakamoto betrayed them," she said, staring ahead at the screen. "He sent Kuroki to kill Masaru."

"He's dead?"

"No, Kuroki couldn't go through with it and begged forgiveness. Masaru has gone completely insane. He's talking about assassinating everyone. Sakamoto, politicians, Imperial advisers. Hundreds."

Aizawa figured his name would eventually wind up on that list too.

"Watanabe-san, where is he? I have to know."

She continued to stare at the screen where the samurai hero fought off waves on oncoming bandits with ease. That is, until the bandit chief rushed back to his tent and returned with a woman, arms tied at her sides.

"My lord's daughter!" the *benshi* said in the samurai's voice. "You villain!"

"Ha ha, surrender now, or she dies!" The bandit slid a dagger underneath the maiden's throat.

The screen faded and the *benshi* cried, "What will become of our heroes?" The pianist upstairs banged out a dramatic score, hinting at their fate.

"Watanabe-san…"

Reiko turned to face him. Illuminated by the projector's pale, flashing lights, she looked as if she'd just stepped out of the movie screen.

"He's nearby," she finally said. "Just a few blocks north. Third *machiya* on the left on Kototoi Street. The one with a Rising Sun flag out in front. You can enter through a side door in the alleyway."

Aizawa scanned every inch of her face for duplicity but her brown eyes shone with a sincerity he often saw in murderers ready to confess.

"Were you followed?" he asked.

"No. They were too busy planning which politician to shoot next to worry about me."

"Wait here," Aizawa said, standing up. "I'll come and get you when it's all over."

Reiko nodded. Onscreen, the bandit chief raised his sword over the maiden's head, who awaited decapitation with a look of dread. Aizawa knew how she felt.

CHAPTER THIRTY-FIVE

As Lieutenant Nakajima neared the Dragonfly Tea House, a toxic mix of emotions swirled in his head: hate and confusion, rage and mistrust, a need for an explanation and a desire to kill. How could General Sakamoto, war hero and future shogun, betray them? Nothing made sense anymore. Perhaps, just perhaps, there was a good reason for all this. But in case there wasn't…he gripped the Army saber at his side.

After a quick phone call to Sakamoto's residence, his wife explained that the General had not returned home yet and even asked where he might be. Nakajima had an idea. Aside from the Army Ministry, the Dragonfly Tea House was where Yori Sakamoto spent most of his time. It was here, back in January, where Lieutenant Nakajima and other staff officers had first met with Sakamoto and hatched their plot to overthrow the government. So many plans and strategies were discussed that the Dragonfly Tea House became a sort of command post for the Showa Restoration.

Twanging *shamisen* music drifted out of the tea house. His khaki cape billowed in the wind, allowing him to view the Nagant revolver stuffed into his belt, which might be fired after all. Nakajima's grip on the saber tightened. Paper lanterns hanging from the tea house's exterior illuminated two enormous men crammed into long gray overcoats. They guarded the entrance with crossed arms and stern faces. Former sumo wrestlers, judging from their size and build.

"Who are you?" one asked.

"Second Lieutenant Hajime Nakajima! Adjutant to General Zakamoto," he said, snapping to attention.

The two traded glances.

"And who are you?" Nakajima asked.

"We work for Takano-san," one said.

Takano? Ah, it made sense now. That *zaibatsu* must have plenty of enemies to station bodyguards wherever he went – the telltale signs of a shameful life.

"I'm here to see the General."

With skeptical eyes, they examined Nakajima. Underneath his cape, he slid his hands over the Nagant, wondering how many bullets it would take to fell a sumo. After a few moments, the two bodyguards stepped aside and he slid open the front doors. Inside, he found a row of shiny leather shoes, *geta* clogs, and a pair of black boots that towered over all of them.

Without removing his own boots, now encrusted with snow, Nakajima walked into the main room. Underneath the paper screen of Mount Fuji, knelt General Yori Sakamoto with an unbuttoned collar and reddened face. A smiling geisha refilled his cup with sake.

Another kneeling geisha strummed her *shamisen* and sang. A pair of grinning fools, the Seiyukai bureaucrats he'd seen a few days before, clapped along like monkeys. But the most nauseating sight was Isamu Takano and his glittering Rolex, coolly smoking a cigarette. Nakajima suppressed an urge to draw the Nagant and open fire.

General Sakamoto threw back the shot of sake before turning his attention to Nakajima. Suddenly, his face erupted in shock.

"Nakajima, my boy!" he said as a geisha helped him to his feet. "What are you doing here? Shouldn't you be enjoying your *sokokai*?"

Traitor or not, Lieutenant Nakajima stood at attention before his superior. "I must talk to you alone." He parted his cape to reveal the Nagant.

General Sakamoto swallowed hard as the red drained from his cheeks. He walked over to Takano and whispered a brief conversation. Through a veil of cigarette smoke, the banker studied Nakajima with contemptuous eyes. The geisha suddenly stopped playing, cutting the bureaucrats off mid-song.

"Hey, sssoldier boy," the geisha said with a drunken slur. "Don't you know better than to leave your boots on inside? Sssuch manners!"

"Oh, leave him alone," the other geisha said. "Welcome to our party! Errr…what rank are you anyway?"

Nakajima said nothing, keeping his eyes focused on Isamu Takano. The banker's high cheekbones, narrow eyes, and pointed face were more fox-like than human. And foxes were often the villains in Japanese fairy tales.

"She asked you a question, sssoldier boy," the drunken geisha fired back. "What's the matter? Too good to talk to a woman?"

Lieutenant Nakajima glared at her.

"Or maybe the only woman he's ever talked to works in Yoshiwara?" the geisha said with a laugh.

The bureaucrats and geisha cackled like cawing crows. Nakajima dashed across the room and grabbed the laughing geisha by her collar like a cat by the scruff of its neck. The *shamisen* fell to the floor and clattered as silence swept over the tea house. The geisha stared back in mute horror.

"Lieutenant! Put her down at once!" General Sakamoto roared.

Nakajima released his grip, and the other geisha rushed over to comfort her.

"I think we should be going, General," Takano said, putting out his cigarette. "Thank you for the party." He stood and looked at Nakajima with a mixture of contempt and pity, like an impudent child about to be spanked. "Come ladies, my Bentley is parked around back. I'll drive you home."

After a round of bows, Takano walked out, followed by the geisha and the Seiyukai bureaucrats. Once they were alone, General Sakamoto rushed Nakajima and struck him with a hard slap across the face.

"How dare you come here uninvited and insult my guests?"

Again, Nakajima showed the Nagant, quieting the General.

"Remember the Nagant revolver that you took off a dead Russian officer during the Battle of Mukden? This wouldn't happen to be it, would it?"

"What are you implying, Lieutenant?"

"That you betrayed us."

"Such impudence," Sakamoto snarled, reaching for the Nagant. Nakajima pulled the revolver out of his belt and turned it on the General. "Lieutenant, put that down. That is an order!"

That might have worked days earlier, but Lieutenant Nakajima only obeyed orders from honorable men. "Is Takano behind this? Did he pay you?"

"It's not what you think, Lieutenant. I didn't do it for money."

Nakajima kept the Nagant aimed at him. "Then why?"

"You wouldn't understand...young men are so hotheaded."

"Explain," Nakajima demanded.

Rubbing his temple, the General sighed. "Japan is not Brazil or Argentina. A military coup won't work here."

"The Showa Restoration is not some vulgar South American coup d'état," Nakajima said. "It will purify Japan from top to bottom!"

General Sakamoto groaned and held up a weary hand. "Consider our past attempts. In March, the plan failed after Ryusaki was arrested. In October, we tried again without any civilians involved, but our plan still met with failure! The political system is already too firmly in place, Lieutenant. It's best to work inside it rather than trying to destroy it."

"And does that mean," Nakajima felt his mouth go dry, "this plan to install you as shogun was all a farce?"

General Sakamoto averted his eyes. "Takano-san has guaranteed me vice-presidency of the Seiyukai. After Inukai-san retires, he will nominate me as his successor. Then, I will reform Japan through legislative means. But first, we had to get Baron Onishi out of the way. He was a threat to Seiyukai leadership in the Diet."

Nakajima's entire frame shook. "Y-you used us as puppets!"

"Be reasonable, Lieutenant! If a horse charges directly at you, you must mount it from the side and take control of the reins. To stand in front only means you'll be trampled. This is why our so-called 'Showa Restoration' has met with failure. The political parties are here to stay."

The words hit Nakajima like a stab in the throat, silencing him.

"Think of it this way, Lieutenant. The campaign in Manchuria is almost over. Another month or two and we'll control the entire region. Our troops will soon share a border with Soviet Russia. What have we mobilized for the Manchurian Incident? Almost nothing. A few units from home, but our overseas forces have carried most of the burden by themselves. Our industry is stagnant. If our nation today engaged in total war, like the one that erupted in 1914, it would break under the strain. Look at what happened to Germany. But total war with Russia *and* America is approaching. Our empire will need the cooperation of all aspects of society; the Army and Navy, the *zaibatsu*, and yes, even the Imperial Diet. As a self-installed shogun, I would earn the resentment of these men. However, as the legitimate prime minister, I would be the rightful head of government, chosen and approved of by His Majesty."

"What about Ryusaki-zensei?" Nakajima asked.

"What about him? The man is an unstable, vainglorious madman," General Sakamoto said, like discussing a dog about to be put down.

"So you bribed Kuroki-zan to assassinate him?"

"I offered Kuroki a chance to join the Army and serve the Emperor on the battlefield. I've given you the same opportunity. Or have you forgotten?"

Lieutenant Nakajima lowered the Nagant and considered his future. Fight for the Emperor in Manchuria, or fight for him here? He begged the gods for clarity. To attain glory on a foreign battlefield was the realization of a lifelong dream. But Sakamoto had issued his transfer, and since the General had been rotted by corruption, that meant all of his commands were now suspect. Though it pained him to entertain the thought, battlefield glory might not be what the gods had planned for Hajime Nakajima.

"I will fight for His Majesty here in Tokyo, by punishing villains wherever they hide…even if it's behind the uniform of an Army general." Nakajima pointed to the General's sheathed saber, lying in the corner of the tea house. "Because you were once an honorable man, I will grant you the dignity of ritual suicide."

A deep somberness carved itself onto Sakamoto's face. "*Seppuku?*"

Nakajima nodded. Ritual suicides were traditionally done with *wakizashi* short swords, but a regulation military saber would have to suffice.

"And…if I refuse?"

"Then your name will be forever cursed as a man who murdered and schemed his way to power before being shot by the very weapon he tried to silence a true patriot with." Nakajima raised the Nagant again. "But if you choose *seppuku* then your honor will be restored."

General Sakamoto panicked eyes darted back and forth between the revolver and his sheathed saber. What an inglorious end for a man who had come so close to leading the Great Japanese Empire! Perhaps he lamented not ordering Lieutenant Nakajima to Manchuria sooner? Or maybe he wondered how he had fallen into such corrupt depths? Face and honor were like food and water to most Japanese, especially military men. How could Yori Sakamoto face his ancestors in the afterlife without them? If anything, the General should thank him for this one last chance at redemption.

"You may write a death poem if you wish, General."

A deep sigh preceded Sakamoto's answer. "No need…"

Unusual, since death poems were one of the most treasured parts of *seppuku*. Perhaps the General wasn't the poetic type? No matter. Sakamoto walked over to the corner and grabbed his sheathed saber. Drawing the blade, he eyed Nakajima for a moment, perhaps planning his escape. But the General soon sank to his knees, a defeated man. Lieutenant Nakajima tucked the Nagant back into his belt and drew his own saber.

"I will act as your second, General."

Sakamoto nodded and unbuttoned his uniform. A surge of confidence animated the General's face, a man determined to prove his bravery by tearing out his own guts. Setting his tunic off to the side, he uttered a prayer. Moments passed until he raised the saber with both hands and with one guttural shout, disemboweled himself.

The blade dug deep into Sakamoto's stomach, releasing a wave of blood onto the floor. The General sawed through his flesh, contorting his face into an agonized sneer. Nakajima stared, stunned by the sheer beauty. *Seppuku* was like a canvas painting with gore as the oils.

After moments of hell, the General looked up with a plea to end his suffering. Because of its long length, the saber wobbled up and down in Sakamoto's gut, as if trying to shake him off. Lieutenant Nakajima snapped out of his awe and raised his sword. It was time to add the finishing strokes to this work of art. With a shout, he brought the saber down, sending General Sakamoto's head rolling across the floor. Across the room, Chitose-oneesan appeared with a pleased smile.

"Well done, Hajime-kun."

CHAPTER THIRTY-SIX

Every ward and neighborhood in Tokyo had at least one *koban*, a police box, and Asakusa was no exception. As Aizawa approached the *koban*, confidence surged through him. Tonight, this private war ended. A few *junsas* would be more than enough backup to deal with Ryusaki and his *soshi*. Uniforms often doubled as bulletproof vests in Japan, since very few would dare assault the Metropolitan Police. However, Sergeant Murayama's dead body flashed into his mind. Army brown must have trumped Police blue.

Aizawa entered and found that this *koban* was larger than it appeared from the outside. It contained a holding cell and a spacious desk where a gray-haired officer sat, sipping a steaming cup of tea. A dark blue uniform hung off his lanky body, and a pair of epaulettes framed the tunic. He was a sergeant and not the callow *junsa* Aizawa had expected. Although he outranked him, Aizawa offered a bow and his *meishi* card as a token of subordination to age.

"Ah, and what brings you out here, Inspector?" the Sergeant asked, handing the *meishi* back.

"Sergeant, I require assistance in making an arrest."

"Who?"

"Masaru Ryusaki."

The Sergeant took another sip of his tea before responding. "I'm afraid that's impossible, Inspector. My orders are to remain at my desk...in case there's a citizen nearby who needs me. I hope you understand."

"Do you have any *junsas* to spare?"

"I'm sorry, but they're out on patrol. You're welcome to use my phone to call your superior for backup."

Aizawa clenched his jaw. Would the Sergeant make a call to Ryusaki after he left, warning him that he was closing in? What was it Baron Onishi had said? *There are so many nationalists in the Police these days.* Then again, maybe the Sergeant was simply obeying the duty that bound him to his desk. Neither was what Aizawa wanted to hear. Best to retreat and save what little face remained.

"Thank you for your time, Sergeant."

Aizawa bowed and walked out. Asakusa was still teeming with humanity that swept him along down Kototoi Street. Passing a crowded stall selling *yakitori* chicken skewers, he considered the only option left, which was to go it alone. The odds were bad, but it was either act now or risk losing that slippery eel into the open sea of Tokyo's back alleys and safe houses forever.

Up ahead, a Rising Sun flag fluttered in the chilly breeze, marking Ryusaki's *machiya.* Aizawa ducked behind an alleyway and drew his Colt automatic, inching his way around. Just as Watanabe-san had promised, a side door led him into the main room. Electric light illuminated a silhouetted, shadowy figure. It was Ryusaki, hunched over a clacking typewriter. What was he writing? Most likely a hit list.

Whatever it was demanded his full attention, allowing Aizawa to creep deeper into the *machiya* behind him. He stepped over and around the empty beer bottles scattered across the floor and closed in. A clear shot soon presented itself, and he aimed the pistol straight at the back of Ryusaki's head.

The gun trembled as Aizawa's finger curled around the trigger. The clacking typewriter keys were soon drowned out by *giri* and *ninjo,* duty and emotion. *Ninjo* demanded that he shoot the murdering dog while *giri* loudly protested that revenge had no part in a police officer's duty.

Suddenly, a heavy blow slammed against Aizawa's head, driving him to the floor. The room was a messy haze for several moments until everything slowly realigned into view. Makoto Kuroki stood over him. The little bastard's face was still swollen from beatings, but somehow glowed in triumph. Aizawa struggled to raise the pistol, but Kuroki's foot was planted over his wrist, while the other pinned down his shoulder.

"Ah, Inspector Aizawa," Ryusaki hissed, finally moving away from the typewriter. "I'm surprised you found out where I live. But I suppose even the lowest order of dog can track a scent. It's a pity that I sent my other patriots away already. They'd be delighted to see your final humiliation."

"Some detective you are," Kuroki said, grinning. "Didn't even see me at that *yakitori* stand just now. But I saw you and followed you right back here! Ready for round two, Inspector?" Kuroki didn't wait for an answer and continued, "That pet gorilla of yours, Sergeant Murayama, nearly knocked my front teeth out. I think I'll remove yours…through your nose."

With his head throbbing, Aizawa wriggled like a giant silkworm, trying to shake Kuroki off, but he only managed to inch closer toward a discarded beer bottle.

"Wait Kuroki-san…it'll be easier if I hack it off so you can dig through the hole," Ryusaki said as he rose with the *katana* blade at his side. He bent down and scooped the Colt automatic out of Aizawa's hand and into his kimono. "During the reign of the Tokugawa shoguns, my ancestors would slice ears and noses off impudent peasants. I think it's time to revive the practice."

Aizawa continued to squirm closer and closer to the bottle. With a sudden flash, the *katana* was unsheathed and Ryusaki angled for position. Kuroki grinned wider, dividing his attention between Aizawa's struggles and Ryusaki's glinting sword. The sword ran along Aizawa's neck, gliding across his jugular, before settling atop his cheek. His death would have all the dignity of a butchered pig if he didn't do something quick.

With an enormous heave, Aizawa wrested one hand loose and snatched the empty beer bottle. In one motion, he hurled it with a pitch that would have made Babe Ruth proud. An explosion of glass engulfed Kuroki's head, sending him toppling backward. Aizawa rolled out from under the *katana*, its tip scraping across his cheek. It took a few moments for Ryusaki to readjust himself and steady his blade, but by then, Aizawa was on his feet again, ready to pounce.

Eyes bulging behind his glasses, Ryusaki lifted the sword for the killing blow. Aizawa sprang forward, slamming his shoulder into Ryusaki's gut and sent them both crashing through the paper door of the *machiya*. They toppled out into the street, against the sidewalk. Releasing a heavy groan, Aizawa pushed himself up, and there, in front of him on the ground, was the pistol. He looked around for Ryusaki, who struggled to upright himself on his *katana* while his face twisted in pain.

More and more people came into view, all frozen and gawking at them like a pair of zoo animals who had escaped their cages. A woman screamed, while a man grabbed the pistol and yelled for the Police. The fall had knocked the wind out of Aizawa, making lengthy explanations impossible. Instead, he turned and threw himself onto Ryusaki, unleashing a fury that had been building since March. One firm punch drove Ryusaki back down into the thin snow.

"S-stop!"

Aizawa looked up. The man now aimed the Colt pistol at him with shaking hands. Most Japanese had never touched a gun – let alone fired one – which meant there was a good chance that it could go off by accident. What could be more shameful than a police officer dying by his own weapon?

"Fool," Aizawa spat out between gasps. "I'm…I'm a police inspector."

The man lowered the gun and bowed for his gross error in judgment. Very few Japanese would ever involve themselves in other's affairs, however, Aizawa couldn't help but admire his bravery.

"Don't apologize!" Aizawa ordered. "Go to the *koban* and get help! Now!"

Several members of the crowd broke away and dashed off, while even more bystanders drew closer to gawk at the scene. Aizawa tried to stand but a peripheral glance caught an oncoming figure. He rolled backward and glimpsed Kuroki slashing at the space where he'd just been. The little bastard's hand grasped a broken beer bottle, stretching out like a shimmering dagger. With blood streaming down his face, Kuroki repositioned himself charged again.

Aizawa fell back and slammed against the snow, using every ounce of muscle to hold Kuroki and his makeshift knife at bay. His back grew stiff against the cold ground as the bottle slowly edged nearer to his throat. He looked at the concerned citizen, still holding the pistol but now wearing a dumbfounded look, as if waiting for a command. Sometimes, the Japanese could be a little *too* obedient...

Screeching whistles cut through the air, distracting Kuroki enough for Aizawa to take advantage of the opening. With one sharp kick, he sent the little bastard tumbling backward next to his *sensei*. Ryusaki released a weary groan and steadied himself on his *katana*. He hoisted Kuroki up by his collar and they dashed off and disappeared into the thick crowd, which had grown to almost fifty or so onlookers.

Hopping to his feet, Aizawa snatched his Colt automatic back from the citizen, who bowed more apologies.

The whistles grew louder as the Sergeant, followed by two *junsas*, parted the crowd and ran toward him.

"Masaru Ryusaki," Aizawa gasped, pointing down the street, "went that way."

The Sergeant nodded. Blowing their whistles again, the *junsas* started off and disappeared back into the crowd.

"What happened here, Inspector? Even in Asakusa, we never have this type of disturbance."

Aizawa shot him a glare more frigid than the temperature. Saying nothing in response, he stormed past the Sergeant and back into the *machiya*. Although his head still ached, he zeroed in on the typewriter, where a single piece of paper jutted out. He bent down and examined it. Not a new book or even a hit list. A political manifesto.

Purity and Patriotism
By Masaru Ryusaki

In my book, 'The New Japan', I called for a modern-day shogun to overthrow the government and reform our nation from above. Ever since the Meiji Era, the apex of Japanese society has been rotting from weakness and greed, so much so that even those who are driven by pure motives are corrupted once they take power. Can nothing be done to free our nation from this poison?

Japan is one body and its 80 million citizens make up the cells and organs. In this national body, the Kusanagi Society will act as the immune system against the poison of corruption! Evil will be purged from our bloodstream with bullets and steel. From now on, every politician, military officer, *zaibatsu* capitalist, newspaper publisher, court adviser, and government official will be under constant threat of assassination.

No matter who they are, a bullet, bomb, or blade from the Kusanagi Society waits for them should they stray from the path of purity and patriotism. But too many innocent people have already suffered because of a few greedy cliques. For retribution, the Kusanagi Society will choose a hundred evil men to die in the coming months, and another hundred if need be. The morning sun is rising over the New Japan!

CHAPTER THIRTY-SEVEN

"Surrender now, villain" the *benshi* said in his best samurai voice. Onscreen, the bandit chief backed up in terror. Reiko couldn't help but smile. It was all over now. Against all odds, the samurai had escaped captivity and saved the maiden before that villain could decapitate her. They'd fled into the woods where he'd taken out the bandits one by one, until only their chief remained.

"No…no…please spare me!" the *benshi* said as the bandit leader laid his sword down.

The samurai approached to accept his surrender, but a close-up revealed a dagger in the villain's hand.

"Watch out," the *benshi* cried in a feminine voice, as the maiden came rushing up.

Before the bandit chief could strike, the samurai slashed his *katana* upwards, ending the villain once and for all. The hero sheathed his sword and accepted the maiden's embrace.

"Whenever the sword of justice is drawn," the *benshi* proclaimed, "the wicked shall always be punished!"

Their adventure concluded, the samurai and maiden hopped on a horse and rode off into the distance.

"Watanabe-san?"

Reiko turned and found a haggard Inspector Aizawa standing over her.

"Inspector? What happened?"

He gestured for her to follow, and they made their way toward the exit. The paltry audience clapped and the *benshi* bowed in gratitude. Out in the lobby, Reiko examined his face more closely. A spot of dried blood dotted his cheek, while a few bruises clung around his jaw. Battered? Maybe, but that squared face was still illuminated by a fighting spirit that even the coldest night couldn't extinguish.

"What happened?"

The Inspector shifted his eyes away. "He escaped. Do you know where else he'd go?"

Reiko searched her memory, but Masaru had lived in that *machiya* ever since she'd first met him. His family's estate in the Roppongi neighborhood had been abandoned shortly after he'd been arrested in March, and now housed a collection of dusty samurai swords and battle armor. He'd probably hide out somewhere closer, but not in Asakusa.

"He won't go back to my apartment, not now anyway. He's feeling vulnerable now, so that means he'll want protection from his men, not his mistress. I'd say he's over at Hajime Nakajima's right now."

"Where's that?"

"I have no idea. Not in Asakusa, I'm sure of that. The Lieutenant hates this place."

"In the barracks?"

"No…Nakajima rents a room in one of those lodging houses for soldiers."

"There are hundreds of those in Tokyo," the Inspector said, turning to face the *Sword of Justice's* lobby card. The yawning audience exited the theater and streamed past like a parade of sleepwalkers. A pair of middle-aged women in muted kimonos and traditional hairstyles examined Reiko's outfit with transparent contempt before shuffling along. During these hard times, such extravagance was frowned upon, even in Asakusa. Last to exit was the *benshi*, who walked out of the theater with an enormous yawn.

"Great show," Reiko said. "Loved the voices."

The *benshi* gave a thankful nod and continued on. An usher in a red jacket and pillbox hat walked up to them and said, "I'm sorry, but the Denkikan will be closing now."

The Inspector turned back around. Forlornness and despair were etched into his face between the bruises. Maybe that fighting spirit from earlier was only temporarily extinguished?

"All right, we'll leave," Aizawa finally said. They walked out of the theater and into the chilly night. Reiko tucked her cloche hat tighter over her ears for warmth and rubbed her gloved hands together. She fumbled for a pack of cigarettes, but the Inspector offered her a lit Golden Bat.

"Thank you," she said, accepting. "It's funny. When I'm a *moga*, men always light cigarettes for me. But as a geisha, all I do is light smokes."

"I've been meaning to ask," he said, lighting a Golden Bat for himself. "How did a woman like you…a geisha *and* a *moga*, become the mistress of Masaru Ryusaki?"

"Would you prefer the long story or the short one?"

"A detective always wants details."

Reiko took a long drag and thought back to that day in March. She'd been at Harlem for hours, and still no one had bought her a drink yet. She glanced over to a dapper *mobo* wearing a pin-striped suit and a deep-set frown. She felt smitten by his studious, handsome face, even though he looked like a man in mourning. The band struck up "The Japanese Sandman" and she asked *him* to dance. He accepted and began singing to her—in English.

"I met him at Harlem, right after you arrested him."

"What were you two doing there?"

"What do you mean?"

"A jazz club is no place for a geisha or the leader of a patriotic society," he said.

She took another puff and giggled. "Some detective you are. Haven't you figured out that it's all just an act?"

"What do you mean?"

"I'm not Masaru Ryusaki's mistress because I'm a good geisha…I'm his mistress because I'm a *lousy* geisha." Aizawa raised a perplexed eyebrow. "Look, have you ever seen that John Barrymore picture from a few years ago? *Dr. Jeykll and Mr. Hyde?*"

The Inspector gave a soft chuckle. "When I got back from Siberia, I took my little sister to see it. Scared the hell out of her."

"Me too. I had nightmares for weeks. But that film is essentially Masaru Ryusaki's life."

Inspector Aizawa said nothing and took another drag, lighting his cigarette up like a firefly.

"You see, there are two Masaru Ryusakis. The Dr. Jeykll studied in San Francisco, speaks English, listens to jazz, watches Hollywood movies; he's the epitome of a modern boy, a *mobo*. But he's also a descendant of twenty generations of samurai. He's seen Tokyo destroyed by the Great Earthquake and a depression ruin the economy. He feels ashamed for his love of modernity as if these calamities were somehow his fault. That's why he created his own Mr. Hyde. This Masaru Ryusaki is a fiery patriot who must prove himself to his ancestors by assassinating politicians and overthrowing the government."

"*Giri* and *ninjo*," Aizawa said with a sigh.

She nodded and took another drag. Across the street, a pair of soldiers sauntered out of a theater while passersby stopped to offer them deep bows.

"Were you in the Army, Inspector?" she asked.

"Yes. I spent two years in Siberia, fighting Bolsheviks and snowstorms." He flicked his cigarette into the snow. "And nobody bowed to us when we got back. Everyone gives a 'banzai' cheer to the Imperial Army today, but when I returned home, three university students surrounded me and demanded that I apologize for murdering fellow workers in Russia." He shook his head. "When I tried to board a streetcar, the conductor sneered that he didn't have any room for 'imperialist soldiers.' As I stood there dumbfounded, a woman in flashy jewelry and a beret told me to take off my 'shit-brown uniform.'"

"And did you?"

"I did, after a few more jeers of 'imperialist assassin' and '*zaibatsu* mercenary.'" He sighed. "Things were different back then. The people blamed the Army for the high taxes needed to pay for the Siberian Expedition. The Versailles Treaty had just been signed. Being a Communist was as fashionable as listening to jazz. Militarism was treated like a bad joke."

"Not like today, huh?"

"Not like today."

After a few moments of silence, Reiko took another drag and said, "Is that why you became a police officer? To teach the Reds a lesson?"

"Nothing so noble. I just needed work," Inspector Aizawa said. "The economy was in a slump, not like today, but bad enough for the labor unions to block returning soldiers from decent jobs. But the Metropolitan Police needed men, especially veterans. I started a few months before the Great Earthquake."

"Now *that* I remember. Before then, I spent whatever time out of school locked up in my parent's cramped *nagaya* row house…which doubled for a textile factory. My father, mother, and I sewed and knitted stockings, socks, underwear, and kimonos. But whatever we sold was still never enough." She swallowed hard, remembering that never-ending pile of silk. "My only pleasure was occasionally sneaking out to watch movies. I prayed that the gods would set me free…I guess they did, though they destroyed Tokyo to do it."

Memories of that day were spotty and fragmented. But certain images would never dull. Her parents underneath a pile of wood, smashed into bloody smears. Her crawling out of her shattered *nagaya* like an earthworm wriggling through the dirt. People with burnt skin wandering about and moaning for water. A squad of firefighters trying to extinguish the fire department building. Worst of all was the enormous tornado of fire that whirled through Tokyo, incinerating anything in its path. She tossed her Golden Bat next to Aizawa's to smolder in the patch of glowing snow.

"After the earthquake, I wandered the streets looking for food. One day, I recognized a geisha who had bought kimonos from my parents. Desperate, I threw myself at her feet and begged for help. She smiled, patted my head, and took me back home out of sympathy," Reiko spread her gloved hands, "or so I thought. All she actually wanted was an apprentice since her last one had burned to death. She

became my *oneesan*, my big sister, and I took on a new name
– Harutora."

"Spring Tiger?"

Reiko couldn't suppress a swelling pride. "It's tradition to
take the first part of your geisha name from your big sister.
Hers was Haruhana, Spring Flower. She named me 'tiger' for
my personality."

"How fitting," the Inspector remarked.

She figured that was a compliment and smiled. "Very.
Haruhana taught me everything from tea ceremonies to fan
dancing and how to attract a client."

"A client? Like a—"

"No, not like that Inspector. A geisha needs a main client
to pay for her lavish lifestyle. The kimonos, the makeup, the
training…it isn't cheap. I was only a child, but already
indebted to Haruhana's geisha house. Without a steady
client, I'd be doomed to forever entertain at New Year's
celebrations and retirement parties."

"It sounds like a terrible fate," Inspector Aizawa said.

"Worse than hell itself. My *oneesan* had a steady client, a
stock trader who worked in Marunouchi." Reiko sighed.
"Then came the financial crisis in 1927. You remember that
April, don't you Inspector? The cherry blossoms were in full
bloom and our banks were spiraling into the abyss. I still
don't understand what caused the panic, but my *oneesan's*
client soon lost his entire fortune."

"A lot of people were ruined during the crisis," Inspector
Aizawa said mournfully.

"Regardless, a year later I became a full-fledged geisha
and my *oneesan* retired. Soon after, she and her client
committed *shinju*, love suicide."

"Every Japanese woman's fantasy…"

Reiko scoffed. "If there's one thing I learned from the
Great Earthquake, there's no beauty in dying."

Inspector Aizawa gave a slow nod. "You're right. Siberia
taught me that."

"So there I was, Inspector. A newborn geisha with no clients and no *oneesan* to help me find one. I wandered the streets in a daze, just like after the earthquake, hoping a rich playboy would save me. I went to Harlem and drowned myself in gimlets and jazz. But the gods must have guided me there because I found my true self in that club. The geisha Harutora became the *moga* Reiko Watanabe."

"*Mogas*," Inspector Aizawa grumbled. "When I was promoted to inspector, one of my first cases involved a modern girl who stabbed a foreign businessman in the crotch. Her excuse was that he'd fondled her and didn't pay the price they had agreed upon."

"She should have gotten the money up front. I probably ran into her at Harlem once or twice. You see, I drank and danced with everything Tokyo had to offer. Stock traders from Marunouchi, yakuza bosses, and *mobo* playboys. After a year as a *moga*, I paid off my debts to the geisha house and never looked back."

"Is the *moga* your Mr. Hyde and the geisha your Dr. Jeykll? Or is it the other way around?"

Reiko ran a gloved hand along her chin. "I haven't figured that out yet." A gust of wind howled through the street and bit into her cheeks.

"And this Harlem club was where you met Masaru Ryusaki?"

She nodded. "After the depression hit, nobody had money to spend. Not for a geisha or even a *moga* mistress. I looked for a job, but when men can't find work, there's little choice for a woman other than the brothels." Reiko shuddered at the thought. "Do you visit Yoshiwara, Inspector?"

"We can't all be *mobo* playboys," he snapped.

Reiko held up supplicating hands. "Sorry. I only meant to say that the women there aren't getting rich. But after almost a year of dwindling finances and few romantic prospects, that was where I was headed. But in March of this year, I met Masaru Ryusaki." She sighed. "He was different then…like my childhood crushes, Sessue Hayakawa and Rudolph Valentino, rolled into one. So kind-hearted and well-traveled. He'd tell me stories about speakeasies and jazz clubs in San Francisco, more magical than any fairy tale I heard growing up."

"You met a different Ryusaki."

"Yes, I met the Dr. Jeykll. You see, your arrest scared him out of politics. He didn't care about saving the nation from corruption anymore. All he wanted to do was write stories, stroll through Ueno Park, take me shopping in Ginza, and listen to jazz. It was heaven on earth."

"Was he your 'steady client'?"

"In a sense." She gave a wistful sigh, full of more melancholy than intended.

"Sounds like you fell for him."

Reiko didn't say anything but peered up at the glittering lights of the Denkikan's marquee. How many nights had Masaru taken her here, during those blissful months of frivolity? What she wouldn't give to have one more night like that.

"Whatever we had, it didn't last long. It ended one night late in October. We'd just come back from seeing *Sword of Justice* and saw an Army officer waiting outside of Masaru's *machiya*."

"Hajime Nakajima?"

"Unfortunately, yes." She shivered, but not because of the cold. "Over tea, he explained how their recent coup d'état attempt had failed and—"

"Wait, there was another attempted coup?" the Inspector asked. "In October?"

Reiko nodded. "Only Army officers were involved this time. No civilians. Regardless, just like the March Incident, this one was called off too. Lack of support, Nakajima explained. But the Lieutenant said that they had a new plan and needed Masaru's help. He begged Masaru to reactivate the Kusanagi Society. I'd never even heard of it or anything else he'd done in politics until that moment. I didn't even know that he had served in the Diet until then!"

Inspector Aizawa chuckled. "Did he tell you the story when he appeared at a session in full samurai armor and threatened other Dietmen with his sword?"

That earned a deep laugh. "No, but I believe it. That's Masaru's Mr. Hyde. And like some magic potion, Nakajima's visit turned him back into the fiery patriot that he is today. At first, Masaru tried to decline but Nakajima kept ranting about the corruption in the government, our soldiers fighting in Manchuria, and the famine ravaging the Tohoku region. Poor Masaru couldn't stand the shame and agreed to help. You see, that rice farmer is everything Masaru Ryusaki wants to be…a selfless patriot, totally devoted to the Emperor."

"And very different from the man you met," Aizawa said.

Reiko nodded again. "Masaru had to change in order to save face in front of Lieutenant Nakajima. No more jazz music, no more Hollywood films, and no more *moga* mistress. An esteemed patriot couldn't fall in love with a creature of Western decadence. But he knew I had once been a geisha, and the geisha is a living piece of Japanese art. He bought me a kimono, makeup, and a wig. What choice did I have, Inspector? Go out into the world alone without any source of income? Or continue on as a geisha and do my best to pry Masaru away from Nakajima?"

"Is that why you called me, Watanabe-san?"

A flurry of answers flooded Reiko's mind. Her love for Masaru and fear of a lack of income had been the main motivation. But this desperate attempt to keep her romance alive had failed, so why did she continue to help the Inspector? The reason presented itself in memories of that horrible September day when the Imperial capital died. It wasn't for Masaru, the Inspector, or even herself. It was for Tokyo, her home.

"I saw what Masaru was planning…I couldn't let this beautiful city of ours become drenched in blood."

Aizawa sighed. "I understand…"

A few moments passed by in silence until a band of musicians in colorful samurai costumes sauntered through, led by a woman in a light green kimono. They stopped on a street corner and began playing old folk songs but with a jazzy twist, as if led by Cab Calloway himself. A typical night for Asakusa. She bit her lip. How she would miss this place.

"But we failed, Inspector. Tokyo will become a bloodbath. I'm...I'm considering leaving town."

"What? You can't leave!"

"Of course I can. There's a late-night express at Tokyo Station."

"You can't run from this, Watanabe-san." He grabbed her by the shoulders and stared into her eyes. In that bruised and blackened squared face was the conviction of a Shinto priest performing an exorcism. "You called me for a reason."

"I was trying to get Masaru away from politics again. Now I realize how strong Nakajima's influence is."

He loosened his grip and let his arms drop. "Meaning?"

"Meaning that since you didn't catch Masaru tonight, he's bound to figure out I've been helping you eventually and when he does—" Reiko rose her hand and chopped the back of her neck.

Inspector Aizawa shook his head. "This isn't about you or me, Watanabe-san. The entire nation is at stake. Take a look." He gestured to the samurai band, now playing the children's song "Cherry Blossoms, Cherry Blossoms" as a jazz standard. "Do any of those fools realize how close Japan is to becoming a dictatorship?"

"Would they even care?"

"That doesn't matter," Aizawa said. "Japan is a nation of laws. It is my sacred duty to the Emperor to enforce them."

"I thought you only joined the Department because you needed a job."

"Maybe, but I later learned what a police officer's duty meant from a man I used to admire."

"Do you mean from Superintendent Shimura?" Reiko asked.

Aizawa ignored the question. "Watanabe-san, I swear that I will protect you. But I need your help." The Inspector ended his speech with a deep bow, arms stiff at his side.

No man had ever shown her such respect with a bow that low. The firmness in his tone suggested a sincerity that she seldom saw. But then again, surely that's what Baron Onishi must have thought. Those horrific photographs flashed through her mind.

"I'll think about it."

Inspector Aizawa straightened up and pulled out a pen along with his *meishi*. After writing something on it, he presented the card with both hands. An address was scribbled on the back.

"If you find anything out, where Ryusaki is staying, who he's seen lately…anything, then please contact me there. It's my home address. Memorize and destroy it."

"No more phone calls?" Reiko asked.

He shook his head. "I don't own a personal telephone and…Superintendent Shimura might have bugged my office. If you have anything to report, just take a one-yen taxi so we can speak in person."

"I'll think about it."

"Watanabe-san—"

"Call me Reiko."

"Reiko-san…thank you."

She studied the address on the *meishi* before putting her lighter to it. A small flame consumed the card and Reiko tossed it to the ground. She stared at the smoldering ash for a few moments before looking up at the samurai band. The woman had stopped playing her trumpet and started to sing.

"Cherry blossoms, cherry blossoms,
Across the spring sky,
As far as you can see.
Is it a mist or clouds?
Fragrant in the air.
Come now, come now!"

Reiko sighed and stared at the snow on the ground. Spring needed to come soon.

CHAPTER THIRTY-EIGHT

Only after Lieutenant Nakajima entered the boarding house did the numbness fade from his body. The journey from the Dragonfly Tea House to his quarters in the eastern Honjo Ward was a misty haze, and the image of General Sakamoto's headless body dominated his mind. The severity of what he had done set in and felt strangely liberating. In this war against evil, he was a shock troop for purity and patriotism.

Nakajima began tugging off his boots when the landlord trotted up.

"Oh, Lieutenant…welcome back," he said with a bow. "Working late at the Army Ministry?"

Nakajima nodded but didn't speak.

"I hope you don't mind, but I allowed some visitors into your room," the landlord said.

"Visitors?" Nakajima asked.

"Yes, Ryusaki-san and Kuroki-san. They said they knew you."

A tightness gripped Nakajima's stomach. Ryusaki-sensei would never pay him a visit so late at night unless something was wrong. He finished removing his boots and dashed down the hallway. Opening his room's *shoji* door, he found Kuroki and Ryusaki-sensei, *katana* in hand, kneeling beside his futon in silence. Several bandages, dotted with blood, were wrapped across Kuroki's forehead. Ryusaki-sensei looked a little better, but dark rings hung under his puffy, reddened eyes.

"Get in here and close the door," Ryusaki-sensei ordered.

Lieutenant Nakajima obeyed and then dropped to his knees. "*Zensei*, what happened?"

The sword rattled in Ryusaki-sensei's hands. "That bastard Aizawa…he found me! Nakajima-san, we have been betrayed! Not only by General Sakamoto but within the Kusanagi Society!"

Nakajima was taken aback.

"*Zensei*…do you mean we have a spy in our group?"

"How else could that miserable detective have found out where I lived?" Ryusaki-sensei snapped.

The past failures replayed in Lieutenant Nakajima's mind. Somehow, the Inspector had discovered Ryusaki-sensei's whereabouts, despite bribing the *koban* police box in Asakusa.

"Who is the spy, *zensei*?"

Ryusaki-sensei shook his head. "I don't know but you must help me uncover him."

Nakajima scanned through a list of suspects in his mind, but only Reiko Watanabe's face stood out.

"Perhaps the Inspector is only obeying his duty, *zensei*."

Ryusaki-sensei scoffed. "His duty is to a corrupt government and he should die with it. We are at war now, Lieutenant…"

Yes, it was war, and Inspector Aizawa was a worthy adversary. So much so, that killing him seemed like a waste. If only he could be enlisted, they would have a valuable ally in their fight against evil. But first, proper punishment must be meted out to the traitor within their ranks.

"*Zensei*, you must consider that the spy is much closer than you think."

Ryusaki-sensei's eyes narrowed. "What do you mean?"

"Who has known of our plot from the beginning?" Nakajima raised his pinky in the gesture for "mistress."

"Reiko wouldn't betray me…" Ryusaki-sensei choked out.

"Why not?" Nakajima demanded.

Ryusaki-sensei averted his eyes. "She…she needs me."

"Does she? Perhaps Inspector Aizawa is paying her now," Nakajima said.

Ryusaki-sensei gave a pained gasp, before biting his lip. It was clear that he was solving the puzzle on his own, even if he didn't want to look at the final picture.

"You don't understand, Lieutenant. We are bound together by the red string of love."

How sad. Flesh reduced even great men to foolish weaklings. Ah, how grateful he was to have remained pure.

"Reiko Watanabe...Harutora...whatever she calls herself, is in love with money, *zensei*. She is a parasite feasting on your money."

Shame lowered Ryusaki-sensei's head and shook his long, thin frame.

"I must think things over. Kuroki-san, assemble my seven most loyal patriots. We'll meet at the Dragonfly Tea House."

General Sakamoto's headless and gutted corpse entered Nakajima's mind.

"*Zensei*, the Dragonfly might not be the best place to meet right now."

Ryusaki-sensei nodded his understanding. "Then we'll meet at the Katsura Inn in Asakusa, two hours from now. And Nakajima-san..."

"Yes, *zensei*?"

"We must throw that barking dog off our scent...and Superintendent Shimura will help us. Pay him a visit and make sure he understands that his assistance is required again."

"But *zensei*, where are you headed?"

A mix of melancholy and fury bubbled behind Ryusaki-sensei's glasses.

"You're right Lieutenant. Before we proceed, I must settle things with Reiko first."

Nakajima let his confusion show.

"If Aizawa is there with her..." he said, tapping sword with a stern face.

"And if he's not?"

Ryusaki-sensei gave a conspiratorial look. "I have a plan to expose the traitor and deal with Aizawa once and for all. Let me explain…"

CHAPTER THIRTY-NINE

A dim light bulb flickered in the foyer, giving Reiko's apartment building a dreamlike feel. After parting ways with Inspector Aizawa, she'd wandered Asakusa for nearly an hour, unsure of what she was looking for before finally returning home. Ascending the stairs, every shadow seemed to belong to sinister beings, aware of her treachery. This whole affair had given her newfound respect for spies. Years from now, future generations would learn of Reiko Watanabe, the Mata Hari of Asia. No, Reiko Watanabe, the poison woman, was a more appropriate title.

Opening her door, she sighed and fumbled for the light switch. Flicking it on, the entire room was illuminated, including Masaru standing underneath the poster of Louise Brooks. Reiko released an involuntary scream as he rushed over and slid his hand tightly over her mouth.

"Be quiet," Masaru ordered in a whisper. "Were you followed?"

Reiko shook her head and he removed his hand. Fatigue was carved into Masaru's handsome face, but his bloodshot eyes darted back and forth, alert and suspicious.

"Not so loud," he said. "The Police could be watching your apartment."

"What were you doing here?" she asked, lowering her voice.

"Forgive me for lurking around like a thief in the night but I have reason to be cautious. My *machiya* was raided by Inspector Aizawa."

She feigned surprise. "Oh no! Are you all right?"

"I'm fine." His pink, puffy eyes narrowed. "Where were you?"

"Just now?"

"After you left my *machiya*. Where did you go?"

Reiko searched for a convincing lie, but the truth sounded more benign. "I went to see a picture. *Sword of Justice*. Remember when we first saw it together?"

She offered a little smile, hoping to prey on any sentimentality he had left. Masaru sank to his knees and grasped her skirt.

"Oh, Reiko…" He looked up at her with moist eyes and a pitiful, aching face. "Have you betrayed me?"

"I would never…"

The lie came easier than she had expected.

"I knew you wouldn't betray me. Because…because…" He gave a flustered but sincere smile. "Reiko Watanabe, I love you. Will you marry me?"

Each word hit her like a fist and left her out of breath. Rarely did the Japanese confess their love for one another. Her parents certainly never did, nor did any of her past lovers. Even the proposal seemed un-Japanese. Most men asked women to marry them with the question, "Will you make me miso soup for the rest of my life?" Still, his words pierced her armor of cynicism. How nice it was to be a romantic idiot, even for just a moment.

She caught her breath and said, "Yes, Masaru. Of course I'll marry you…"

He stood and wrapped his arms around her. It was shocking how much she actually missed this, like an invalid discovering her legs worked again. They were lovers again, transported back in time before everything was ruined. The other three million people disappeared and Tokyo became a city of two.

He kissed her deeply before pulling her onto the bed. Hollywood had taught the Japanese how to kiss, which was almost unheard of in the past. Few men knew this art, but Masaru Ryusaki was an expert.

"I…I love you, Masaru…"

Did she really say that? It all seemed too staged. She looked around her apartment for cameras and lighting. But there was only Masaru Ryusaki, caressing her as if it were their first time. Within moments, he had disrobed and was working through her layers. Off came her leather gloves, cloche hat, coat, skirt, and stockings, tossed aside on the floor. She tore off her sweater and pulled him on top. They had done this dance many times before, but this was the first in weeks that she'd felt something other than mechanical lust. Each passionate thrust sent waves of pleasure rippling throughout her body.

Masaru collapsed beside her, ending this round with a deep kiss. It was moist and warm this time, but no less passionate. He reached his arm around and held her, running his long fingers across her delicate skin. Moments went by in silence until she couldn't suppress a nagging question.

"Why, Masaru? Why now?"

Rolling over, he stared at the ceiling with a serene expression. "Tonight I experienced true terror. I saw myself in prison, separated from you forever."

As if he couldn't be any more charming. But she couldn't pretend that she wasn't flattered.

"Does that mean you've given up politics again?"

He turned to face her. His serenity evaporated, replaced by a grim fatalism.

"Not yet," Masaru said.

"Why not?"

"Reiko, I must fulfill my duty…to my men and the Emperor," he said, stroking her cheek. "Only then will I be free to spend my life with you."

"Masaru, this can't go on…"

"I know. It will end soon. And then it will be you," he leaned over and kissed her deeply, "and me, forever."

"I need a cigarette," she said with a sigh. "And a bath."

"Later," he said, hopping out of bed. "My men are waiting, and I want you to come with me."

She sat up and gave a confused look. "Why?"

"The supposed champion of the Kusanagi Society, General Sakamoto, has betrayed us. My men are confused, angry, and downtrodden. A geisha would lift their spirits."

She sighed. It was nice to have the old Masaru back, if only for a moment.

CHAPTER FORTY

Superintendent Shimura's *machiya* was more spacious than most houses in Tokyo, made even larger by its near emptiness. Photographs on tables and dressers showed a young Joji Shimura in an Army uniform, Joji Shimura with his bride, Joji Shimura and his children, and even Joji Shimura with a fresh-faced Inspector Aizawa.

"You have a beautiful family, Superintendent," Lieutenant Nakajima said, accepting a steaming cup of green tea.

Shimura, clad in a thick kimono, frowned and grunted. "The Great Earthquake took my wife and two daughters."

Nakajima gave a sympathetic nod and glanced over at the photograph of young Shimura in an old dark blue Army uniform, probably taken during the Russo-Japanese War. Ah, if only he could taste the glory of battle before…no. He needed to concentrate on why Ryusaki-sensei had sent him here.

"Superintendent, I come bearing a request from our *zensei*…"

"That's why you've come calling at this hour? Couldn't it have waited until morning?"

"It's a matter of urgency."

"Haven't I already done everything requested of me?"

"Yes, and Ryusaki-zensei thanks you," Nakajima said before taking a sip of tea.

"Then why haven't I been appointed superintendent-general of the Metropolitan Police yet? Where is this coup d'état that Ryusaki-san promised?"

"Our original plan has been…altered."

"Is that so?"

Nakajima nodded. "Before any coup d'état begins, we must know one thing. Who is the informant that Inspector Aizawa has in the Kusanagi Society?"

Shimura's eyebrows raised. "I have no idea."

Nakajima took another sip of tea and tried to remain calm. "Are you sure? What about Reiko Watanabe?"

"That *moga*?"

"*Moga*, geisha…a traitor's heart beats inside her no matter what outfit she wears."

"I don't know any more than you do. The first I ever heard of her was when she and Ryusaki-san arrived at my office last night."

Nakajima gripped the teacup tighter. "Fine then. Ryusaki-zensei has decided to deal with Inspector Aizawa once and for all."

Shimura's face clouded with worry. "What do you mean?"

"Tonight, we want you to order Aizawa somewhere remote…with no witnesses…"

Shimura swallowed as his entire frame began to shake. "I didn't agree to this. Assassinating that villain Baron Onishi was one thing, but Aizawa?"

Nakajima held up placating hands. "I don't want him killed either. He's an honorable man, simply doing his duty. But Ryusaki-zensei has decided he is too dangerous to be allowed to continue running around."

"Isn't there some other way? Take him prisoner…without killing him…"

"I would prefer that, but if he resists, we'll have no other choice. Will you help us?"

Shimura's entire frame began to shake. Tears formed behind his glasses. "I believe in Masaru Ryusaki and the New Japan, Lieutenant, but Kenji Aizawa is like a little brother to me. He's the only family I have left…and…he was my partner." After a deep breath, Shimura steadied himself and with a face harder than granite, he said, "I cannot take part in this insidious plot."

Ah, such loyalty filled Nakajima with a burst of warmth.

"Now if that's all, Lieutenant," Shimura snarled. "Please leave my house."

Nakajima took another sip of tea and contemplated what to do next. Neither he nor Ryusaki-sensei even considered that Superintendent Shimura would disobey an order. Although Nakajima admired the comradery between two former partners, Shimura was now a liability. He had proven to be a strong ally but would make an even more dangerous enemy. Without Shimura's help, they would have to rely on Ryusaki-sensei's contingency plan to eliminate Aizawa.

"Kill him, Hajime-kun," Chitose-oneesan whispered as her spindly form rose up from behind the Superintendent. The otherworldly presence had an almost hypnotic effect on Nakajima, prompting him to set the teacup aside and stand up. Shimura stood too and gave a farewell bow.

Lieutenant Nakajima grabbed his saber handle and with one fluid motion, slashed the blade across Shimura's upper torso. The Superintendent shrieked out pained, gurgling noises as he stumbled to the side, bleeding out all over the photographs. Nakajima stepped aside to avoid any splatter.

After a few moments of writhing, Shimura vomited out a death rattle and collapsed onto the floor with a wet thud. Nakajima sighed and bowed deeply, reminding himself that Joji Shimura was simply an unfortunate casualty of war. Straightening up, he looked at the wispy form of Chitose-oneesan and knew there would be many more to follow.

CHAPTER FORTY-ONE

It usually took hours for Reiko to don her entire regalia, but Masaru insisted that they hurry. He helped apply her makeup, straightened her *shimada* wig, and tied her *obi* belt, something no man had ever helped her with before. The transformation from *moga* to geisha took a little under an hour and Harutora returned to the streets of Asakusa.

Shuffling in her tight kimono and *geta* clogs, she looked over at Masaru who slowed his pace. He also chivalrously carried her *shamisen* since singing was essential for any geisha party. But this was a party for the Kusanagi Society, which meant there'd be songs, games, and probably a hit list. She sighed.

"Anything wrong?" Masaru asked.

"I'm just cold. That's all."

He smiled. "We're almost there." A few blocks later, they ducked into the Katsura Inn and were greeted by a tiny woman in a near-permanent bow. Though geisha usually performed at tea houses, Reiko remembered several inns she had visited while training. There she and her *oneesan* would entertain wealthy foreigners whose entire Japanese vocabulary consisted of *konnichiwa* and *arigatou*.

After removing their shoes, they were led into a private room where the seven founding members of the Kusanagi Society knelt along the sides. Kneeling at the opposite end were Makoto Kuroki and, unfortunately, Lieutenant Nakajima. After bows were exchanged, Masaru shut the door behind them and knelt like a good *sensei* rejoining his class. Reiko took a spot beside him as Masaru set the *shamisen* aside.

"Before we begin, I have an announcement to make." Masaru cleared his throat. "I have asked for

Harutora…Reiko Watanabe…to be my wife. We will be married before the year is out."

Stunned gasps were the initial response until Kuroki threw up his hands and yelled, "Banzai! To the future daughter of the Ryusaki family! Banzai!"

The patriots cheered and banzaied in celebration but across the room, Lieutenant Nakajima looked ill.

"*Zensei*," he said, slamming his hands on the floor. "This woman will be your downfall!"

Masaru examined this challenge to his authority with a stern gaze.

"I understand your concern, Lieutenant. But I can see with unmistakable clarity that her soul is pure."

Nakajima divided his quick, panicked glances between Masaru and her. The country monkey was in such humiliating agony that Reiko couldn't suppress a smile.

"*Zensei*, she has blinded you with lust!"

"Enough!" Masaru roared, slapping the floor.

"Please *zensei*, let me speak to you alone."

Masaru stood and followed Nakajima to a private room. From behind a *shoji* door, they looked like enormous shadow puppets come to life. After a minute of hushed words, Nakajima returned, his boyish face twisting in pain.

Masaru reappeared, stern and implacable.

"*Zensei*, please…" Nakajima said, lowering his head.

"Go now," Masaru ordered, pointing to the door.

Lieutenant Nakajima bowed an apology and kept his gaze planted on the floor while walking out, like a dishonored child. A sadistic glee welled up inside Reiko. Such humiliation must have been devastating.

"*Sensei*," Kuroki said. "What happened?"

Masaru knelt back down and said, "Lieutenant Nakajima is no longer a member of the Kusanagi Society. We'll carry on without him."

"What will we do without the Lieutenant? We have no access to weapons now," Kuroki said.

Masaru waved his hand. "We do not need him. My family's estate has all the weapons we'll need for the coming war. You see, men, I have already decided upon our next target."

"Who, *sensei*?" one of the patriots asked, leaning closer.

"During his confrontation with General Sakamoto, Nakajima-san learned who has been pulling the strings from the shadows – Isamu Takano!" Masaru almost spat the name. "Apparently, that *zaibatsu* banker promised General Sakamoto that he would become prime minister after Inukai-san. But he must learn that the Kusanagi Society is not his personal weapon to be used and discarded! Takano must pay for this treachery…with his life."

The Kusanagi Society men growled like tigers in a cage. Their anger was contagious and Reiko's hands began to tremble. Only the Great Earthquake had made her feel so insignificant. Isamu Takano was worse, an earthquake that could scheme and plot.

"Kuroki-san!" Masaru said.

"Yes, *sensei*!"

"I am giving you a chance to redeem yourself. Tomorrow morning, outside of the Marunouchi Building, you shall strike Isamu Takano dead!"

Kuroki's bruised face glowed with joy. "*Sensei*! I am honored!"

"Takano's assassination will serve as the Kusanagi Society's declaration of war against evil," Masaru said, his face steadfast.

The patriots threw up their arms and roared another round of banzais.

"This night will be Makoto Kuroki's *sokokai*," Masaru said before gesturing to one of the patriots. "Fetch us some sake. Kuroki-san should have a proper send-off to war."

The man bowed and dashed out of the room. Reiko took that as her cue. The men expected a geisha after all. She opened with the Dance of Spring, entrancing the Kusanagi Society with each graceful movement and delicate pose.

Minutes later, one of the patriots returned with a bottle of sake, opening the door for drinking games. Rock-paper-scissors followed by *konpira fune fune* lubricated the *sokokai* even further. Maybe she wasn't such a lousy geisha after all.

"Sing us a song, Harutora" Masaru ordered.

Reiko remembered how days earlier, he'd begged for jazz, like ointment for a wound. But now, something patriotic seemed more appropriate. She grabbed her *shamisen* and strummed out the steady, haunting melody of Japan's national anthem.

"May the reign of the Emperor
continue for a thousand, nay, eight thousand generations
and for the eternity that it takes
for small pebbles to grow into a great rock
and become covered with moss."

It'd been years since she'd played *Kimigayo*, but the lyrics came out effortlessly. The simple display of trite patriotism moistened several eyes in the room. Even Masaru looked ready to weep.

A good geisha always wore a mask to conceal her true emotions. But that song had reawakened a love, not just for Tokyo, but all of Japan. Not for this Japan, a strange nation rotting from militarism, corruption, and assassinations. No, it was for the Japan of a few years ago, carefree and peaceful. That was *her* Japan. And she'd do anything to bring it back to life.

CHAPTER FORTY-TWO

An outside banging stirred Aizawa awake. He sat up and rolled off his futon. After clicking on a nearby lamp, he checked his wristwatch. It was 5:50 in the morning. *Junsas* knew better to knock on his door this early, so it had to be Reiko. After a deep yawn and a satisfying stretch, he answered the door.

Reiko Watanabe stared back at him with half-closed eyes. Gone were her cloche hat, pea coat, and skirt, replaced with a black kimono, *shimada* hairstyle, and white face paint that couldn't hide the bright red in her cheeks. The *moga* caterpillar had become the geisha butterfly, Harutora. Across the street, a taxicab had parked behind Baron Onishi's Rolls-Royce. Its driver smoked a cigarette and warmed his hands near the engine as a light sprinkling of snow drifted to the ground.

"Yer right, Inspector. These one-yen taxis are great," she slurred. "Mind if I come in?"

After she removed her *geta* clogs, Aizawa led Reiko to the main room of the *nagaya* where she almost collapsed into a kneeling position.

"Do you want any tea?"

"No, thank you."

"Are you sure? You look ready to pass out."

She scoffed. "If I couldn't handle my alcohol, I couldn't be a geisha."

"You're a very unconventional one."

Reiko's stomach gave a loud grumble. She covered her mouth with a paper fan and asked, "On second thought, do you have anything to eat?"

Aizawa retreated to his pantry and presented Reiko with a small box of Glico Caramel Candies. Still holding her paper fan with one hand, she opened the box and shoved a handful of sweets into her mouth. After a few loud chews, she swallowed and expelled a satisfied sigh. She cooed her thanks and set the box aside with a contented smile.

Reiko Watanabe was a new species of woman. A Frankenstein monster assembled from discarded parts of *mogas* and geisha. Their alliance was something that could have only been arranged by the gods — as a practical joke.

"Why are you here, Reiko-san?" he asked, kneeling across from her.

"I'm sorry! Maybe I am drunker than I thought." She laughed. "When I returned to my apartment, guess who was waiting for me?"

"Masaru Ryusaki."

She nodded. "And like something out of a Rudolph Valentino picture, he asked me to marry him."

"What did you say?"

"Of course I agreed."

Aizawa tensed, half-expecting her to call their alliance off. Instead, she laughed and shook her head.

"If he'd asked a month ago, I might have actually meant it," she said with a wistful sigh. "But still, it's nice that he finally proposed."

"Is that all?"

"I'm getting to the most important part, Inspector."

"Please do."

"Masaru wanted me to entertain his men," she gestured to the makeup and kimono with her paper fan, "but when Lieutenant Nakajima began to whine, Masaru kicked him out! Just like that!" She snapped the fan shut and lapsed into a fit of laughter.

Aizawa sighed with relief. Lieutenant Nakajima was almost untouchable without involving the *Kempeitai*. Now that the strings to the Army were cut, the Kusanagi Society was an entirely civilian organization, making it easy prey for the Metropolitan Police.

"Where are they now?"

"I don't know. I just came from Asakusa. We all went our separate ways after the party. Masaru said he'd contact me later. Right now, he's probably staying with one of his many admirers. He wouldn't tell me where in case I was picked up and tortured by the Police." She laughed again. "My Masaru…such a trusting fool!"

"Is that all?"

She waved the fan. "You're not very patient, Inspector. I was just going to say that they've picked their first target. Isamu Takano. Kuroki-san is going to kill him."

"When? Where?"

"Whenever the workday starts outside the Marunouchi Building," she said.

That meant around 7:00. Aizawa glanced back at his watch. 6:00.

"Why Takano?"

As if he needed to ask. All *zaibatsu* capitalists were hated by the patriotic societies, but bankers earned a special contempt.

"Because all of this was Takano's doing. Lieutenant Nakajima found out it was that banker who was really controlling General Sakamoto. He offered the General the chance to become prime minister after Inukai." Reiko leaned closer. "Takano isn't just some *zaibatsu*…he's a shadow shogun."

That made sense. After all, Takano was a major donor to the Seiyukai and must have had the influence to choose its leadership. Even the powerful General Sakamoto was a mere puppet of Isamu Takano. What schemes was this banker plotting in the shadows? Aizawa searched his memory for any clues and remembered the conversation with Baron Onishi.

Reviving full trade with America was an issue that stood out. What else had the Baron sneered at? Oh yes, Takano's insistence on returning to the gold standard. Baron Onishi had mentioned that the banker had been speculating in American currency, and if Japan was no longer tied to gold, he'd double his profits when he converted his dollars into yen.

Money was motive enough for most people to kill, but to orchestrate a political assassination? That took a certain kind of audacity. Japanese politics was loaded with intrigue left over from the old shoguns, but this was something new. Part of him wanted to go back to bed and step out of Kuroki's way. But assassination was still a crime even if the victim was a villain like Takano. Besides, the banker couldn't testify at his own trial if he was dead.

"I have to get ready," he said, standing up. "You should go."

Reiko rose with a yawn. "Good idea. I think I actually *am* about to pass out."

"If you get any more information, especially where Ryusaki is, please let me know." He led her to the door. "And Reiko-san…"

"Yes?"

"Thank you. For everything," he said with a deep bow. "I am in your debt."

"You can pay me back now," she said, extending an open palm. "I don't have enough for the fare back to my apartment."

Aizawa sighed. The gods must have been laughing at their handiwork.

CHAPTER FORTY-THREE

Marunouchi crackled with an energy that rivaled Asakusa. The workday was just beginning, and salarymen poured out of electric trams while executives emerged from gleaming sedans and limousines. Many filed into the concrete buildings of the four major *zaibatsu* – Mitsui, Sumitomo, Mitsubishi, and Yasuda. If Asakusa was a terminally ill patient, then Marunouchi was a corpse that had risen from the dead. Since the depression began, most of the smaller *zaibatsu* went under, but Takano Bank had somehow thrived. However, its survival now seemed less miraculous and more like the product of black magic.

Aizawa circled the Rolls-Royce around the eight-story Marunouchi Building – the Maru-Biru – searching the streets for anyone with a Charlie Chaplin mustache. Damn it all. It had stopped snowing, but it was near impossible to identify anyone out in these crowds. A squad of *junsas* would make his job much easier. But that request would have to be approved by Superintendent Shimura. He gave a resigned sigh and kept driving.

At least in the financial district, a Rolls-Royce was inconspicuous among all the imported foreign cars. Even in a depression, the *zaibatsu* traveled in style. Unsurprising since there had always been a wide gulf between rich and poor in Japan. During the Tokugawa Shogunate, society was organized in four clearly defined castes – *daimyo* lords at the top, followed by samurai, then farmers, and finally, the merchants.

That would place Baron Onishi at the apex, followed by Masaru Ryusaki, then Lieutenant Nakajima, and finally Kenji Aizawa. But the title of police inspector was a prestige that none of his ancestors could ever have reached. His grandfather had peddled tofu but his father died a railway switchman. Each generation crawled a little higher on the social ladder.

What caste would Isamu Takano be part of? As a *niwaka narikin* – a new rich – he would still technically be at the bottom of the pyramid. But Takano was far more powerful than any *daimyo* lord or samurai warrior during the Tokugawa Era. He deserved his own caste – a shadow shogun, as Reiko had called him.

Aizawa circled a few more times but Kuroki was nowhere to be found. Parking the Rolls-Royce near the Marunouchi Building, he looked at his watch: 6:50. He peered into the swarms of salarymen, all of whom looked far too well dressed to be anyone in league with Ryusaki and none sported that ridiculous mustache.

He viewed a sleek Bentley pulling up behind him in the rearview mirror. The doors sprang open and out hopped two enormous men in long gray overcoats. Most wealthy men hired off-duty police officers for protection, but from the looks of it, Takano's bodyguards were former sumo.

Isamu Takano himself emerged, wearing a stylish homburg and a fur-trimmed black coat. Another elegantly dressed man followed him out of the automobile, but this one wasn't even Japanese. A white foreigner towered over Takano and his sumo bodyguards like a giant among pygmies.

Aizawa hopped out of the Rolls-Royce and walked straight toward Takano. The bodyguards took notice and blocked his path. He dug into his coat and pulled out his *meishi* card, holding it up like a token sacrifice. But the two sumo stared at him like stone Buddhas, unmoving and implacable. A few meters away, Takano and his foreign friend looked over and chatted in what sounded like English.

"Metropolitan Police. I need to speak to Takano-san."

"Takano-san is with a very important guest," one of the sumo said.

"From New York City," the other emphasized.

Takano continued chatting with the foreigner, occasionally shooting quick glances at Aizawa. Bodyguards were deterrent enough for most crooks but the fact that Takano needed them at all must have been an embarrassment. Especially in front of such an important gentleman from New York City. Perhaps it was a weakness that could be exploited.

"You can either let me speak with Takano-san now, or I will come back here with the entire Police Department. I have no qualms about interrogating him in front of his American friend."

The bodyguards edged closer, backing Aizawa up. He'd never grappled with a sumo before but had seen enough wrestling matches to know he was about to be thrown from the ring. Behind the advancing sumo, Aizawa saw Takano give an apologetic bow to the American and then begin walking toward them.

"Stop this now," Takano said, parting the bodyguards. "Leave us."

The sumo bowed and walked back toward the foreigner. Takano drew himself up and glared.

"Inspector Aizawa, isn't it?"

He nodded. "You and I have much to discuss, Takano-san."

The banker's face betrayed no emotion as he gestured to the American.

"Do you know who that is?"

"Hebert Hoover?"

Takano chuckled. "No, more important. He's from Wall Street."

Aizawa looked back at the foreigner. There wasn't anything remarkable about him; a large nose, wide eyes, and taut face turned pink from the cold. Only his height was impressive. But weren't all Americans supposed to be tall? Regardless, he was much taller than the sumo bodyguards. He also dwarfed another Japanese man who approached with rapid steps.

A gust of wind billowed the man's tattered overcoat. Although his face was partly obscured by a threadbare flat cap, he obviously wasn't Makoto Kuroki. He didn't even have a mustache. And unlike Kuroki, he actually managed to draw his weapon and aimed it with both hands like a cannon.

"*Tenchu!*"

Divine Punishment. The typical battle cry for *soshi* nationalists.

Like a human avalanche, one of the sumo bodyguards tackled the would-be assassin and hit the pavement with a loud thud. Despite an impressive hold, the *soshi* slithered out and drew his pistol again, struggling to get a bead. Pushing Takano aside, Aizawa pulled out his Colt automatic and, in one fluid motion, aimed and fired.

The *soshi's* chest exploded and he fell backward, painting the sidewalk with a gruesome red. Aizawa walked closer and examined the dead man. It wasn't Makoto Kuroki, but his face still possessed an eerie familiarity. Where was it from? The way he fell backward bore a resemblance to the first man he'd killed, a Bolshevik soldier back in Siberia. There'd been a few others since then, but even now he could still see that Russian boy falling backward, cushioned by a pillow of bloody snow.

No, it wasn't that. Recognition set in. He'd seen this *soshi* only yesterday in Ueno Park, one of the original Kusanagi Society men. But where was Makoto Kuroki? Aizawa grabbed the pistol, half-buried in snow. It wasn't a Nambu or Japanese, but rather a Nagant, the sidearm of choice for Bolshevik commissars.

He stood up, holstered his Colt, and shoved the Nagant into his waistband. A few horrified salarymen stared at him and crowded around the body. He looked over at Takano, surrounded by his sumo bodyguards. They pushed aside the salarymen, leading both the banker and his American guest into the Maru-Biru.

As a group of salarymen ringed the scene, Aizawa cast his attention back to the *soshi's* corpse, who – even in death – stared back with wide, hateful eyes.

CHAPTER FORTY-FOUR

A series of sharp knocks shook Reiko awake. Sunlight trickled in through the windows and illuminated the clock next to her bed. 7:42. The knocking continued, now in rapid bursts. Who could be at her door at this hour? She heaved herself out of bed and stole a glance in the mirror. A haggard-looking ghost in a night slip squinted back, her face still painted white. Last night had left her so exhausted that she didn't even bother to remove her makeup before passing out. Now she looked like a sad clown who'd been kicked out of the circus.

Reiko opened the door. Masaru stood there, fresh-faced and alert. He'd even managed to change out of his kimono and into a *mobo* outfit: blue suit, red tie, and fedora. How did he still look so handsome this early in the morning?

"I apologize for my appearance, Masaru," she said with a bow.

He waved a hand. "Even in rags, you're as radiant as sunlight."

She giggled. "You look quite dashing yourself."

"Thank you," he said.

"Do you want some tea, Masaru?"

"No, thank you." He removed his shoes and followed her into the apartment. "I'm here to request your presence as a geisha."

Reiko groaned. "Again?"

"You're still wearing the makeup, *darling*." He said the last word in English. "Another one of my patriots will have his *sokokai* today. I've chosen the next target to assassinate."

"Who?"

A knowing smile broadened Masaru's face. "Our greatest enemy."

Whoever that was, he sounded important. Reiko sat on the bed with a defeated sigh. Part of her wanted to make another appeal to Masaru's better side, but there was no point now. The only thing she could do was find out where the entire Kusanagi Society would be later and tell Inspector Aizawa. That would put an end this madness once and for all.

"Okay. I'll do it. Where and when should I meet you?"

"The Dragonfly Tea House," he said, sitting next to her.

"There? But General Sakamoto—"

"Has been dealt with. So get ready. I'll help you change."

Her stomach tightened, realizing there was no way to warn Inspector Aizawa in time. Grabbing her pack of Golden Bats from the nightstand, she lit one up and wracked her brain for some excuse to leave early.

"What's wrong?" Masaru asked, concern shining behind his glasses.

She forced a weak smile between drags. "Nothing. I'm just so tired from last night. Can we postpone this? I need to get some sleep."

He met her smile with a deep frown. "I'm sorry, Reiko. I know how tired you must be entertaining my men. But it is your duty as a geisha and my wife."

She sighed and turned away.

"We're not married yet, Masaru."

"Soon. I promise."

The proposal might have meant something a few months ago. Even up until last week, her acceptance would have been genuine. But now, despite his *mobo* clothes, Masaru Ryusaki's war mask had become his face. And what about her? Her makeup hid many Reiko Watanabes; geisha, *moga*, and poison woman. She finished her cigarette and stubbed it out on the ashtray.

"Masaru, I—"

He cut her off with a kiss, melting her.

"Don't talk, Reiko. Just listen."

Masaru walked over to the Sharp radio and turned the dial. The blissful melody of "My Blue Heaven" filled the room. He held out his hand and beckoned her like a hypnotized doll. Dutifully, she obeyed, intoxicated by the sweet nectar of jazz. She rested her head on his shoulders as they rocked back and forth, like a little ship in the open sea.

They moved as one, slow and steady, animated by the flow of music from the radio. "My Blue Heaven" was replaced by "Sing Me a Song of Araby," and finally, "The Japanese Sandman." Just an instrumental version, but he filled in the lyrics by singing to her. For weeks, she'd tried to seduce him with jazz, never expecting the same tactic to be used on her with such devastating effectiveness.

The bastard. After everything that had happened, why did he do this to her now? She couldn't hold the tears back that soon wetted his jacket. Dual suicides were how many Japanese romances ended, but she'd already figured out that death was a scam. Besides, Reiko Watanabe wouldn't die. She would just get tired of living one day.

Still, shame rose in her throat like bile as she stared into the eyes of the man she loved. What was that old saying? Oh yes, bound together by red string. Not that it mattered, since their red string of love would be cut in a few hours. So long as she could warn Inspector Aizawa in time.

The melody faded out and so did Masaru's singing.

He was right. The lyrics were just nonsense.

*****

The ambulance closed its doors and drove off with a screeching whine. The workday had started, and the only ones left on the street were a dozen or so reporters from the *Asahi, Nichi Nichi,* and *Yomiuri,* along with a few smaller papers. Standing in front of the Marunouchi Building, Aizawa took questions from the press.

"Inspector," the *Yomiuri* reporter called out. "Who was this man?"

"I don't know. We'll find out soon."

"Any idea why he wanted Isamu Takano dead?" the *Nichi Nichi* man asked.

Aizawa shrugged. "Who hasn't thought about killing a banker these days?"

Laughter rippled through the crowd. Aizawa was about to call on another reporter when a bulky shadow enveloped him. He turned around and stared at one of Takano's sumo bodyguards.

"Excuse me, Inspector. But Takano-san wishes to see you right away."

"So, all I had to do was save his life to get an appointment with him?" Aizawa asked.

The sumo gave an offended look.

"Never mind. Tell Takano-san I'll be right up." He turned back to the reporters. "I must ask a favor from all of you. I've treated you all with fairness in the past, but I need you to bury this story. At least for a few days."

Confused stares were the immediate response.

"Inspector, shootings in the financial district don't happen often. We can't keep this buried," the *Asahi* man remarked.

"And Inspector, what were you doing here? Has Takano-san been threatened before?" the *Yomiuri* reporter asked.

What didn't they understand? Most police officers viewed the press as an enemy, or at best, a puppet. He couldn't have the details of this investigation showing up in the evening papers. Not unless he wanted Ryusaki to figure out he had an informant in his midst.

"This is outrageous Inspector. After all, we have a duty to our readers!"

"If you don't keep quiet, then your paper will be in violation of the Peace Preservation Law," Aizawa said.

A hostile silence swept over the reporters. Freedom of the press was a privilege in Japan and something that the Metropolitan Police could easily take away. All that was needed was to invoke the Peace Preservation Law, the legislation that made even "dangerous thoughts" illegal. It seemed like something out of the mind of a Bolshevik commissar, even though it was used specifically to crush the Japanese Communist Party. For the most part, newspapers practiced self-censorship, if only because they realized how easy it would be to close them down, one by one.

The reporters gave submissive nods, understanding their place, except the *Asahi* man, who broke away and stormed off. Aizawa sympathized but reminded himself that a police officer must uphold the law, even that one. All that mattered now was Masaru Ryusaki. This battle of theirs had ceased being a conflict between men. Two concepts warred for superiority now. Order against revolution, law against crime, *giri* against *ninjo*, and Japan's future hung in the balance.

CHAPTER FORTY-FIVE

The elevator dinged, depositing Aizawa and his sumo escort on the third floor of the Marunouchi Building. A tense stillness hung in the lobby, amplifying their footsteps and the secretary's clacking typewriter to an almost deafening pitch. She looked up with a nervous glance before returning to work.

Down the hallway, a gold plaque reading "Isamu Takano, President" in both English and Japanese ornamented the heavy wooden doors of the banker's private office. The sumo knocked and said, "Inspector Aizawa to see you, sir."

"Enter."

Aizawa followed the sumo inside and found Takano standing beneath that majestic portrait of the Emperor, coolly smoking a cigarette. Returning to his personal kingdom must have revived his confidence. He wore a mask of composure while his stone-faced American guest sat in the exact spot where Baron Onishi had only days earlier. A final indignity to the dead.

The American rose and said a few words of clipped English to Takano, who responded with a supplicating bow and polite smile. Takano escorted the American to the door, who gave a curt nod to Aizawa as they walked past. Aizawa hadn't seen many Americans up close, but this one looked strange as most white men did. His skin was pale with splotches of pink, offset by his head of snowy-white hair, and a large, sharp nose. They made an odd couple. Takano, smiling and diminutive. The American, stern and towering. Their only commonality was a taste for elegant three-piece suits and flashy Rolex wristwatches.

They shook hands and the American walked out, followed by the lumbering sumo bodyguard, who closed the heavy doors behind him. Once they were alone, Takano turned his attention to Aizawa.

"My sincerest apologies, Inspector."

"A friend of yours?"

Takano continued to smile. "A business associate. He arrived a few days ago from New York City. He represents an American bank that has a branch here in Tokyo. After the Great Earthquake, he secured huge loans for our nation to rebuild."

"Is that so? Please tell them I said 'thanks.'"

The banker laughed. "It was a form of payback, really. When San Francisco was destroyed by an earthquake in 1906, it was the Japanese who sent the most foreign loans for reconstruction. Even the Meiji Emperor donated over 200,000 yen."

"Don't many Japanese live in San Francisco?"

Takano's smile remained frozen. "You doubt the sincerity of our people?"

"Forgive me, Takano-san. Dealing with criminals makes me see shadows everywhere."

Takano led him to the table and gestured for him to take a seat, now as an equal. He pulled out a pack of foreign cigarettes and offered one.

"I smoke Chesterfields, but I also have Lucky Strikes and Pall Malls."

"No thanks," Aizawa said, lighting up a Golden Bat, a subtle reminder to the banker that they were Japanese. They smoked their cigarettes in silence for several moments while eyeing each other through the thin haze.

"Thank you for your bravery out there, Inspector," Takano finally said. "Such an unfortunate incident. It reminds me of when Prime Minister Hamaguchi was shot last year."

"Baron Onishi was also shot," Aizawa said, "just a few days ago."

Takano gave a brief contorted look, like a man in pain.

"Oh, yes. Such strange times we live in."

"Tell me, Takano-san. Why anyone would want to kill you?" Aizawa asked.

"Many people blame the banks for the state of the economy." He shrugged. "We're an easy target."

This would take all day if he went the standard path of Japanese politeness. He could already see how it would end. Takano would deny everything and promise to aid the investigation with the utmost sincerity. However, to outright accuse him of murder seemed unthinkable. After all, he only had a hunch based on what Reiko Watanabe had told him. He took a long drag on his Golden Bat and thought. Would shame work for someone like Isamu Takano?

"That is true," Aizawa said. "But these *soshi* nationalists are so imaginative. They invent wild stories about the *zaibatsu*. They even have one about you, Takano-san."

"Is that so?" Takano asked, taking a puff on his Chesterfield. "What are these fantasies they entertain about me, Inspector?"

"It's ridiculous really," Aizawa continued. "Something about you manipulating General Sakamoto into ordering the Kusanagi Society to assassinate Baron Onishi. After all, you fund the Seiyukai, so it stands to reason that you would want them in power for selfish reasons. At least, that's what these *soshi* say."

Takano stared at his smoldering Chesterfield as if entranced by the curls of smoke. What was he thinking? Maybe the most polite way to have his bodyguards throw him out? Or maybe shame had penetrated this cynical man. International banker or not, Takano was still Japanese.

"Inspector Aizawa," the *zaibatsu* said, returning his attention to him. "I just had a satisfying conversation with my colleague from Wall Street. I feel the Americans have a much better way of discussing business. Direct and to the point. Would you be offended if I suggested we acted like Americans?"

"No."

"Good," Takano said, taking a drag. "Please tell me what you're really thinking."

Under normal circumstances, Aizawa would never directly insult such a powerful man without hard evidence. But they were Americans now.

"I know that you orchestrated the assassination of Baron Onishi for financial gain."

Takano took another drag. "Did I?"

"I also know that your bank has bought millions in American currency. Going off the gold standard will allow you to double your profits when you convert your dollars back into yen."

"You know more about economics than most policemen," Takano said, flashing a hollow smile.

Aizawa forced his own phony smile and took a drag on his cigarette. "Money is the primary motivation for most criminals. Even well-dressed ones like yourself."

Takano frowned and said, "Inspector, I am grateful for your actions today. But I will not allow you to insult my patriotism."

Aizawa scoffed. "You? Patriotic?"

"Yes...everything I did was for Japan," Takano stated without a hint of insincerity. "Tell me, Inspector, how much do you know about the Smoot-Hawley Tariff?"

Aizawa searched his memory for every newspaper article he'd read about the subject. "It's why we're in this depression now. These import taxes are too high, so the Americans aren't buying what we make."

Takano sneered. "Ridiculous! Two fools in America wrote a law to protect their industry, and the world's economy collapses. That's democracy for you."

Aizawa chuckled. "Spoken like a true shadow shogun, Takano-san!"

"A shadow shogun?" Takano scoffed. "You think too highly of me, Inspector. I'm simply a patriot who wants to use his influence to help Japan."

"You own the Seiyukai Party, correct?"

Takano flicked his cigarette ash and said, "I don't own anything. Several *zaibatsu* fund the party, but yes, I'm the largest donor."

"And Prime Minister Inukai?"

Takano pursed his lips. "He takes my advice."

"You mean he takes your orders," Aizawa said.

The banker sighed and stubbed out his Chesterfield. Aizawa took an enormous drag and followed suit.

"Come over here, please," Takano said as he stood up. They walked over to a massive desk, where a beige globe was planted. The banker's thick, weathered hands ran across the sprawling Pacific Ocean until it reached the United States. "What do you see, Inspector?"

"Your palm over America."

"You see just a nation. But it's more than that. It's oil, wheat, tobacco, scrap metal, coal, and cotton. And more importantly, a hundred million consumers." Takano swished the globe back across the Pacific, settling on the tiny string of islands labeled "Japan."

"Now, look at our paltry nation and its worthless colonies, Korea and Taiwan," the banker continued. "What do we produce? Rice and silk. An empire cannot run on food and garments alone."

Aizawa pointed to the vast region of northeast China. "What about Manchuria? Isn't it supposed to be the 'lifeline of our empire?'"

Takano nodded. "True, it does have large quantities of coal and iron ore. But those fools in the Kwantung Army didn't consider how much a military occupation would cost Japan, considering that we're almost bankrupt."

"The Army leadership says Manchuria will pay for itself."

The banker gave the globe a hard spin. "We don't have the money. But we will soon." Takano looked up. "Do you remember the financial panic of 1927?"

"I remember helping with crowd control during all the bank runs."

"That's all it was. One gigantic run on the banks. After the Great Kanto Earthquake, the government issued bonds to prop up unstable banks. But during the spring of 1927, rumors circulated that a bank had failed, and a wave of runs ensued." Takano shook his head. "My bank would have gone under, if not for emergency loans from my American colleague."

Aizawa wondered where this was headed but didn't wish to interrupt a full confession. "You seem to be doing well now," he simply said.

Takano waved his hand. "If we continued our old economic policies, I'd go out of business in a year. The panic scared enough people to return to the gold standard as a way to stabilize the market. That outdated system is what's choking the world economy today. But back in September, while the Kwantung Army started its little adventure in Manchuria, Britain went off gold."

"Why?"

"Without being tied to gold, Britain can print as much money as they want and spend their way out of the depression. It's working. British employment is on the rise."

Economics was out of a police officer's element. The maddened frenzy on the Tokyo Stock Exchange was an affront to any policeman's sense of order. But still, Aizawa remembered what Baron Onishi had said days before.

"Aren't you worried about inflation? Like what happened in Germany?" he asked.

Takano frowned. "I'm more worried about a military occupation of Manchuria bankrupting the nation. Despite our posturing in the League of Nations, Japan is poor and the depression has made us poorer."

Aizawa fixed Takano with an accusing gaze. "And that's why you had Baron Onishi assassinated?"

For several moments, the office was silent aside from the belching stock ticker.

"The man was a relic. A puffed-up *daimyo* lord who still thought it was the Tokugawa Era," Takano said, shaking his head. "His adherence to the gold standard was only because of his family fortune. He cared nothing for common people like us."

Aizawa was taken aback. "Us?"

"We're both commoners," Takano said. "Men who have worked our way up. Too many of the Emperor's advisers have a bias against our class. They favor aloof aristocrats like the honorable Baron."

"I'm sure you can buy yourself a title."

Takano hissed like a tea kettle. "You laugh, but the Japanese Empire was almost handed over to that incompetent fool just because of his family name. Not only would he have remained on the gold standard, dooming millions to the abyss of unemployment, he would have even ended trade with the United States. All because his feelings were hurt."

Aizawa thought back to Baron Onishi's study and remembered the books that all detailed a future American-Japanese war. All the snide comments and warnings took the shape of a dark fortune.

Takano sighed and said, "America and Japan should maintain a symbiotic relationship."

"They give us baseball and we give them silk?"

"A simplification, but in a sense…yes." Takano walked behind his desk and sat. The Emperor's portrait seemed to stare down at them.

"Is that what your friend from Wall Street was here for?" Aizawa asked.

"Partly. Other *zaibatsu* and I have purchased dollars from the bank he represents. The Americans have no intention of going off gold yet." Aizawa was about to speak, but Takano held up a hand. "I can sense your righteous anger now, Inspector. How dare these *zaibatsu*, already bloated with money, make millions while poverty festers in our nation?"

"You said it," Aizawa said, gritting his teeth. "Not me."

"The other *zaibatsu* and I tried to convince Prime Minister Wakatsuki to abandon the gold standard, but that fool wouldn't listen."

Aizawa thought back to the past few days. What was it that had forced Reijiro Wakatsuki to resign as prime minister? Oh yes, one of his cabinet members – Kenzo Adachi – refused to attend cabinet meetings.

"You bribed Adachi-san," Aizawa said flatly.

Takano sighed. "Adachi wanted to start his own political party. Regardless, it forced Wakatsuki's resignation. But that eliminated only one of our problems."

"What was the other?"

"Baron Onishi possibly becoming prime minister. He was unacceptable to many parties...my New York colleague, for instance, since most of our raw materials come from the United States. Onishi's foolish embargo on American goods would have made the depression even worse. He had some ridiculous plan to appeal to the League of Nations and negotiate fairer trade agreements." Takano shook his head in disgust. "America isn't even part of the League! Onishi didn't realize that organization is a fantasy. Our invasion of Manchuria proved what a farce it is."

A valid point. Baron Onishi's faith in the League seemed borderline religious.

"But if the tariff is lifted, then the door will be opened for further exports," Takano continued. "It's only a matter of time. President Hoover is despised by his own people...he'll be out of power soon."

"What does this have to do with Japan?"

Takano gave a proud, knowing smile. "Simply this. We, the hated bankers of Japan, will use the money we've made speculating in American dollars to purchase government bonds. These will not only pay for the occupation of Manchuria, they will also be reinvested in Japanese industry and subsidize exports. Our unemployed masses will go back to work making consumer goods, cheaper and quicker than any other nation. A struggling American family won't care if their textiles, spark plugs, toothbrushes, toys, or teacups have the words 'Made in Japan' on them. And even if the tariff remains, we'll just label our products 'Made in the USA. '"

Aizawa let the words sink in. "In order to get out of the depression, we'll flood American markets with cheap Japanese-made trinkets?"

Takano's face turned downward, almost in a pout. "Not just America, but all of Europe and Asia will buy Japanese goods. Who cares what we're producing, so long as our people get back to work? Have you heard the expression, 'if goods don't cross borders then armies will'? The only real antidote to war is open trade."

"It didn't stop the Manchurian Incident."

Takano scoffed. "The only reason we're in Manchuria is because of trade. We've been in that region for decades, building railroads, farms, and factories. But the Army was fearful that the Chinese might kick us out, or even worse, the Russians might take it over. They were so afraid that our own soldiers faked an attack on the South Manchurian Railway and invaded…the fools."

For some reason, Aizawa never considered that the Imperial Army had lied about its reasons for invading Manchuria. Odd, since he knew of its complicity in the March Incident, its ties to patriotic societies, and, from his own service in the Siberian Expedition, its willingness to exaggerate body counts to impress the press back home. And still, like most Japanese, he couldn't see through the paper screen of war songs and news reports. Some detective he was.

Takano gave a taunting smile. "As you can see, Inspector, my motives were entirely patriotic," he said, reaching for the phone. "Now, if you will excuse me, I have work to do."

No, it couldn't end like this. Not with all the blood that had stained Tokyo. Proper punishment needed to be meted out. Aizawa's fingers slid inside his coat and curled around the Colt pistol. It was a good gun, sturdy and reliable. Now, he'd need it one more time.

Aizawa took aim and said, "Isamu Takano, you're under arrest!"

CHAPTER FORTY-SIX

An oppressive silence filled the office, interrupted only by the chirping stock ticker. Takano backed away from the phone and stared at the pistol with blank eyes. There was no fear in his expression, just cold calculation of the risk in front of him.

"You have no proof," the banker said, reviewing him up and down. "Just the words of a dead man."

Aizawa steadied the pistol. "I can go to your puppets...General Sakamoto and Prime Minister Inukai."

Takano scoffed and leaned forward. "General Sakamoto is indebted to me. A week ago, he came to me wanting to turn some patriotic society that he was secretly funding—"

"The Kusanagi Society?"

"Yes, that's the one. He wanted to turn it into a legitimate political party. It was led by some former Dietman—"

"Masaru Ryusaki."

"Ah, yes. This Ryusaki could draw in more members, mostly unemployed riff-raff but all eligible voters. Instead, I offered General Sakamoto a top position in the Seiyukai. After Inukai, the General would become the next prime minister...providing he gave us an assassin from his Kusanagi Society."

"Makoto Kuroki."

"Whatever his name was, when Ryusaki had chosen him, I arranged the fall of the Wakatsuki cabinet. Someone as vainglorious as Baron Onishi would bask in press conferences, making him an easy target."

"Sorry I spoiled your plans," Aizawa hissed, hoping his contempt showed.

"You were only doing your duty," Takano said. "Regardless, General Sakamoto had the clever idea to bring the Baron to my office while his adjutant waited across the street. Had Baron Onishi agreed to abandon the gold standard, I would have called the assassination off. But as I suspected, he remained firm in his archaic beliefs. Yet somehow, you managed to sneak him out safely. But in the end, everything worked out."

Such aloof arrogance galled Aizawa more than any *soshi* nationalist or yakuza hoodlum. General Sakamoto was a dead end, even if he was still alive.

"And Prime Minister Inukai?"

Takano leaned back in his chair. "You inferred that he takes my orders. Regardless, he's been kept ignorant of much of these machinations."

Aizawa's arm began to ache, but he kept the gun level. "I could go to the press."

"You could, but one word from the Prime Minister's office and whatever editor printed the story would be picked up by the Police. Then he'll cheerfully retract it with sincere apologies."

Aizawa pictured a long line of prime ministers, bought and sold by the *zaibatsu*.

"I don't care if you own the government. It's my duty to the Emperor to uphold the law," Aizawa said, digging into his coat for his handcuffs.

Takano gave a sly smile. "Inspector…who do you think ordered this?"

Aizawa stopped digging. "What do you mean?"

"It was the Emperor who gave his approval to…remove Baron Onishi from the political stage."

"The Baron seemed to think the Emperor wanted him to become prime minister," Aizawa said.

"I'm sure he did," Takano said, rising from his seat. "His Majesty can hold two differing opinions at once. Regardless, I was recently summoned to the Imperial Palace and had an audience with the Emperor himself about financial matters. I told him that Japan could only stand another year of this depression or else there might be a revolution…either from the Left or the Right. He agreed that something drastic needed to be done in order to save the nation."

Aizawa scanned Takano's face for any hint of deceit, but found only a proud sincerity. The banker had fulfilled his own duty to the Emperor, just like the patriot he claimed to be. A sudden tightness took hold of Aizawa's chest. Events and clues aligned with frightening clarity. No wonder Takano had been so casual with his confession. His accomplice sat atop the Chrysanthemum Throne.

The pistol began to lower as Aizawa spat out, "The Emperor...ordered the assassination..."

Takano's face was solemn and stoic. "Not in words, since most of his advisers favored appointing Baron Onishi as prime minister. He was an aristocrat and his criticism of the Army gave the impression he could control further military adventures. Choosing Inukai instead might cause a loss of face in front of his advisers. But the Emperor knew the empire could not weather this depression much longer. He told me to bring about my economic plan...no matter what." Takano lifted his head high and said, "Do you see now, Inspector? We both serve the Emperor...in our own way."

Could the Emperor have predicted all of this bloodshed when he gave his implicit order? Instead of a military dictator, Ryusaki's assassins had installed a shadow shogun who ruled through finance instead of steel. Numbly, Aizawa looked up at the portrait. His Imperial Majesty, the Son of Heaven, was no longer there. He'd been replaced by a bespectacled little man wearing a garish uniform.

A sense of shame overwhelmed Aizawa. Such dangerous thinking was illegal. But he couldn't have been the first police officer to see who was really sitting upon the Chrysanthemum Throne. *Giri,* his duty, had been revealed as a paper screen behind which the real criminals hid. *Ninjo* stepped in and demanded surrender. He looked down. The automatic hung limply at his side, impotent and harmless.

"Guards!" Takano cried.

Aizawa spun around. The bodyguards burst into the office and took massive strides toward him. Aizawa raised the gun, but one of the sumo slapped it away with a heavy swat. The other closed in from behind and imprisoned him with a suffocating bear hug. The sumo swung him back to face the banker.

"I admire your fighting spirit, Inspector," Takano said. "But the nation needs me. I will have to be more cautious in case these foolish *soshi* try again. Like the old saying goes, 'In a moment of victory, tighten your helmet straps.'"

Aizawa squirmed, but it was no use. Unlike with the assassin from earlier, the sumo had a firm grip this time. Each breath grew shorter and stabbed like a dagger.

"Perhaps you'd be interested in becoming a bodyguard? I'll need more security in the future." A sly smile curled Takano's thin lips. "Do you need time to consider?"

Aizawa strained against the sumo's hold but it was no use. His fingers grew numb and breaths became weak gasps.

Takano's mouth moved again, but there was no sound. Aizawa couldn't hear anymore or feel anything. He glanced down. His arms hung like limp jellyfish tentacles. The office grew fuzzy. Darkness closed in and turned out the lights.

CHAPTER FORTY-SEVEN

As always, Asakusa vibrated with life. The hawking merchants, the tattooed yakuza, and clattering rickshaws were out in full force today. A line of men stretched out the door of an employment agency, all of whom glared at Reiko and Masaru as they walked past. But Reiko barely noticed any of them. Instead, she focused on how to warn Aizawa. The most probable way was to excuse herself after the first bottle of booze ran out and then call Aizawa from the nearest phone booth. After all, it had worked before.

"Is something wrong?" Masaru asked.

Reiko looked over at him, still in his *mobo* outfit.

"I'm just tired," she said.

Thankfully, he'd helped her don her geisha regalia once again. With tender fingers, he repainted her face, tied her *obi* belt, and adjusted her *shimada* wig. He was the old Masaru again, kind-hearted and attentive. The poor fool. He didn't suspect that his loyal mistress was a poison woman pointing a dagger at his throat.

As they walked, Reiko stayed three steps behind as tradition dictated. Months before, they flouted convention even further by walking around Ginza arm and arm and even stole an occasional kiss in public. She shook her head. Better not to remember those days. It would make what she had to do all the more painful.

The Dragonfly Tea House came into view, and they paused in front of the entrance.

"Reiko, is something wrong?"

"Nothing's wrong," she said with a smile. "I promise."

Masaru's face twisted into a cruel, accusing mask. "Reiko, this is your last chance to tell me. Is there something wrong?"

No. He couldn't know anything. Or could he? She tried to speak, but no words came. She wanted to run but knew she couldn't get very far in this kimono. Was this why he made her play geisha again? Masaru slid the door open and shoved her into the tea house with a forceful push. A horrible stench clawed at her nose. She gagged and covered her mouth. It was even worse than the carts of night soil that carried the shit of Tokyo far away. She'd smelled that same stench for days after the Great Earthquake. Rotting flesh.

Masaru's hands seized her shoulders and guided her into the main room. There were others in there, but all she could focus on was a headless body that lay on the floor. A brown stain of dried blood collected underneath the severed head of General Sakamoto, mouth agape in an eternal scream.

Reiko soon found herself on the floor beside the body, supported by her hands and knees. Despite the cold, sweat oozed down her neck. She wanted to scream, but her throat was dry. Still reeling, she managed to lift her gaze upward to take in the rest of the room. Kneeling in front of the Mount Fuji wall scroll, were some of the patriots she'd entertained last night, including Makoto Kuroki. And there, kneeling in the center, like a nightmare in daylight, was Lieutenant Nakajima.

She turned back to Masaru, now blocking the exit. His angry stare seemed to drill into her skull and left her mind hollow.

"What do you have to report?" Masaru asked, shifting his attention to his men.

One of the patriots slid a newspaper in front of Reiko. It was a special morning edition of the *Asahi Shimbun* with the headline: "Madman Gunned Down In Marunouchi!" Each breath she took grew tighter than the last.

"Just hit the newsstands," the *soshi* said with a sneer.

Masaru snatched up the newspaper and scanned it.

"Interesting, don't you think, Reiko?" He asked, tucking the newspaper under his arm. "Inspector Aizawa was there just in time to protect Takano. He also prevented Baron

Onishi's assassination...twice! *And* he discovered where I lived. How strange. I suppose he must have an informant in our group." His lips curled into a sadistic smirk. "Who do you think it is?"

A pitiful whimper escaped her throat. "Masaru…"

"I really didn't know who to believe," he said as his smirk turned into a bitter snarl. "Lieutenant Nakajima suggested that you might be the traitor, but I had to be sure. So we hatched a little trap. I made you aware of Kuroki's orders to kill Takano to see if the information would get back to Aizawa. But unknown to you, I sent another assassin, just in case."

Reiko swallowed. That explained why Nakajima had to talk to Masaru in private last night. She cursed herself for being so naïve.

"Masaru…please…"

"But Aizawa still ruined everything. Just like before." He sank to his knees and gripped her shoulders. "I didn't want to believe it was you. I prayed the whole way over here that Takano would be dead and you really would entertain my men. Then…we could have been married." His eyes flickered with warmth before icing back over. "Just tell me one thing. Did Aizawa pay you?"

"No..."

Masaru took a deep breath and stood. "If you did it for money, your betrayal would be unforgivable. At least your motives were sincere."

"Masaru…please, I just wanted our old life back. Before," she spun and pointed at that devil soldier, "before *he* came along and ruined everything!"

She turned back to Masaru for help but he paid her no attention.

"Patriots of the Kusanagi Society! The war against corruption and evil has begun," Masaru said. "We will need weapons for coming battles. My family's estate in Roppongi has the weapons we will need for the battle ahead."

The patriots filtered by, who each shot her brief, hateful glares as they exited the tea house. But Hajime Nakajima stayed put, clutching his saber. When Masaru turned to follow his men, Reiko's arms flailed out and locked around his leg.

"Please, Masaru! Have mercy! If you love me, don't leave me here with him!"

Her moans filled the tea house like a wounded animal. Masaru knelt down and took her by the shoulders, steadying her shaking frame.

"Darling," he said in English with a mournful look. "It's *because* I love you that I'm leaving you here with Lieutenant Nakajima. Only he can rehabilitate you."

The bastard. His proposal, the 'I love you', and the romantic dance; all a charade to dope her up so she'd be too numb to see the dagger pointed right at *her* throat. Masaru stood and, without a second glance, walked out.

Reiko placed a hand over her mouth to muffle her cries and steeled herself for what was coming. If she really was going to die, she'd deny Nakajima the pleasure of slaughtering a whimpering child. He'd have to stick his saber through the belly of a poison woman.

CHAPTER FORTY-EIGHT

Still on her knees, Reiko turned around to face him. Kneeling with erect military posture, Lieutenant Nakajima stared back with transparent contempt.

"Take a good look, Watanabe-zan," he said, gesturing to the headless corpse that once was General Sakamoto. "The General's death was with honor. He saved face through *seppuku*. How will you die?"

"You tell me."

He curled his upper lip. "That depends on you. I promised Ryusaki-zensei to rehabilitate you through purity and patriotism. The Police sometimes turn Communists into honorable men through this method, so perhaps there is hope for you, Watanabe-zan. Tell me, how old are you?"

Bastard. He was just toying with her now. "I'm twenty-four, Nakajima-san. And you?"

"Twenty-two. That means you're old enough to remember the Rice Riots of 1918…"

"Around that time, I was just learning how to use a thread and needle."

"Then let me remind you. The war in Europe was almost over. Britain, France, America, and Japan all dispatched troops to Ziberia in an effort to strangle the Bolshevik Revolution in its cradle. However, thanks to unscrupulous stock traders in Marunouchi, rice prices rose to obscene amounts."

"Yes, I remember people marching in the streets while I went to bed hungry."

Nakajima's fingers clutched the saber handle. "A pampered city girl complains of hunger? You know nothing of it! Famine plagues my family and the entire Tohoku region as we speak! Hunger is a constant pain, like a dagger slowly cutting into your stomach. It is the torture of having to plant, harvest, and stare dumbly at rice you are unable to eat since it will hurt profits. Did you ever eat bark from trees or gorge yourself on dried crickets?"

The nerve of that bastard. Did he actually expect sympathy from her? No, she wouldn't let herself be shamed by *him*.

"You think your childhood was harsh?" she snapped. "Imagine that every minute you were out of school, your parents made you sew pretty kimonos and stockings that you could never wear. Imagine being beaten for every misaligned seam or tear. Then, picture your entire life collapsing under the greatest earthquake in history and seeing your hometown burnt to a cinder." She swallowed hard. "Your suffering is not unique."

Nakajima remained still for several moments, except for a trembling bottom lip. "I will not take such disrespect from…from—"

"From what? A geisha? A *moga*? A woman? You're pathetic. Even Masaru understands you."

The trembling stopped. He flashed a confused expression. "What do you mean?"'

"You hate women. That's why you've never been with one." She looked him over. "You're just a boy, wearing a man's clothes."

For the first time, Hajime Nakajima removed that mask of contempt and looked at her with a human face.

"You misjudge," he said. "I am fighting for the men *and* women of Japan. Our sisters groan under the heel of poverty even louder than men. I don't doubt your childhood was a collection of miseries, but imagine yourself sold by your own parents to the brothels after the rice harvest failed to bring in enough money."

She kept quiet. Better not to poke a barking dog.

"It was during the Rice Riots when they took my older sister Chitose away from us," Nakajima continued. "A man from Tokyo came to our rice farm, looking for country girls to fill the Yoshiwara brothels. Chitose was nineteen at the time, but still a virgin, so she fetched a good price. With the money she was sold for, we were able to pay the rest of the year's rent. She actually bowed and thanked my parents for giving her a chance to honor the family."

Nakajima shook his head.

"The brave little fool," he said with a whimper. "Of course, my parents couldn't part with my older brother or I. We were needed for the next year's crop. At the time, I was jealous of her for having left. Long summers of toil passed. I begged the gods to let me drown in those never-ending paddy fields."

Nakajima released a morose sigh as his head drooped.

"But I escaped years later. As a boy, I read countless novels about the wars against China and Russia. Ah, how I longed for the opportunity to fight for the Emperor! Even the battlefield was more appealing than life in the rice paddies. At least there my death would mean something.

"I studied and was accepted into the Imperial Army Academy, here in Tokyo. It was over a year ago, right before I graduated, when I finally tracked my sister down. Not to a brothel in Yoshiwara, but to an insane asylum." He shook his head. "She was wrapped up in a straightjacket like a fly in a spider web. Her face was an enormous open sore. Syphilis had rotted her mind. This was the fate of my older sister and thousands of other women. Fortunately, the gods had mercy and ended her wretched existence a month later."

He looked up. His eyes were glassy and distant, sending waves of terror down Reiko's spine.

"Soon after, I read Ryusaki-zensei's book. Not just I, but all my brother officers studied it from cover to cover. It became clear to us that something drastic needed to be done to save the nation. So we enlisted Ryusaki-zensei to our cause." He sighed. "But in March, Inspector Aizawa ruined our plans..."

"So you tried again."

"Yes, without any civilians that time. But the October plot failed too. I knew we had to enlist Ryusaki-zensei once more. Imagine my disgust when I found him in the arms of a...*moga*." He curled his upper lip at the word.

"I felt the same way when I first saw you."

Nakajima scoffed. "Ryusaki-zensei and I are swords to be used by the Emperor's divine hand. Sex, individualism, luxury, and frivolity...these are all corrosives that dull our blade. *You* embody all of these evils, Watanabe-zan."

Under normal circumstances, she'd take that as a compliment. But now such accusations were tantamount to a death sentence. She kept kneeling with elegant poise, determined to die in a refined position. Nakajima removed his grip from the saber and stretched across the room, running his fingers down her face. The sweep was firm, peeling off the face paint until stopping at her bottom lip. White paint clung to his fingertips and he smeared it across the floor.

"I have always seen past your disguise...but I had to convince Ryusaki-zensei first," he continued, rubbing his fingers together. "At first, we tried to enlist Superintendent Shimura to order Aizawa into a trap...but he declined and had to be...disposed of. So now, you'll have to be his replacement."

A chill swept over her, realizing her purpose as bait for Inspector Aizawa.

"But I don't hate you...and neither does Ryusaki-zensei." Nakajima gestured to the butchered meat across the room. "I didn't hate General Zakamoto either. I hate the evil you both represent."

Nausea seized Reiko's stomach. Partly from fear, partly from the stench of Sakamoto's bloated husk, but mostly from humiliation. Some spy she'd been. Taken in by a performance and sweet words. She'd have to be more skeptical in her next life.

Nakajima donned his service cap and stood up. That brown uniform had always made him look like a walking wall of shit, but now it radiated the ferocity of a stampeding horse.

"Get up," he said, grabbing her collar. "Your rehabilitation begins now."

Had General Sakamoto been "rehabilitated" before or after he lost his head? With shaking legs, she rose and steadied herself with a prayer. But one glance at that headless corpse on the floor told her that none of the gods could save her now.

CHAPTER FORTY-NINE

"Wake up, Inspector."

The words cut through the dark waves where Aizawa lay submerged. Deeper and deeper they plunged, wrapping around his body and raised him up to the surface.

Aizawa opened his eyes and looked out a car window. The proud structure of the Metropolitan Police Headquarters stood across the street. A *junsa* holding a formidable *keijo* stick stood guard outside. Morning sunlight cast a bright glare on the snowy sidewalks, forcing him to turn away. In the front seat were the two sumo bodyguards, staring back with amused grins. No doubt they had a good laugh out of almost crushing his insides. Aizawa's entire body was still numb but soon prickled with sensation. Once feeling had returned to his arms, he felt inside his coat for the Colt and the Nagant.

"Looking for these?" the sumo in the passenger seat asked, holding both guns up by their barrels. "Don't worry, we'll give them back. After all, what would a police inspector be without his gun?"

"A private detective," Aizawa groaned, rubbing his temple. How long had he been out? He checked his wristwatch: half past noon.

"You should consider Takano-san's offer. He pays very well."

"I'll bet," Aizawa said.

"Takano-san is an honorable man," the driver sumo said. "He spared your life out of gratitude for saving his."

"Tell him I said 'thanks.'"

The two sumo looked at each other with smug grins before tossing the guns out the window.

"Have fun playing hero, Inspector."

Aizawa opened the door and hopped out. The car sped off, merging into the steady flow of traffic. With a sigh, he bent down and scooped up the pistols. After tucking them back into his coat, he started across the street. Hopefully, the *junsa* standing guard hadn't seen him get tossed out on the curb like a drunk.

Aizawa entered Metropolitan Police Headquarters and paused to absorb the warmth. Once defrosted, he started for the elevator. A pair of conversing *junsas* walked by and gave half-hearted salutes. Another inspector passed without acknowledgment. He'd been losing face ever since the arrest of Masaru Ryusaki had been reversed back in March. The past few days had dealt a death blow to his status. Joji Shimura's once-favorite pupil was now the most unpopular boy in class. He needed to regroup in the safety of his own office.

Aizawa entered the elevator and took it to the third floor. Walking out, he caught the attention of two detectives, staring at him with eyes colder than anything he'd felt outside.

"Hey, Aizawa-san," one called out from behind a desk, overcrowded from files. "Come here."

Aizawa was all too aware that these detectives were both senior men who resented his rapid rise through the ranks and, above all else, his private office. A small, vocal part of him wanted to ignore their summons, but he started toward them anyway. After all, he was still just a rookie compared to these hardened veterans and protocol demanded appropriate subordination. Aizawa had always worn his duty like a uniform but now it felt more like a dog collar around his throat. Nevertheless, he presented himself with a low, supplicating bow.

"Superintendent Shimura is dead," one of the senior detectives said.

Aizawa's throat and fists tightened. "W-what happened?"

"He was found murdered in his *machiya* this morning. Someone nearly cut him in half. I'm sorry...I know you and he used to be close."

The room felt colder and emptier. Aizawa wanted to sit down but maintained his poise. An image of Masaru Ryusaki holding a bloody *katana* entered his mind. Their private war had claimed yet another casualty.

"It's Ryusaki...it has to be him," Aizawa said.

"Who?"

"Masaru Ryusaki..."

"Oh yes, that playboy with the little *moga* girlfriend. We heard about how you tried to pin Baron Onishi's assassination on him."

"It is Ryusaki! I can prove it," Aizawa said, slamming his fist on the desk. The other detective gave a skeptical grunt.

"Focus on your own case, Inspector. We'll solve this one. Congratulations on saving that banker today."

Aizawa's eyes widened.

"Oh yes, one of the *junsas* mentioned it to us," the senior detective said. "If only you could have saved Baron Onishi and Sergeant Murayama as well..."

Aizawa wanted to crawl deep inside his overcoat. The shame couldn't reach him there. Instead, he turned around and continued down the hall. There was no time for self-pity.

Aizawa closed the office door behind him. Turning to the framed newspaper on the wall, tears swarmed around his eyes as he read its headline over and over – "Inspectors Shimura and Aizawa Raid Yakuza Gambling Den!" He wiped them clean and returned to his desk, wondering what to do next. Visit a temple and pray for the soul of Joji Shimura? He'd have to pray for Sergeant Murayama and the Onishis too. No, not yet. Ryusaki was his first priority. But even if he managed to apprehend Ryusaki...then what? Takano and his co-conspirators had won. Aizawa finally understood how insignificant his duty was. Still, he was bound to follow it, like a wind-up toy soldier marching toward the edge of the table.

A shrill telephone ring cut through the silence.

"Inspector Aizawa," he answered.

Reiko's worried voice broke through. "It's me."

That damn fool.

"Reiko-san, I told you not to call here anymore."

"Just listen. Masaru's planning something even worse than what we thought. I found out only moments ago and escaped with my life."

"What are you talking about?"

"No time to explain. I'm on the run."

"What happened?"

"There's no time to explain! I have to keep moving."

"Meet me at my *nagaya* and—"

"No! Masaru's men might follow me there! Meet me at Ueno Park after sundown. Around nine o'clock. I'll be near the statue of Takamori Saigo."

"Reiko-san, I—"

The line went dead. Aizawa clicked the receiver down as a typhoon of thoughts swirled in his head. Another death on his shoulders was more than he could bear. He'd see Reiko Watanabe tonight but only to tell her to leave town. He looked at his watch. Almost one o'clock. He'd have to return to Marunouchi and retrieve Baron Onishi's Roll-Royce if he wanted to be at Ueno Park at nine. From there, he'd drive Reiko to Tokyo Station, allowing her to escape from this city of shadows forever.

CHAPTER FIFTY

Ueno Park was ugly in the daytime, but it possessed an eerie stillness after dark, like a frosted nightmare. Aizawa parked the Rolls-Royce near the south entrance and dashed up the flight of stairs, powdered with snow. Reaching the top, he scanned the meeting square for Reiko Watanabe. However, there was only the statue of Takamori Saigo and his faithful dog, glowing a pale bluish-green in the electric light of a nearby lamppost.

In fact, the only person in sight was a sleeping tramp on a nearby bench, blanketed by a newspaper. Pitiful sights like this always reminded Aizawa that no matter how low you fell, there was always somebody lower.

Aizawa scanned the path for any oncoming figure. Had Ryusaki discovered her? He remembered his promise from last night with a slight feeling of shame.

'Watanabe-san, I swear that I will protect you.'

The best way to protect Reiko now was to get her out of town. Aizawa checked his watch again. Ten after nine. Where was she?

The tramp stirred underneath an issue of the *Asahi Shimbun* but kept his face covered. Walking closer, Aizawa could make out the words more clearly. It was a special morning edition with the headline "Madman Gunned Down in Marunouchi!" Those fools at the *Asahi* went ahead and ran the story anyway. Ryusaki had probably read this over his morning tea and realized there was an informant within the Kusanagi Society. All of a sudden, Reiko's desperate pleas over the telephone sounded mechanical and forced.

He'd been lured into a trap. Aizawa whipped out his Colt automatic and began a quick retreat back to the staircase. Before he could reach it, a samurai in full armor stepped out of the darkness and blocked his path. Like a ghost from the

Tokugawa Era, he clutched a full-sized *katana* like an executioner's blade. Armored in red-and-black lacquer and a metal breastplate, he looked like a demon ready for the battlefield. Two horns jutted out of a black helmet that shadowed his face. But there was no mistaking his true identity. Only someone as vainglorious as Masaru Ryusaki could orchestrate this.

Aizawa stood in numb disbelief for several moments before the samurai gave a guttural cry and charged. The night air was quiet except for the incessant clanking of armor. Instinct took control and rolled Aizawa out of the way just as Ryusaki swung his sword. Tumbling to the side, Aizawa straightened himself up and saw Ryusaki stumble a few steps, but he soon steadied himself for another attack.

Aizawa aimed his gun and fired three quick shots. The bullets connected and forced Ryusaki back, but not enough to stop his advance. Wearing that armor didn't seem so vainglorious now, since it also doubled as a bulletproof vest. Aizawa steadied the pistol again but before he could fire, out of his peripheral, he saw the tramp rise from the bench and leap toward him. They both slammed against the cold pavement, leaving Aizawa out of breath.

Seeing him up close, Aizawa recognized this "tramp" as one of the seven founding members of the Kusanagi Society. Aizawa's arms were soon pinned to the ground as Makoto Kuroki sprang forth from the shrubbery and stood over him with a taunting grin.

"Looks like you're the one under arrest now, Inspector," he said before taking both the Colt from Aizawa's shoulder holster and the Nagant from his waistband.

Kuroki shoved the weapons into his coat and helped the tramp hoist Aizawa off of the ground. With firm grips, they locked Aizawa's arms at his sides. Five other *soshi* stepped out of the shadows and shrubbery, each clutching a *wakizashi* short sword, forming a wall of steel and blocking the exit to the staircase. Fitting that Ryusaki would enact his revenge before the statue of the disgruntled samurai who plunged Japan into a civil war.

Aizawa struggled against Kuroki and the tramp's grip, to no avail. "You put on a costume just to kill me?" he called out.

"Oh, it's no costume," Ryusaki said. "This is the armor of the Ryusaki family, worn for generations into battle. But it's more than that. It is the uniform of purity and patriotism!"

"Not to mention bulletproof. Isn't that the same armor you wore to threaten your fellow Dietmen?"

Ryusaki laughed. "Arrogant to the end! I'm actually glad that you dodged my blade just now. Now, each of my men can slice off a piece of you…before I end your miserable life with one quick stroke."

With their short swords glinting in the moonlight, the five *soshi* began advancing. Aizawa twisted and turned but couldn't break loose. Part of him wanted to stick his neck out and be done with it. But another, more vocal part reminded him that this was Masaru Ryusaki he was dealing with. If that bastard wanted him dead, he'd have to hack him to pieces while he fought to the end.

Aizawa twisted and turned but still couldn't break loose. Despite being a head taller, these two *soshi* held him like a vice. Only his hands remained free and with one motion, Aizawa grabbed the back of his captor's kneecaps, dug his fingers into vulnerable pressure points, and slammed the entirety of his weight backward.

Kuroki and the tramp buckled and hit the ground hard, cushioning his fall. Still atop of them, Aizawa reached over to Kuroki, searching for the pistols. The tramp let out a strained groan, but Kuroki recovered quickly and pushed Aizawa off before he could recover the guns. The other five *soshi* rushed toward them, holding their *wakizashi* swords high in a battlefield charge.

There was no other option but to make a break for it and lose them inside Ueno Park. Aizawa spun around and dashed northward, his stride quickening with every step. Behind him, a symphony of laughter arose.

"Run Inspector!" Ryusaki called out. "Run for your life!"

CHAPTER FIFTY-ONE

Aizawa ran north, stealing quick glances behind him. Ryusaki and his *soshi* hadn't caught up yet. Not that it mattered. In a few minutes he'd be able to call for backup and end this war forever. Reiko Watanabe entered his mind. First as a *moga*, then as a geisha, and finally as a severed head. Hopefully, Ryusaki's arrest would be a token of penance.

He soon passed Kiyomizu Temple on the left and the baseball field approached on his right. The *koban* police box appeared in the distance, a tiny outpost for law and order. There he could call for reinforcements and haul Ryusaki out of Ueno Park like a rat in a cage. He dashed across the deserted baseball field and past the dugout with neatly stacked bats, glancing to and fro for any oncoming *soshi*. Still nothing.

Aizawa soon reached the *koban* and opened the door. A young *junsa*, sitting behind a tiny desk, stared back at him. Aizawa leaned against the door for several moments, drawing in huge breaths to steady himself. The *junsa* stood and looked him over.

"You're Inspector Aizawa, right?"

Aizawa nodded and gasped for air. After licking his dry, cold lips, he choked out, "Call Police Headquarters…tell them Masaru Ryusaki…is here…"

The *junsa* nodded but did nothing.

Aizawa walked toward the desk and asked, "Didn't you hear me?"

The *junsa's* eyes narrowed as he drew his saber. Only too late did Aizawa realize that the Kusanagi Society had gained another member.

"Does your duty mean nothing?" Aizawa asked, edging backward to the door. The *junsa* stepped around the desk, sword in hand.

"My duty is to rid the Metropolitan Police of corrupt careerists like you, Inspector. My duty is to the New Japan!"

As the *junsa* drew closer, Aizawa retreated out the door and back into the bitter night. Moonlight illuminated the snowy ground, revealing several elongated shadows rushing toward him. The *soshi* were closing in quick. He ran westward, cursing himself for being so careless. No wonder, Ryusaki had lured him here. All of Ueno Park was his enemy now.

Aizawa didn't look back, but the *junsa's* footsteps crunched behind him. So much for calling in reinforcements. Ueno Zoo soon came into view, offering more places to hide. He climbed the paltry gate and hopped the turnstile. The zoo was mostly asleep, but the few animals that were awake followed him in silence with curious, stalking eyes.

Passing the rhinoceros exhibit, he still hadn't come across a single employee or watchman. Those underpaid zookeepers were probably kept away by bribes, not that he could fault them in this depression. Aizawa moved past a yellow-eyed lion, who watched silently from inside its cage. Indecipherable conversations drew nearer, confirming that the *soshi* were now inside the zoo. Several creatures began to stir from the intrusion, filling the chilly night air with shrieks, growls, and caws.

The background chattering grew louder, and Aizawa ducked behind some nearby shrubbery.

"Look around the rhinoceros enclosure! I'll check the lion cage!" Kuroki ordered.

From behind the leaves and branches, Aizawa saw Kuroki – holding the Colt automatic – step in front of the caged lion and gawked at the beast. As if sensing easy prey, the animal roared, causing Kuroki to stumble and back up. Now would be the only chance Aizawa had to take his weapon back.

Aizawa sprang up and ran straight toward the startled Kuroki. Shifting his entire weight to his shoulder, he slammed the little bastard against the cage bars, sending the pistol flying into the air.

The lion watched them struggle in silence, swishing its tail back and forth like a ticking clock. Kuroki seemed energized with fear and fought like a demon, flailing and striking out at anything he could. Somehow, he managed to land a heavy punch against Aizawa's face and sent him tumbling backward.

How could such a little man hit so hard? Suddenly, Aizawa remembered the gun. Kuroki dashed past in a blur and snatched it up. There was no other choice but to run for it. Ignoring his stinging cheek, Aizawa turned and ran. He made his way past the rhinoceros exhibit, hopped the gate, and was soon out of Ueno Zoo and back into the park proper.

Pausing for a moment, he sucked in as much air as he could. In the distance, Kuroki's harsh commands chattered away like a machine gun. The *soshi* were regrouping. There were eight of them now, not including Ryusaki. That *junsa* probably wouldn't be the only surprise he'd encounter. Every park exit might be guarded by an armed *soshi*.

In that case, he needed a weapon. The baseball bats he saw earlier might work. He started running again, retracing his steps from before. Soon, the baseball field appeared and Aizawa headed straight for the dugout. Several wooden bats were lined up for the next round of players in typical Japanese courtesy. Grabbing one, Aizawa took up a defensive position outside of the dugout. Two *soshi* were closing in from opposite outfields.

As they neared, their features came into focus. On his right was the tramp from earlier, brandishing a shimmering *wakizashi* short sword. From the left came the *junsa*, holding his saber. He sized the two *soshi* up before planning an attack. Those tin swords issued to *junsas* were anything but sharp, at least compared to a *wakizashi*. Aizawa gripped the baseball bat and rushed left. Even if the attack failed, beating this traitorous police officer would at least give him some satisfaction.

The *junsa* raised the sword for a killing, blow but Aizawa caught it with the bat. The blade lodged deep inside the wood, and with one circular twist, the *junsa* was disarmed. Aizawa jerked the bat again, sending the blade spinning out and into the distance. He followed up and swung the baseball bat sideways, landing a shattering blow across the *junsa's* face, filling the night air with a loud crunch. Hitting the ground, the *junsa* gave a few violent twitches before releasing a gurgling death rattle.

There was still the other *soshi* to contend with. Aizawa turned and gripped the bat tighter, but the tramp stood off to the side, deferring to Masaru Ryusaki, still encased in that demonic armor. Aizawa tried to reassure himself that he was only facing a madman in a costume, but the centuries blurred until there was only samurai and peasant. Ryusaki pointed his *katana* straight at Aizawa, like an accusation for an unforgivable crime and charged forward.

Plumes of snow and dirt kicked up from behind Ryusaki. Aizawa spun around and ran toward the shrubbery at the edge of the baseball field. Sprinting into the thicket, Aizawa searched for a suitable hiding spot. But the only foliage were snow-encrusted shrubs that barely came up to his knees. He glanced over his outfit: black overcoat, black fedora, black suit. An easy target in this snowy landscape.

Only the skeletal, bare trees offered cover. Aizawa ducked behind one and cooled his burning lungs with deep inhales of crisp air. Crunching snow cut through the air. He tightened his jaw and held his breath. There were several footsteps echoing around him, in different rhythms and beats. He kept himself pressed against the tree, waiting for the moment to strike.

A glinting sword came into view on his left, followed by the ragged figure of the tramp. Like a searchlight, his head swung to the left, then to the right. Aizawa slammed the baseball bat hard into the *soshi's* gut. The tramp dropped his sword and sank to his knees, gasping for air, allowing Aizawa to bend down and grab the *wakizashi*.

Clanking armor rang out rhythmically like war drums. Aizawa looked up and zeroed in on Ryusaki heading straight toward him, *katana* raised for the kill. He managed to bring the *wakizashi* up in defense and caught the incoming blade halfway.

Aizawa threw what strength remained into holding the *katana* at bay. Every muscle and tendon strained in agony. Sheer exhaustion should have overtaken him by now, but a deep fighting spirit had been ignited and was kindled with every near miss and escape.

Ryusaki's face blazed with the same fighting spirit, coupled with a hate and bitterness that had been growing since March. Aizawa wasn't a man who asked the gods for much, but now he begged for help. The Onishis, Sergeant Murayama, Superintendent Shimura, and now Reiko Watanabe filled his mind. The fire inside him grew with every passing corpse.

Somehow, he summoned enough strength to disengage from the *katana*. But the jerking movement also sent the *wakizashi* somersaulting out of his hands and into the darkness. Still clutching his own sword, Ryusaki stumbled backward, offset from the cumbersome armor. He soon steadied himself and resumed his advance, going from a turtle on its back to an oncoming tank within moments. There were also the other *soshi*, who'd finally spotted him and now rushed in like vultures.

Aizawa turned and ran. Every one of his crunching footsteps was amplified with four or five more behind him. After several yards, he came out of the foliage and saw the statue of Takamori Saigo, glowing a murky green underneath the lampposts.

Bolting around the statue, his peripheral caught a stream of *soshi*. Ryusaki led his men like an army of devils escaping from a haunted forest. Aizawa dashed down the steps, almost slipping on the wet, powdery snow. The *soshi* poured down the staircase after him with Ryusaki leading the charge.

Aizawa yanked open the door to the Rolls-Royce and started the engine. The automobile roared to life. He flipped on the headlights and hit the gas, but a heavy figure slammed onto the hood, almost jerking Aizawa out of his seat. Ryusaki held onto the speeding car with one hand while the other clutched his *katana*, angling for another try at impalement.

With a shrill cry of *"Tenchu!"* he drove the sword through the front window. The blade missed Aizawa, but lodged itself into the leather upholstered seat right above his shoulder. Shards of glass splattered all over like glistening rain.

Ryusaki slid the *katana* out and repositioned himself for another strike. He wouldn't miss this time. Aizawa slammed on the brakes. A thin glaze of ice caused the car to fishtail, flinging Ryusaki off the hood. In the rearview mirror, Aizawa saw him catapult off the car and slam against the road with clanking thuds. Turning the steering wheel hard finally broke the spin and the Rolls-Royce came to a jarring halt.

Aizawa looked back and found Ryusaki lying off to the side, immobile and hopefully dead. What remained of his samurai armor was chipped, twisted, and cracked open, as if someone had stomped on an enormous insect. He was soon surrounded by his loyal *soshi*, looking like men in mourning. All except for Makoto Kuroki, who took aim and opened fire at the Rolls-Royce.

A gunshot tore through the back window and shattered what remained of the front. The cold night wind hit him with full force, making him even more alert. Aizawa hit the gas and sped forward. Behind him, the Kusanagi Society shrank into specks, like nightmares banished by the dawn.

CHAPTER FIFTY-TWO

After a call to Headquarters, Aizawa returned to Ueno Park an hour later with a squad of *junsas*. They fanned out with flashlights, but Aizawa knew the Kusanagi Society were long gone by now.

A senior *junsa* stayed behind and took notes.

"How many *soshi* were there, Inspector?"

"Seven…and Masaru Ryusaki. He's the leader."

The *junsa* nodded, writing on his notepad. "We'll put out a bulletin to arrest on sight."

"Try Reiko Watanabe's apartment in Asakusa," Aizawa said before giving the address. He shuddered, picturing a butchered body lying underneath those posters of Louise Brooks and Anna May Wong. Or maybe she was lying at the bottom of the Sumida River like a yakuza hit.

"His mistress?"

Aizawa nodded. "Your men will find one of our own in there…"

"A police officer?"

"Yes. He worked for Ryusaki. I had no choice…"

The *junsa* sucked air between his teeth but said nothing. After all, it wasn't every day an inspector confessed to killing a fellow policeman. Aizawa dreaded the inevitable meeting with an inquiry board almost as much as another confrontation with the Kusanagi Society.

"Do you need anything else?" Aizawa asked.

"No, sir. We'll notify you if anything is found here or at Watanabe-san's apartment." The *junsa* snapped his notebook shut and gave a salute.

Aizawa nodded and returned to the Rolls-Royce, hoping that it wouldn't break down on the ride back to his *nagaya*. Fatigue gnawed at his muscles and left him exhausted. He didn't know what his next course of action should be but for now, the only thought that dominated his mind was sleep. He started the car and sped off into the night.

*****

It was well past midnight when Aizawa parked the Rolls-Royce and returned to his *nagaya* row house. A bleak future played out in his mind. Tomorrow, he would be summoned before an inquiry board and dismissed. Baron Onishi was dead, and so was his informant, both of whom he'd sworn to protect. And now he'd even killed a police officer. They'd probably blame him for Superintendent Shimura's death too. On top of everything, he'd lost his pistol, perhaps for good. Some police officers committed suicide over the shame of losing their firearms. However, all of these failures could have been forgiven if only he had brought Masaru Ryusaki to justice.

After his disgrace, Kenji Aizawa would probably be drafted into the army of Tokyo's unemployed, drifting from one menial job to the next for the rest of his days. But suicide wasn't in his future, no matter how bleak. He'd deny Ryusaki that victory.

But for now, his body yearned for sleep. One last rest before the deluge. Aizawa entered the *nagaya* and removed his shoes, caked with powdery snow. He slid open the *shoji* door and fumbled for the overhead light. Despite his grogginess, he felt a trace of icy water seeping into his socks. Someone else was there. He grasped the chain and pulled.

The room flooded with light and Aizawa spun around, searching for the intruder. A blurry figure appeared in his peripheral and lashed out like a snake, striking Aizawa hard against the base of his neck. A deafening crack filled the *nagaya* and Aizawa's knees buckled. He sank to the floor as darkness smothered him.

*****

"Kenji-onisan, are you okay?"

He glanced over to Tokiko Aizawa and smiled. It had been years since he'd been called *onisan*, big brother. She knelt beside him, wearing a summer kimono and cutting a plump watermelon into slices. Strangely enough, they were in his childhood *machiya*, somehow standing again. How odd. Aizawa looked himself over. Gone was his black overcoat and suit, replaced by the white summer uniform of a *junsa*.

"Oh, Kenji is up," a woman's chipper voice cried out before sliding open a *shoji* door. The gray-haired figures of his mother and father entered and bowed. "Have a good day at work, Kenji."

"But Kenji-onisan promised to split a watermelon with me!" Tokiko whined.

"There will be time for that later," his father said, helping Aizawa to his feet. "Kenji has duty now! Right, son?"

Aizawa focused his eyes and examined his family. The healthy color in their faces dulled into a sallow, ghostly hue. A surreal atmosphere covered the *machiya* like a veil.

"You're all dead," he said.

They nodded.

"Am I?"

They exchanged uncertain looks.

"Are you, Kenji-onisan?" Tokiko asked.

He considered the possibility. Either he was dead or dreaming. Or maybe both. Growing up, he'd heard a Buddhist story about a man who dreamt that he was a butterfly. Or was he actually a butterfly dreaming that he was a man? Was Kenji Aizawa dreaming he was dead or a dead man who thought he was asleep? Regardless, there was something he'd wanted to tell them for years. He sank to his knees and kowtowed.

"Mother…Father…Tokiko-chan…please forgive me…"

"Kenji," his mother cooed. "There's nothing to forgive."

"I failed to protect you. After the earthquake struck…I ran back to our *machiya* but it was already burning. If I had gotten there a few minutes earlier..." He lowered his head deeper.

"You did your duty. There was nothing else you could have done," his father said, guiding him to the front door. "Now hurry up or you'll be late for work!"

Suddenly, Aizawa was standing outside in Ueno Park. Strangely enough, it was springtime and swarms of cherry blossoms fluttered through the air. The sheer beauty of it summoned a flurry of happy memories: playing baseball with friends, viewing the cherry blossom festival with his family, and taking a stroll with a pretty girl right before shipping out to Siberia.

But in one howling gust of wind, Ueno Park vanished in a swirl of cherry blossoms, replaced by the landscape of Tokyo set ablaze. Aizawa turned around, just in time to see his family's *machiya* collapse into rubble for a second time. It was September 1st, 1923 again, and he had failed his family once more.

The rest of that day was a blur of tripping over charred corpses and leading panicked survivors to safer ground. There were also scores of Korean immigrants and suspected Communists massacred by angry mobs who claimed they were poisoning wells and setting fires as part of a vast Bolshevik plot to overthrow the government. Aizawa could only stand aside with his little tin sword; helpless, frustrated, impotent, and too frightened to stop any of it.

The inferno was expanding, torching rows of wooden *machiyas* and swallowing people in a mammoth, convulsing conflagration. He looked up toward the horizon and gasped. There, in the center of Tokyo, was that swirling pillar of fire, even larger than he remembered. Now it climbed past the clouds, soaring deep into outer space. It grew wider and wider until it had consumed the entire city. Then, everything went white.

CHAPTER FIFTY-THREE

Aizawa blinked several times and focused in on a figure standing where the tornado of flames had been. With every passing moment the details sharpened, from the rank insignia on the figure's dark brown uniform to his black boots, gleaming in the electric light. It was those boots that must have traipsed in wet snow into the *nagaya*. The figure's face took a definitive shape and formed Lieutenant Nakajima, looming over him. He'd awoken from a dream and into a nightmare.

"Good morning, Inspector."

"Good morning, Lieutenant," Aizawa said, pushing himself up with a strained groan. He looked down and found his black overcoat and suit were now a blanket of wrinkles. After running his hand over a face full of stubble, he looked back up at Nakajima. The Lieutenant stretched out a Nambu pistol, execution-style. It was all over now. But if he was going to die, at least he wouldn't go lying down. Summoning the last bit of his strength, he rose to his feet and braced himself.

"You can shoot me now."

"You misjudge," Lieutenant Nakajima said as his face softened. "I don't want to hurt you, Inspector."

Aizawa rubbed his throbbing head. "Is that so?"

"I'm sorry, but I had to incapacitate you in case you were armed. You were knocked out for longer than I intended. It's almost 0600 hours." The Lieutenant gave an apologetic bow. "Rest assured, I'm not here to kill you…but to ask for your surrender."

"I'm to become a prisoner of war?"

Nakajima gave emphatic nods and said, "We're soldiers on opposite sides of the battlefield. As such, you're entitled to fair treatment."

"Shouldn't a Japanese soldier prefer death before dishonor?"

"Only if he is stained with dishonor. *You* have fought honorably, Inspector."

That was news to him. But praise from a murderer sent waves of nausea rippling to the pit of his stomach.

"You served in the Imperial Army, right?" Nakajima asked as he lowered his weapon, but still keeping it at a threatening height.

"Yes, during the Siberian Expedition."

"Ah, the glorious war against Communism!"

"Not exactly what I would call freezing my ass off and getting shot at by Bolsheviks."

Nakajima gave a sullen look. "I'm envious, Inspector. My only regret is that I was not able to join my comrades in Manchuria and fight for the Emperor there…like a true soldier." He gave a deep sigh, full of forlorn and regret. "Regardless, your cause in Ziberia was an honorable one. We could have eliminated the Bolshevik threat if only those weak-kneed politicians hadn't ordered our forces out. And for such cowardice, the gods punished us."

Inside Aizawa's pounding head, the answer came. "With the Great Kanto Earthquake?"

Nakajima nodded. "What else could have caused it? The god Kashima is the only being who can restrain the great catfish, Namazu, upon whose back the Japanese islands rest. If let loose, the ground trembles from his mighty tail."

"So, Kashima let Namazu go because we pulled out of Siberia?"

"There were other causes too. Our society became corrupt, greedy, and decadent, which poisoned the Great Japanese Empire."

"Things went back to the way they were after the earthquake, though."

"And the gods punished us again! This economic depression is divine punishment for the immorality that infests Japan like lice."

Aizawa nodded. Gods were a part of everyday life in Japan, but Lieutenant Nakajima seemed the type unable to separate prayer from fairy tales.

"How do you know this, Lieutenant?"

Nakajima beamed. "My sister relays messages from the sun goddess herself."

"That's right, the dead one." Aizawa rubbed his coarse chin and wondered whether the Lieutenant had gone insane before or after he met Masaru Ryusaki. "And what does your sister say?"

Lieutenant Nakajima gave another smile, full of dark secrets. "That Japan must be purged of evil. We have struck the first blow by killing Baron Onishi. But Chitose-oneesan has told me that the gods demand more assassinations until not a villain or traitor remains. Only then will Japan be saved."

"That could lead to civil war."

The Lieutenant held his head high. "We follow the paths of the Meiji Emperor and Takamori Zaigo."

"That was a different era. Back then, there weren't even telephones or automobiles, let alone airplanes, tanks, and poison gas."

Lieutenant Nakajima smiled. "A civil war might be what Japan needs right now. The Meiji Restoration modernized the nation. Zaigo's rebellion gave the Imperial Army its first real test. Bullets and blood are nourishment for our people."

"You'd really start a war in the home islands when our troops are still fighting in Manchuria?"

"There are more wars to come, Inspector. We cannot face the northern threat of Russia or fight a transpacific war against America while the maggots of corruption and greed wriggle in Tokyo. The government must be cleansed. Preferably with swords and pistols, but if not, then with bombs and machine guns."

"The government controls the Police, the Army, and the Navy," Aizawa countered.

"We are prepared to fight," Nakajima said.

"It'll be a very short war."

"Will it? I've been in contact with artillery officers who will gladly order their batteries to shell the Diet Building. Tank commanders who will storm the Prime Minister's residence. Pilots who will drop bombs and burn this corrupt city to ashes."

The Lieutenant's words resonated deep. Maybe that enormous tornado of fire stretching into the sky wasn't an image of the past, but a vision of the future. Aizawa swallowed hard and tightened his jaw. The past few days had left him with so many uncertainties. Perhaps the Emperor wanted Baron Onishi to become prime minister and ordered him to be assassinated. Maybe His Majesty was only a man but also a god. However, there was only one thing he knew for certain – Tokyo was on the verge of becoming a sea of flames for the second time in his life.

"You'd kill your own people?" Aizawa hissed, almost spitting out the words. "And yet you have the audacity to wear the uniform of the Imperial Army?"

Nakajima frowned and gave a wounded expression. "We act to save the Japanese people."

"Save them from what?" Aizawa demanded.

"From unemployment. From greed. From selling their daughters to fill their rice bowls. Corruption has tainted almost everyone. What man hasn't fastened the chains of our women by visiting Yoshiwara?"

For a country boy, Hajime Nakajima spoke with surprising lyricism. Aizawa wondered what passage of Ryusaki's book he'd just quoted. Still, the words conjured up memories of that Tohoku girl – Yuki – enslaved to the brothels.

"You can't save the people if you kill them," Aizawa said.

"Better to die with honor than live in shame," Nakajima said, raising the Nambu again. "But civil war is a last resort. We will use assassination to carry out reform first. Then, Ryusaki-zensei and the Kusanagi Society will build the New Japan founded on purity and patriotism."

That husk of samurai armor flashed in his mind.

"Ryusaki is still alive?"

Nakajima nodded and said, "My sister told me that the sun goddess spared both of your lives. Don't you see, Inspector? We are destined to become allies!"

Aizawa cursed himself for not circling the Rolls-Royce around to make sure. He sighed and stopped himself. He'd drive himself mad with regret if he went down that path. Instead, he focused on how to get out of this mess alive. He glanced around the cramped *nagaya* for some way to escape, but Lieutenant Nakajima blocked the only exit. Rushing him was out of the question. Aizawa's only chance was to appeal to that code of purity he kept going on about. Self-righteousness was the only weakness he could exploit.

"If Ryusaki is still alive, then what's to prevent him from killing me after I surrender?"

Nakajima's expression softened. "I've convinced Ryusaki-zensei to accept your surrender with impunity. I give you my word of honor."

"Your 'word of honor' means nothing to me. You murdered Sergeant Murayama and the Onishis. Superintendent Shimura was found slashed to death, which means either Ryusaki and his *katana* or you and that saber had something to do with it."

"Superintendent Shimura was…uncooperative. He refused to help us lure you into an ambush," Nakajima said without emotion. "I had to rely on Reiko Watanabe to do that…albeit with a gun to her head."

Aizawa gritted his teeth. "What kind of soldier kills an unarmed woman?"

"Watanabe-zan is not dead. She gave me directions to your *nagaya* just this morning."

Aizawa fell silent for a moment. Someone as obsessed with purity as Lieutenant Nakajima was didn't seem like the lying type. A glimmer of hope shined through.

"Let me see her," Aizawa said.

Nakajima smiled and gestured with the Nambu to walk outside.

"Certainly. You can drive us there, Inspector."

Aizawa nodded and began putting his shoes on. He muttered a prayer of thanks to the gods for giving him another reprieve, figuring it would be his last.

CHAPTER FIFTY-FOUR

Although the Rolls-Royce wheezed and rattled with every passing meter, the vehicle somehow remained serviceable. Gusts of crisp morning air blew through the shattered front window, keeping Aizawa alert behind the steering wheel. Not that he needed it. Lieutenant Nakajima sat in the passenger seat and held the Nambu pistol against his side, jabbing him in the ribs from time to time.

"Keep driving," Nakajima snapped.

Easier said than done. They were deep into Asakusa now, where the streets narrowed and – even at this early hour – pedestrians sauntered about. Some opened up shops and kiosks, while others in tattered coats and rumpled kimonos looked for a new place to sleep for the day.

"This city," Nakajima sneered, shaking his head. "When I first arrived here, it felt as if I'd traveled to a foreign country."

"I've never been to the Tohoku region, so I can't compare," Aizawa said.

"As a boy, I pictured Tokyo with the splendor of old Peking. Imagine my disappointment when I saw that it was just a mass of paper houses clustered around the Imperial Palace and a few concrete buildings."

Feeling a need to defend his hometown, Aizawa said, "In just a few years this city rebuilt itself after the worst earthquake in history."

The Lieutenant held up his free hand. "I used to admire Tokyoites for that. But they've been poisoned by a corruption and decadence so thick that you can smell it in the air. Now, I pity them. Turn here."

Aizawa turned a corner and swerved around a cart selling *yakitori* chicken skewers. A few onlookers stared at the shattered and ragged Rolls-Royce, but only with a tempered

curiosity. They were still in Asakusa and the day for oddities
was just starting.

"Stop here."

Aizawa pulled the car over and they hopped out. A khaki
cape hid most of Nakajima's frame, including his Nambu, as
they walked down the street in relative obscurity. The
passersby glanced over, and while most just yawned, a few
gave deep bows to Nakajima.

"Big difference from when I was a soldier," Aizawa said.

The Lieutenant nodded. "Things have even changed
since I was a cadet. Only a few years ago, some restaurants
denied us service and merchants overcharged us for
everything." He shook his head. "But since the Manchurian
Incident began, the people have recognized the Imperial
Army as the defenders of the nation."

"Until the economy recovers, that is," Aizawa countered.

The Lieutenant said nothing, but kept herding him past
nagaya row houses and storefronts. Two men in long coats
and flat caps stood outside of a humble tea house named
"Dragonfly." As they neared, Aizawa recognized them as
two *soshi* from the night before. They soon spotted him and
gave wolfish grins.

The *soshi* slid the doors open and guided them inside. The
genkan vestibule was full of shoes, *geta* clogs, and oddly
enough, a pair of black riding boots. Aizawa glanced back
over at the Lieutenant, still in full uniform. Nakajima's pistol
emerged from underneath his cape and dug deep into his
back.

"No time for proper custom, Inspector," Nakajima
ordered, pushing him past the rows of footwear. "Ryusaki-
zensei is waiting."

After the two *soshi* opened another pair of sliding doors,
the Lieutenant shoved him inside. A sickening stench
permeated the room, easily recognizable as rotting flesh. He
looked around for a corpse but couldn't find any. Despite a
few scrapes and scratches, Masaru Ryusaki sat underneath a

wall scroll of Mount Fuji, very much alive. As usual, he gripped that *katana*, secure in its sheath...for the moment.

Stacked off to the side, like the wreckage from a scrap yard, was the chipped and broken armor from last night. Nakajima and his cohorts offered deep bows. Four other *soshi* knelt around their *sensei* and returned the gesture. Ryusaki, however, remained motionless, an invisible fire burning behind his horn-rimmed glasses.

Aizawa looked around the room for the source of the smell and came across a small man, clad in the dark brown uniform of an Army officer. Despite the change of clothes and a shaved mustache, Makoto Kuroki was unmistakable. He bolted upright and snapped a salute at Nakajima, who reciprocated. Well, he did say it was his boyhood dream to join the Imperial Army. Dressing up must have been the next best thing.

Sitting next to him was Reiko Watanabe, or was she Harutora now? It was hard to tell them apart. She wore a black kimono with bobbed hair in a strange hybrid of both identities. Her face was coated with white face paint, but the makeup couldn't hide the bluish tint of bruised and battered skin that crisscrossed her cheeks. Deep swelling settled around her eyes, so puffy they had almost vanished. The *moga* caterpillar emerged from her cocoon as a geisha butterfly but got stuck halfway through.

Clutching a small white box, the geisha-*moga* fixed a hollow gaze on Aizawa, sending an involuntary chill through him. He tried to decipher what was behind that stare, searching for any subtle gesture. But there was nothing. Even a fiery anger would have been better than the blankness that confronted him. He'd seen that numb, vacant expression painted on survivors after the Great Earthquake, on soldiers after a battle, and on prisoners after torture sessions.

"Welcome, Inspector," Ryusaki hissed, beckoning him closer. A firm hand from the Lieutenant forced Aizawa to kneel down.

"You would do that," he gestured to Reiko, "to your own lover?"

Ryusaki scoffed. "She's lucky to still be alive. If this was the Tokugawa Era, I'd have cut out her tongue for treachery and hung her upside down to bleed dry." A smile creased his long face. "Instead, I ordered Lieutenant Nakajima to rehabilitate her."

"Is that what you call torture?"

Nakajima knelt beside him. "Don't the Police use the same method on Reds?"

A valid point. Rather than prosecuting Communists and other thought criminals, it was less expensive to torture and shame them into patriotism. The ones who held out wasted away in Sugamo Prison, the national dungeon of Japan.

"The Lieutenant is a firm believer in rehabilitation. It saved me from foreign devils, and he believes it will save you from this corrupt government," Ryusaki continued.

"I don't recall Nakajima-san beating your face to a pulp in order to 'rehabilitate' you," Aizawa said.

"Watanabe-zan needed to be punished for her treachery," Nakajima cut in. "Once she understood how hopeless both of your situations are, she broke like glass."

"You see, Inspector, the Japanese soul is sensitive to shame," Ryusaki said. "Reiko realized how shameful her betrayal was and that, not the Lieutenant's beatings, allowed her to be rehabilitated. That is why Kuroki-san would never confess, no matter how hard you beat him. He had nothing to be ashamed of."

Aizawa glanced over to Kuroki in his officer's uniform, looking like a child in his father's clothes, and said, "They finally let you into the Army?"

Kuroki braced his tiny frame. "I am a soldier in the Kusanagi Society."

"Wearing your brother's uniform?"

He nodded. "Harutora-san tailored it for me."

Still holding that mysterious white box, the geisha-*moga* gave Aizawa another haunting, empty stare. What had been his plan anyway? Somehow escape with her and call for backup? Maybe he just wanted to see her once more, to make sure he hadn't failed as badly as he'd thought. But instead, shame now covered his body like grime and forced him to look away.

Suicide was the common escape from such unmitigated failure. But just like Reiko Watanabe, he'd long ago figured out there was nothing honorable about dying. All death left behind was a greasy smear and an awful stench.

"Who did you kill in here? The smell is still ripe," Aizawa said, looking up at Ryusaki's grinning face.

Ryusaki beckoned his mistress closer. Shuffling over, she handed over the white box and kept her head low. Opening the lid, Ryusaki pulled out a human head and held it up in sadistic triumph. Its cheeks were rouged, and any signs of gore had been washed away, but General Yori Sakamoto was easily recognizable, even without a body.

"We dumped his body in the Sumida last night, but I decided to keep this as a trophy," Ryusaki said, snickering.

Aizawa turned to the Lieutenant. "You murdered your commanding officer?"

"I gave General Zakamoto the choice between assassination and *seppuku*. I'm pleased that he chose an honorable death," Nakajima said. "Other villains will not be so lucky."

Not much had changed since the feudal era when samurai presented the severed heads of enemies to their *daimyo* lords. The *soshi* grinned and glowed with bloodlust. Aizawa stole a quick glance at Reiko Watanabe's pulpy face. A lot more would look like her soon.

"Speaking of villains, how do you plan on assassinating Isamu Takano?" Aizawa asked. "He'll be on his guard now after—"

"After you murdered one of my men yesterday?" Ryusaki said, stuffing the head back inside the box.

Aizawa kept quiet, not wanting to press his luck. Ryusaki gestured to Kuroki, who shuffled over to another large box, tucked away in the corner. He opened it and slid a long tube out, encased in brown paper. After a few seconds of showing it off, Kuroki put it back in with a delicate grace.

"Dynamite?" was all Aizawa could say.

Ryusaki nodded and laughed. "Leftovers from the plans we hatched back in March."

Aizawa found his voice and said, "And now you'll use it to blow the Marunouchi Building sky high, killing Isamu Takano in the process?"

The Kusanagi Society gave eager nods.

"I shall lead these brave men," Nakajima said, gesturing to the *soshi* around him, "straight into that den of devils and slaughter every villain we see!"

Aizawa sized the Kusanagi Society up. They were even more ragged than he remembered them back in March. But after nearly a year without work and a steady diet of patriotic violence, the resolve in their ashen, unshaven faces had become firmer and boasted an eagerness to kill and die.

"Dynamiting the Marunouchi Building will kill a lot more people than just Takano," Aizawa said.

"Casualties are to be expected in war," Ryusaki said, slamming his hand on the *tatami* flooring. "But the people are with us. They scream for us to crush that nest of wasps! Japan cannot begin to heal until the poisonous stingers of capitalism, corruption, and liberalism are torn out of our national flesh!"

"And what will you do while your men are blowing up the Maru-Biru, Ryusaki-san? Write your second book?"

Ryusaki frowned and Nakajima answered for him.

"Ryusaki-zensei is too important to our movement to die. He'll go underground and recruit more followers to the cause."

Aizawa's throat and frame tightened at the thought. Blowing up the Maru-Biru was just the beginning. Tokyo was about to enter an era of violence that would make the Meiji Restoration look tame. Even more ominous was

Lieutenant Nakajima's threat of enlisting his fellow Army officers to turn the Imperial capital into a battlefield.

"I spoke to Takano-san yesterday," Aizawa said. "He claims his motives were entirely patriotic."

Ryusaki scoffed. "Men like him only salute money, not our sacred flag."

"Maybe, but he says he'll use his money to rebuild the economy and make Japan strong again."

"And you believed that?" Ryusaki snapped.

"He claimed to have some powerful backers," Aizawa said.

"Who?"

"His Imperial Majesty."

The *soshi* widened their eyes and shifted nervous glances to their *sensei*.

Ryusaki gave a harsh laugh, like a croaking frog. "The Emperor is misled by his corrupt advisers. Men who are in the pocket of Takano and the other *zaibatsu*." His face darkened. "Men like you, Inspector."

Lieutenant Nakajima leaned over and said, "Inspector, the Kusanagi Society and the Metropolitan Police should not be enemies. We both serve the Emperor in different ways. If we unite, the dark clouds that swirl over our nation will be driven away by the sunlight of purity and patriotism!"

The Lieutenant's soft face glowed with an eager naïveté in stark contrast to Ryusaki, who frowned with narrowed eyes. Despite Nakajima's assurance of safety, to outright refuse this offer might be enough of an excuse for Ryusaki to draw his *katana*.

"Let me think about it," Aizawa said.

Lieutenant Nakajima gave a placated nod.

"I'm sure the Inspector will make the right decision in time," Ryusaki said. "But until then, restrain him."

Kuroki jumped up and dug through Aizawa's coat before finding his handcuffs. His hands were pulled behind him and shackled into place. Kuroki resumed his search until discovering a pair of keys, and presented them to Ryusaki.

Aizawa gave a few sharp strains against the cuffs, searching for any looseness to exploit. But the metal dug deep into his wrists, payback for Kuroki's earlier treatment. Whatever chance of escape he had was gone now.

Like an animated puppet, Reiko-Harutora shuffled through and passed out cups. She then poured ritual sake, a ceremony that all Japanese men enjoyed before battle, be they samurai, soldiers, or *soshi*. Ryusaki gave a triumphant smile and raised his glass.

"To the New Japan. Banzai."

CHAPTER FIFTY-FIVE

Lieutenant Nakajima peered out the back of the taxicab's rear window as Asakusa faded from view. Kuroki sat next to him, stern-faced and stiff in his dark brown uniform, as if he'd just graduated from the Imperial Army Academy. Another patriot sat in the front passenger seat, tight-lipped and staring straight ahead. Behind them trailed another one-yen taxi, crammed with the five other patriots. Not as glorious as leading a platoon across Manchuria, but it would have to suffice.

With a sigh, Nakajima glanced out the side window. Ueno Park appeared in the distance, cold and gray in the early morning light. Somehow Inspector Aizawa had escaped from there last night, despite the best efforts of Ryusaki-sensei. Such a miraculous escape was evidence that the gods had intervened on his behalf, and demanded his enlistment into the Kusanagi Society. Since the Inspector was a man of honor, patriotism would convert him into a useful ally in the coming war. It was, after all, the will of the gods.

Tokyo passed by, its features melting together into one drab blur. How he hated this city. Here was the epicenter of greed and corruption, like a diseased heart pumping out poisoned blood. The Kusanagi Society would try to remove the virus through assassination, but if that didn't work, a mercy killing might be best for Tokyo. The capital of the New Japan would be erected on its ashes.

A loud screech jarred Nakajima from his thoughts as the car braked hard. Tires squealed behind them as the other one-yen taxi skidded to a halt behind them, nudging the car's bumper with a firm push. He gave a relieved sigh. A faster speed would have surely detonated the box of dynamite they had stored in the taxicab's trunk. Yet another sign the gods supervised their mission.

"Be more careful," Nakajima said, clutching his saber for added emphasis.

"Sorry about that," the driver replied, offering a slight bow. "I hope your box didn't break. What do you have in there anyway?"

Nakajima traded a glance with Kuroki and said, "We are not at liberty to discuss that."

The driver nodded with understanding. "Sorry about the rough stop. I guess there's some soldiers shipping out today."

Nakajima peered out the window at Tokyo Station in front of them. Not only was it the largest railway terminal in the empire, but patriots had also struck down two treacherous prime ministers there. Ah, another good omen for their mission. The Marunouchi Building was now just blocks away.

However, an enormous throng clustered around the station's entrance and slowed their advance to a crawl. Most were civilians waving Rising Sun flags, but a line of brown-uniformed soldiers streamed past them to endless chants of "banzai!" while a brass band played "If Ten Thousand Enemies Should Come."

A twinge of jealousy stabbed at Lieutenant Nakajima's heart. He briefly pictured himself shipping out with them but shook his head. No time for self-pity. Such selfishness was exactly what they were fighting against. He'd have to meet his death here and take as many of the enemy with him.

*****

"It's over, Inspector. I've won," Ryusaki said before downing another cup of sake. Aizawa kept quiet and continued to strain against the handcuffs. Each tug bit the metal deeper into his skin.

Reiko-Harutora sat beside Ryusaki and refilled the cup of sake. Aizawa scanned for any hints of rebellion, a wink or a nod to escape. But her glassy eyes shone only a submissive defeat. Ryusaki sat his cup down and dug into his kimono and slid out the Colt pistol, missing since last night.

"Careful, that's not a toy," Aizawa said.

"Such arrogance from a man who lost a weapon entrusted to him by the Emperor," Ryusaki said, shaking his head. "But I expect nothing less from you, Aizawa-san. I'll make sure to put this to good use and shoot a few politicians with it."

"And what do you plan on doing with her?" Aizawa asked, nodding in Reiko-Harutora's direction. She made no movement.

Ryusaki plunged the Colt back into his kimono before returning full attention to his *katana*. "My Reiko was led astray and corrupted. I should have suspected her sooner. Betrayal comes more naturally for women. But now she is coming to grips with the crimes that she's committed. A few more rehabilitation sessions will beat out any treachery left in her. Then, she'll make a fine wife for me!" He smiled. "All Japan must undergo rehabilitation to be saved." Ryusaki gripped the sword and slammed its hilt under Aizawa's chin. "Except you, Inspector."

"Me?"

"Rehabilitation won't work on you. Lieutenant Nakajima might be fooled, but I see what you really are."

Aizawa gave a hard swallow. "And that is?"

"Our greatest enemy. Not the *zaibatsu* or the politicians, but you. We would have succeeded months ago…if only *you* hadn't interfered."

"I have a way of doing that."

"Yes, you do." Each breath grew tighter as the hilt pressed deeper into Aizawa's throat. "But why? Why do you risk your life to defend this corrupt government? Can't you see that *we* are the selfless patriots who serve the Emperor? Why do you resist?"

Everyone had the best of intentions. Baron Onishi was content to let the masses wallow in unemployment to save face. Isamu Takano and the Emperor wanted to save the economy by assassinating Onishi. Even Ryusaki wanted to reform the nation, though there might not be much of Japan left standing afterward. No matter how patriotic or selfless the motives were, there would always be innocents who would suffer.

Reiko-Harutora's chewed-up face summoned *ninjo* back to life. A lot more would end up like her if he did nothing. Reiko's simple words from the other night haunted him.

'I saw what Masaru was planning…I couldn't let this beautiful city of ours become drenched in blood.'

Not only *ninjo*, but *giri* had returned and presented both his duty and desire with sudden clarity.

"Tokyo," Aizawa said.

Confusion clouded Ryusaki's face as he pulled the *katana* back. "For *this* city?" he said. "For a heap of paper houses, tea houses, and electric trams?"

Why couldn't Aizawa see it earlier? It had always been Tokyo. His duty was not to any man or to the government, but to his home. His purpose in life was to protect the Imperial capital and its inhabitants, from Reiko Watanabe to the Emperor of Japan. For that, he had no qualms. *Giri* and *ninjo* had merged into one.

"Yes, for Tokyo," he said.

Ryusaki gave an empty, vapid expression before anger twisted his face into a violent mask.

"Is that so? Well, I'll make sure to burn it to the ground then. Too bad you won't live to see it," Ryusaki said. Standing up, he unsheathed the *katana* like a metallic snake slithering out of its nest.

"Lieutenant Nakajima gave me his word that I wouldn't be harmed."

"I'm not that rice farmer who you made a deal with. I am Masaru Ryusaki, the descendant of twenty generations of samurai. I will not allow my family name to be disgraced by some *peasant* detective."

Aizawa's jaw tightened. "I always knew you to be the type of a man who would forsake honor for vanity."

A wicked smile curled Ryusaki's face. "Oh, but this *is* a matter of honor, Inspector. Can you imagine the loss of face I suffered when you arrested me? Or when you saved Baron Onishi? And when you," he choked back a sob, "when you turned the woman I love against me?"

"She did that on her own."

The blade began to tremble in Ryusaki's hands.

"Damn you! It's your head I want most of all. Only then will my honor be avenged."

Aizawa balled his fists and tensed his muscles. Ryusaki would have to hack through a maze of sinew and bone before claiming his head.

"Make sure to raise the sword high above your head. After all, you've never actually killed a man with your bare hands before, have you?"

Ryusaki sneered. "You have the honor of being my first, Inspector. But not the last. Soon, Tokyo will become a mass grave before I turn it into a funeral pyre."

Aizawa cast a pitiful, helpless glance at the geisha-*moga*. A pained expression cracked her catatonic gaze. Ryusaki grabbed Aizawa by his hair and forced his head downward. A practice swing released a whoosh of air that bristled against his neck. The next one would be real. He bit his lip and prayed to the gods for strength.

The screech of cracking glass filled the tea house. Aizawa snapped up and twisted around. Reiko-Harutora stood with the shattered sake bottle, crumpling in her hand like melting ice. Ryusaki – head soaked with a mixture of blood and booze – stumbled backward with large, panicked eyes behind his cracked and broken glasses.

"I...I can't see!" he said, regaining his balance.

Ryusaki slashed the open air with his sword awkwardly and blindly, like a cornered animal. Cursing, he squinted, trying in vain to focus on his attacker. Despite the tight kimono, Reiko-Harutora dodged each lethal slash with such elegant grace, she may as well have been dancing.

She crouched down and launched herself like a coiled spring, slamming them both onto the floor. The *katana* rose again in a desperate defense, but Reiko-Harutora dug her hands into Ryusaki's kimono and removed the Colt. Instead of firing, she held it by the muzzle and brought it down like a hammer. After another crackle of glass, she slammed it again and again, until the *katana* dropped from Ryusaki's hand and rattled harmlessly on the *tatami* mats.

Reiko-Harutora's dainty frame grew and shrank in enormous heaves of breath. After searching through Ryusaki's kimono, she stood and turned toward Aizawa, holding the handcuff key. Ryusaki's face was visible now; bloodied pulp framed by a pair of shattered glasses.

"Is he…?"

"No," she said through clenched teeth. "I want him in locked away in Sugamo Prison for the rest of his life."

Reiko-Harutora uncuffed Aizawa and handed the Colt over. Her swollen face was aflame with a fighting spirit he'd never seen in a woman, or even in a man. Well, there was the reason why she took the name *Spring Tiger*. With rapid shuffles, she returned to Ryusaki and cuffed his hands together. With his bondage came her freedom.

"Reiko-san…I…I…," Aizawa stammered, holstering the pistol. Her stern, bruised face tightened his throat and left him speechless. Instead, he bowed an apology.

"Don't apologize," she spat out, teeth still locked. "Do your duty."

CHAPTER FIFTY-SIX

Free of the throngs that choked Tokyo Station, the Marunouchi Building – the Maru-Biru – finally came into full view like some overgrown termite mound. It was here, in one explosive act of purity and patriotism, where Second Lieutenant Hajime Nakajima, the humble son of rice farmers, would attain godhood.

But why couldn't he shake this feeling of regret? He was about to slay one of the nation's greatest villains and yet, he felt inadequate. The battle would be little more than blowing up a building full of bankers and salarymen. Meanwhile, his comrades in Manchuria faced Chinese bombs and bullets. It was in that distant land where he could attain *true* glory and honor. If only he had accepted that transfer. If only he could see the New Japan dawn. If only he had experienced a woman before he died. If only things had turned out differently. Ah, if only…

But there was no time for sentimental drivel.

"Stop here," he ordered.

The taxi came to a halt, and Nakajima handed over a yen coin.

"Sorry, Lieutenant," the driver said. "But since yesterday we've had to raise our price. It's one yen and five sen now."

Nakajima grumbled. Growing inflation was yet another reason to send Takano and his ilk straight to hell. He handed over a five-sen coin and hopped out. The workday had already started, clearing the streets of curious onlookers. Nakajima opened the trunk, revealing the box containing over thirty sticks of dynamite. More than enough firepower to demolish the entire building. The other patriots filed out of their taxi and gathered around. Two of them removed the box and waited for instructions.

Between the gaps of the financial towers and office buildings, the Imperial Palace stood in the distance, shimmering in the morning sun. Such an omen made it clear they had His Majesty's support! Nakajima turned back to the patriots and pulled out his Nambu. On cue, they reached into their kimonos and overcoats and drew their *wakizashi* short swords for the fight ahead.

Kuroki brandished the Nagant revolver, recaptured from Aizawa in last night's battle. They would be the only two with firearms, but it didn't matter. With the gods behind them, they could kill a thousand capitalists if needed. Nakajima fastened the chinstrap on his peaked cap, signaled for the men to follow, and then dashed into the Maru-Biru as if it were an enemy fort. No opposition greeted them in the lobby, so he ordered four men to guard each entrance.

"Only let the women out. If someone wearing an expensive suit or Rolex watch tries to escape, kill them on the spot."

They nodded and marched off, swords drawn and faces grim. Lieutenant Nakajima entered a nearby elevator, followed by Kuroki and the remaining two patriots, straining with the box of explosives. A female operator stared at them with wide, fearful eyes.

"The Takano Bank Office, please," Nakajima said. Trembling, the elevator girl pulled the lever, depositing them on the third floor. Before they exited, Nakajima said to her, "Go to the ground floor and get out. This is no place for a woman."

The elevator operator nodded and slid the gate shut. Nakajima ordered the dynamite handlers to stay put and gestured for Kuroki to follow. Their footsteps smacked against the tile and echoed throughout the lobby like artillery shells. He was Takamori Saigo fighting in the Southwestern War. He was Admiral Togo sinking the Russian fleet at Tsushima. He was Peach Boy Taro storming the island of *oni* devils with his animal friends.

A dumbfounded secretary greeted them in the lobby with a horrified stare.

"Be quiet and leave," Nakajima said, pointing to the stairs with his pistol.

Instead, she released a shrill scream and bolted out from behind her desk, as if trying to warn Takano.

Kuroki raised his Nagant and fired. The secretary crumpled to the floor, letting out a choked gurgle. A nauseated unease settled in Nakajima's gut. Women were utterly blameless for the evil that went on here. However, Chitose-oneesan appeared over the body and gave a firm nod, reassuring him. In war, there would always be innocents who suffered. Nakajima refocused his attention to the target.

To his right held another hallway with more offices, including a set of heavy oak doors with the words "Isamu Takano, President," written in English and Japanese on a golden plaque.

The thick doors creaked open, allowing a head to pop out. It wasn't the banker, but one of his massive sumo bodyguards. Kuroki fired again, missing the sumo who retreated back behind the doors. A few salarymen filed out of their offices and inspected the commotion with horrified expressions.

Lieutenant Nakajima nodded to Kuroki, who forced them back into their offices, brandishing his Nagant like a farmer herding livestock. Nakajima drew his saber and summoned the other two patriots closer. They hobbled forth, carrying the box of dynamite. Kuroki returned and snapped a salute.

"Your orders, sir?"

"Blow those doors apart," Lieutenant Nakajima roared, pointing with his sword. Kuroki and the patriots nodded and went to work like true sappers. A single stick of dynamite was placed against the double oak doors and lit. With a heavy strain, Nakajima overturned the secretary's desk, converting into a makeshift bunker. The patriots took refuge beside him; Kuroki clutching his Nagant with a steady grip while the other two drew their *wakizashi* swords.

For a moment, they weren't in Marunouchi, Tokyo, or even Japan. They were in far away Manchuria, where icy winds howled alongside screaming mortars. These weren't just ragged men from the Kusanagi Society, but comrades in arms fighting a foreign foe. And he would be decorated by the Emperor himself before returning back to the front to die a beautiful death, like a cherry blossom on the last day of spring. Ah, if only…

An explosion ripped through the air and shook the floor like a small earthquake. Nakajima stood and thrust his saber toward the smoldering pair of doors, now splintered in half.

"Forward!"

They sprinted over the desk and charged into Takano's office. Smoke hovered around the entrance, obscuring his vision. But across the room, from behind another fortified desk, two enormous figures were visible, taking aim with pistols.

A crackle of shots filled the office. Instincts learned from years of drilling pulled Lieutenant Nakajima to the ground and forced him into a low crawl. The other two patriots stormed ahead, *wakizashi* blades raised above their heads and shouting, "*Tenchu!*" Halfway across the room, gunfire ripped through their bodies. The patriots shook with violent convulsions before hitting the floor, already stained red with their blood.

Nakajima stared in horror, unable to move. Already he'd lost two of his men. But Chitose-oneesan returned and reminded him that to die in combat was the highest achievement for a soldier. He nodded and turned to Kuroki, who low-crawled beside him with a determined expression.

"Hajime-kun, there's your opening!" Chitose-oneesan said.

Nakajima peered through the stinging smoke and found the two sumo bodyguards reloading their pistols. A new fighting spirit burned inside and propelled him to his feet.

Like a good soldier, Kuroki followed his commanding officer as he took aim and opened fire.

Another volley of gunshots cut through the office. The desk exploded in a violent maelstrom of splinters and bullets. The thick frames of the two sumo bodyguards twitched and collapsed with heavy thuds. Lieutenant Nakajima sheathed his saber and took in a deep breath. The acrid smell of smoke burned his lungs, but it didn't matter. Now he understood the thrill of combat and what it meant to conquer an enemy. But the battle was not over. Not yet. Where was that money-hungry devil, Isamu Takano?

Nakajima started toward the fortified oak desk, now riddled with holes. A stationary globe was smashed into pieces and to the left, a stock ticker groaned after its glass had been cracked by a stray bullet. He looked up. Luckily, the portrait of His Majesty was unharmed, another good omen.

His gaze swept across the office, but Takano was nowhere to be found. At least Baron Onishi was man enough to stand his ground. A pained moan drifted up from behind the splintered desk. Nakajima inspected and found one of the sumo staring upward with an empty gaze. The back of his head had been blown wide open, splattering gore just below the Emperor's portrait.

But the other sumo, lying next to him, sputtered and coughed up a mouth full of blood. Beside him, just out of reach was his pistol, an American 1911 Colt automatic. Even the weapons here were foreign. Nakajima reached over and grabbed his lapel, putting the muzzle of the Nambu underneath his pudgy chin.

"Where's Takano?"

The sumo chuckled, spitting droplets of blood onto Lieutenant Nakajima's tunic. "Gone," he said.

Nakajima's finger tightened around the trigger. "Where?"

"Fool," he wheezed. "He's…not even in Tokyo."

No, it couldn't be true. "You're lying! Where is he?"

The sumo gave another fit of bloody coughs. "Left for America this morning…with his friend from Wall Street."

They were too late. That scheming banker had outsmarted them again. No. It couldn't end like this. Nakajima looked up at the Emperor, who stared back with a sullen, disappointed gaze.

Nakajima wanted to cry, but his eyes only blinked in surprise. His grip loosened around the sumo's lapel and the man slammed back onto the floor. After another fit of coughing, the sumo's eyes slid shut with a grim finality.

"Kill them, Hajime-kun," Chitose-oneesan said, appearing beside him. "Kill them all."

She was right. As long as the Maru-Biru was blown to rubble, his mission would be accomplished. But a queer melancholy stabbed his heart and invigorated a desire to live. Ah, if only he could stay alive to fight again. However, one look at Chitose-oneesan's wispy face quelled that rebellion.

Nakajima stood up and turned to Kuroki, standing at attention with the Nagant attentively at his side. What a fine soldier he would have made.

"Your orders, Lieutenant?"

"Follow me."

Nakajima stepped around the desk and walked back into the lobby. The salarymen were still held up in their offices, evidenced by audible conversations from behind the closed doors. Leave it to the Japanese to obey orders from a superior, even if it meant their own deaths.

"They're calling the Police," Kuroki said.

"Then we don't have much time. Stand guard here. Shoot anyone who tries to enter or exit."

Kuroki saluted and assumed a sentry position with his Nagant. Lieutenant Nakajima returned to the box and opened it. The dynamite was arranged neatly in bundles of seven. Thankfully, he'd learned enough about explosives from his education at the Imperial Army Academy. With an explosion of this magnitude so close to the foundation, the entire building would come crashing down on itself. Ah, divine punishment for the corruption and greed that festered here! But the Metropolitan Police would be closing in soon. He begged the gods for just a few minutes more.

CHAPTER FIFTY-SEVEN

Although it sputtered and shook with each passing meter, Aizawa pushed the Rolls-Royce faster and faster. He swerved around street vendors, cut off rickshaws, and almost sideswiped an electric tramcar. But he was almost there. Tokyo Station was around the corner, the gateway to the financial district.

But his heart sank when he turned the car. A mass of civilians and soldiers swarmed around the station, as if put there by the cruelest of gods. Aizawa slammed his fists against the steering wheel. He'd have to walk the rest of the way. There was no time for any more delays. The Kusanagi Society had enough dynamite to level a city block, including all of Tokyo Station.

Aizawa cut the engine and hopped out of the Rolls-Royce. Rising Sun flags fluttered everywhere while the brass band banged out martial music. The crowd was thick and delirious. He shoved, elbowed, and pushed his way through the banzai-ing crowds. At last, he emerged on the other side with the Marunouchi Building now in clear sight. He dashed down the street, only to find another crowd gathering. Reporters and curious salarymen ringed the Maru-Biru, held back by a few *junsas*.

After clearing another path for himself, Aizawa called out to the most senior officer.

"Inspector Aizawa? Is that you?"

Aizawa nodded and rubbed the stubble on his chin. That – combined with the lack of sleep and the recent beatings he'd endured – must have given him the look of a wild man.

"Has the Maru-Biru been evacuated?" he asked.

The *junsa* shook his head. "No, sir. Each entrance is guarded by those *soshi*. We heard gunfire, so the suspects must be armed. Whoever they came to assassinate must be dead by now, but we can't even get in there...not with these…" the *junsa* said, resting a hand on his short sword. Aizawa shook his head. The Metropolitan Police wasn't prepared for this level of insanity.

"This area needs to be cleared," Aizawa said. "They plan on blowing the entire building up."

The *junsa's* eyes bulged. "Y-yes, sir. The Army should be here any minute."

"The Army?"

"Yes, sir. We requested their assistance. They're better equipped to handle this situation."

That may have been true, but Lieutenant Nakajima's words haunted him. Perhaps the approaching soldiers were also members of the Kusanagi Society. No reason to wait around and find out. Drawing his pistol, Aizawa leaned over to the *junsa* and said, "Make sure the area is clear. I'm going in."

As he passed by, the *junsas* saluted him with a certain reverence he'd seen at award ceremonies and funerals. His odds of survival were low, but that didn't matter. The fighting spirit he saw in Reiko Watanabe proved contagious.

Aizawa entered the Maru-Biru and kept the Colt close to his face. Shutting the door behind him, a grim-faced *soshi* in a flat cap and ratty overcoat advanced with rapid steps. He held a *wakizashi* short sword that glinted in the hallway's electric lights and aimed it directly at Aizawa's chest. With one mechanical motion, Aizawa brought the pistol into position and fired.

The *soshi* groaned and slammed face-first into the floor, still clutching the sword. An impressive shot, but there was no time for pride or pity for the dead. He focused on the situation. There were four main entrances to the Maru-Biru and each one probably had its own guard. The gunshot would probably attract attention so he needed to move quickly. The offices of Takano Bank were on the third floor, which now lay wide open. Chances were that's where

Lieutenant Nakajima would still be. The elevator looked out of order, so he'd have to walk.

Stepping over the fallen *soshi*, Aizawa made a beeline for the stairs and dashed up to the third floor. He threw open the door and there, in the lobby, stood Makoto Kuroki in his little brown uniform. Rushing to a nearby hallway for cover, he fired a few shots from the Nagant revolver. Aizawa ducked as bullets tore into the lobby's plaster walls, sprinkling him with white powder.

Aizawa was about to return fire when a woman's corpse – Takano's secretary – strewn out on the floor, jarred him. Her desk had been moved and was now propped up against Takano's office door as a makeshift barricade. Kuroki reappeared from behind the corner and renewed his fire. But the shot went wide, allowing Aizawa time to retreat into the stairs to gain cover.

"That bullet came nowhere near me. Good thing they never let you into the Army," Aizawa called out.

A few more shots erupted, missing him again.

"I'm surprised Ryusaki sent you to kill Baron Onishi. What would your brother say about such terrible shooting?"

"Shut up! Don't talk about my brother!" Kuroki snapped.

Aizawa kept his gun steady and close. A few more taunts would rattle Kuroki enough and leave him wide open.

"No wonder he killed himself. If I was related to such a pathetic imp, I'd have put a gun to my head too."

Kuroki rushed from behind his cover, charging head-on with the Nagant outstretched. A shot whizzed by Aizawa, puncturing the stairwell behind him, but was followed by only an empty clicking sound. Out of ammunition! Instincts and training took control of Aizawa. He turned the corner and took aim. Kuroki tossed the revolver aside and leaped toward him, just as Aizawa pulled the trigger.

Kuroki's small frame slammed into Aizawa, knocking the Colt away. They toppled backward and Kuroki's fingers wrapped around Aizawa's throat. Each moment pressed more air out of Aizawa's lungs. Blood rushed to his face and his vision began to dim.

But a gruesome red splotch soon grew on Kuroki's tunic and his grip loosened. Aizawa threw him off with one heavy push. Kuroki rolled to the side and gazed upward with a grotesque facsimile of a smile.

"B-banzai …to…the…" Kuroki tried to finish the slogan, but a pool of blood collected in his mouth, choking any final words. Instead, he released a loud gurgle as his eyes glazed over. It was like death in Siberia, inglorious and anticlimactic. But this unemployed cannery worker had finally gotten his wish – to die for the Emperor in uniform. Aizawa almost felt sorry for the little bastard, but another glance at the dead woman discouraged that thought.

Aizawa shook his head and caught his breath. He snatched up his automatic and sprinted over to the barricaded doors of Takano's office. The desk would take precious time and strength to remove. And the doors, while heavily damaged, were still thick enough to catch his bullets.

Regardless, he drew himself up and shouted, "This is Inspector Kenji Aizawa of the Tokyo Metropolitan Police Department! Lieutenant Nakajima, you're under arrest!"

CHAPTER FIFTY-EIGHT

There was no answer for several moments. Had the Lieutenant committed *seppuku* already? Aizawa hopped on the desk and gave a sharp kick to the doors, releasing a light crunching sound. He kicked again, again, and again.

"I'm disappointed in you, Inspector," Nakajima called out from the other side. "Have you come to defend your *zaibatsu* masters?"

Aizawa replied with another kick. The doors groaned but didn't budge.

"Don't bother doing that, Inspector. The dynamite has already been set. Four minutes left. You'll never get through in time."

Aizawa took in deep breaths and focused on his next move. Lieutenant Nakajima was insane, but honest. Brute strength wouldn't work. Aizawa considered emptying his weapon into the door on the off chance he might actually hit this madman. But more likely, if his shots managed to get past the door, he'd end up striking the dynamite and send the Maru-Biru up in fireworks anyway. He slammed his fist against the door.

Had it really come to this? Blown to bits alongside hundreds of salarymen, bankers, and Masaru Ryusaki's protégé? There'd be other Ryusakis too, inspired to carry out his mission, and he wouldn't be there to stop them. The thought of Tokyo becoming a city of bombings and assassinations burned shame into his soul.

That was it! It was his last weapon, but if used right, it was far more potent than his Colt automatic. He'd use shame to deliver the final blow.

"Don't you understand, Lieutenant? This explosion won't just kill people in the Maru-Biru. Didn't you see that crowd at Tokyo Station?"

"A small price to pay for the decimation of this snake pit," Nakajima said.

"Fool! Half of Tokyo is made of paper and wood! A fire started here can spread! Hundreds more could die! Innocent men, women, and children!"

Several moments passed by in agonized silence. Lives apparently didn't matter anymore to Lieutenant Nakajima. Better to change strategies. But how could he shame a murderer? Aizawa searched his memory and focused on the portrait of His Imperial Majesty, hanging above Takano's desk.

"The Emperor!" he shouted, banging his fists against the door. "The Emperor's picture is in there!"

There had been suicides over accidentally dropping the Emperor's photograph or from handling it uncovered. Blowing it to pieces would be unforgivable. Perhaps shame would force Nakajima to stop the timer just long enough to remove it and give Aizawa the opening he needed.

"Chitose-oneesan tells me the Emperor will forgive such an offense, so long as my motives are pure."

Aizawa groaned. How could he counteract a ghost? Chances are this "Chitose" was only Nakajima's *ninjo* in disguise. Emotion and desire had hypnotized another victim. But if "Chitose" was his *ninjo*, then what was Lieutenant Nakajima's *giri*? What was his duty?

A symphony of gunshots rang out, punctuated by shrieks and groans. So much for the other three *soshi* guarding the entrances. A percussive drumbeat of heavy boots thundered throughout the stairwell, growing louder until a dozen soldiers in dark brown uniforms burst into the office lobby.

Most were enlisted men but their commanding officer stood out — Major Takumi Hatsu of the *Kempeitai*. Like a flustered mole, he scanned the room, squinting from behind his thick glasses. The other *kempei* exuded a more impressive appearance. With their rifles at the ready and the chin straps on their service caps tightly fastened, they looked as if they'd just returned from the Manchurian front. The image recalled the Lieutenant's words from earlier.

'I'm envious, Inspector. My only regret is that I was not able to join my comrades in Manchuria and fight for the Emperor there…like a true soldier.'

For all that self-righteous talk about purity and patriotism, Hajime Nakajima was still a little boy who wanted to play war. Not that Aizawa could blame him. After all, every soldier knew the highest honor was to fight for the Emperor on the field of battle.

"Why do you insist on suicide, Lieutenant? Do you fear the battlefield? Are you scared of the enemy? Or maybe you can't take the harsh life of the campaign?"

A brief hiss shot through the doors from the other side, but there was still no clear response.

"Inspector," Major Hatsu said, marching toward him. "Stand aside! We're going to open fire."

Aizawa hopped off the desk and said, "There's no time! He's rigged the building to explode in a few minutes!"

Hatsu's eyes widened behind his glasses but more in rage than surprise.

"Such impudence!"

"Did you hear that, Lieutenant?" Aizawa called out. "Even Major Hatsu thinks that you've neglected your duty. Is the Manchurian winter too much for your delicate skin? My fallen comrades in Siberia would sneer at such a coward wearing the Army uniform!"

Hatsu pushed him aside and roared, "This is Major Hatsu of the *Kempeitai*! Lieutenant Nakajima, I order you to open the door and surrender!"

Several moments passed in silence, full of anxiety and apprehension. Nakajima might have been through taking orders, but perhaps he could be bribed.

Aizawa leaned over to the Major and with a low, firm voice said, "Offer him a pardon and a posting in Manchuria. Anything. Just get him out of that office."

A look of shock swept over Major Hatsu's face. Then, after a moment, he gave a conspiratorial nod and stepped forward to the barricaded doors.

"Lieutenant Nakajima…" Hatsu paused and took a deep breath. "If you surrender now, I guarantee you a full pardon and immediate transfer to Manchuria."

A few more moments passed. Aizawa checked his wristwatch. Less than two minutes left. He could sense Nakajima's apprehension, even from behind the doors. All he needed was a final push.

"Lieutenant, this is Inspector Aizawa. I give you my word of honor that I will not arrest you or block your transfer. As long as you surrender, you can leave Japan with full impunity!"

The words filled Aizawa's mouth with the bile of shame. But personal feelings and honor were meaningless. Tokyo was the only thing that mattered now.

*****

"Empty promises," Chitose-oneesan whispered into Nakajima's ear. "The only thing that matters is to punish the evil inside of this building."

Nakajima looked at his sister. The morning sun shone in through the windows and blurred with her white kimono and pale face. She was right. His duty was to the poor, the downtrodden, and the victimized. He remembered how pathetic she looked before she died, a diseased heap of flesh. The total destruction of the Maru-Biru would be retribution for her miserable fate.

Yet, a thirst for life parched his soul. Every war novel from childhood flooded back. His duty was in far-off Manchuria, alongside his freezing comrades. Perhaps Hatsu and Aizawa were telling the truth. The Inspector was a man of honor, after all. Maybe he really would be allowed to go to Manchuria and fight. Then, only after the laurels of battle were his, could he take his rightful place at the Yasukuni Shrine.

"Your Majesty," he said, turning to the Emperor's portrait. "Please…guide me."

The picture did nothing but stare into unending space. But in its blank gaze, Lieutenant Nakajima felt the cold sting of disapproval and shame. He spun back toward his sister, but she was gone, replaced by the pale glow of the morning sunlight. A dangerous thought crept into his mind. Had she ever been there?

"Lieutenant, this is your last chance," Inspector Aizawa called out from the other side. "Die like a coward in the luxury of Tokyo or join your men in Manchuria like a true soldier!"

Each taunt bit into his flesh like a wasp sting. Why did the gods make him so weak? Where were they now? Tears blotted his eyes. He couldn't resist any longer. The shame was too great and numbed his body. Before he could think, he reached down and cut the main fuse.

*****

"I'm coming out!"

Major Hatsu nodded to his men, who dislodged the overturned desk from the office entrance. The doors parted in a loud creak, revealing Lieutenant Nakajima, arms up in surrender. The leather visor on his service cap shadowed most of his face, but it couldn't hide the tears that wetted his cheeks. The saber rattled beside him, his cape billowed slightly as he stepped forward, and his shoulder rank insignia gleamed in the electric lights. Every step he took made him look like a soldier marching toward the Manchurian front.

But his moment of gallantry was brief. Major Hatsu and his men slammed the Lieutenant against the wall and snapped handcuffs on him. There was no resistance as they led him from the lobby and down the stairs. But before disappearing, Nakajima cast a gaze that hit Aizawa hard.

It wasn't hatred or fear but something more mysterious. It took Aizawa a few moments to decipher, but it was the same expression he must have given when *giri* and *ninjo* had merged into one – gratitude. Lieutenant Nakajima was thankful for having been reminded of his *true* duty.

After they left, a few salarymen trickled out into the lobby and viewed the corpses of Kuroki and Takano's secretary with horrified gasps. Ignoring their incessant questioning, Aizawa walked over to the main window and stared out at the city. Tokyo, his home, stared back.

CHAPTER FIFTY-NINE

Aizawa rarely entered the fifth floor of the Metropolitan Police Headquarters, where the top brass lurked. But today he'd been summoned to see the Superintendent-General himself to – as he put it – "discuss" certain matters in his report. As he stepped off the elevator and walked down the hallway, Aizawa caught his reflection in several glass doorframes. He cut an impressive figure in his peaked cap and dark tunic, pressed and starched like a suit of armor.

Inspectors hardly ever wore uniforms, but this past week he'd worn his for a number of funerals. And just like armor, it shielded him against the mournful sobs of the widow Murayama and her children. It deflected the hostile glares from Baron Onishi's son, who had arrived by airplane from Washington DC to attend both of his parents' funerals. And it shielded him from sorrow engulfing him at the funeral of Superintendent Joji Shimura.

Aizawa needed whatever protection it could offer, since he fully expected to be dismissed or at least demoted. How many deaths was he responsible for now? Sergeant Murayama, the Onishis, Takano's two sumo bodyguards, and Takano's secretary. Takano himself, that sly fox, was nowhere to be found.

Taking a deep breath and straightening his tunic, he stood before the Superintendent-General's office and announced, "Inspector Kenji Aizawa, sir!"

"Enter," a sharp voice commanded.

Aizawa opened the door and found his way into the spacious office, befitting the highest of ranks. Like Superintendent Shimura's office, it had sparse décor: a bookshelf, plaques for awards, and of course, a portrait of the Emperor. Unlike Shimura's office, several chairs clustered around the main desk. A hodgepodge of faces stared back at him. Behind the desk sat the Superintendent-General, head of the entire Tokyo Metropolitan Police Department. He was magnificently attired with glittering epaulettes set against a dark uniform, the sight of which stiffened every police officer's spine.

Major Hatsu sat across from his desk. That dark brown tunic of his made for an all too common sight these days. Aizawa averted his eyes to a *junsa*, standing stiffly next to a handcuffed Masaru Ryusaki. The *sensei* of the Kusanagi Society had seen better days, but despite half-repaired glasses and a face raw from beatings, he still wore an implacable grin of triumph.

Aizawa stepped forward and saluted.

"Welcome Inspector," the Superintendent-General said, beckoning him in. "I'd like to go over some items here." He tapped an open manila folder on the desk. "The press wants more information about what they're calling the 'Kusanagi Society Incident.' I would like to make sure we're all in agreement on the details."

That sounded cordial enough.

"For starters, your report makes mention of a," the Superintendent-General squinted at the report, "Second Lieutenant Nakajima. But Major Hatsu has informed me that is impossible."

Hatsu bolted upright and presented Aizawa with an official Army telegram. It read "Lieutenant Nakajima has taken command of his platoon and joined the Kwantung Army's Tenth Infantry Division." He looked at the date. December 16th, Showa 6.

"You see, Inspector?" Major Hatsu said, betraying no emotions. "Lieutenant Nakajima couldn't have had anything to do with this regrettable incident because he was en route to Manchuria. His unit is now involved in the final advance on Chinchow."

A lovely story. More likely he received an impromptu court-martial in the cellars of the Army Ministry and was executed by a pistol shot to the head. Not surprising, since having one of their own so close to the "Kusanagi Society Incident" would prove embarrassing for the Imperial Army.

Or perhaps Nakajima really had been sent to Manchuria. The Army could use men like him, already experienced with killing. And what better way to dispose of a troublesome junior officer than by exiling him to that barren wilderness? If he didn't die from Chinese bombs or bullets, those subzero winters would silence him eventually.

There was no reason to protest. Any piece of paper with the Army's seal was far more convincing than a dozen eyewitnesses.

"Yes, I understand."

"Excellent," the Superintendent-General said, flipping through the report. "However, a man identified as Makoto Kuroki was found dead at the Maru-Biru, wearing the uniform of an Imperial Guard lieutenant. Ryusaki-san has confirmed that this man was responsible for the deaths of Sergeant Murayama, Baron Onishi, and the others. Isn't that right?"

Ryusaki glanced over at Aizawa with knowing eyes. Ever since his arrest at the Dragonfly Tea House, he'd been held at Sugamo Prison, well out of Aizawa's jurisdiction. Sympathetic guards probably fawned over the esteemed patriot and coached him on what to say.

"Yes," Ryusaki mustered with obvious difficulty. "Kuroki-san is the man who assassinated Baron Onishi."

"And General Sakamoto?" Aizawa interjected.

"The General's death will be listed a suicide," Hatsu said.

"And what about his involvement?"

A hush swept over the room until the Superintendent-General said, "Simply this. Ryusaki-san sent Makoto Kuroki, an intensely patriotic yet disturbed young man, to assassinate Baron Onishi, over his remarks about the Manchurian Incident. You thwarted his first attempt, but when Superintendent Shimura released him, Kuroki-san put on his brother's old uniform and went to the Baron's *yashiki*. This explains the servants' description about an Army officer.

Ryusaki-san has also confessed to sending Kuroki to assassinate General Sakamoto, who he also felt was corrupt. The General committed *seppuku* instead. Most regrettably, this Makoto Kuroki also killed Superintendent Shimura in his own home."

"I see. There was also a *junsa* in Ueno Park, in league with Ryusaki."

The Superintendent-General nodded. "A shame one of our own was involved. No doubt, you acted in self-defense. Regardless, after ambushing you in the park, Ryusaki-san sent certain members of his Kusanagi Society to assassinate Isamu Takano and blow up the Maru-Biru as an act of protest. Isn't that right, Ryusaki-san?"

A slight nod was Ryusaki's only response. It was a simple version and easily digestible, but it remained sensational enough to satiate the newspapers. At least, Reiko Watanabe's name would be kept out of it, allowing her some life of peace. Still, one question remained.

"What happened to Isamu Takano?"

The Superintendent-General smiled. "Takano-san set sail for America with his Wall Street colleague on the morning of the attack. Prime Minister Inukai appointed him trade liaison to President Hoover. Something to do with getting that ridiculous Smoot-Hawley Tariff repealed."

Surely the attempt on his life must have influenced his decision. Or maybe this was his plan all along. With the money he and the other *zaibatsu* cliques would make from the "Dollar Buying Incident," as the newspapers had titled it, they could now purchase government bonds which would then be reinvested in the economy. That would help pay for the Manchurian Incident and future military adventures. But more importantly, if the trade barriers were lifted, cheap Japanese goods could flood the shores of the United States from sea to shining sea.

Aizawa sighed. There was no reason to fight. His mind had been decided for him.

"I understand," he said.

"Good. So, then this is the final version, correct?" the Superintendent-General said.

Major Hatsu and Aizawa nodded. Although the Kusanagi Society Incident was over, custom dictated that someone should be sacrificed for all of the lives lost. Since it had been Aizawa's case, his career would serve as atonement.

"Sir, in light of the deaths that have occurred, I hereby resign from the Tokyo Metropolitan Police Depart—"

"Your resignation is not accepted," the Superintendent-General said.

"Sir?"

"The Emperor himself has heard of your heroic deeds and extends his gratitude," the Superintendent-General continued. "He has even awarded you this."

The Superintendent-General reached into his desk and retrieved a small box, decorated with a sixteen leaf chrysanthemum – the official crest of the Imperial family. Aizawa took it with both hands and opened it with delicate fingers. Inside was a medal; a red jewel centered in a sea of jutting white rays.

"The Order of the Rising Sun, fourth class." The Superintendent-General took the medal and pinned it on Aizawa's chest, then snapped a salute.

Aizawa stiffened. Even after everything he'd been through, a medal from the Emperor was still humbling. This little trinket placed him in a long brotherhood of men who had given their all for Japan. Tears wetted his cheeks. Major Hatsu and the *junsa* gave respectful salutes. Ryusaki glared with contempt.

"I-I'm honored, sir," Aizawa said, drying his eyes.

"You're dismissed, Inspector," the Superintendent-General said. "Take the rest of the week off. Return to duty by New Years."

A hiss of disgust leaked out of Ryusaki's swollen lips. Aizawa turned and snapped, "I hope you like Sugamo Prison, Ryusaki-san, because you'll be there for the rest of your life."

Ryusaki's puffy face molded a smile. "That would be fine. The guards salute when they pass my cell. They've even given me a typewriter so I can respond to all the mail I've received."

"The mail?" the Superintendent-General asked with nonchalant curiosity.

"Oh yes, over four hundred letters in the past week. All of which thanked me for killing that self-serving aristocrat and attempting to obliterate that dung heap in Marunouchi. One letter told me that sales for my book have doubled." Ryusaki turned to Aizawa, his swollen smile growing more sinister. "You see Inspector? The final victory will be mine."

Failure and arrest had somehow made Masaru Ryusaki even more popular. Not that he should be surprised, but the sheer volume of praise seemed almost unreal. Over four hundred in one week? At that rate, he'd receive a thousand by New Years. How many angry men were eager to become the next Ryusaki and start their own patriotic murder squad? 1931, the sixth year of the Showa Era, was almost over, but a new dark age was dawning in Japan.

After a round of salutes, Aizawa turned and walked toward the door.

CHAPTER SIXTY

As the trancelike melody of "Mood Indigo" floated from the radio and filled her apartment, Reiko Watanabe scanned the main article that dominated today's *Asahi Shimbun* — "Chinchow Offensive Begins!" The Kwantung Army was marching toward the Headquarters of Chang Hsüeh-liang to kick the bandit warlord out of Manchuria forever. By New Years, the Rising Sun flag would flutter over Chinchow's walls. After that, Harbin would fall within a week or two. But what if the League of Nations didn't approve? Then to hell with them, argued the *Asahi*. Japan didn't need the world's approval anymore.

It was a surprising read, considering the paper's moderate history. But victory after victory in Manchuria had converted most people. Reiko wondered if the next war would be as easy. Below was a brief summary of the infamous "Kusanagi Society Incident" that everyone had been talking about. Until the advance on Chinchow started, that is. It was a sanitized version, sparing many details, namely her involvement. A good thing too. If she became known as a geisha who couldn't keep secrets, she'd be out of work forever.

A chill ran through Reiko at the thought of a future without a stable income. She reached over and turned the electric heater up. It was going to be a long winter. But according to the *Asahi*, Japan's economy would fully recover by this time next year, thanks to Finance Minister Takahashi and men like Isamu Takano.

A knock at the door interrupted further reading. Reiko set the *Asahi Shimbun* aside and hopped out of bed. Her apartment was a mess and she had barely left it in the past few days. Newspapers and old issues of *Kinema Junpo* lay scattered across the floor, but as long as the posters of Anna May Wong and Louise Brooks still hung, the little apartment retained some class. She stole a quick glance in the mirror. A dark blue sweater and skirt overshadowed the bruises on her face that grew fainter with each passing day. Luckily, she had a tough hide underneath such soft skin.

Reiko opened the door and reviewed the dark uniform that stood across from her. A peaked cap shadowed Inspector Aizawa's warm face. Although her cheeks were still sore, she smiled. Aizawa had visited her every day for the past week, bringing hot miso soup and other soft foods. His white-gloved hands wrapped around a small purple box. After they exchanged bows, she led him inside and cleared away some clutter for a proper place to kneel.

"How are you feeling?" he asked.

"Better. I saw the doctor again yesterday. None of my teeth are broken and the swelling should be gone soon."

Aizawa smiled. "I'm glad to hear it." He presented the box to her with both hands. "Something soft to eat while you recuperate."

She opened the lid and found rows of *mochi* rice cakes, filling her with a childlike glee.

"A man after my heart," she said before plopping a *mochi* cake into her mouth. After a few chews, she remembered her manners and offered one to the Inspector.

"They're all for you," he said, waving a gloved hand.

Despite the pain, Reiko gave another smile and looked him over. The only color in that dark uniform was a twinkling medal pinned on his breast.

"The Order of the Rising Sun? Congratulations, Inspector. It looks good on you."

His head lowered. "You deserve it more than I do."

"Too tacky for my taste. Besides, I prefer to remain anonymous."

"But if it wasn't for you, Ryusaki would still be free."

"Speaking of him…"

"He'll be going to trial soon. Just a formality, since he's already confessed to everything. You won't need to be called as a witness, and I'll see to it your name is kept out of the newspapers. With any luck, he'll rot in Sugamo Prison for the rest of his days."

"Thank you. Geisha are supposed to keep their mouths shut, after all. It'd be bad for business if word got around that I can't."

The Inspector gave a concerned look. "Unfortunately, imprisonment has only increased his prestige among the other patriotic societies..."

Reiko swallowed hard as she saw the dark future that lay on Japan's horizon. "What about Lieutenant Nakajima?"

Inspector Aizawa sighed. "The Army claims he was sent to Manchuria...but I don't know for certain."

Despite the warmth from the electric heater blasting at full force, another chill ran down her spine. She would pray to the gods that Hajime Nakajima would be swallowed up by the vast Chinese wilderness, if he wasn't dead already. But somehow she knew it wouldn't be enough. With Masaru more popular than ever and the possibility that devil soldier could still be alive, her sense of purpose rose like the bright morning sun.

"Inspector, I want to help."

He gave a warm smile. "You've helped enough."

"No, I haven't. I've been hiding in Asakusa, hoping the world would pass me by. Everything with," she bit her lip, briefly mourning her past life, "everything with Masaru has made that clear."

"What are you saying?"

"I want to be an undercover agent for you. I'll be the eyes and ears of justice, you'll be the fist."

"No, it's too dangerous for a woman."

"Inspector, how many of your men can you still trust?"

Aizawa sighed and said, "After everything you went through...you still want to return to this world?"

Reiko nodded. "I'm a natural spy, Inspector. As a geisha, I can attend lavish parties. As a *moga*, I'll slink around nightclubs and gambling dens. After a few drinks, I can pry secrets out of any man."

He fell silent for a few moments, rubbing his squared chin. An honorable man like Inspector Aizawa would no doubt balk at putting a civilian – much less a woman – in danger without a good reason.

"Inspector, acting as your informant will not only give me a source of income…it might very well save the Imperial capital again."

Aizawa's eyes softened with understanding.

"After Nakajima's," Reiko said, pausing to swallow, "rehabilitation, I was numb, unable to think for myself. But when Masaru threatened Tokyo…our home, his hold over me snapped. I couldn't let it die again. I just couldn't."

"Reiko-san…"

"It's my city too, Inspector. I want to protect it with you."

Aizawa gave a slow nod in agreement. Reaching into his pocket, he withdrew a green pack of Golden Bat cigarettes. He lit two of them and handed one over. Reiko stared at the wisps of smoke that poured from the glowing ember. It reminded her of the incense she'd lit yesterday while praying for the souls of Baron Onishi and his wife, that poor Sergeant Murayama, his family, and for Japan's future, which looked so uncertain. But now, there would be no more hiding. Alongside Inspector Aizawa, she would protect Tokyo.

Afterword

Although *Shadows of Tokyo* is entirely fictitious, elements of it are rooted in fact. Inspector Aizawa, Reiko Watanabe, Masaru Ryusaki, Lieutenant Nakajima, General Sakamoto, Isamu Takano, and Baron Onishi are all fictional characters. However, others like Reijiro Wakatsuki and Tsuyoshi Inukai were historical figures. The Manchurian Incident (*Manshu Jiken*) which began on September 18th 1931 is common knowledge. Less well-known is the Dollar Buying Incident (*Doru Bai Jiken*) which also occurred in late 1931.

Japan had returned to the gold standard in January 1930, which only worsened the effects of the Great Depression. When Britain left the gold standard in September 1931, several *zaibatsu* bankers engaged in wild speculation against the yen by purchasing US dollars. They correctly guessed that Tsuyoshi Inukai would leave the gold standard, allowing them to exchange their US currency for inflated Japanese yen, thus doubling their investment.

Under Finance Minister Korekiyo Takahashi, Japan began its long climb out of the Great Depression. The increased money supply helped stimulate economic growth, aided further by government bonds. However, the political damage of the Dollar Buying Incident had already been done.

The scandal enraged the Japanese Far-Right, which had blamed the economic turmoil on corrupt politicians colluding with greedy capitalists. As the decade continued, they plotted more assassinations such as the 5-15 Incident (*Go Ichi Go Jiken*) of 1932. The events of this novel were inspired by various assassination and coup d'état plots along with the very real corruption scandals that plagued Japanese politics during the 1930s.

Thank You

Thank you for reading *Shadows of Tokyo*, the first book of the Reiko Watanabe/Inspector Aizawa series. If you enjoyed this novel, please leave a review on Amazon and Goodreads! Honest reviews from readers like you are absolutely essential for authors to survive in today's marketplace.

Thanks in advance and sign up for my mailing list for updates! Just visit:

www.matthewlegare.com

Reiko Watanabe and Inspector Aizawa will return in *Smoke Over Tokyo*!

About the Author

Matthew Legare has always loved reading, writing, and history. He's combined his passions to tell stories set during little-known, but fascinating, events of the past. His style is a smooth blend of old pulp magazines and contemporary thrillers, which makes for a pulsating read.

Matthew would love to hear from his readers! Please contact him at:

Website: www.matthewlegare.com

Twitter: @mlegareauthor

Printed in Great Britain
by Amazon